SEVASTOPOL

SEVASTOPOL
AND OTHER STORIES

BY

LEO TOLSTOY

METHUEN & CO. LTD.
36 ESSEX STREET W.C.
LONDON

First Published, by Methuen & Co. Ltd., at 1s. net, in 1912

CONTENTS

CONTENTS

TRANSLATOR'S PREFACE

In presenting Count Tolstoy's story of "The Cossacks" to the English reader it may be remarked that none of his works enjoy a higher reputation among the Russians than this narrative of love and war in the Caucasus, in which realism and poetry are so admirably blended. The late Ivan Turgenieff, who, despite passing estrangement, remained until his death Tolstoy's chief mentor in literary matters, pronounced this to be a perfect work. In his published correspondence he frequently refers to it. Again and again, at various periods when Count Tolstoy had forsaken letters for politics, or for the prosecution of his schemes of social reform, Turgenieff urged him to return to literature and to give the world such another story as "The Cossacks." The high opinion that Tolstoy's admitted master formed of this work will probably be shared by the English reader; and for the latter "The Cossacks" will possess an especial attraction since it pictures life in the wild region of the Terek, amid scenes and races of which we still know so little. In the same way a peculiar interest attaches to the "Prisoner of the Caucasus," a short story which is included in the present volume, and in which Count Tolstoy recounts the perilous adventures of a Russian officer captured by the Tartars.

In "Recollections of Sevastopol" we are presented with a series of historical pictures which cannot be too highly commended. We have our own histories of the Crimean war, but if we are acquainted with the offensive and defensive movements of our adversaries we know but little of what was passing in their hearts and minds. In this respect Count Tolstoy, skilfully combining his reminiscences with a touch of romance, raises the veil as it were ; and the student of history, after perusing Kinglake, should turn to these pages if he would acquire an adequate idea of the life led in the beleaguered city, and of the sentiments that swayed its defenders. The reader's emotions are not spared. War, with all its horror and heroism, could not be more forcibly delineated. And yet Count Tolstoy never exaggerates ; while praising the qualities of his countrymen he points out their failings ; and for this reason his reminiscences, although presented in the form of fiction, are invested with especial value.

RECOLLECTIONS OF SEVASTOPOL

SEVASTOPOL IN DECEMBER, 1854

DAWN tinges the horizon above Mount Sapoun; the shadows of the night have left the surface of the sea, which, now dark-blue in colour, only awaits the first ray of sunshine to sparkle merrily; a cold wind blows from the fog-enveloped bay; there is no snow on the ground, the soil is black, but frost stings the face and cracks underfoot. The quiet of the morning is disturbed by the incessant murmuring of the waves, and is broken at long intervals by the dull roar of cannon. All is silent on board the men-of-war; the hour-glass has just marked the eighth watch. Towards the north the activity of day replaces little by little the tranquility of night. On this side a detachment of soldiers is going to relieve the guard, and the click of their guns can be heard; a surgeon hurries towards his hospital; a soldier crawls out of his hut, washes his sunburnt face with icy water, turns towards the east, and repeats a prayer, making rapid signs of the cross. On that side a huge, heavy cart with creaking wheels reaches the cemetery where the corpses, heaped almost to the top of the vehicle, are about to be buried. Approach the harbour and you are disagreeably surprised by a mixture of odours; you smell coal, manure, moisture, meat. There are thousands of different objects—wood, flour, gabions, beef, thrown in heaps here and there; soldiers of different regiments, some provided with guns and with bags, others with neither guns nor bags, crowd together; they smoke, they quarrel, and they carry loads on to the steamer stationed near the plank bridge and ready to start. Small private boats, filled with all sorts of people—soldiers, sailors, traders, and women—are constantly arriving and departing. " This way for Grafskaya ! " and two or three retired sailors rise in their boats and offer you their services. You choose the nearest one, stride over the half-decomposed body of a black horse lying in the mud at two steps from the boat, and seat yourself near the helm. You push off from the shore; all around you the sea sparkles in the morning sun; in front of you an old sailor in an overcoat of camel's-hair cloth and a lad with fair hair are diligently rowing. You turn your eyes towards the gigantic ships with striped hulls scattered over the harbour, upon the shallops—black dots on the sparkling azure of the water—upon the pretty houses of the town, to whose light-coloured walls the rising sun gives a rosy tinge, upon the hostile fleet standing like lighthouses in the crystalline distance of the sea, and, at last, upon the foaming waves, where play the salt drops which the oars dash into the air. You hear at the same time the regular sound of voices which comes over the water, and the grand roar of the cannonade at Sevastopol, which seems to increase in strength as you listen.

At the thought that you, you also, are in Sevastopol, your whole soul is filled with a sentiment of pride and valour, and your blood runs more quickly in your veins.

" Straight towards the *Constantine*, your excellency," says the old sailor, turning round to watch the direction you are giving to the helm.

" Look ! she has still got all her cannons," remarks the lad with the fair hair, as the boat glides along the side of the ship.

"She is quite new, she ought to have them. Korniloff lives on board," repeats the old man, examining in his turn the man-of-war.

"There! it has burst!" cries the lad, after a long silence, his eyes fixed upon a small white cloud of drifting smoke suddenly appearing in the sky above the south bay, and accompanied by the strident noise of a shell explosion.

"They are firing from the new battery to-day," adds the sailor, calmly spitting in his hand. "Come along, Nichka; pull away. Let's pass the shallop."

And the small boat moves rapidly over the undulating surface of the bay, passes the heavy shallop laden with bags and soldiers, unskilful rowers who are pulling awkwardly, and at last makes for land in the middle of a great number of skiffs moored to the shore in the harbour of Grafskaya. A crowd of soldiers in grey overcoats, sailors in black jackets, and women in motley gowns passes to and fro on the quay. Some peasants are selling bread; others, seated beside their samovars, offer warm drink to customers.

Here, on the upper steps of the landing, rusty shot, shell, canister, cast-iron cannon of different calibres are strewn about pell-mell; there, farther away, in a great open square, enormous joists, gun-carriages, sleeping soldiers, are lying. On one side there are wagons, horses, cannon, artillery caissons, stacks of muskets; farther on, soldiers, sailors, officers, women, and children, are moving about; carts full of bread, bags, and barrels, a Cossack on horseback, a general in his droshky, are crossing the square. A barricade looms up in the street to the right, and in its embrasures are some small cannon, beside which a sailor sits quietly smoking his pipe. On the left stands a pretty house, on the pediment of which numerals are scrawled, and above can be seen soldiers and bloodstained stretchers. The dismal traces of a camp in war-time meet the eye everywhere. Your first impression is, doubtless, a disagreeable one; the strange amalgamation of town life with camp life, of an elegant city and a dirty bivouac, strikes you like a hideous incongruity. It seems to you that all are acting vacuously, overcome by terror ; but if you examine the faces of the men who are moving about you, you will think differently. Look well at this soldier of the wagon-train who is leading his bay troika horses to drink, humming through his teeth, and you will find that he does not go astray in this confused crowd, which, in fact, does not exist for him, for he is full of his own business, and will do his duty, whatever it be—will lead his horses to the watering-place or drag a cannon along with as much calm and assured indifference as if he were at Toula or at Saransk. You notice the same expression on the face of this officer, with his irreproachable white gloves, who is passing before you, of that sailor who sits on the barricade smoking, of the soldiers who wait with their stretchers at the door of what was lately the Assembly Hall, even upon the face of the young girl who crosses the street, leaping from stone to stone for fear of soiling her pink dress. Yes, a great deception awaits you on your arrival at Sevastopol. In vain do you try to discover upon any face traces of agitation, fright, indeed even enthusiasm, resignation to death, or resolution ; there is nothing of all that. You see the course of everyday life ; you see people occupied with their daily toil, so that, in fact, you blame yourself for your exaggerated exaltation, and doubt not only the truth of the opinion you have formed from hearsay about the heroism of the defenders of Sevastopol, but also doubt the accuracy of the description which has been given you on the north side and the sinister sounds which fill the air there. Before doubting, however, go up to a bastion, see the defenders of Sevastopol on the very spot of the defence, or rather go straight into this house at whose door stand the stretcher-bearers. You will see there the heroes of the army, you will there see horrible and heartrending sights, both sublime and comic, but wonderful and of a soul-elevating nature. Enter this

great hall, which before the war was the hall of the
Assembly.   Scarcely have you opened the door before
the odour exhaling from forty or fifty amputations
and severe wounds turns you sick.   You must not
yield to the feeling which keeps you on the threshold
of the room, it is an unworthy feeling ; go boldly in,
and do not blush at having come to look at these
martyrs.   You may approach and speak with them.
The wretches like to see a pitying face, to relate their
sufferings, and to hear words of charity and sympathy.
Passing down the middle between the beds, you look
for the face which is the least rigid, the least contracted by pain, and on finding it you decide to go
near and put a question.

   " Where are you wounded ? " you hesitatingly ask
an old, emaciated soldier, seated on his bed, watching
you with a kindly look, and apparently inviting you
to approach.   You have, I say, put this question hesitatingly, because the sight of the sufferer inspires not
only a lively pity, but also a sort of dread of hurting
his feelings, coupled with profound respect.

   " On the foot," replies the soldier ; and nevertheless you notice by the folds of the blanket that his leg
has been cut off above the knee.

   " God be praised ! " he adds, " I shall be discharged."

   " Were you wounded long since ? "

   " It is the sixth week, your excellency."

   " Where do you feel badly now ? "

   " Nowhere, only in the calf when it is bad weather
nothing but that."

   " How did it happen ? "

   " On the fifth bastion, your excellency, in the first
bombardment.   I had just sighted the cannon, and
was going quietly to the other embrasure, when
suddenly something struck my foot.   I thought I had
fallen into a hole.   I looked—my leg was gone ! "

   " You didn't feel any pain at first, then ? "

   " None at all, only just as if I had scalded my leg ;
that's all."

" And afterwards ? "

" None afterwards, only when they stretched the skin ; that was a little rough. First of all things, your excellency, we mustn't think. When we don't think we don't feel. When a man thinks, it is the worse for him."

Meanwhile, a woman dressed in grey, with a black kerchief tied around her head, approaches, joins in the conversation, and begins to give a detailed account of the sailor ; how he has suffered, how his life was despaired of for four weeks, how, when wounded, he made them stop the stretcher on which he was being carried to the rear in order to watch the discharge of our battery, and how the grand-dukes had spoken with him, had given him twenty-five roubles, and how he had replied that, not being able to serve any more himself, he would like to come back to the bastion to train the conscripts. The good woman, her eyes sparkling with enthusiasm, relates all this in one breath, looking at you and then at the sailor, who turns away and pretends not to hear, busy with picking lint on his pillow.

" It is my wife, your excellency," says the sailor at last, with an intonation of voice which seems to say : " You must excuse her ; all that is woman's foolish prattle, you know."

You then begin to understand what the defenders of Sevastopol are, and you feel ashamed of yourself in the presence of this man. You would have liked to express all your admiration for him, all your sympathy, but the words will not come, or those which do come are worthless, and you can only bow in silence before this unconscious grandeur, before this firmness of soul and this exquisite modesty as to his own merit.

" Ah, well, may God speedily cure you ! " you say, and you stop before another wounded man lying on the floor, who, suffering horrible pain, seems to be awaiting his death. He is fair, and his pale face is greatly swollen. Stretched on his back, his left hand thrown up, his position indicates acute suffering. His hissing breath escapes with difficulty from his parched, half-open mouth. The glassy blue pupils of his eyes are rolled up under the eyelids, and a mutilated arm, wrapped in bandages, sticks out from under the tumbled blanket. A nauseating, corpse-like odour rises to your nostrils, and the fever which burns the sufferer's limbs seems to penetrate your own body.

" Is he unconscious ? " you ask the woman who kindly accompanies you, and to whom you are no longer a stranger.

" No ; he can still hear, but he is very bad ; " and she adds, under her breath, " I have just made him drink a little tea. He is nothing to me, only I pity him ; indeed, he has only been able to swallow a few mouthfuls."

" How do you feel ? " you ask him.

At the sound of your voice the wounded man's eyes turn towards you, but he neither sees nor understands.

" It burns my heart ! " he murmurs.

A little farther on an old soldier is changing his clothes. His face and his body are both of the same brown colour, and he is as thin as a skeleton. One of his arms has been amputated at the shoulders. He is seated on his bed, he is out of danger, but from his dull, lifeless look, from his frightful thinness, from his wrinkled face, you see that he has already passed the greater part of his existence in suffering.

On the opposite bed you see the pale, delicate, pain-contracted face of a woman whose cheeks are flushed with fever.

" She is a sailor's wife. A shell hit her on the foot while she was carrying dinner to her husband at the bastion," says the guide.

" Has she been amputated ? "

" Above the knee."

Now, if your nerves are strong, enter there on the left. It is the operating-room. There you see the surgeons with pale and serious countenances, their arms blood-splashed to the elbows, beside the bed of a wounded man, who, stretched on his back with open eyes, is delirious under the influence of chloroform, and utters broken phrases, some unimportant, others touching.   The surgeons are busy with their repulsive but beneficent task, amputation.   You see the curved and keen blade penetrate the healthy white flesh.   The wounded man suddenly comes to himself with heartrending cries and curses.   The assistant-surgeon throws the arm into a corner, while another wounded man on a stretcher who sees the operation turns and groans, more on account of the mental torture of expectation than from the physical pain he feels.   You will here witness horrible, heartrending scenes ; you will see war without the brilliant and accurate alignment of troops, without music, without the drum-roll, without standards flying in the wind, without galloping generals—you will see it as it is, in blood, in suffering, and in death !   Leaving this house of pain, you will experience a certain impression of well-being, you will take long breaths of fresh air, and will feel glad to find yourself in good health ;   but at the same time the contemplation of these misfortunes will have convinced you of your own insignificance, and you will go up to a bastion without hesitation.   What are the sufferings and the death of an atom like me, you will ask yourself, in comparison with these innumerable sufferings and deaths ?   Besides, in a short time the sight of the pure sky, of the bright sun, of the pretty city, of the open church, of the soldiers coming and going in all directions, raises your spirits to their normal state. Habitual indifference, pre-occupation with the present and with its petty interests, resume the ascendant. Perhaps you will meet on your way the funeral procession of an officer—a red coffin followed by a band and unfurled standards—and perhaps the roar of the cannonade on the bastion will strike your ear, but your thoughts of a few moments before will not come back again.   The funeral will only be a pretty picture for you, the growl of the cannon a grand military accompaniment, and there will be nothing in common between this picture, these sounds, and the clear, personal impression of suffering and death called up by the sight of the operating-room.

Pass the church and the barricade, and you enter the most animated, the liveliest quarter of the city. On both sides of the street are shop signs, eating-house signs.   Here are traders, women with bonnets or handkerchiefs on their heads, and officers in elegant uniforms.   Everything testifies to the courage, the assurance, the safety of the inhabitants.

Enter that restaurant on the right.   If you want to listen to the sailors' and the officers' talk, you will hear them relate the incidents of the night before, of the affair of the 24th ; hear them grumble at the high price of the badly-cooked cutlets, and mention the comrades recently killed.

" Devil take me ! we are badly off where we are now," says the bass voice of a pale, fair-haired, beardless, newly-appointed officer, his neck wrapped in a green knit scarf.

" Where is that ? " some one asks.

" At the fourth bastion," replies the young officer ; and at this reply you attentively look at him, and feel a certain respect for him.   His exaggerated carelessness, his violent gestures, his over-loud laughter, which shortly before would have seemed to you impudent, become in your eyes the signs of a certain kind of combative spirit common to all young people who are exposed to great danger, and you are sure he is going to explain that it is on account of the shells and the bullets that they are so badly off in the fourth bastion.   Nothing of the kind !   They are badly off there because the mud is deep.

" Impossible to get up to the battery," he says, pointing to his boots, muddied even to the upper-leathers.

" My best gunner was shot dead to-day by a ball in his forehead," rejoins a comrade.

" Who was it ?   Mituchine ? "

" No, another man.—Look here ! are you never going to bring me my chop, you villain ? " says he, speaking to the waiter. " It was Abrossinoff, as brave a man as lived. He took part in six sorties."

At the other end of the table two infantry officers are eating veal cutlets with green peas, washed down by sour Crimean wine, by courtesy called Bordeaux. One of them, a young man with a red collar and two stars on his coat, is telling his neighbour, with a black collar and no stars, the details of the fight on the Alma.   The first is a little the worse for liquor. His frequently interrupted tale, his uncertain look, which reflects the lack of confidence which his story inspires in his auditor, the fine part he gives himself, the heightened colour of his picture, lead you to guess that he is wandering away from the absolute truth. But you haven't anything to do with these tales, which you will hear for a long time yet in the farthest corners of Russia ; you have one wish alone, that is, to go straight to the fourth bastion, which you have heard so many and such varied reports about.   You will notice that whoever tells you he has been there says it with pride and satisfaction ; that whoever is getting ready to go there either shows a little emotion or affects exaggerated calmness. If one man is joking with another, he will invariably tell him, " Go to the fourth bastion," If a wounded man on a stretcher is met, and he is asked where he comes from, he will answer, almost without fail, " From the fourth bastion ! " Two completely different notions of this terrible earthwork have been circulated ; the first by those who have never set their foot upon it, and for whom it is the inevitable tomb of its defenders ; the second by those who, like the little fair-haired officer, live there and simply speak of it, saying it is dry or muddy there, warm or cold.

During the half hour you have been in the restaurant the weather has changed, and the fog which spreads over the sea has risen. Thick, grey, moist

clouds hide the sun. The sky is gloomy, and a fine
rain mixed with snow is falling, wetting the roofs, the
sidewalks, and the soldiers' overcoats. After passing
one more barricade you go along up the main street.
There are no more shop-signs ; the houses are unin-
habitable, the doors fastened up with boards, the
windows broken. On this side the corner of a wall
has been carried away, on that side the roof has been
broken in. The buildings look like old veterans tried
by grief and misery, and stare at you with pride,
one might say with disdain even. On the way you
stumble over cannon-balls and into holes, filled with
water, which the shells have made in the stony ground.
You pass detachments of soldiers and officers. You
occasionally meet a woman or a child ; but here the
woman does not wear a bonnet. As for the sailor's
wife, she wears an old fur cloak, and has soldiers' boots
on her feet. The street now leads down a gentle de-
clivity, but there are no more houses around you,
nothing but shapeless masses of stones, boards, beams,
and clay. Before you, on a steep hill, stretches a
black space, all muddy, and cut up with trenches.
What you are looking at is the fourth bastion.

Passers become rare, no more women are met. The
soldiers walk with rapid step. A few drops of blood
stain the path, and you see coming towards you four
soldiers bearing a stretcher, and on the stretcher a
face of a sallow paleness and a bloody coat. If you
ask the bearers where the man is wounded, they will
reply, in an irritated tone, without looking at you,
that he has been hit on the arm or on the leg. If his
head has been carried away, if he is dead, they will
keep a morose silence.

The near whiz of bullets and shells gives you a disagreeable impression while you are climbing the hill,
and suddenly you have an entirely different idea
from the one you recently had of the meaning of the
cannon-shots heard in the city. I do not know what
placid and sweet souvenir will suddenly shine out in
your memory. Your intimate *ego* will occupy you

so actively that you will no longer think of noticing your surroundings. You will permit yourself to be overcome by a painful feeling of irresolution. However, the sight of a soldier who, with extended arms, is slipping down the hill in the liquid mud, and who passes near you, running and laughing, silences your small inward voice, the cowardly counsellor which arises in you in the presence of danger. You straighten up in spite of yourself, you raise your head, and in your turn you scale the slippery slope of the clay hill. You have scarcely gone a step before musket-balls hum in your ears, and you ask yourself if it would not be preferable to get under cover of the trench thrown up parallel with the path. But the trench is full of a yellow, fetid, liquid mud, so that you are obliged to follow the path ; all the more since it is the way everybody takes. At the end of two hundred paces you come out on a spot surrounded by gabions, embankments, shelters, platforms supporting enormous cast-iron cannon, and heaps of symmetrically piled cannon-balls. These heaps of things give you the impression of a strange and aimless disorder. Here on the battery assembles a group of sailors ; there in the middle of the enclosure lies a dismounted cannon, half-buried in the sticky mud, through which an infantryman, musket in hand, is going to the battery, with difficulty pulling out first one foot and then the other. Everywhere in this liquid mud you see broken glass, unexploded shells, cannon-balls—every trace of camp life. You seem to hear the noise of a cannon-ball falling only two yards away, and from all sides comes the sound of balls, which sometimes hum like bees, sometimes groan and rend the air, which vibrates like a violin-string, the whole dominated by the sinister rumbling of cannon, which shakes you from head to foot and fills you with terror.

This is, then, the fourth bastion, this really terrible place, you say to yourself, feeling a little pride and a great deal of repressed fear. Not at all ! You

are the sport of an illusion.   This is not yet the fourth
bastion ; it is the Jason redoubt, a place which, com-
paratively, is neither dangerous nor frightful.   In
order to reach the fourth bastion you enter the narrow
trench which the infantryman follows, stooping over.
You will perhaps see more stretchers, sailors, soldiers
with spades, wires leading to the mines and earth-
shelters equally muddy, into which only two men
can crawl, and where the battalions of the Black Sea
sharpshooters live, eat, smoke, and pull their boots
on and off, in the midst of fragments of cast-iron of
every form scattered here and there.   You will perhaps find here four or five sailors playing cards in the
shelter of the parapet, and a naval officer, who, seeing
a new face come up, that of a spectator, will be really
pleased to initiate you into the details of the arrange-
ments and give you an explanation of them.   This
officer seats himself on a cannon, rolls a cigarette
with such coolness, passes so quietly from one embrasure to another, and talks with you with such
natural calmness, that you recover your own *sang-
froid*, in spite of the balls which are whistling here in
greater numbers.   You ask him questions, and even
listen to his tales.   The officer will describe to you,
if you will only ask him, the bombardment of the
5th, the state of his battery with a single serviceable
cannon, his men reduced to eight, and yet, on the
morning of the 6th, the battery fired with every gun.
He will tell you also how, on the 5th, a shell penetrated a shelter-place and struck down eleven sailors.
He will show you through the embrasure, the enemy's
trenches and batteries, which are only thirty or forty
fathoms distant.   I fear, however, that, on leaning
out of the embrasure in order to examine the enemy
better, you will see nothing, or that, if you perceive
something, you will be very much surprised to learn
that the white and rocky rampart a few steps away,
and from which little clouds of smoke are spouting,
is really the enemy—" *him*," as the soldiers and
sailors say.

It is very possible that the officer, either through vanity or simply to amuse himself, will tell his men to fire in your presence. At his order the chief gunner and the men, fourteen sailors all told, gaily approach the cannon to load it, some chewing biscuits, others cramming their short pipes in their pockets, while their hob-nailed boots clatter on the platform. Notice the faces of these men, their bearing, their movements, and you will detect in each of the wrinkles on their sunburnt faces with high cheek-bones, in each muscle, in the breadth of their shoulders, in the thickness of their feet, shod with colossal boots, in each calm and bold gesture, the principal elements that make up the strength of the Russian—simplicity and obstinacy. You will also see that danger, misery, and suffering in the war have imprinted on these faces the conscious-ness of their dignity, of high thoughts, of a sentiment.

Suddenly a deafening noise makes you quake from head to foot. You at the same instant hear the shot whistling away, while a thick powder-smoke envelops the platform and the black figures of the sailors mov-ing about. Listen to their conversation, notice their animation, and you will discover among them a feel-ing which you would not expect to meet—that of hatred of the enemy, of vengeance. " It fell straight into the embrasure ; two killed. Look ! they are carrying them away," and they shout for joy. " But he is getting angry now, he is going to hit back," says a voice, and in truth at the same instant you see a flash and spurting smoke, and the sentinel on the parapet calls " Cannon ! " A ball whizzes in your ears and plunges into the ground, digging it up and casting a shower of earth and stones around. The commander of the battery gets angry, renews the order to load a second, a third gun. The enemy replies, and you experience interesting sensations. The sentinel again calls " Cannon ! " and the same sound, the same blow, and the same throwing up of earth are repeated. If, on the other hand, he cries " Mortar ! " you will be struck by a regular, not

disagreeable hissing, which has no connection in your
mind with anything terrible. It comes nearer and
with greater rapidity. You see the black spheroid
fall to the ground, and the bombshell burst with a
metallic cracking. The pieces fly into the air, whistling and screeching ; stones hit each other, and mud
splashes over you. You feel a strange mixture of
pleasure and fright at these different sounds. At
the instant the projectile reaches you, you invariably
think it will kill you. But pride keeps you up, and
no one notices the dagger that is digging into your
heart. So when it has passed without grazing you you
live again ; for an instant a feeling of indescribable
sweetness possesses you to such a degree that you find
a special charm in danger, in the game of life and
death. You would like to have a ball or a shell fall
nearer, very near you. But the sentinel announces
with his strong, full voice, " Mortar ! " The hissing,
the blow, the explosion are repeated, but accompanied this time by a human groan. You go up to
the wounded man at the same time as the stretcher-
bearers. He has a strange look, lying in the mud
mingled with his blood. Part of his chest has been
carried away. At the first moment his mud-splashed
face expresses only fright and the premature sensation
of pain, a feeling familiar to man in this situation.
But when they bring the stretcher to him, and he
unassisted lies down on it on his uninjured side, an
exalted expression, elevated but restrained thoughts,
enliven his features. With brilliant eyes and closed
teeth he raises his head with an effort, and at the
moment the stretcher-bearers move he stops them,
and addressing his comrades in a trembling voice
says : " Good-bye, brothers ! " He would like to
say something more, he seems to be trying to find
something touching to say, but he limits himself to
repeating, " Good-bye, brothers ! " A comrade approaches the wounded man, puts his cap on his head
for him, and turns back to his cannon with a gesture
of perfect indifference. At the sight of your terrified

expression of face the officer, yawning, and rolling between his fingers a cigarette in yellow paper, says : " So it is every day, up to seven or eight men."

You have just seen the defenders of Sevastopol on the very spot of the defence, and, strange to say, you will retrace your steps without paying the least attention to the bullets and balls which continue to whistle the whole length of the road as far as the ruins of the theatre.   You walk with calmness, your soul elevated and strengthened, for you bring away the consoling conviction that never, and in no place, can the strength of the Russian people be broken ; and you have gained this conviction not from the solidity of the parapets, from the ingeniously combined entrenchments, from the number of mines, from the cannon heaped one on the other, and all of which you have not in the least understood, but from the eyes, the words, the bearing, from what may be called the spirit of the defenders of Sevastopol.

There is so much simplicity and so little effort in what they do that you are persuaded that, if it were necessary, they could do a hundred times more, that they could do everything.   You judge that the sentiment that impels them is not the one you have experienced, mean and vain, but another and more powerful one, which has made men of them, living tranquilly in the mud, working and watching among the bullets, with a hundred chances to one of being killed, contrary to the common lot of their kind.   It is not for a cross, for rank ; it is not that they are threatened into submitting to such terrible conditions of existence.   There must be another, a higher motive power.   This motive power is found in a sentiment which rarely shows itself, which is concealed with modesty, but which is deeply rooted in every Russian heart—patriotism. It is now only that the tales that circulated during the first period of the siege of Sevastopol, when there were neither fortifications, nor troops, nor material possibility of holding out there, and when, moreover, no one admitted the thought of surrender—it is now only that the anecdote of Korniloff, that hero worthy of antique Greece, who said to his troops, " Children, we will die, but we will not surrender Sevastopol," and the reply of our brave soldiers, incapable of using set speeches, " We will die, hurrah ! "—it is now only that these stories have ceased to be to you beautiful historical legends, that they have become truth, facts. You will easily picture to yourself, in the place of those you have just seen, the heroes of the period of trial, who never lost courage, and who joyfully prepared to die, not for the defence of the city, but for the defence of the country. Russia will long preserve the sublime memory of the epopœia of Sevastopol, of which the Russian people were the heroes !

Day closes ; the sun, disappearing on the horizon, shines through the grey clouds which surround it, and lights up with purple rays both the rippling sea, tinted with green reflections and covered with ships and boats, and the white houses of the city, and the population stirring there. On the boulevard a regimental band is playing an old waltz, which sounds far over the water, and to which the cannonade of the bastions forms a strange and striking accompaniment.

SEVASTOPOL IN MAY, 1855

SIX months had rolled by since the first bomb-shell thrown from the bastions of Sevastopol ploughed up the soil and cast it upon the enemy's works. Since that time thousands of bombs, bullets, and balls had never ceased flying from bastions to trenches, from trenches to bastions, and the angel of death had constantly hovered over them.

The self-love of thousands of human beings had been sometimes wounded, sometimes satisfied, sometimes soothed in the embrace of death! What numbers of red coffins with coarse palls!—and the bastions still continued to roar. The French in their camp, moved by an involuntary feeling of anxiety and terror, examined in the soft evening light the yellow and burrowed earth of the bastions of Sevastopol, where the black silhouettes of our sailors came and went; they counted the embrasures bristling with fierce-looking cannon. On the telegraph tower an under-officer was watching through his field-glass the enemy's soldiers, their batteries, their tents, the movements of their troops on the Mamelon-Vert, and the smoke ascending from the trenches. A crowd, composed of heterogeneous races, moved by quite different desires, converged from all parts of the world towards this fatal spot. Powder and blood had not succeeded in solving the question which diplomats could not settle.

CHAPTER I

A REGIMENTAL band was playing in the besieged city of Sevastopol; a number of soliders and women in Sunday clothes were promenading

in the avenues. The clear sun of spring had
risen upon the English works, had passed over the
fortifications, over the city, and over the Nicholas
barracks, sheding its joyous light everywhere ; and
now it was setting into the blue distance of the
sea, which gently rippled, sparkling with silvery
reflections.

An infantry officer of tall stature and with a slight
stoop, who was putting on some gloves of doubtful
whiteness, though still presentable, came out of one
of the small houses built on the left side of Marine
Street. He directed his steps towards the boulevard,
fixing his eyes in a careless manner on the toes of his
boots. The expression of his ill-favoured face did
not denote a high intellectual capacity, but traits of
good-fellowship, good sense, honesty, and love of
order were to be plainly recognised there. He was
not well-built, and seemed to feel some confusion at
the awkwardness of his own motions. He had a
well-worn cap on his head, and on his shoulders a
light cloak of a curious purplish colour, under which
could be seen his watch chain, his trousers with straps,
and his clean and well-polished boots. If his features
had not clearly indicated his pure Russian origin he
would have been taken for a German, for an aide-de-
camp, or for a regimental baggage-master—he wore
no spurs, to be sure—or for one of those cavalry
officers who had exchanged in order to take part in
the campaign. In fact, he was one of the latter, and
while going up to the boulevard he was thinking of a
letter he had just received from an ex-comrade, now
a landholder in the Government of F——; he was
thinking of his comrade's wife, pale, blue-eyed Natacha, his best friend ; he was especially recalling the
following passage :

" When they bring us the *Invalide*,* Poupka (that
was the name the retired lancer gave his wife) rushes
into the ante-chamber, seizes the paper, and throws

---

* The Russian military gazette.—TRANS.

herself upon the sofa in the arbour* in the parlour, where we passed so many pleasant winter evenings in your company while your regiment was in garrison in our city. You can't imagine the enthusiasm with which she reads the story of your heroic exploits! ' Mikhaïloff,' she often says in speaking of you, ' is a pearl of a man, and I shall throw myself on his neck when I see him again ! *He is fighting on the bastions, he is !* He will get the cross of St. George, and the newspapers will be full of him.' Indeed, I am beginning to feel jealous of you. It takes the papers a very long time to get to us, and although a thousand bits of news fly from mouth to mouth, we can't believe all of them. For example : your good friends the *musical girls* related yesterday how Napoleon, taken prisoner by our Cossacks, had been brought to Petersburg—you understand that I couldn't believe that ! Then one of the officials of the War Office, a fine fellow, and a great addition to society now that our little town is deserted, assured us that our troops had occupied Eupatoria, *thus preventing the French from communicating with Balaclava ;* that we lost two hundred men in this business, and they about fifteen thousand. My wife was so much delighted by this that she celebrated it all night long, and she has a feeling that you took part in the action and distinguished yourself."

In spite of these words, in spite of the expressions which I have put in italics and the general tone of the letter, Captain Mikhaïloff took a sweet and sad satisfaction in imagining himself with his pale provincial lady friend. He recalled their evening conversations on *sentiment* in the parlour arbour, and how his brave comrade, the ex-lancer, became vexed and disputed over games of cards with copek stakes when they succeeded in starting a game in his study, and how his wife joked him about it. He recalled

---

* A sort of arbour covered with ivy was then erected in most fashionable parlours.—TRANS.

the friendship these good people had shown for him ; and perhaps there was something more than friendship on the side of the pale friend !   All these pictures in their familiar frames arose in his imagination with marvellous softness.   He saw them in a rosy atmosphere, and, smiling at them, he affectionately handled the letter in the bottom of his pocket.

These memories brought the captain involuntarily back to his hopes and his dreams.   " Imagine," he thought, as he went along the narrow alley, " Natacha's joy and astonishment when she reads in the *Invalide* that I have been the first to get possession of a cannon, and have received the Saint George !   I shall be promoted to be captain-major : I was proposed for it a long time ago.   It will then be very easy for me to get to the command of a battalion in the course of a year, for many among us have been killed, and many others will be during this campaign.   Then, in the next battle, when I have made myself well-known, they will entrust a regiment to me, and I shall become lieutenant-colonel, commander of the Order of Saint Anne—then colonel, ———"   He was already imagining himself a general, honouring with his presence Natacha, his comrade's widow—for his friend would, according to the dream, have to die about this time—when the sound of the band came distinctly to his ears.   A crowd of promenaders attracted his gaze, and he came to himself on the boulevard as before, a second-captain of infantry.

CHAPTER II

HE first approached the pavilion, by the side of which several musicians were playing.   Other soldiers of the same regiment served as music-stands by holding the open music-books before them, and a small circle surrounded them—quarter-masters, under-officers, nurses, and children—engaged in watching rather than in listening. Around the pavilion sailors, aides-de-camp, officers with white gloves were standing, or sitting, or promenading. Farther off in the broad avenue could be seen a confused crowd of officers of every branch of the service, women of every class, some with bonnets on, the majority with kerchiefs on their heads ; others wore neither bonnets nor kerchiefs, but, astonishing to relate, there were no old women, all were young. Below, in fragrant paths shaded by white acacias, were seen isolated groups, seated and walking.

No one expressed any particular joy at the sight of Captain Mikhaïloff, with the exception, perhaps, of Objogoff and Souslikoff, captains in his regiment, who shook his hand warmly. But the first of the two had no gloves ; he wore trousers of camel's-hair cloth, a shabby coat, and his red face was covered with perspiration ; the second spoke with too loud a voice, and with shocking freedom of speech. It was not very flattering to walk with these men, especially in the presence of officers with white gloves. Among the latter was an aide-de-camp, with whom Mikhaïloff exchanged salutes, and a staff-officer whom he could have saluted as well, having seen him a couple of times at the quarters of a common friend.

There was positively no pleasure in promenading with these two comrades, whom he met five or six times a day, and shook hands with each time. He did not come to the band concert for that.

He would have liked to go up to the aide-de-camp with whom he exchanged salutes, and to chat with those gentlemen, not in order that Captains Objogoff and Souslikoff, Lieutenant Paschtezky, and others might see him in conversation with them, but simply because they were agreeable, well-informed people who could tell him something.

Why is Mikhaïloff afraid ? and why can't he make up his mind to go up to them ? It is because he distrustfully asks himself what he will do if these gentlemen do not return his salute, if they continue to chat together, pretending not to see him, and if they go away, leaving him alone among the *aristocrats*. The word *aristocrat*, taken in the sense of a particular group, selected with great care from various classes of society, has lately gained a great popularity among us in Russia—where it never ought to have taken root. It has entered into all the social strata where vanity has crept in—and where does not this pitiable weakness creep in ? Everywhere ; among the merchants, the officials, the quarter-masters, the officers ; at Saratoff, at Mamadisch, at Vinitzy—everywhere, in a word, where men are. Now, since there are many men in a besieged city like Sevastopol, there is also a great deal of vanity ; that is to say, *aristocrats* are there in large numbers, although death, the great leveller, hovers constantly over the head of each, be he aristocrat or not.

With Captain Objogoff, Second-captain Mikhaïloff is an *aristocrat ;* with Second-captain Mikhaïloff, Aide-de-camp Kalouguine is an *aristocrat*, because he is an aide-de-camp, and says thee and thou familiarly to other aides-de-camp ; lastly, with Kalouguine, Count Nordoff is an *aristocrat*, because he is an aide-de-camp of the Emperor.

Vanity, vanity, nothing but vanity ! even in the presence of death, and among men ready to die for an exalted idea. Is not vanity the characteristic trait, the destructive evil of our age ? Why has this weakness not been recognised hitherto, just as small-pox or cholera has been recognised ? Why in our time are there only three kinds of men—those who accept vanity as an existing fact, necessary, and consequently just, and freely submit to it ; those who consider it an evil element, but one impossible to destroy ; and those who act under its influence with unconscious servility ? Why have Homer and Shakespeare spoken of love, of glory, and of suffering, while the literature of our century is only the interminable history of snobbishness and vanity ?

Mikhaïloff, unable to make up his mind, passed

twice in front of the little group of *aristocrats*. The third time, making a violent effort, he approached them. The group was composed of four officers—the aide-de-camp Kalouguine, whom Mikhaïloff was acquainted with ; the aide-de-camp Prince Galtzine, an *aristocrat* for Kalouguine himself ; Colonel Neferdoff, one of the *Hundred and Twenty-two* (a group of society men who had re-entered the service for this campaign ; and, lastly, Cavalry-captain Praskoukine, who was also among the Hundred and Twenty-two. Happily for Mikhaïloff, Kalouguine was in charming spirits ; the general had just spoken very confidentially to him, and Prince Galtzine, fresh from Petersburg, was stopping in his quarters, so he did not find it compromising to offer his hand to a second-captain. Praskoukine did not decide to do as much, although he had often met Mikhaïloff at the bastion, had drunk his wine and his brandy more than once, and owed him twelve roubles and a half, lost at a game of preference. Being only slightly acquainted with Prince Galtzine, he had no wish to call his attention to his intimacy with a simple second-captain of infantry. He merely saluted slightly.

"Well, captain," said Kalouguine, "when are we going back to the little bastion ? You remember our meeting on the Schwartz redoubt ? It was warm there, eh ? "

"Yes, it was warm there," replied Mikhaïloff, remembering that night when, following the trench in order to reach the bastion, he had met Kalouguine marching with a grand air, bravely clattering his sword. "I should not have to return there until to-morrow, but we have an officer sick." And he was going on to relate how, although it was not his turn on duty, he thought he ought to offer to replace Nepchissetzky, because the commander of the eighth company was ill, and only an ensign remained, but Kalouguine did not give him time to finish.

"I have a notion," said he, turning towards Prince Galtzine, "that something will come off in a day or two."

" But why couldn't something come off to-day ? " timidly asked Mikhaïloff, looking first at Kalouguine and then at Galtzine.

No one replied. Galtzine made a slight grimace, and glancing on one side over Mikhaïloff's cap, said, after a moment's silence :

" What a pretty girl, yonder, with the red kerchief ! Do you know her, captain ? "

" It is a sailor's daughter. She lives close by me," he replied.

" Let's look at her closer."

And Prince Galtzine took Kalouguine by the arm on one side and the second-captain on the other, sure that by this action he would afford the latter lively satisfaction. He was not deceived. Mikhaïloff was superstitious, and to have anything to do with women before going under fire was in his eyes a great sin. But that day he was posing for a libertine. Neither Kalouguine nor Galtzine was deceived by this, however. As for the girl with the red kerchief, she was very much astonished, having more than once noticed that the captain blushed when he passed her window. Praskoukine marched behind and nudged Galtzine, making all sorts of remarks in French ; but the path being too narrow for them to march four abreast, he was obliged to fall behind, and in the second file to take the arm of Serviaguine—a naval officer known for his exceptional bravery, and very anxious to join the group of *aristocrats*.

This gallant officer very gladly laid his honest and muscular hand upon Praskoukine's arm, though he knew the latter to be not quite honourable. Explaining his intimacy with the naval officer to Prince Galtzine, Praskoukine whispered that he was a well-known, brave man ; but Prince Galtzine, who the evening before had been on the fourth bastion, and had seen a shell burst twenty paces from him, considered himself equal in courage to this gentleman ; and so, being convinced that most reputations were exaggerated, he paid no attention to Serviaguine.

B

Mikhaïloff was so happy to promenade in this brilliant company that he thought no more of the dear letter received from F——, nor of the dismal forebodings that assailed him each time he went to the bastion. He remained with the others until they had visibly excluded him from their conversation, avoiding his eye, as if to make him understand that he could go on his way alone. At last, indeed, they left him in the lurch.

In spite of all that, the second-captain was so satisfied that he was quite indifferent to the haughty expression with which the yunker Baron Pesth straightened himself up and took off his cap to him. This young man had become very proud since he had passed his first night in the bomb-proof shelter-place of the fifth bastion, an experience which, in his own eyes, transformed him into a hero.

CHAPTER III

NO sooner had Mikhaïloff crossed his own threshold than entirely different thoughts came into his mind. He again saw his little room, where beaten earth took the place of a wooden floor ; his warped windows, in which the broken panes were replaced by paper ; his old bed, beside which there was nailed to the wall a rug with a pattern portraying an amazon ; his brace of Toula pistols, hanging near the head-board, and on one side a second untidy bed with an Indian coverlet belonging to the yunker, who shared his quarters. He saw also his valet Nikita, who rose from the ground where he was crouching, scratching his head bristling with greasy hair. He saw his old cloak, his second pair of boots, and the bundle prepared for the night at the bastion, wrapped in a cloth from which protruded the end of a piece of cheese and the neck of a bottle filled with brandy. Suddenly he remembered that he had to lead his company into the casemates that very night.

" I shall be killed, I'm sure," he said to himself ; " I feel it. Besides, I offered to go myself, and a man who does that is certain to be killed. And what is the matter with this sick man, this cursed Nepchissetzky ? Who knows ? Perhaps he isn't ill at all. And, thanks to him, a man will get killed—he'll get killed, surely. However, if I am not shot I shall be put on the list for promotion. I noticed the colonel's satisfaction when I asked permission to take the place of Nepchissetzky if he was ill. If I don't get the rank of major, I shall certainly get the Vladimir Cross. This is the thirteenth time I go on duty at the bastion. Oh, oh, unlucky number ! I shall be killed, I'm sure ; I feel it. Nevertheless, some one must go. The company cannot go with an ensign ; and if anything should happen, the honour of the regiment, the honour of the army would be compromised. It is my duty to go—yes, my sacred duty. No matter, I have a presentiment——"

The captain forgot that he had this presentiment, more or less strong, every time he went to the bastion; and he did not know that all who go into action have this feeling, though in very different degrees. His sense of duty, which he had particularly developed, calmed him at last, and he sat down at his table and wrote a farewell letter to his father. In about ten minutes the letter was finished. He thereupon arose with moist eyes and began to dress, repeating all the prayers which he knew by heart. His servant, a dull fellow, three-quarters drunk, helped him to put on his new tunic, the old one he was accustomed to wear at the bastion not being mended.

" Why hasn't that coat been mended ? You can't do anything but sleep, you beast ! "

" Sleep ! " growled Nikita, " when I am running about like a dog all day long. I tire myself to death, and after that I am not allowed to sleep ! "

" You are drunk, I see."

" I didn't drink with your money ; why do you find fault with me ? "

" Silence, fool ! " cried the captain, ready to strike him.

He was already nervous and troubled, and Nikita's rudeness made him lose all patience. Nevertheless, he was very fond of the fellow, he even spoiled him, and had kept him with him a dozen years.

" Fool ! fool ! " repeated the servant. " Why do you abuse me, sir—and at this time ?   It isn't right to abuse me."

Mikhaïloff thought of the place he was going to, and felt ashamed of himself.

" You would make a saint lose patience, Nikita," he said with a softer voice. " Leave that letter addressed to my father lying on the table. Don't touch it," he added, blushing.

" All right," said Nikita, weakening under the influence of the wine he had taken, at his own expense, as he said, and blinking his eyes ready to weep.

Then when the captain shouted, on leaving the house, " Good-bye, Nikita ! " he burst into a violent fit of sobbing, and seizing the hand of his master, kissed it, howling all the while, and saying, over and over again, " Good-bye, master ! "

An old sailor's wife at the door, good woman as she was, could not help taking part in this affecting scene. Rubbing her eyes with her dirty sleeve, she mumbled something about masters who, on their side, have to put up with so much, and went on to relate for the hundredth time to the drunken Nikita how she, poor creature, was left a widow, how her husband had been killed during the first bombardment and his house ruined, for the one she lived in now did not belong to her, etc., etc.   After his master was gone, Nikita lighted his pipe, begged the landlord's daughter to fetch him some brandy, quickly wiped his tears, and ended by quarrelling with the old woman about a little pail he said she had broken.

" Perhaps I shall only be wounded," the captain

thought at nightfall, as he approached the bastion at the head of his company. " But where—here or there ? "

And he placed his finger on his stomach and then on his chest.

" If it were only here," he thought, pointing to the upper part of his thigh, " and if the ball passed round the bone ! But if it is a fracture it will be all over."

Mikhaïloff, by following the trenches, reached the casemates safe and sound. In perfect darkness, assisted by an officer of the sappers, he set his men to work ; then he sat down in a pit in the shelter of the parapet. They were only firing at intervals ; now and again, first on our side and then on *his*, a flash blazed forth, and the fuse of a shell traced a curve of fire across the dark, starlit sky. But the projectiles fell far off, behind or to the right of the quarters in which the captain hid at the bottom of a pit. He ate a piece of cheese, drank a few drops of brandy, lighted a cigarette, and having said his prayers, he tried to sleep.

CHAPTER IV

PRINCE GALTZINE, Lieutenant-Colonel Nefer-doff, and Praskoukine—whom nobody had invited, and with whom no one chatted, though he followed them just the same—left the boulevard to go and take tea at Kalouguine's quarters.

" Finish your story about Vaska Mendel," said Kalouguine.

Having thrown off his cloak, he sat down beside the window in a stuffed easy-chair, and unbuttoned the collar of his well-starched fine linen shirt.

" How did he get married again ? "

" It's quite incredible, I tell you ! There was a time when there was nothing else talked about at Petersburg," replied Prince Galtzine, laughing.

He left the piano where he had been sitting, and drew near the window.

" Yes, indeed, it's quite incredible !   I know all the details——"

And gaily and wittily he set about relating the story of an amorous intrigue, which we will pass over in silence, because it offers us little interest.   The striking thing about these gentlemen was, that one of them seated at the window, another at the piano, and a third on a chair with his legs doubled up, seemed to be quite different men from what they were a moment before on the boulevard.   No more conceit, no more of that ridiculous affectation towards the infantry officers.   Here between themselves they showed what they really were—good fellows, gay, and in high spirits.   Their conversation related to their comrades and their acquaintances in Petersburg.

" And Maslovsky ? "

" Which one—the lancer or the horse guardsman ? "

" I know them both.   In my time the horse guardsman was only a boy just out of school.   And the oldest, is he a captain ? "

" Oh, yes, he has been one for a long time."

" Is he always with his gipsy girl ? "

" No, he left her——"

And the talk went on in this way.

Then Galtzine sang in a charming manner a gipsy song, accompanying himself on the piano.   Praskoukine, without being asked, sang second, and so well too that, to his great delight, they begged him to do it again.

A servant brought some tea, cream, and rusks on a silver tray.

" Give some to the prince," said Kalouguine.

" Isn't it strange to think," said Galtzine, drinking his glass of tea near the window, " that we are here in a besieged city, that we have a piano, tea with cream, and all this in lodgings which I would be glad to live in at Petersburg ? "

" If we didn't even have that," said the old

lieutenant-colonel, always discontented, "existence would be intolerable. This continual expectation of something, or this seeing people killed every day without stopping, and this living in the mud without the least comfort——"

"But our infantry officers," interrupted Kalouguine, "those who live at the bastions with the soldiers, and share their soup with them in the bomb-proof shelter places, how do they get on ?"

"How do they get on ? They don't change their linen, to be sure, for ten days at a time, but they are astonishing fellows ; true heroes !"

Just at this moment an infantry officer entered the room.

"I—I have received an order—to go to general— to his excellency, from General N——," he said, timidly saluting.

Kalouguine rose, and without returning the salute of the new-comer, without inviting him to be seated, begged him with cruel politeness and an official smile to wait a while ; then he went on talking in French with Galtzine, without paying the slightest attention to the poor officer, who stood in the middle of the room, and did not know what to do with himself.

"I have been sent on an important matter," he said at last, after a moment's silence.

"If that is so, be kind enough to follow me." And Kalouguine threw on his cloak and turned towards the door. An instant later he came back from the general's room.

"Well, gentlemen, I believe they are going to make it warm to-night."

"Ah, what—a sortie ?" they all asked together.

"I don't know, you will see yourselves," he replied, with an enigmatical smile.

"My chief is at the bastion ; I must go there," said Praskoukine, putting on his sword.

No one replied ; he ought to know what he had to do. Praskoukine and Neferdoff went out to go to their posts.

"Good-bye, gentlemen, *au revoir!* we shall meet again to - night," cried Kalouguine through the window, while they set off at a rapid trot, bending over the pommels of their Cossack saddles. The sound of their horses' shoes quickly died away in the dark street.

"Come, tell me, will there really be something going on to-night?" said Galtzine, leaning on the window-sill near Kalouguine, whence they were watching the shells rising over the bastions.

"I can tell you, you alone. You have been in the bastions, haven't you?"

Although Galtzine had only been there once, he replied by an affirmative gesture.

"Well, opposite our lunette there was a trench "—and Kalouguine, who was not a specialist, but who was satisfied of the value of his military attainments, began to explain confusedly, and making a wrong use of various engineering terms, the state of our works, the situation of the enemy, and the plan of the affair which had been prepared.

"There! there! They have begun to fire heavily on our quarters; is that coming from our side or from *his*—the one that has just burst there?" And the two officers, leaning out of the window, watched the lines of fire which the shells traced as they crossed in the air, the white powder-smoke, the flashes which preceded each report and illuminated for a second the blue-black sky; they listened also to the roar of the cannonade, which increased in violence.

"What a charming panorama!" said Kalouguine, attracting his guest's attention to the truly beautiful spectacle. "Do you know that sometimes one can't tell a star from a bombshell?"

"Yes, it is true; I just took that for a star, but it is coming down. Look! it bursts! And that large star there yonder—what do they call it? One would say it was a shell!"

"I am so accustomed to this that when I go back to Russia a starry sky will seem to me to be sparkling with bombshells. One gets so used to it."

" Ought I not to go and take part in this sortie ? "
said Prince Galtzine, after a pause.

" My dear fellow, what an idea ! Don't think of
it. I won't let you go ; you will have time enough."

" Seriously, do you think I ought not to ? "

At this moment, in the direction in which these
gentlemen were looking, one could hear, above the
roar of artillery, the rattle of a terrible fusillade ; a
thousand little flames spurted and sparkled along the
whole line.

" Look, it is in full swing," said Kalouguine. " I
can't calmly listen to this fusillade ; it stirs my soul !
They are shouting ' Hurrah ! ' " he added, stretching
his ear towards the bastion, from which arose the
distant and prolonged clamour of thousands of voices.

" Who is shouting ' Hurrah '—*he* or we ? "

" I don't know ; but they are surely fighting at
the sword's point, for the fusillade has stopped."

An officer on horseback, followed by a Cossack,
galloped up under their window, and dismounted.

" Where do you come from ? "

" From the bastion, to see the general."

" Come, what is the matter ? Speak ! "

" They have attacked—have taken the quarters.
The French have pushed forward their reserves—ours
have been attacked—and there were only two battalions of them," said the officer, out of breath.

It was the same one who had come in the evening,
but this time he went towards the door with confidence.

" Then we retreated ? " asked Galtzine.

" No," replied the officer, in a surly tone, " a battalion arrived in time. We repulsed them, but the
colonel of the regiment is killed, and many officers
besides. They want reinforcements."

So saying, he went with Kalouguine into the
general's room, whither we will not follow them.

Five minutes later Kalouguine set out for the
bastion on a horse, which he rode in the Cossack
fashion, a kind of riding which seems to give a
particular pleasure to the aides-de-camp. He was

the bearer of certain orders, and had to await the
final result of the affair. As to Prince Galtzine,
agitated by the painful emotions which the signs of a
battle in progress usually excite in the idle spectator,
he hastily went out into the street to wander aimlessly
to and fro.

CHAPTER V

SOLDIERS passed carrying the wounded on
stretchers, and supporting others under the
arms. It was dark in the streets; here and there
shone the lights in the hospital windows or in the
quarters of a wakeful officer. The uninterrupted
sound of the cannonade and the fusillade came from
the bastions, and the same fires still lighted up the
black sky. From time to time one could hear the
gallop of a staff-officer, the groan of a wounded man,
the steps and the voices of the stretcher-bearers, and
the exclamations of doting women who stood on the
thresholds of their houses and watched in the direction of the firing.

Among these last we find our acquaintance Nikita,
the old sailor's widow with whom he had made peace,
and the little daughter of the latter, a child ten years
old.

" Oh, my God! holy Virgin and Mother! " murmured the old woman with a sigh; and she followed
with her eyes the shells which flew through space
from one point to another like balls of fire. " What
a misfortune! what a misfortune! The first bombardment was not so hard. Look! one cursed thing
has burst in the outskirts of the town right over our
house! "

" No, it is farther off; they are falling in Aunt
Arina's garden," said the child.

" Where is my master? where is he now? "
groaned Nikita, still drunk, and drawling out his

words. " No tongue can tell how I love my master ! If, God forbid, they commit the sin of killing him, I assure you, good aunt, that I won't be answerable for what I may do ! Really, he is such a good master that—— There is no word to express it, you see. I wouldn't exchange him for those who are playing cards inside there. Really ! " concluded Nikita, pointing to the captain's room, in which the yunker Yvatchesky had arranged with some ensigns a little festival to celebrate the decoration he had just received.

" What a lot of shooting-stars there are ! what a lot of shooting-stars there are ! " cried the child, breaking the silence which followed Nikita's speech. " There ! there ! another one is falling ! What is that for ? Say, mother."

" They'll destroy our cabin ! " sighed the old woman without replying.

" To-day," resumed the little prattler, in a sing-song voice—" to-day I saw in uncle's room, near the wardrobe, an enormous ball ; it had come through the roof and had fallen right into the room. It is so large that they can't lift it."

" The women who had husbands and money are gone away," continued the old woman. " I have only a cabin, and they are destoying that ! Look ! look how they are firing, the wretches ! Lord, my God ! "

" And just as we were coming out of uncle's house," the child went on, " a bombshell came straight down ; it burst, and threw the earth about on all sides ; one little piece almost struck us ! "

CHAPTER VI

PRINCE GALTZINE met wounded men in constantly increasing numbers, some borne on stretchers, others dragging themselves along on foot or supporting each other, and talking noisily.

" When they fell upon us, brothers," remarked a tall, deep-voiced soldier, who carried two muskets on his shoulder—" when they fell upon us, shouting ' Allah ! Allah ! '* they pushed one another on. We killed the first, and others climbed over them. There was nothing to be done ; there were too many of them —too many of them."

" You come from the bastion ? " asked Galtzine, interrupting the orator.

" Yes, your excellency."

" Well what happened there ?   Tell me."

" This happened, your excellency—*his strength* surrounded us ; he climbed up the ramparts and had the best of it, your excellency."

" How ? the best of it ? But you beat them back ? "

" Ah, yes, beat them back ! But when all *his strength* came down upon us, *he* killed our men, and we had no help ! "

The soldier was mistaken, for the trenches were ours ; however, strange but well-authenticated fact, a soldier wounded in a battle always believes it a lost and a terrible bloody one.

" I was told, nevertheless, that you beat him back," continued Galtzine, good-naturedly ; " perhaps it was after you came away. Did you leave there long ago ? "

" This very moment, your excellency. The trenches must belong to him ; *he* had the upper hand——"

" Why, aren't you ashamed of yourselves ? Abandon the trenches ! It is frightful," said Galtzine, irritated by the indifference of the man.

" What could be done when *he* had the *strength*."

" Ah, your excellency," said a soldier borne on a stretcher, " why not abandon them when he had killed as all ? If we had had the *strength* we would

---

* The Russian soldiers, accustomed to fight the Turks and to hear their battle-cries, always asserted that the French had the same shout, " Allah ! "

never have abandoned them! But what was to be done? I had just stuck one of them when I was hit —Oh softly, brothers, softly! Oh, for mercy's sake!" groaned the wounded man.

"Hold on; far too many are coming back," said Galtzine, again stopping the tall soldier with the two muskets. "Why don't you go back, eh? Halt!"

The soldier obeyed, and took off his cap with his left hand.

"Where are you going to?" sternly demanded the prince, "and who gave you permission, you good-for——" But coming nearer, he saw that the soldier's right arm was covered with blood up to the elbow.

"I am wounded, your excellency."

"Wounded! where?"

"Here, by a bullet," and the soldier showed his arm; "but I don't know what hit me a crack there." He held his head down, and showed on the back of his neck some locks of hair glued together by coagulated blood.

"Whose gun is this?"

"It is a French carbine, your excellency: I brought it away. I wouldn't have come away, but I had to lead that little soldier, who might fall down," and he pointed to an infantryman who was walking some paces ahead of them, leaning on his gun, and dragging his left leg with difficulty.

Prince Galtzine felt cruelly ashamed of his unjust suspicions, and conscious that he was blushing, he turned round. Without questioning or looking after the wounded any more, he directed his steps towards the field-hospital. Making his way to the entrance with difficulty through soldiers, litters, and stretcher-bearers who came in with the wounded and went out with the dead, Galtzine proceeded as far as the first room, took one look about him, recoiled involuntarily, and then precipitately fled into the street. What he had seen was far too horrible.

CHAPTER VII

THE lofty, sombre hall, lighted only by four or five candles, which the surgeons moved about while examining the wounded, was literally crammed with people. Stretcher-bearers continually brought more wounded and placed them side by side in rows on the ground. The crowd was so great that the poor fellows pushed against one another and bathed in their neighbours' blood. Pools of stagnant gore stood in empty places; from the feverish breath of several hundred men, and the perspiration of the bearers, rose a heavy, thick, fetid atmosphere in which the candles burned dimly in different parts of the hall. A confused murmur of groans, sighs and death-rattles, was interrupted by piercing cries. Sisters of Charity, whose calm faces did not express woman's futile and tearful compassion, but an active and lively interest, glided here and there in the midst of bloody coats and skirts, sometimes striding over the wounded, carrying medicines, water, bandages, and lint. Surgeons with their sleeves turned up, on their knees before the wounded, examined and probed the wounds by the flare of the lights held by their assistants, and in spite of the terrible cries and supplications of the patients. Seated at a little table beside the door a surgeon wrote down number 532.

"Ivan Bogoïeff, private in the third company of the regiment from C—— *fractura femuris complicata* !" shouted another surgeon, who was dressing a broken limb at the other end of the hall. "Turn him over."

"Oh, oh, good fathers !" gasped the soldier, begging them to leave him in peace.

"*Perforatio capitis*. Simon Neferdoff, lieutenant-colonel of the infantry regiment from N——. Have a little patience, colonel. There is no way of—— I shall be obliged to leave you there," said a third surgeon, who was fumbling with a sort of hook in the head of the unfortunate officer.

"In Heaven's name, get done quickly!"

"*Perforatio pectoris*. Sebastian Sereda, private—what regiment? But it is no use, don't write it down. *Moritur*. Carry him off," added the surgeon, leaving the dying man, who with upturned eyes was already gasping.

Forty or fifty stretcher-bearers awaited their burdens at the door. The living were sent to the hospital, the dead to the chapel. They waited in silence, but sometimes a sigh escaped them as they contemplated this picture.

CHAPTER VIII

KALOUGUINE met many wounded on his way to the bastion. Knowing by experience the bad influence of this spectacle on the spirits of a man who is going under fire, he not only did not stop to ask questions, but he tried not to notice those he met. At the foot of the hill he ran across a staff-officer coming down from the bastion at full speed.

"Zobkine! Zobkine! one moment!"

"What?"

"Where do you come from?"

"From the quarters."

"Well, what is going on there? Is it hot?"

"Terribly!"

And the officer galloped off. The fusillade seemed to weaken; on the other hand, the cannonade began again with renewed vigour.

"Hum—a bad business!" thought Kalouguine. He had an indefinite but very disagreeable feeling; he had even a presentiment, that is to say, a very common thought—the thought of death.

He, however, possessed self-love and nerves of steel. He was, in a word, what is commonly called a brave man. He did not give way to this first impression; he raised his courage by recalling the story of one of Napoleon's aides-de-camp, who came to his chief with his head bloody, after carrying an order with all speed.

"Are you wounded?" asked the emperor.

"I crave pardon, sire, I am dead!" replied the aide-de-camp, and falling from his horse, he died on the spot.

This anecdote pleased Kalouguine. Picturing himself in the place of the French aide-de-camp, he lashed his horse, put on a still more "Cossack" gait, and rising in his stirrups to cast a look upon the platoon that followed him at a trot, he reached the place where they had to dismount. There he found four soldiers sitting on some rocks, smoking their pipes.

"What are you doing here?" he cried.

"We have been carrying a wounded man, your excellency, and we are resting," said one of them, hiding his pipe behind his back and taking off his cap.

"That's it—you are resting! Forward! to your post!"

He put himself at their head and proceeded with them along the trench, meeting wounded men at every step. On the top of the plateau he turned to the left, and, a few steps farther on, found himself completely isolated. A piece of shell whistled near him and buried itself in the trenches; a mortar-bomb rising in the air seemed to fly straight for his breast. Seized by a sudden terror, he rushed on several steps and threw himself down. When the bomb had burst some distance off he felt very angry with himself and got up. He looked around to see if any one had noticed him lying down; no one was near.

Let fear once get possession of the soul, and it does not readily yield its place to another sentiment. He who had boasted of never bowing his head, now went along the trenches at a rapid pace, and almost on his hands and feet.

" Ah ! it is a bad sign," thought he, as his foot tripped. " I shall be killed, sure ! "

He breathed with difficulty ; he was bathed with sweat, and he was astonished that he made no effort to overcome his fright. Suddenly, at the sound of a step which approached, he quickly straightened up; raised his head, clinked his sabre with a swagger, and lessened his pace. He met an officer of sappers and a sailor. The former shouted, " Lie down ! " pointing to the luminous point of a bomb-shell, which came nearer, redoubling in speed and brightness.

The projectile struck the side of the trench. At the cry of the officer, Kalouguine made a slight, involuntary bow, but continued on his way without even winking.

" There's a brave fellow," said the sailor, who coolly watched the fall of the bomb. His practised eye had calculated that the pieces would not fall into the trench. " He wouldn't lie down."

To reach the bomb-proof shelter occupied by the commander of the bastion, Kalouguine only had one more open space to pass when he felt himself again overcome by a stupid fear. His heart beat as if it would burst, the blood-rushed to his head, and it was only by a violent effort of self-control that he reached the shelter at a run.

" Why are you so out of breath ? " asked the general, after he had delivered the order he brought.

" I walked very quickly, your excellency."

" Can I offer you a glass of wine ? "

Kalouguine drank a bumper and lit a cigarette. The engagement was finished, but a violent cannonade continued on both sides. The commander of the bastion and several officers, among them Praskoukine, were assembled in the shelter-place ; they were talking over the details of the affair. The interior, covered with figured paper with a blue ground, was furnished with a lounge, a bed, a table covered with papers, and decorated with a clock hanging on the wall and an image, before which burned a small lamp. Seated in this comfortable room, Kalouguine saw all the signs of a quiet life ; he measured with his eye the great beams of the ceiling half a yard thick ; he heard the noise of the cannonade, deafened by the bomb-proofs, and he could not understand how he could have twice yielded to unpardonable attacks of weakness. Angry with himself, he would have liked to expose himself to danger again to put his courage to the proof.

A naval officer with a great moustache and a cross of Saint George on his staff overcoat came up at this moment to beg the general to give him some workmen to repair two embrasures in the battery.

" I am very glad to see you, captain," said Kalouguine to the new-comer ; " the general charged me to ask you if your cannon can fire grape into the trenches."

" One single gun," replied the captain with a morose air.

" Let's go back and look at them ! "

The officer frowned and growled out :

" I have just passed the whole night there, and I have come in to rest a little ; can't you go there alone ? You will find my second in command, Lieutenant Kartz, who will show you everything."

The captain had commanded this same battery for fully six months, and it was one of the most dangerous posts. He had not left the bastion, indeed, since the beginning of the siege, prior to the construction of the bomb-proof shelters. He had gained among the sailors a reputation for invincible courage. On this account his refusal was a lively surprise to Kalouguine.

" That's what reputations are ! " thought the latter. " Then I will go alone, if you allow me," he added aloud, in a mocking tone, to which the officer paid no attention.

Kalouguine forgot that this man counted six whole months of service at the bastion, while he, altogether, at different times, had not passed more than fifty hours there. Vanity, a desire to shine, to get a reward and make a reputation, even the delight of danger, still incited him, whereas the captain had become indifferent to all that. He also had made a show, had performed courageous deeds, had uselessly risked his life, had hoped for and had received rewards, had established his reputation as a brave officer. But to-day these stimulants had lost their power over him ; he looked at things differently. Well understanding that he had little chance of escaping death after six months at the bastions, he did not thoughtlessly risk his life, but limited himself to fulfilling his duty strictly. In fact, the young lieutenant appointed to his battery only eight days ago, and Kalouguine to whom this lieutenant showed it in detail, seemed ten times braver than the captain. Rising in each other's estimation, these two hung out of the embrasures and climbed over the ramparts.

His inspection ended, Kalouguine was returning to the bomb-proof, when he ran against the general, who was going to the observation tower, followed by his staff.

" Captain Praskoukine," ordered the general, " go down, I beg, into the quarters on the right. You will find there the second battalion from M——— which is working down there. Order it to stop work, to retire without any noise, and to rejoin its regiment in the reserve force at the bottom of the hill. You understand ? Lead it yourself to the regiment."

" I'm off," replied Praskoukine, and he departed on the run.

The cannonade was diminishing in violence.

CHAPTER IX

" IS yours the second battalion of the regiment from M———? " asked Praskoukine of a soldier who was carrying sand-bags.

" Yes."

" Where is the commander ? "

Mikhaïloff, supposing that the captain of the company was wanted, came out of his pit, raised his hand to his cap, and approached Praskoukine, whom he took for a commanding officer.

" The general orders you—you must—you must retire at once—without any noise—to the rear ; that is, to the reserve force," said Praskoukine, stealthily looking in the direction of the enemy's fire.

Having recognised his comrade, and having gained an idea of the manœuvre, Mikhaïloff dropped his hand and gave the order to the soldiers. They took their muskets, put on their coats, and marched off.

He who has never felt it cannot appreciate the delight which a man experiences on leaving, after three hours' bombardment, a place as dangerous as these quarters were. During those three hours Mikhaïloff, who, not without reason, was thinking of death as an inevitable thing, had had time to get accustomed to the notion that he would surely be killed, and that he no longer belonged to the living world. In spite of that, it was by a violent effort that he refrained from running when he came out of the quarters at the head of his company, side by side with Praskoukine.

" *Au revoir !* a good journey," shouted the major who commanded the battalion left in the quarters. Mikhaïloff had shared his cheese with him, both of them seated in a pit in shelter of the parapet.

" The same to you ; good luck ! It seems to me it is getting quieter."

But scarcely had he uttered these words than the enemy, who had doubtless noticed the movement, began to fire his best ; our side replied, and the cannonade began again with violence. The stars were shining, but gave little light, for the night was dark. The shots and the shell explosions alone lighted up the surrounding objects for an instant. The soldiers marched rapidly and in silence, some hurrying past the others; only the regular sound of their steps could be heard on the hardened soil, accompanied by the incessant roar of the cannonade, the click of bayonets striking one another, the sigh or the prayer of a soldier : " Lord ! Lord ! "

Occasionally a wounded man groaned, and a stretcher was called for. In the company which Mikhaïloff commanded the artillery fire had disabled twenty-six men since the day before.

A flash illuminated the distant darkness of the horizon ; the sentinel on the bastion cried " Can—non ! " and then a ball, whistling over the company, plunged into the ground, which it ploughed up, sending the stones flying about.

" The devil take them ! How slowly they march ! " thought Praskoukine, who, following Mikhaïloff, was looking behind him at every step. " I could run ahead, since I have delivered the order—but no ! they would say I was a coward ! Whatever happens I will march along with them."

" Why is he following me ? " said Mikhaïloff, on his side. " I always noticed that he brings bad luck. There comes another shell, straight towards us, it seems to me."

A few hundred steps further on they met Kalouguine on his way to the quarters, bravely rattling his sword. The general had sent him to ask how the work went on, but at the sight of Mikhaïloff he said to himself, that instead of exposing himself to this terrible fire, he could just as well find out by asking the officers coming from the place. Mikhaïloff gave him, in fact, all the details. Kalouguine accompanied him to the end of the path, and then re-entered the trench which led to the bomb-proof shelter.

" What's the news ? " asked an officer, who was supping alone in the earthwork.

" Nothing. I don't believe there will be any more fighting."

" How ! no more fighting ? On the contrary, the general has just gone up to the bastion. A new

regiment has arrived. Besides—listen !—the fusillade is beginning again. Don't go. What's the use
of it ?" added the officer, as Kalouguine made a
movement.

"Nevertheless, I ought to go," said the latter
to himself. "However, haven't I been exposed
to danger long enough to day ? The fusillade is
terrible."

"It is true," he continued aloud, "I had better
wait here."

Twenty minutes later the general came back, accompanied by his officers, among whom was the
yunker, Baron Pesth, but Praskoukine was not with
them. Our troops had retaken and reoccupied the
quarters. After having heard the details of the affair,
Kalouguine went out of the shelter with Pesth.

CHAPTER X

"YOU have some blood on your overcoat ; were
you fighting hand-to-hand ?" asked Kalouguine.

"Oh ! it is frightful ! Imagine——" And Pesth
began to relate how he had led his company after the
death of his chief, how he had killed a Frenchman,
and how, without his assistance, the battle would
have been lost. The foundation of the tale (that is,
the death of the chief and the Frenchman killed by
Pesth) was true, but the yunker, elaborating the
details, enlarged on them and boasted.

He boasted without premeditation. During the
whole affair he had lived in a fantastic mist, so much
so that everything that had happened seemed to him
to have taken place vaguely, God knows where or
how, and to belong to some one besides himself.
Naturally enough he tried to invent incidents to his
own advantage. However, this is the way the thing
happened :

The battalion to which he had been detailed to take part in the sortie remained two hours under the enemy's fire, then the commander said a few words, the captains began to move about, the troops left the shelter of the parapet and were drawn up in columns a hundred paces farther on. Pesth was ordered to place himself on the flank of the second company. Neither understanding the situation nor the movement, the yunker, with restrained breath and a prey to a nervous tremor which ran down his back, placed himself at the post indicated, and gazed mechanically before him into the distant darkness, expecting something terrible. However, the sentiment of fear was not the dominating one in his case, for the firing had ceased. What appeared to him strange and uncomfortable, was to find himself in the open field outside the fortifications.

The commander of the battalion once more pronounced certain words, which were again repeated in a low voice by the officers, and suddenly the black wall formed by the first company sank down. The order to lie down had been given ; the second company did the same, and Pesth in lying down pricked his hand with some sharp thing. The small silhouette of the captain of the second company alone remained standing, and he brandished a naked sword without ceasing to talk and to walk up and down in front of the soliders.

"Attention, children ! Show yourselves brave men ! No firing ! get at the wretches with the bayonet ! When I shout ' Hurrah ! ' follow me— closely and all together—we will show them what we can do. We won't cover ourselves with shame, will we, children ? For the Czar, our father ! "

"What's the name of the captain ? " asked Pesth of a yunker next to him. "He is a brave one ! "

"Yes, he's always so under fire. He is called Lissinkoffsky."

Just at this moment a flame spurted out, followed by a deafening report ; splinters and stones flew in the air.   Fifty seconds later one of the stones fell from a great height and crushed the foot of a soldier.   A shell had fallen in the middle of the company, a proof that the French had noticed the column.

" Ah ! you are sending us shells now !   Let us get at you and you will taste the Russian bayonet, curse you ! "

The captain shouted so loud that the commander of the battalion ordered him to be silent.

The first company rose up, after that the second ; the soldiers took up their muskets and the battalion advanced.

Pesth, seized by a foolish terror, could not remember how far they marched ; he went on like a drunken man.   Suddenly thousands of sparks flashed on all sides, with whizzings and crackings.   He gave a yell, and ran forward because they all yelled and ran ;   then he tripped and fell over something.   It was the captain, wounded at the head of his men, who, taking the yunker for a Frenchman, seized hold of his leg.   Pesth pulled his feet away and got up. Some one threw himself on him in the darkness, and he was almost knocked over again.   A voice shouted to him: " Kill him, then !   What are you waiting for ? "

Then a hand seized his musket, and the point of his bayonet penetrated into something soft.

" Ah ! God ! "

These words were spoken in French, with an accent of pain and fright.   The yunker knew he had just killed a Frenchman.   A cold sweat moistened his whole body ;   he began to tremble, and threw down his musket.   But that only lasted a second ;   the thought that he was a hero came to his mind.   Picking up his gun, he left the dead man, running and shouting " Hurrah ! " with the rest.   Twenty steps farther on he reached the trench where our troops and the commander of the battalion were.

" I have killed one ! " said he to the latter.

" You are a brave fellow, baron," was the reply.

CHAPTER XI

" DID you know that Praskoukine is dead ? " said
Pesth to Kalouguine on the way back.

" It isn't possible ! "

" Why not ?   I saw him myself."

" Good-bye ; I am in a hurry."

" A lucky day ! " thought Kalouguine, as he was
entering his quarters. " For the first time I am
lucky. It has been a brilliant affair ; I have come out
of it safe and sound ; there will be recommendations
for decoration. A sword of honour will be the least
they can give me. Faith, I have well deserved it ! "

He made his report to the general, and went to his
room. Prince Galtzine was reading a book at the
table, and had been waiting for him a long time.

It was with an inexpressible joy that Kalouguine
found himself at home, far from danger. Lying on
his bed in his night-shirt, he related the incidents of
the fight to Galtzine. These incidents naturally
arranged themselves so as to make it appear that he,
Kalouguine, was a brave and capable officer. He
discreetly touched on this because no one could be
ignorant of it, and no one, with the exception of the
defunct Captain Praskoukine, had the right to doubt
it. The latter, although he had felt very much
honoured to walk arm-in-arm with the aide-de-camp,
had whispered to one of his friends only the evening
before that Kalouguine—a very good fellow, no doubt
—did not like to walk on the bastions.

We left Praskoukine coming back with Mikhaïloff.
He had reached a less exposed place and begun to
breathe again, when on turning around he perceived
the sudden light of a shot. The sentinel shouted,
" Mor—tar ! " And one of the soldiers who followed
added : " It is coming straight into the bastion ! "

Mikhaïloff looked. The luminous point of the bomb-shell seemed to stop directly over his head, at the very moment when it was impossible to tell what direction it was going to take. That lasted for the space of a second. Suddenly, redoubling its speed, the projectile came nearer and nearer. The sparks of the fuse could be seen flying out, the dismal hissing was plainly audible. It was going to drop right in the midst of the battalion. "To the ground!" shouted a voice. Mikhaïloff and Praskoukine obeyed. The latter, with his eyes closed, heard the shell fall some-where on the ground very near him. A second, which appeared to him an hour, passed, and the shell did not burst. Praskoukine was frightened! then he asked himself what cause he had for fear. Perhaps it had fallen farther away, and he wrongly imagined that he heard the fuse hissing near him. Opening his eyes, he was satisfied to see Mikhaïloff stretched motionless at his feet; but at the same time he perceived, a yard off, the lighted fuse of the shell, which was spinning round like a top. A glacial terror, which stifled every thought, every sentiment, took possession of his soul. He hid his face in his hands.

Another second passed, during which a whole world of thoughts, of hopes, of sensations, and of souvenirs passed through his mind.

"Whom will it kill? Me or Mikhaïloff, or indeed both of us together? If it is I, where will it hit me? If in the head, it will be all over; if on the foot, they will cut it off, then I shall insist upon having some chloroform, and I may get well. Perhaps Mikhaïloff alone will be killed, and later on I will tell how we were close together, and how I was covered with his blood. No, no! it is nearer me—it will be I!"

Then he remembered the twelve roubles he owed Mikhaïloff, and another debt left at Petersburg, which ought to have been paid long ago. A gipsy air that he had sung the evening before came to his mind. He also saw in his imagination the lady he was in love with in her lilac trimmed bonnet; the man who had insulted him five years before, and whom he had never taken vengeance on. But in the midst of these and many other souvenirs the present feeling—the expectation of death—did not leave him. "Perhaps it isn't going to explode!" he thought, and he was on the point of opening his eyes with desperate boldness. But at this instant a red fire flashed upon his eyeballs through the closed lids, something hit him in the middle of the chest with a terrible crash, he ran forward at random, entangled his feet in his sword, stumbled, and finally fell on his side.

"God be praised, I am only bruised."

This was his first thought, and he wanted to feel his breast, but his hands seemed as if they were tied. A vice griped his head, soldiers ran before his eyes, and he mechanically counted them:

"One, two, three soldiers, and also an officer, who is loosing his cloak!"

A new light flashed; he wondered what had fired. Was it a mortar or a cannon? Doubtless a cannon. Another shot, more soldiers—five, six, seven. They passed in front of him, and suddenly he became terribly afraid of being crushed by them. He wanted to cry out, to say that he was bruised, but his lips were dry, his tongue was glued to the roof of his mouth. He experienced burning thirst. He felt that his breast was damp, and the sensation of this moisture made him think of water. He would have liked to drink that which drenched him.

"I must have knocked the skin off in falling," he said to himself, more and more frightened at the idea of being crushed by the soldiers who were running in crowds before him. He then again tried to cry out:

"Take me——"

But instead of that he uttered so terrible a groan that he was frightened at it himself. Then red sparks danced before his eyes; it seemed as if the soldiers were piling stones on him. The sparks danced more rapidly, the stones piled on him stifled him more and more. He stretched himself out, he ceased to see, to hear, to think, to feel. He had been killed by a splinter of the shell striking him full on the breast.

CHAPTER XII

MIKHAÏLOFF also threw himself down on seeing the shell. Like Praskoukine, he thought of a crowd of things during the two seconds which preceded the explosion; He said his prayers mentally repeating :

" May Thy will be done ! Why, O Lord, am I a soldier ? Why did I exchange into the infantry to make this campaign ? Why did I not remain in the lancer regiment, in the province of F———, near my friend Natacha ? and now see what is going to happen to me."

He began to count—" One, two, three, four," saying to himself that if the shell exploded at an even number he would live, if at an odd one he would be killed.

" It is all over, I am killed ! " he thought, at the sound of the explosion, without thinking any more of odd or even. Struck on the head, he felt a terrible pain.

" Lord pardon my sins ! " he murmured, clasping his hands.

He tried to rise, but fell unconscious, face downward. His first sensation when he came to himself was of blood running from his nose. The pain in his head was much lessened.

" My soul is departing. What will there be over *yonder ?* My God, receive my soul in peace ! It is nevertheless strange," he reasoned, " that I am dying, for I can distinctly hear the footsteps of the soldiers and the sound of shots ! "

" A stretcher this way ! The captain is killed ! " now cried a voice which he recognised as that of the drummer Ignatieff.

Some one raised him up by the shoulders ; he

opened his eyes with an effort and saw the dark-blue sky over his head, with myriads of stars, and two shells flying through space, as if they were racing with each other. He saw Ignatieff, soldiers loaded with stretchers and muskets, the slope of the intrenchment, and then suddenly he understood he was still in the world.

A stone had slightly wounded him on the head. His first impression was almost a regret. He felt so well, so quietly prepared to go over *yonder*, that the return to reality, the sight of the shells, of the trenches, and of blood, was painful to him. The second impression was involuntary delight at feeling himself alive, and the third was a desire to leave the bastion as quickly as possible. The drummer bandaged his chief's head and led him towards the field-hospital, supporting him under his arm.

" Where am I going, and what for ? " thought the captain, coming to himself a little. " My duty is to remain with my company—all the more," whispered a little voice within him, " since it will shortly be out of range of the enemy's fire."

" It's no use, my friend," he said to the drummer, taking away his arm. " I won't go to the field-hospital ; I will stay with my company."

" You had better let yourself be properly attended to, your Excellency.   It don't seem to be anything at first, but it may grow worse.   Indeed, your Excellency——— "

Mikhailoff stopped, undecided what to do.   He would have followed Ignatieff's advice, perhaps, but he saw what a number of wounded men crowded the hospital, almost all of them seriously hurt.

" Perhaps the doctor will make fun of my scratch," he said to himself, and without listening to the drummer's arguments he went with a firm step to join his company.

" Where is officer Praskoukine, who was beside me a short time ago ? " he asked of the sub-lieutenant whom he found at the head of the company.

" I don't know ; I think he was killed," hesitatingly replied the latter.

" Killed or wounded ? Why don't you know ? He was marching with us. Why didn't you bring him off ? "

" It wasn't possible in that furnace."

" Oh ! why did you abandon a living man, Mikhaïl Ivanovitch ? " said Mikhaïloff, with a vexed tone " Even if he is dead, we must bring off his body."

" How can he be alive ? Indeed I tell you, I went up to him, and I saw—— What would you have ? We scarcely had time to bring off our own men. Ah ! the devils, how they are firing shell now ! "

Mikhaïloff sat down, and held his head in his hands ; The walk had increased the violence of the pain.

" No," said he, " we must certainly go and get him. Perhaps he is alive. It is our duty, Mikhaïl Ivanovitch."

Mikhaïl Ivanovitch did not reply.

" He didn't think of bringing him off at the time, and now I must detail men for it. Why send them into this hell-fire, which will kill them, for nothing ? " thought Mikhaïloff.

" Children, we must go back to get that officer who is wounded yonder in the ditch," he said, without raising his voice, and in a tone which lacked authority, for he guessed how disagreeable the execution of this order would be to the men.

But since he addressed himself to no one in particular, not one of them came forward at this call.

" Who knows ? he is dead, perhaps, and it isn't worth while to risk our men uselessly. It is my fault ; I ought to have thought of it. I will go alone ; it is my duty. Mikhaïl Ivanovitch," he added aloud, " lead on the company ; I will overtake you."

Gathering up the folds of his cloak with one hand, he touched the image of St. Mitrophanes with the other. He wore this on his breast as a sign of special devotion to the blessed one.

He then retraced his steps, assured himself that Praskoukine was really dead, and came back holding in his hand the bandage which had become unwound from his own head. The battalion was already at the foot of the hill, and almost out of reach of the balls, when he rejoined it. A few stray shells still came in their direction.

"I must go to-morrow and be registered at the field-hospital," he said to himself while the surgeon was dressing his wound.

CHAPTER XIII

HUNDREDS of mutilated, freshly-bleeding bodies, which two hours before were full of hopes and of different desires, sublime or humble, lay with stiffened limbs in the flowery and dew-bathed valley which separated the bastion from the intrenchment, or on the smooth flags of the little mortuary chapel of Sevastopol. The dry lips of all of these men murmured prayers, curses, or groans. They crawled, they turned on their sides, some were abandoned among the corpses of the blossom-strewn valley, others lay on stretchers, on cots, and on the damp floor of the field-hospital. Notwithstanding all this, the heavens shed their morning light over Mount Saponn as on the preceding days; the sparkling stars grew pale; a white mist rose from the sombre and plaintively swelling sea; the east grew purple with the dawn, and long, flame-coloured clouds stretched across the blue horizon. As on the days before, the grand torch mounted slowly, powerful and proud, promising joy, love, and happiness to the awakened world.

CHAPTER XIV

ON the following evening the band of an infantry regiment again played upon the boulevard. Around the pavilion officers, yunkers, soldiers, and young women promenaded with a festive air in the paths, shaded by white flowering acacias.

Kalouguine, Prince Galtzine, and another colonel marched arm-in-arm along the street, talking of the affair of the day before. The chief subject of this conversation was, as it always is, not the affair itself, but the part that the talkers had taken in it. The expression of their faces, the sound of their voices, had something serious in it, and it might have been supposed that the losses profoundly affected them. But, to tell the truth, since no one among them had lost any one dear to him, they put on this officially-mournful expression for propriety's sake. Kalouguine and the colonel, although they were very good fellows, would have asked nothing better than to be present at a similar engagement every day, in order to receive each time a sword of honour or the rank of major-general. When I hear a conqueror, who sends millions of men to their destruction in order to satisfy his personal ambition, called a monster, I always want to laugh. Ask sub-lieutenants Petrouchef, Antonoff, and others, and you will see that each is a little Napoleon, a monster ready to engage in battle, to kill a hundred men, in order to obtain one more little star or an increase of pay.

"I beg pardon," said the colonel, "the affair began on the left flank. *I was there.*"

"Perhaps so," replied Kalouguine, "for I was almost all the time on the right flank. I went there twice, first to seek the general, then simply of my own accord to look on. It was there it was hot!"

"If Kalouguine says so, it is a fact," continued the colonel, turning towards Galtzine. "Do you know that only to-day V—— told me you were a brave man? Our losses are truly frightful. In my own regiment four hundred men disabled! I don't understand how I came out alive."

At the other end of the boulevard they saw Mikhaïloff's bandaged head arise. He was coming to meet them.

" Are you wounded, captain ? " asked Kalouguine.

" Slightly—by a stone," said Mikhaïloff.

" Is the flag down ? " said Prince Galtzine, in French, looking over the head of the captain, and addressing himself to no one in particular.

" Not yet," said Mikhaïloff, in the same language, very anxious to show that he knew it.

" Does the armistice still go on ? " then asked Galtzine, addressing himself politely in Russian, as if to say to him, " I know that you speak French with difficulty, why not simply speak Russian ? " Upon this the aides-de-camp went away from Mikhaïloff, who, as on the evening before, felt very lonesome. Not wishing to come in contact with some of them, and not making up his mind to approach others, he limited himself to saluting certain officers, and sat down near the Kazarsky monument to smoke a cigarette.

Baron Pesth also made his appearance on the boulevard. He related that he had taken part in the negotiations of the armistice, that he had chatted with the French officers, and that one of them had said to him :

" If daylight had come an hour later the ambuscades would have been retaken."

To which he had replied :

" For politeness' sake, sir, I will not say the contrary ; " and this remarkable answer had filled the yunker with pride.

In reality, although he had been present at the conclusion of the armistice, and had been very desirous of talking with the French, he had said nothing remarkable. He had simply promenaded about for a long time in front of the lines, asking the nearest Frenchman :

" What regiment do you belong to ? "

They answered him, and that was all. As he advanced a little beyond the neutral zone, a French sentinel, who did not imagine that the Russian understood his language, flung a formidable curse at him.

C

"He is coming to examine our works, this damned——"

After that the yunker returned home, composing along the road the phrase which he had just retailed to his acquaintances.

Captain Zobkine was also seen on the promenade, shouting with a loud voice ; Captain Objogoff, with his torn uniform ; a captain of artillery, who asked no favours of any one ; a yunker, in love—in a word, all the personages of the day before swayed by the same eternal moving forces. Praskoukine, Nefer-doff, and several others were alone absent. Nobody thought of them. Nevertheless, their bodies were neither washed nor dressed nor buried in the earth.

CHAPTER XV

WHITE flags were flying on our fortifications and in the French intrenchments. In the blossom-covered valley mutilated bodies, clothed in blue or grey, and with bare feet, lay in heaps, and the men were carrying them off to place them in carts. The air is poisoned by the odour of the corpses. Crowds of people poured out of Sevastopol and out of the French camp to witness the spectacle. The different sides met with each other on this ground with eager and kindly curiosity.

Listen to the words exchanged between them. On this side, in a small group of French and Russians, a young officer is examining a cartridge-box. Although he speaks bad French he can make himself under-stood.

"And why that—that bird ? " he asks.

"Because it is the cartridge-box of a regiment of the guard, sir. It is ornamented with the imperial eagle."

"And you—you belong to the guard ? "

" No, sir, to the sixth regiment of the line."

" And this—where was this bought ? " And the officer points to the little wooden mouth-piece which holds the Frenchman's cigarette.

" At Balaklava, sir.   It is only palm-wood."

" Pretty," replies the officer, obliged to make use of the few words he knew, and which, *nolens volens*, intrude into the conversation.

" You will oblige me if you will keep that as a souvenir of this meeting."

Then the Frenchman throws away his cigarette, blows into the mouth-piece, and politely presents it to the officer with a salute.   The latter gives him his in exchange.   All the French and Russian bystanders smile and seem delighted.

Here comes a shrewd-looking infantryman in a red shirt, his overcoat thrown over his shoulders.   His face is full of good spirits and curiosity.   Accompanied by two comrades, whose hands are behind their backs, he approaches and asks a Frenchman for a light.   The latter blows into his pipe, shakes it, and offers a light to the Russian.

" Tobacco good ! " says the soldier wearing the red shirt, in French, and the bystanders smile.

" Yes, good tobacco—Turkish tobacco ! " answers the Frenchman ; " and with you Russian tobacco good ? "

" Russian good ! " repeats the soldier in the red shirt, and this time the spectators burst out laughing.

" Frenchmen not good ; good-day, *mousiou*," continues the soldier, making a show of all he knew in French, and laughing, and tapping on the stomach of the man who was talking with him.   The Frenchmen also laugh.

" They are not pretty, these Russian fellows," said a Zouave.

" What are they laughing at ? " asks another, with an Italian accent.

" The jacket good ! " the bold soldier begins again, examining the embroidered uniform of the Zouave.

" To your places, *sacré nom !* " shouts a French corporal at this instant.

The soldiers sulkily disperse.

Nevertheless, our young cavalry lieutenant is strutting in a group of the enemy's officers.

" I knew Count Sasonoff well," says one of the latter. " He is one of the true Russian counts, such as we like."

" I also knew a Sasonoff," replies the cavalry officer, " but he wasn't a count, as far as I know. He is a short, dark man about your age."

" That's it, sir—that's he. Oh, how I would like to see the dear count ! If you see him, give him my regards, Captain Latour," he adds, bowing.

" What a miserable business we are carrying on ! It was hot last night, wasn't it ? " continues the cavalry officer, anxious to keep up the conversation, and pointing to the corpses.

" Oh, sir, it is frightful. But what fine fellows your soldiers are ! It is a pleasure to fight with fine fellows like them."

" It must be confessed that your fellows are up to snuff also," replies the Russian officer, with a salute, satisfied that he has given him a good answer.

But enough on this subject. Let us watch that ten-year-old boy, with an old worn cap on his head which doubtless belonged to his father, with naked legs and large shoes on his feet, and wearing a pair of cotton trousers, held up by a single brace. He came out of the fortifications at the beginning of the truce. He has been walking about ever since on the low ground, examining with stupid curiosity the French soldiers and the dead bodies lying on the ground. He is gathering the little blue field-flowers with which the valley is strewn. He retraces his steps with a great bouquet, holding his nose so as not to smell the fetid odour that comes on the wind. Stopping near a heap of corpses, he looks a long time at a headless, hideous, dead man. After an examination, he goes near and touches with his foot the arm stretched stiffly in the air. As he presses harder on it the arm moves and falls into place. Then the boy gives a cry, hides his face in the flowers, and enters the fortifications, running at full speed.

Yes, flags of truce float over the bastions and on the intrenchments; the brilliantly-shining sun is setting beyond the blue sea, which ripples and sparkles under the golden rays. Thousands of people assemble, look at each other, chat, laugh. These people, who are Christians, who profess to obey the great law of love and devotion, are looking at their work without throwing themselves down in repentance at the knees of Him who gave them life, and with life the fear of death, the love of the good and the beautiful. They do not embrace each other like brothers, and shed tears of joy and happiness! We must at least take consolation in the thought that we did not begin the war, that we are only defending our country, our native land. But the white flags are lowered; the engines of death and suffering thunder once more; again a flood of innocent blood is shed, and groans and curses can be heard.

I have said what I have wanted to say for this time at least, but a painful doubt overwhelms me. It would have been better, perhaps, to have kept silent, for possibly what I have uttered is among those pernicious truths, obscurely hidden away in every one's soul, which, in order to remain harmless, must not be expressed; just as old wine must not be disturbed lest the sediment rise and make the liquid turbid. Where, then, in my tale do we see the evil we must avoid, and the good towards which we must strive to go? Where is the traitor? Where is the hero? All are good and all are bad. It is not Kalouguine with his brilliant courage, his gentlemanly bravado, and his vanity—the chief motive power of all his actions; it is not Praskoukine, an inoffensive cipher, although he fell on the battle-field for his faith, his ruler, and his country ; nor timid Mikhaïloff ; nor Pesth, that child with no conviction and no moral sense, who can pass for traitors or for heroes.

No ; the hero of my tale, the one I love with all the power of my soul, the one I have tried to reproduce in all his beauty, just as he has been, is, and always will be beautiful, is Truth.

SEVASTOPOL IN AUGUST, 1855

CHAPTER I

TOWARDS the end of the month of August there was slowly moving along the stony Sevastopol road between Douvanka* and Baktchisaraï an officer's carriage of peculiar form, unknown elsewhere, which in construction was a queer compound of a basket-chaise, a Jewish britchka, and a Russian country cart.

In this carriage a servant, dressed in linen, with a soft and shapeless officer's cap on his head, held the reins. Behind him, on various parcels and bags covered with a soldier's overcoat, sat an officer in a summer cloak, who was small in stature, as well as could be judged from his position, and who was less remarkable for the massive squareness of his shoulders than for the thickness of his body between his chest and his back.

His neck was largely developed, and the muscles were firmly extended. What is commonly spoken of as a waist did not exist ; and yet he was not cor- pulent, being far from fat ; indeed, his face, upon which was spread a layer of yellow and unhealthy sunburn, was noticeable by its thinness. It would have passed for an attractive one if it had not been for a certain bloating of the flesh, and for its skin furrowed by deep wrinkles, which, interweaving, distorted the features, took away all freshness, and imparted a brutal expression. His small, brown, extraordinarily keen eyes had an almost impudent look. His very thick moustache, which he was in

* The last station before Sevastopol.

the habit of biting, did not extend much in breadth. His cheeks and his chin, which he had not shaved for two days, were covered with a black and thick beard. Wounded on the head by a piece of shell on the 10th of May, and still wearing a bandage, he nevertheless felt entirely cured, and had left the hospital at Sympheropol to join his regiment, posted somewhere in the direction where firing could be heard ; but he had not been able to find out whether it was at Sevastopol itself or at Severnaïa or at Inkerman. The cannonade was distinctly heard, and seemed very near when the hills did not intercept the sound which was brought by the wind. Occasionally a tremendous explosion shook the air and made you tremble in spite of yourself. Now and then less violent noises, like a drum-beat, followed each other at short intervals, intermingled with a deafening rumble ; or perhaps all was confounded in a hubbub of prolonged rolls, like peals of thunder at the height of a storm when the rain begins to fall. Every one said, and indeed it could be heard, that the violence of the bombardment was terrible. The officer urged his servant to hasten on. They met a line of carts driven by Russian peasants, who had carried provisions to Sevastopol, and who were on their way back, with sick and wounded soldiers in grey overcoats, sailors in black pilot-coats, volunteers in red fez caps, and bearded militiamen. The officer's carriage was forced to stop, and he, grimacing and blinking his eyes amid the impenetrable and motionless cloud of dust raised by the carts, which flew into the eyes and ears on all sides, examined the faces as they passed by.

" There is a sick soldier of our company," said the servant, turning towards his master and pointing to a wounded man.

Seated sidewise on the front of his cart a Russian peasant, wearing a full beard, with a felt cap on his head, was tying a knot in an enormous whip which he held by the handle under his elbow. He turned his back to four or five soldiers shaking and tossing about in the vehicle. One of them, with his arm tied up, his overcoat thrown on over his shirt, sat erect and firm, although he was somewhat pale and thin, in the middle place. Perceiving the officer, he instinctively raised his hand to his cap, but remembering his wound, he made believe he wanted to scratch his head. Another one was lying down beside him at the bottom of the cart. All that could be seen of him was his two hands clinging to the wooden bars, and his two raised knees swinging nervelessly like two hempen dish rags. A third, with swollen face, his head wrapped up in a cloth on which was placed his soldier's cap, sat sidewise, his legs hanging outside and grazing the wheel, and he dozed, with his hands resting on his knees.

" Doljikoff ! " the traveller shouted at him.

" Present ! " replied the latter, opening his eyes and taking off his cap. His bass voice was so full, so tremendous, that it seemed to come out of the chest of twenty soldiers together.

" When were you wounded ? "

" Health to your Excellency ! "* cried the soldier in his strong voice, his glassy and swollen eyes growing animated at the sight of his superior officer.

" Where is the regiment ? "

" At Sevastopol, your Excellency. They are thinking of going away from there on Wednesday."

" Where to ? "

" They don't know—to Severnaïa, no doubt, your Excellency. At present," he continued, dragging his words, " *he* is firing straight through everything, especially with shells, even away into the bay. *He* is firing in a frightful manner ! " And he added words which could not be understood ; but from his face and from his position it could be guessed that,

---

* This is the literal translation of the common phrase used by the soldiers in reply to a greeting from their superior officers.

with a suffering man's sense of injury, he was saying something of a not very consoling nature.

Sub-lieutenant Koseltzoff, who had just asked these questions, was neither an officer of ordinary stamp nor one of those who live and act in a certain way simply because others live and act thus. He had been richly endowed with various inferior qualities. He sang and played the guitar in an agreeable manner, he conversed well, and wrote with facility, especially official letters, of which he had acquired the trick during his service as battalion aide-de-camp. His energy was remarkable, but this energy only received its impulse from self-love, and grafted on this second-rate characteristic, it formed a salient and characteristic trait of his nature. That kind of self-love which is most commonly developed among men, especially among military men, had so penetrated into his existence, that the only choice he conceived possible was between "first or nothing." Self-love was then the motive force of his most intimate enthusiasms. Even when quite alone he was fond of considering himself superior to those with whom he compared himself.

"Come! I am not going to be the one to listen to 'Moscow's'* chatter!" murmured the sub-lieutenant, whose thoughts had been troubled somewhat by meeting the train of wounded; and the soldier's words, the importance of which was increased and confirmed at every step by the sound of the cannonade, weighed heavily on his heart.

"They are curious fellows these 'Moscows.' Come, Nicolaïeff, forward! you are asleep, I think," he angrily shouted at his servant, throwing back the lappels of his coat.

Nicolaïeff shook the reins, made a little encouraging sound with his lips, and the vehicle went off at a trot.

"We will only stop to feed them," said the officer, "and then off again—forward!"

---

* In certain regiments the officers nicknamed the soldiers "Moscow," half in scorn, half in kindly sport.

CHAPTER II

JUST as he entered the street of Douvanka, where everything was in ruins, sub-lieutenant Koseltzoff was stopped by a wagon-train of cannon-balls and shells for Sevastopol, which had halted in the middle of the road.

Two infantrymen, seated in the dust on the stones of an overthrown wall, were eating bread and watermelon.

" Are you going far, fellow-countrymen ? " said one of them, chewing his mouthful. He was speaking to a soldier standing near them with a small knapsack on his shoulder.

" We are going to join our company ; we have come from the country," replied the soldier, turning his eyes from the water-melon and arranging his knapsack. " For three weeks we have been guarding the company's hay, but now they have summoned everybody, and we don't know where our regiment is to-day. They tell us that since last week our fellows have been at Korabelnaïa. Do you know anything about it, gentlemen ? "

" It is in the city, brother, in the city," replied an old soldier of the wagon-train, busy cutting an unripe melon with his pocket-knife. " We just came from there. What a terrible business, brother ! "

" What is that, gentlemen ? "

" Don't you hear how *he* is firing now ? No shelter anywhere ! It is frightful how many of our men *he* has killed ! " added the speaker, making a gesture, and straightening up his cap.

The soldier on his travels pensively shook his head, clacked his tongue, took his short pipe out of its box, stirred up the half-burned tobacco with his finger, lighted a bit of tinder from the pipe of a comrade who was smoking, and lifting his cap, said :

" There is no one but God, gentlemen.   Good-bye to you," and putting his knapsack in place he went his way.

" Ah ! it would be better to wait," said the water-melon eater, in a tone of conviction.

" It is all the same," murmured the soldier, settling the knapsack on his back, and worming his way between the wheels of the halted carts.

CHAPTER III

AT the posting station Koseltzoff found a crowd of people, and the first person he perceived was the postmaster in person, very young and very thin, quarrelling with two officers.

" You will not only wait twenty-four hours but ten times twenty-four hours. Generals wait too," he said, evidently with the wish to stir them up in a lively manner.   " And I am not going to hitch myself in, you understand ! "

" If this is so, if there are no horses, they can't be given to any one. Why, then, are they given to a servant who is carrying baggage ? " shouted one of the two officers, holding a glass of tea in his hand.

Although he carefully avoided using personal pronouns, it could easily be guessed that he would have liked to say thee and thou to his interlocutor.

" I want you to understand, Mr. Postmaster," hesitatingly said the other officer, " that we are not travelling for our pleasure. If we have been sum-moned it is because we are necessary. You can be sure I shall tell the general, for it really seems as if you had no respect for the rank of officer."

" You spoil my work every time, and you are in my way," rejoined his comrade, half vexed.   " Why do you talk to him about respect? You ought to speak to him in another manner. Horses!" he suddenly shouted; "horses, this instant."

"I wouldn't ask better than to give them to you, but where can I get them? I understand very well, my friend," continued the postmaster, after a moment of silence, and warming up by degrees as he gesticulated, "but what do you want me to do? Let me just"—and the officers' faces at once had a hopeful expression—"keep soul and body together till the end of the month, and then I shan't be seen any longer. I would rather go to the Malakoff than remain here, God knows! Do what you like, but I haven't a single conveyance in good condition, and for three days the horses haven't seen a handful of hay."

At these words he disappeared. Koseltzoff and the two officers entered the house.

"So!" said the elder to the younger in a calm tone, which strongly contrasted with his recent wrath. "We have already been three months on the road. Let's wait. It is no misfortune; there isn't any hurry."

Koseltzoff with difficulty found an empty corner near the window in the room of the post-house, all smoky, dirty, and filled with officers and trunks. He sat down there, and, rolling a cigarette, began to examine faces and to listen to conversations. The chief group was placed on the right of the entrance, around a shaky and greasy table on which two copper tea-urns, stained here and there with verdigris, were boiling; lump-sugar was strewn about in several paper wrappings. A young officer without a moustache, in a new Circassian coat, was pouring water into a teapot; four others of about his own age were scattered in different corners of the room. One of them, with his head placed on a cloak which served as a pillow, was sleeping on a divan; another, standing near a table, was cutting some mutton into small mouthfuls for a one-armed comrade. Two officers, one in an aide-de-camp's overcoat, the other in an infantry overcoat of fine cloth, and carrying a saddle-bag, were sitting beside the stove ; and it could be readily divined by the way they looked at the others, by the manner the one with the saddle-bag was smoking, that they were not officers of the line, and that they were very glad of it. Their manner did not betray scorn but a certain satisfaction with themselves, founded partly on their intercourse with the generals, and on a feeling of superiority developed to such a point that they tried to conceal it from others. There was also in the place a doctor with fleshy lips, and an artilleryman with a German cast of countenance, who sat almost on the feet of the sleeper, counting money. Four men-servants, some dozing, some fumbling in the trunks and the packets heaped up near the door, completed the number of those present, among whom Koseltzoff did not find a face he knew. The young officers pleased him. He guessed at once from their appearance that they had just come from school, and this called to his mind that his young brother was also coming straight therefrom to serve in one of the Sevastopol batteries. On the other hand, the officer with the saddle-bag, whom he believed he had met somewhere before, displeased him. He found that he had so anti-pathetic and so insolent an expression of face that he went to sit down on the large base of the stove, with the intention of putting him in his proper place if he happened to say anything disagreeable. In his quality as a brave and honourable officer at the front he did not like the staff-officers, and for such he took this one at the first glance.

CHAPTER IV

" IT is bad luck," said one of the young fellows, " to be so near the end and not be able to get there. There will perhaps be a battle to-day, and we shall not be in it."

The sympathetic timidity of a young man who fears to say something out of place could be guessed from the slightly sharp sound of his voice, and from the youthful rosiness which spread in patches over his fresh face.

The one-armed officer looked at him with a smile.

" You will have time enough, believe me," he said.

The young officer respectfully turned his eyes upon the maimed man's thin face, which was lighted up by a smile, and continued to pour out the tea in silence. Indeed the figure, the position of the wounded man, and, above all, the fluttering sleeve of his uniform, gave him that appearance of calm indifference which seemed to reply to everything said and done about him : " All this is very well, but I know it all, and I could do it if I wanted to."

" What shall we decide upon ? " asked the young officer of his comrade with the Circassian coat. " Shall we pass the night here, or shall we push on with our single horse ? "

" Just think of it, captain," he continued, when his companion had declined his suggestion (he spoke to the one-armed man, picking up a knife he had dropped), " since they told us that horses could not be had at Sevastopol at any price, we bought one out of the common purse at Sympheropol."

" Did they skin you well ? "

" I don't know anything about it, captain. We paid for the whole thing, horse and wagon, ninety roubles. Is it very dear ? " he added, addressing all who looked at him, Koseltzoff included.

" It isn't too dear if the horse is young," said the latter.

" Isn't it ? Nevertheless, we have been assured it was dear. He limps a little, it is true, but that will go off. They told us he was very strong."

" What institution are you from ? " Koseltzoff asked him, wishing to get some news of his brother.

" We belong to the regiment of the nobility. There are six of us who are going of our own accord to Sevastopol," replied the loquacious little officer, " but we don't exactly know where our battery is.   Some say at Sevastopol, but this gentleman says it is at Odessa."

"Wouldn't you have been able to find out at Sympheropol?" asked Koseltzoff.

"They didn't know anything there.   Imagine it! They insulted one of our comrades who went to the government office for information!   It was very disagreeable.   Wouldn't you like to have this cigarette already rolled?" he continued, offering it to the one-armed officer, who was looking for his cigar-case.

The young man's enthusiasm even entered into the little attentions he showered on him.

"You have also just come from Sevastopol?" he rejoined.   "Heavens, how astonishing!   At Petersburg we did nothing but think of you all, you heroes!" he added, turning to Koseltzoff with good-fellowship and respect.

"What if you are obliged to go back there?" asked the latter.

"That's just what we are afraid of, for after having bought the horse and what we had to get— this coffee-pot, for example, and a few other trifles— we are left without a penny," he said, in a lower tone, casting a look at his companion on the sly, "so that we don't know how we shall get out of it."

"You haven't received any money for the road, then?" Koseltzoff asked him.

"No," murmured the young man, "but they promised to give it us here."

"Have you the certificate?"

"I know that the certificate is the chief thing. One of my uncles, a Senator at Moscow, could have given it to me, but I was assured I should receive it here without fail."

"Doubtless."

"I believe it also," replied the young officer, in a tone which proved that after having repeated the same question in thirty different places, and having received different replies everywhere, he no longer believed any one.

CHAPTER V

" WHO ordered beet soup ? " shouted the house-keeper at this moment, a stout, slovenly-dressed wench, about forty years old, who was bring-ing in a great earthen dish.

There was a general silence, and every eye was turned towards the woman.   One of the officers even winked, exchanging with his comrade a look which plainly referred to the matron.

" But it was Koseltzoff who ordered it," rejoined the young officer ; "we must wake him up.   Hallo ! come and eat," he added, approaching the sleeper, and shaking him by the shoulder.

A youth of seventeen, with black, lively, sparkling eyes and red cheeks, rose with a bound, and having involuntarily pushed against the doctor said : " A thousand pardons," then rubbed his eyes and stood still in the middle of the room.

Sub-lieutenant Koseltzoff immediately recognised his younger brother, and went up to him.

" Do you know me ? " he asked.

" Oh, oh, what an astonishing thing ! " cried the younger, embracing him.

Two kisses were heard, but just as they were about to give each other a third, as the custom is, they hesitated a moment.   It might have been said that each asked himself why he must kiss three times.

" How glad I am to see you ! " said the elder, leading his brother outside.   " Let's chat a bit."

" Come, come !   I don't want any soup now.   Eat it up, Federson," said the youth to his comrade.

" But you were hungry——"

" No, I don't want it now."

Once outside on the piazza, after the first joyous outbursts of the youth, who began to ask his brother questions without speaking to him of what concerned himself, the lieutenant, profiting by a moment of silence, asked him why he had not gone into the guard, as they had expected him to do.

" Because I wanted to go to Sevastopol. If everything comes out all right, I shall gain more than if I had remained in the guard. In that branch of the service you have to count ten years to reach the rank of colonel, while here Todtleben has gone from lieutenant-colonel to general in two years. And if I am killed, well, then, what's to be done ? "

" How you do argue," said the elder brother, with a smile.

" And then, what I have just told you is of no importance. The chief reason "—and he stopped, hesitating, smiling, in his turn, and blushing as if he were going to say something very shameful—" the chief reason is that my conscience bothered me. I felt scruples at living in Petersburg while men were dying here for their country. I also relied on being with you," he added, still more bashfully.

" You are a curious fellow," said the brother, without looking at him, but hunting for his cigar-case. " I am sorry we can't stay together."

" Come, pray tell me the truth about the bastions. Are they horribly frightful ? "

" Yes, at first ; then one gets used to it. You will see."

" Tell me also, please, do you think Sevastopol will be taken ? It seems to me that such a thing cannot happen."

" God only knows ! "

" Oh, if you only knew how annoyed I am ! Imagine my misfortune. On the road I have been robbed of different things, among others my helmet, and I am in a fearful position. What shall I do when I am presented to my chief ? "

Vladimir Kolsetzoff, the younger, looked very like his brother Mikhaïl, at least as much as a spray of budding eglantine can resemble one which has lost its flower. He had similar blonde hair, but thicker, and curly around the temples ; while one long lock strayed down his white and delicate neck behind—a sign of happiness, as the old women say. Rich young blood suddenly tinged his habitually creamy complexion at each impression of his soul ; a veil of moisture often swept over his eyes, which were like his brother's, but more open and more limpid ; a fine blonde down began to show on his cheeks and on his upper lip, which, purplish red in colour, often extended in a timid smile, exposing teeth of dazzling whiteness. As he stood there in his unbuttoned coat, under which could be seen a red shirt with Russian collar ; slender, broad-shouldered, a cigarette between his fingers, leaning against the balustrade of the piazza, with his face lighted up by unaffected joy, and his eyes fixed on his brother, he was really the most charming and sympathetic youth it is possible to see, and one ceased gazing at him reluctantly. Frankly happy to find his brother, whom he looked upon with pride and respect as a hero, he was, nevertheless, a little ashamed of him on account of his own more cultivated education, his acquaintance with French, his association with people in high places, and considering himself superior to his elder brother, he hoped to succeed in civilising him. His impressions, his judgments, were formed at Petersburg under the influence of a woman, who, having a weakness for pretty faces, made him pass his holidays at her house. Moscow had also contributed its part, for he had danced there at a great ball at the house of his uncle the Senator.

CHAPTER VI

AFTER having chatted long enough to prove, as often happens, that, while loving each other very much, they had few common interests, the brothers remained silent for a moment or two.

"Come, get your traps and we'll go," said the elder.

The younger blushed and became confused.

"Straight away to Sevastopol?" he asked, at length.

"Of course. I don't suppose you have many things with you; we will find room for them."

"All right, we'll go," replied the younger, as he went into the house sighing.

Just as he was opening the door of the hall he stopped and held down his head.

"Go straight to Sevastopol," he said to himself, "be exposed to shells—it is terrible! However, isn't it all the same whether it be to-day or later? At least with my brother——"

To tell the truth, at the thought that the carriage would carry him as far as Sevastopol in a single trip, that no new incident would delay him any longer on the road, he began to appreciate the danger he had come to meet, and the proximity of it profoundly moved him. Having at last succeeded in calming himself he rejoined his comrades, and remained such a long time with them that his brother, out of patience, opened the door to call him, and saw him standing before an officer, who was scolding him like a school-boy. At the sight of his brother his countenance fell.

"I'll come at once," he shouted, making a gesture with his hand; "wait for me, I'm coming!"

A moment later he went to find him.

"Just think," he said, with a deep sigh, "I can't go off with you."

"Stuff and nonsense! Why not?"

"I am going to tell you the truth, Micha. We haven't a penny; on the other hand, we owe money to that captain. It is horribly shameful!"

The elder brother scowled and kept silent.

"Do you owe much?" he asked at last without looking at him.

"No, not much; but it worries me awfully. He paid three posts for me. I used his sugar, and then we played at preference, and I owe him a trifle on that."

" That's bad, Volodia! What would you have done if you hadn't met me?" said the elder, in a stern tone, never looking at him.

" But you know I count on receiving my travelling expenses as Sevastopol, and then I shall pay him. That can still be done; and so I had rather go there with him to-morrow."

At this moment the elder brother took a purse out of his pocket, from which his trembling fingers drew two notes of ten roubles each and one of three.

" Here's all I have," said he. " How much do you want?" He exaggerated a little in saying that it was all his fortune, for he still had four gold-pieces sewn in the seams of his uniform, but he had promised himself not to touch them.

It was found, on adding up, that Koseltzoff owed only eight roubles—the loss on the game and the sugar together. The elder brother gave them to him, making the remark that one never ought to play when he had not the wherewithal to pay. The younger said nothing; for his brother's remark seemed to throw a doubt on his honesty. Irritated, ashamed of having done something which might lead to suspicions or reflections on his character on the part of his brother, of whom he was fond, his sensitive nature became so violently agitated that, feeling it impossible to stifle the sobs which choked him, he took the note without a word and carried it to his comrade.

CHAPTER VII

NIKOLAÏEFF, after refreshing himself at Dou-vanka with two glasses of brandy, which he bought from a soldier who was selling it on the bridge, shook the reins, and the carriage jolted over the stony road which, interspersed with shadow at rare intervals, led along the Belbek to Sevastopol ; while the brothers, seated side by side, their legs knocking together, kept an obstinate silence, each thinking about the other.

" Why did he offend me ? " thought the younger. " Does he really take me for a thief ?   He seems to be still angry.   Here we have quarrelled for good, and yet we two, how happy we could have been at Sevastopol !   Two brothers, intimate friends, and both fighting the enemy—the elder lacking cultivation a little, but a brave soldier, and the younger as brave as he, for at the end of a week I shall have proved to all that I am no longer so young.   I shan't blush any more ;   my face will be more manly and my moustache will have time to grow so far," he thought, pinching the down which was visible at the corners of his mouth.   " Perhaps we shall get there to-day, even, and take part in a battle.   My brother must be very headstrong and very brave ;   he is one of those who talk little but act better than others. Is he continually pushing me on purpose towards the side of the carriage ?   He must see that it annoys me, and he makes believe he does not notice it.   We shall surely get there to-day," he continued to himself, keeping close to the side of the carriage, fearing if he stirred that he might show his brother that he was not well seated.   " We go straight to the bastion —I with the artillery, my brother with his company. Suddenly the French throw themselves upon as. Then I fire, I kill a crowd of them, but they run just the same, straight upon me.   Impossible to fire—I am lost ! but my brother dashes forward, sword in hand.   I seize my musket and we run together ; the soldiers follow us.   The French throw themselves on my brother.   I run up ; I kill first one, then another, and I save Micha.   I am wounded in the arm ;   I take my musket in the other hand and run on.   My brother is killed at my side by a bullet ; I stop a moment, I look at him sadly, I rise and cry, ' Forward with me ! let us avenge him ! '   I add.   ' I loved my

brother above everything ; I have lost him. Let us
avenge ourselves, kill our enemies, or all die together ! '
All follow me, shouting. But there is the whole
French army. Pélissier at their head. We kill all
of them, but I am wounded once, twice, and the
third time mortally. They gather around me.
Gortschakoff comes and asks what I wish for. I
reply that I wish for nothing—I only desire one thing,
to be placed beside my brother and to die with him.
They carry me and lay me down beside his bloody
corpse. I raise myself up and say, ' Yes, you could
not appreciate two men who sincerely loved their
country. They are killed—may God pardon you ! '
and thereupon I die.''

Who could tell to what point these dreams were
destined to be realised ?

"Have you ever been in a hand-to-hand fight ? "
he suddenly asked his brother, entirely forgetting
that he did not want to speak to him again.

"No, never. We have lost two thousand men in
our regiment, but always in the works. I also was
wounded there. War is not carried on as you
imagine, Volodia.''

This familiar name softened the younger. He
wished to explain matters to his brother, who did
not imagine he had offended him.

"Are you angry with me, Micha ? " he asked, after
a few moments.

"Why ? "

"Because—nothing. I thought there had been
between us——''

"Not at all,'' rejoined the elder, turning toward
him and giving him a friendly tap on the knee.

"I ask pardon, Micha, if I have offended you,''
said the younger, turning aside to hid the tears which
filled his eyes.

CHAPTER VIII

"IS this really Sevastopol?" asked Volodia, when they had reached the top of the hill.

Before them appeared the bay with its forest of masts, the sea, with the hostile fleet in the distance, the white shore batteries, the barracks, the aqueducts, the docks, the buildings of the city. Clouds of white and pale lilac-coloured smoke continually rose over the yellow hills that surrounded the city, and stood out sharp against the clear blue sky, lighted by the rosy rays, which were brilliantly reflected by the waves ; on the horizon the sun was sinking towards the sea.

It was without the least thrill of horror that Volodia looked upon this terrible place he had thought so much about. He experienced, on the contrary, an æsthetic joy, a feeling of heroic satisfaction at thinking that in half an hour he would be there himself, and it was with profound attention that he gazed uninterruptedly, up to the moment when they arrived at Severnaïa, at this picture of such original charm. There was the baggage of his brother's regiment, and there also he had to find out where his own regiment and his battery were.

The officer of the wagon-train lived near to what they called the new little town, composed of wooden shanties built by sailors' families. In a tent adjoining a shed of considerable size, made of leafy oak branches which had not yet had time to wither, the brothers found the officer sitting in a shirt of a dirty yellow colour before a rather slovenly table, on which a cup of tea was cooling beside a plate and a decanter of brandy. A few crumbs of bread and caviare had fallen here and there. He was carefully counting a package of notes. But before bringing him on the stage we must necessarily examine closer the interior of his place, his duties, and his mode of life. The quarters were large, solid, and conveniently arranged, provided with turf tables and seats, the same as they provided for the generals ; and in order to keep the leaves from falling, three rugs, of bad design, although new, and probably, very dear, were stretched on the walls and the ceiling of the building. On the iron bed placed under the principal rug, which represented the everlasting amazon, could be seen a red coverlet of shaggy stuff, a soiled torn pillow, and a cloak of genet-skin. On a table were scattered a mirror in a silver frame, a brush with a back of the same metal in a very dirty state, a candlestick, a broken horn comb full of greasy hair, a bottle of liquor ornamented with an enormous red and gold label, a gold watch with the portrait of Peter the Great, some gilt pen-holders, boxes holding percussion-caps, a crust of bread, old cards thrown about in disorder, and finally, under the bed, several bottles, some empty, others full. It was this officer's duty to attend to the wagon-train and the forage for the horses. One of his friends occupied with financial work, shared his dwelling, and was asleep in the place at this moment, while he was making out the monthly accounts with government money. He had an agreeable and martial appearance. He was distinguished by his great stature, a large moustache, and a fair amount of corpulence. But there were two unpleasant things in him which struck the eye at once. First, a constant perspiration on his face, joined with a puffiness which almost hid his little grey eyes and gave him the look of a leather bottle full of porter, and secondly, extreme slovenliness, which was apparent from his thin grey hair to his large naked feet, shod in ermine-trimmed slippers.

"What a lot of money !—heavens, what a lot of money," said Koseltzoff the elder, who, on entering, cast a hungry look at the notes. "If you lend me half, Vassili Mikhaïlovitch ! "

The officer of the wagon-train looked sour at the sight of the visitors, and gathering up the money, saluted them without rising.

"Oh, if it were mine, but it is money belonging to the crown, brother! But whom have you here?"

He looked at Volodia while he piled up the papers and placed them in an open chest beside him.

"It is my brother just out of school. We come to ask where the regiment is."

"Sit down, gentlemen," said the official, rising to go into the tent. "Can I offer you a little porter?"

"I agree to porter, Vassili Mikhaïlovitch."

Volodia, on whom a profound impression was produced by the grand airs of the officer, as well as by his carelessness and by the respect his brother showed him, said to himself timidly, as he sat on the edge of the lounge: "This officer, whom everybody respects, is doubtless a good fellow, hospitable, and probably very brave."

"Where is our regiment, then?" asked the elder brother of the officer, who had disappeared in the tent.

"What do you say?" shouted the latter.

The other repeated his question.

"I saw Seifer to-day," he replied; "he told me it was at the fifth bastion."

"Is it certain?"

"If I say so it is sure. However, devil take him! he lies easily enough! I say," he added, "will you have some porter?"

"I would gladly take a drink," replied Koseltzoff.

"And you, Ossip Ignatievitch," continued the same voice in the tent, addressing the sleeping commissary, "will you have a drink? You have slept enough; it is almost five o'clock."

"Enough of that old joke. You see well enough that I am not asleep," replied a shrill and lazy voice.

"Get up, then, for I am tired of it," and the officer rejoined his guests. "Give us some Sympheropol porter!" he shouted to his servant.

The latter, pushing proudly against Volodia, as it appeared to the young man, pulled out from under the bench a bottle of the porter called for.

The bottle had been empty some time, but the conversation was still going on when the flap of the tent was pushed aside to admit a small man in a blue dressing-gown with girdle and tassels, and a cap trimmed with red braid and ornamented with a cockade.

With lowered eyes, and twisting his black moustache, he only replied to the officers' salute by an imperceptible movement of the shoulders.

" Give me a glass," he said, sitting down near the table. " Surely you have just come from Petersburg, young man ? " he resumed, addressing Volodia with an amiable air.

" Yes, and I am going to Sevastopol."

" Of your own accord ? "

" Yes."

" Why in the devil are you going there ? Gentlemen, really I don't understand it," continued the commissary. " It seems to me, if I could, I would go back to Petersburg on foot. I have had my bellyful of this cursed existence."

" But what are you grumbling at ? " asked the elder Koseltzoff. " You are leading a very enviable life here."

The commissary, surprised, cast a look at him, turned around, and addressing Volodia, said : " This constant danger, these privations, for it is impossible to get anything—all that is terrible. I really cannot understand you, gentlemen. If you only got some advantage out of it ! But is it agreeable, I ask you, to risk becoming at your age maimed and good-for-nothing for the rest of your days ? "

" Some try to make money, some serve for honour," replied Koseltzoff the elder, vexed.

" What is honour when there is nothing to eat ? " rejoined the commissary, with a disdainful smile, turning towards the officer of the wagon-train, who

followed his example. " Wind up the music-box,"
he added, pointing to a box. " We'll hear ' Lucia ' ;
I like that."

" Is this Vassili Mikhaïlovitch a brave man ? "
Volodia asked his brother, when, twilight having
fallen, they again rolled along the Sevastopol road.

" Neither good nor bad, but a terribly miserly
fellow. As to the commissary, I can't bear to see
even his picture. I shall knock him down some day."

CHAPTER IX

WHEN, at nightfall, they arrived at the great
bridge over the bay, Volodia was not exactly
in a bad humour, but a terrible weight lay on his
heart. Everything he saw, everything he heard,
harmonised so little with the last impressions that
had been left in his mind by the large, light examina-
tion-hall with its polished floor, the voices of his
comrades and the gaiety of their sympathetic bursts
of laughter, his new uniform, and his beloved Czar,
whom he had been accustomed to see during seven
years, and who, taking leave of them with tears in
his eyes, had called them " his children "—yes, everything he saw little harmonised with his brilliant
dreams sparkling from a thousand facets.

" Here we are ! " said his brother, getting out of
the carriage in front of the M—— battery. " If they
let us cross the bridge we will go straight to the
Nicholas barracks. You will stop there until to-
morrow morning. As for me, I shall go back to my
regiment to find out where the battery is, and to-
morrow I will go and hunt you up."

" Why do that ? let's rather go together," said
Volodia. " I will go to the bastion with you ; won't
that be the same thing ? One must get accustomed
to it. If you go there, why can't I go ? "

" You would be better not to go."

" Let me go—please do. At least I shall see what it is——"

" I advise you not to go there ; but, nevertheless——"

The cloudless sky was sombre, the stars, and the flashes of the cannon, and the bombs flying in space, shone in the darkness. The bridge-facing and the great white pile of the battery came out sharply in the dark night. Every instant reports, explosions, shook the air, together or separately, ever louder and more distinct. The mournful murmur of the waves played an accompaniment to this incessant roll. A fresh breeze filled with moisture blew from the sea. The brothers approached the bridge. A soldier awkwardly shouldered arms and shouted :

" Who comes there ? "

" A soldier."

" You can't pass."

" Impossible—we must pass ! "

" Ask the officer."

The officer was taking a nap, seated on an anchor. He arose and gave the order to let them pass.

" You can go in, but you can't come out. Attention ! Where are you getting to all together ? " he shouted to the wagons piled up with gabions, which were stopping at the entrance to the bridge.

On the first pontoon they met some soldiers talking in a loud voice.

" He has received his outfit ; he has received it all."

" Ah ! friends," said another voice, " when a fellow gets to Severnaïa he begins to revive. There is quite another air there, by heavens ! "

" What nonsense are you talking now ? " said the first. " The other day a cursed bombshell carried away the legs of two sailors. Oh ! oh ! "

The water in several places was dashing into the second pontoon, where the two brothers stopped to await their carriage. The wind, which had appeared light on the land, blew here with violence and in gusts. The bridge swayed, and the waves, madly dashing against the beams, broke upon the anchors and the ropes and flooded the flooring. The sea roared with a hollow sound, forming a black, uniform, endless line, which separated it from the starry horizon, now lighted by a silvery glow. In the distance twinkled the lights of the hostile fleet. On the left rose the dark mass of a sailing ship, against the sides of which the water dashed violently ; on the right, a steamer coming from Severnaïa, noisily and swiftly advanced. A bombshell burst, and lighted up for a second the heaps of gabions, revealing two men standing on the deck of the ship, a third in shirt-sleeves, sitting with swinging legs, busy repairing the deck, and showing the white foam and the dashing waves with green reflections raised by the steamer in motion.

The same lights continued to furrow the sky over Sevastopol, and the fear-inspiring sounds came nearer. A wave driven from the sea broke into foam on the right side of the bridge and wet Volodia's feet. Two soldiers, noisily dragging their legs through the water, passed by. Suddenly something burst with a crash and lighted up before them the part of the bridge along which a carriage was passing, followed by a soldier on horseback. The splinters fell whistling into the water, which spouted up in jets.

" Ah, Mikhaïl Semenovitch ! " said the horseman drawing up before Koseltzoff the elder, " here you are—well again ? "

"Yes, as you see. Where in God's name are you going ?"

" To Severnaïa for cartridges. They send me in place of the aide-de-camp of the regiment. They are expecting an assault every moment."

" And Martzeff, where's he ? "

" He lost a leg yesterday in the city, in his room. He was asleep. You know him, perhaps."

" The regiment is at the fifth, isn't it ? "

" Yes ; it relieved the M——. Stop at the

field-hospital, you will find our fellows there; they will show you the way."

"Have my quarters in the Morskaïa been kept?"

"Ah, brother, the shells destroyed them long since! You wouldn't recognise Sevastopol any longer. There isn't a soul there; neither women, nor band, nor eating-house. The last café closed yesterday. It is now so dismal! Good-bye!" and the officer went away on the trot.

A terrible fear suddenly seized Volodia. It seemed to him that a shell was going to fall on him, and that a splinter would surely strike him on the head. The moist darkness, the sinister sounds, the constant noise of the wrathful waves, all seemed to advise him not to take another step, and to tell him that no good awaited him there; that his foot would never touch the solid earth on the other side of the bay; that he would do well to turn back, to flee as quickly as possible from this terrible place where death reigned. "Who knows? Perhaps it is too late. My lot is fixed." He said to himself, trembling at the thought, and also on account of the water which was running into his boots. He sighed deeply, and kept away from his brother a little.

"My God! shall I really be killed—I? Oh, my God, have mercy on me!" he murmured, making the sign of the cross.

"Now we will push on, Volodia," said his companion, when their carriage had rejoined them. "Did you see the shell?"

Farther on they met more wagons carrying wounded men and gabions. One of them, filled with furniture, was driven by a woman. On the other side no one stopped their passage.

Instinctively hugging the wall of the Nicholas battery the two brothers silently went along, with ears attentive to the noise of the shells which exploded over their heads and to the roar of the splinters thrown down from above; and at last they reached the part of the battery where the holy image was placed.

There they learned that the Fifth Light Artillery Regiment, which Volodia was to join, was at Korabelnaïa. They consequently made up their minds to go and sleep at the fifth bastion in spite of the danger, and to proceed to their battery on the next day. Passing through the narrow passage, stepping over the soldiers who were sleeping along the wall, they at last reached the hospital.

CHAPTER X

ENTERING the first room, filled with beds on which the wounded were lying, they were struck by the heavy and nauseating odour which is peculiar to hospitals. Two Sisters of Charity came to meet them. One of them, about fifty years old, had a stern face : she held in her hands a bundle of bandages and lint, and was giving orders to a very young assistant-surgeon who was following her. The other, a pretty girl of twenty, had a blonde, pale and delicate face. She appeared particularly gentle and timid under her little white cap ; she followed her companion with her hands in her apron-pockets, and it could be seen that she was afraid of stopping behind. Koseltzoff asked them to show him Martzeff, who had lost a leg the day before.

" Of the P—— regiment ? " asked the elder of the two sisters. " Are you a relative ? "

" No, a comrade."

" Show them the way," she said in French to the younger sister, and left them, accompanied by the assistant-surgeon, to go to a wounded man.

" Come, come, what are you looking like that for ? " said Koseltzoff to Volodia, who had stopped with raised eyebrows, and whose eyes, full of painful sympathy, could not leave the wounded, whom he watched incessantly, at the same time following his brother, and repeating, in spite of himself, " Oh, my God ! my God ! "

" He has just arrived, has he not ? " the young sister asked Koseltzoff, pointing to Volodia.

" Yes, he has just come."

She looked at him again and burst into tears, despairingly repeating, " My God ! my God ! when will it end ? "

They entered the officers' room.   Martzeff was there lying on his back, his muscular arms bare to the elbow and held under his head.   The expression on his yellow visage was that of a man who is clenching his teeth so as not to cry out with pain.   His un-injured leg, with a stocking on, stuck out from under the coverlet, and the toes worked convulsively.

" Well, how do you feel ? " asked the young sister, raising the wounded man's hot head and arranging his pillow with her thin fingers, on one of which Volodia espied a gold ring.   " Here are your comrades come to see you."

" I am suffering, you know," he replied, with an irritated air.   " Don't touch me ; it is well as it is," and the toes in the stocking moved with a nervous action.   " How do you do ?   What's your name ? Ah, pardon ! " when Koseltzoff had told his name. " Here everything is forgotten.   Nevertheless we lived together," he added, without expressing the least delight, and looking at Volodia with a question-ing air.

" This is my brother ; he has just come from Petersburg."

" Ah ! and I have done with it, I believe.   Heavens, how I am suffering !   If that would only stop quicker ! "

He pulled his leg in with a convulsive movement. His toes worked with increased restlessness.   He covered his face with both hands.

" He must be left quiet ; he is very ill," the sister whispered to them.   Her eyes were full of tears.

The brothers, who had decided to go to the fifth

D

bastion, changed their minds on coming out of the hospital, and concluded, without telling each other the true reason, to separate, so as not to expose themselves to useless danger.

"Will you find your way, Volodia?" asked the elder. "However, Nikolaïeff will lead you to Korabelnaïa. Now I am going alone, and to-morrow I will see you."

That was all they said at this last interview.

CHAPTER XI

THE cannon roared with the same violence, but Ekaterinenskaïa Street, along which Volodia went, accompanied by Nikolaïeff, was empty and quiet. In the darkness he could only see the white walls standing in the midst of the great overthrown houses, and the stones of the sidewalk he was on. Sometimes he met soldiers and officers, and going along the left side, near the Admiralty, he noticed, by the bright light of a fire which burned behind a fence, a row of dark-leaved acacias, covered with dust, recently planted along the sidewalk and held up by green painted stakes. His steps and those of Nikolaïeff, who was loudly breathing, alone resounded in the silence. His thoughts were vague. The pretty Sister of Charity, Martzeff's leg, with his toes moving convulsively in his stocking, the darkness, the shells, the different pictures of death, passed confusedly in his memory. His young and impressionable soul was irritated and wounded by his isolation, by the complete indifference of every one to his lot, although he was exposed to danger. "I shall suffer, I shall be killed, and no one will mourn me," he said to himself. Where, then, was the life of the hero full of energetic ardour and rich in the sympathies he had so often dreamed off? The shells whistled and burst nearer and nearer and Nikolaïeff sighed oftener without speaking. In crossing the bridge which led to Korabelnaïa he saw something two steps off plunge whistling into the gulf, illuminating the violet-tinted waves for a second with a purple light, and then bound off, throwing a shower of water into the air.

"Curse it ! the villain is still alive," muttered Nikolaïeff.

"Yes, answered Volodia, in spite of himself, and surprised at the sound of his own voice, so shrill and harsh.

They now met wounded men carried on stretchers, carts filled with gabions, a regiment, men on horseback. One of the latter, an officer followed by a Cossack, stopped at the sight of Volodia, examined his face, then, turning away, hit his horse with his whip and continued on his way. "Alone, alone ! whether I am alive or not, it is the same to all ! " said the youth to himself, ready to burst into tears. Having passed a great white wall, he entered a street bordered with little ruined houses, and continually lighted up by the flash of the shells. A drunken woman in rags, followed by a sailor, came out of a small door, and stumbled against him, "I beg pardon, your Excellency," she murmured. The poor boy's heart was more and more oppressed, while the flashes continually lit up the black horizon and the shells whistled and burst about him. Suddenly Nikolaïeff sighed, and spoke in a voice which seemed to Volodia to express a restrained terror.

"It was well worth our while to hurry from home to come here ! We went on and on, but what was the use of hurrying ? "

"But, thank the Lord ! my brother is cured," said Volodia, hoping that by talking he would drive away the horrible feeling which had seized hold of him.

"Finely cured, when he is still ill ! Even those who are well would find themselves much better off in the hospital in times like these. Do we, perchance, take any pleasure in being here ? Now an arm is

D 2

lost, now a leg, and then——— And yet it is better here
in the city than at the bastion, Lord God ! On the
way a man has to say all his prayers. Ah, scoundrel !
it just hummed in my ears," he added, listening to
the whirr of a piece of shell which had passed close to
him. " Now," continued Nikolaïeff, " I was told to
lead your Excellency, and I know I must do what I
am ordered to, but our carriage is in the care of a
comrade, and the bundles are undone. I was told to
come, and I have come. But if any one of the things
we have brought is lost, it is I, Nikolaïeff, who must
answer for it."

A few steps farther on they came out on an open space.

"Here is your artillery, your Excellency," he
suddenly said. "Ask the sentinel, he will show you."

Volodia went forward alone. No longer hearing
Nikolaïeff's sighs behind him, he felt himself abandoned for good and all. The feeling of this desertion
in the presence of danger, of death, as he believed,
oppressed his heart with the glacial weight of a stone.
Halting in the middle of the space, he looked all about
him to see if he was observed, and taking his head in
both hands, he murmured, in a voice broken by terror :
" My God ! am I really a despicable poltroon, a
coward ? I who so lately dreamed of dying for my
country, for my Czar, and that with joy ! Yes, I am
an unfortunate and despicable being ! " he cried, in
profound despair, and quite undeceived about himself.
Having however, finally overcome his emotion, he
asked the sentinel to show him the house of the
commander of the battery.

CHAPTER XII

THE commander of the battery lived in a little
two-storey house. It was entered through a
court-yard. In one of the windows, in which a pane
was missing, being replaced by a sheet of paper, there

shone the feeble light of a candle. The servant, seated in the doorway, was smoking his pipe. Having announced Volodia to his master, he showed him into his room. There, between two windows, beside a broken mirror, was seen a table covered with official papers, several chairs, an iron bed with clean linen and a rug before it. Near the door stood the sergeant-major, a fine man, with a splendid pair of moustaches, his sword in his belt. On his coat sparkled a cross and the medal of the Hungarian campaign. The commander, small in stature, with a swollen and bandaged cheek, walked up and down, dressed in a frock-coat of fine cloth which bore marks of long wear. He was decidedly corpulent, and appeared about forty years old. A bald spot was clearly marked on the top of his head; his thick moustache, hanging straight down, hid his mouth; his brown eyes had an agreeable expression; his hands were fine and white, a little fat; his feet, which turned out, were set down with a certain assurance and affectation which proved that bashfulness was not the weak side of the commander.

"I have the honour to present myself. I am attached to the Fifth Light Battery—Koseltzoff the younger; ensign," said Volodia, who, entering the room, recited in one breath this lesson learnt by heart.

The commander of the battery replied by a somewhat dry salute, and without offering him his hand begged him to be seated. Volodia then sat down timidly near the writing-table, and in his distraction took hold of a pair of scissors, and began to play with them mechanically. With his hands behind his back and his head bowed, the commander of the battery continued his promenade in silence, casting his eyes from time to time on the fingers which continued to juggle with the scissors.

"Yes," he said, stopping at last in front of the sergeant-major, "from to-morrow forward we must give another measure of oats to the caisson horses they are thin. What do you think of it?"

"Why not? It can be done, your Excellency; oats are now cheaper," replied the sergeant-major, with his arms hanging beside him, and his fingers stirring—an habitual movement with which he usually accompanied his conversation.

"Then there is the forage-master, Frantzouc, who wrote me a line yesterday, your Excellency. He said that we must buy some axle-trees without fail; they are cheap. What are your orders?"

"Well, they must be bought; there is money," answered the commander, continuing to walk. "Where are your traps?" he suddenly said, pausing before Volodia.

Poor Volodia, pursued by the thought that he was a coward, saw in each look, in each word, the scorn he must inspire; and it seemed to him that his chief had already discovered his sad secret, and that he was jeering at him. Then he replied in confusion that his things were at Grafskaia, and that his brother would send them to him on the following day.

"Where shall we lodge the ensign?" the lieutenant-colonel asked the sergeant-major, without listening to the young man's answer.

"The ensign?" repeated the sergeant-major. A rapid glance thrown on Volodia, and which seemed to say, "What sort of an ensign is that?" finished disconcerting the latter. "Down there, your Excellency, with the second-captain. Since the captain is at the bastion his bed is empty."

"Will that do for you while you are waiting?" asked the commander of the battery. "You must be tired, I think. To-morrow it can be more conveniently arranged for you."

Volodia arose and saluted.

"Will you have some tea?" added his superior officer. "The samovar can be heated."

Volodia, who had already reached the door, turned around, saluted again, and went out.

The lieutenant-colonel's servant conducted him downstairs, and showed him into a bare and dirty room where different broken things were thrown aside as rubbish, and in which, in a corner, a man in a red shirt, whom Volodia took for a soldier, was sleeping, wrapped in his overcoat, on an iron bed without sheets or coverlet.

" Peter Nikolaïevitch "—and the servant touched the sleeper's shoulder—" get up ; the ensign is going to sleep here. It's Vlang, our yunker," he added, turning to Volodia.

" Oh, don't disturb yourself, I beg," cried the latter, seeing the yunker, a tall and robust young man, with a fine face, but one entirely devoid of intelligence, rise, throw his overcoat over his shoulders, and drowsily go away, murmuring, " That's nothing ; I will go and sleep in the yard."

CHAPTER XIII

LEFT alone with his thoughts, Volodia at first felt a return of the terror caused by the trouble which agitated his soul. Relying upon sleep to be able to cease thinking of his surroundings and to forget himself, he blew out his candle and lay down, covering himself all over with his overcoat, even his head, for he had kept his fear of darkness since his childhood. But suddenly the idea came to him that a shell might fall through the roof and kill him. He listened. The commander of the battery was walking up and down over his head.

" It will begin by killing him first," he said to himself, " then me. I shall not die alone ! " This reflection calmed him, and he was going to sleep when this time the thought that Sevastopol might be taken that very night, that the French might burst in his door, and that he had no weapon to defend himself, completely waked him up again. He rose and walked about the room. The fear of real danger had stifled the mysterious terror of darkness. He hunted and found to hand only a saddle and a samovar. "I am a coward, a poltroon, a wretch," he thought again, filled with disgust and scorn of himself. He lay down and tried to stop thinking; but then the impressions of the day passed again through his mind, and the continual sounds which shook the panes of his single window recalled to him the danger he was in. Visions followed. Now he saw the wounded covered with blood; now bursting shells, pieces of which flew into his room; now the pretty Sister of Charity who dressed his wounds weeping over his agony, or his mother, who, carrying him back to their provincial town, praying to God for him before a miraculous image, shed hot tears. Sleep eluded him; but suddenly the thought of an all-powerful Deity who sees everything and who hears every prayer flashed upon him distinct and clear in the midst of his reveries. He fell upon his knees, making the sign of the cross, and clasping his hands as he had been taught in his childhood. This simple gesture aroused in him a feeling of infinite, long-forgotten calm.

"If I am to die, it is because I am useless! Then, may Thy will be done, O Lord! and may it be done quickly. But if the courage and firmness which I lack are necsssary to me, spare me the shame and the dishonour, which I cannot endure, and teach me what I must do to accomplish Thy will."

His weak, childish, and terrified soul was fortified, was calmed at once, and entered into new, vast, and luminous regions. He thought of a thousand things: he experienced a thousand sensations during the short time this feeling lasted; then he quietly went to sleep, heedless of the dull roar of the bombardment and of the shaking windows.

Lord, Thou alone hast heard, Thou alone knowest the simple but ardent and despairing prayers of ignorance, the confused repentance asking for the

cure of the body and the purification of the soul—
the prayers which rise to Thee from these places
where death resides ; beginning with the general,
who with terror feels a presentiment of approaching
death, and a second after thinks only of wearing a
cross of Saint George on his neck, and ending with
the simple soldier prostrate on the bare earth of the
Nicholas battery, supplicating Thee to grant him for
his sufferings the recompense he unconsciously has a
glimpse of.

CHAPTER XIV

THE elder Koseltzoff, having met a soldier of his
regiment in the street, was accompanied by
him to the fifth bastion.

" Keep close to the wall, your Excellency," the
soldier said.

" What for ? "

" It is dangerous, your Excellency. *He* is always
passing over us," replied the soldier, listening to the
whistling of a ball, which with a sharp sound struck
the other side of the hard road. But Koseltzoff
remained in the middle of the road without heeding
this advice. There were the same streets, the same
but more frequent flashes, the same sounds and the
same groans, the same meeting of wounded men, the
same batteries, parapets, and trenches, just as he
had seen them in the spring. But now their aspect
was more dismal, more sombre and more martial, so
to speak. A greater number of houses were riddled,
and there were no more lights in the windows—the
hospital was the only exception—no more women in
the streets ; and the character of everyday, careless
life formerly imprinted upon everything was effaced,
and replaced by the element of anxious, weary expectation, and of redoubled and incessant efforts.

He came at last to the farthermost intrenchment

and a soldier of the P—— regiment recognised his former captain. There was the third battalion as could be guessed in the darkness by the constrained murmur of voices and the clicks of the muskets placed against the wall, which the flash of the discharges lit up at frequent intervals.

"Where is the commander of the regiment?" asked Koseltzoff.

"In the bomb-proof shelter, with the sailors, your Excellency," replied the obliging soldier. "If you would like to go I will show you the way."

Passing from one trench to another, he led Koseltzoff to the moat, where a sailor was smoking his pipe. Behind him was a door, through the cracks of which shone a light.

"Can we go in?"

"I will announce you," and the sailor entered the bomb-proof shelter, where two voices could be heard. "If Prussia continues to keep neutral, then Austria ——" said one of them.

"What is Austria good for when the Slavs——" said the other. "Ah, yes! ask him to come in," added this same voice.

Koseltzoff, who had never before set his foot in these bomb-proof quarters, was struck by their elegance. A polished floor took the place of common boards, a screen hid the door. In a corner was a great icon representing the holy Virgin, with its gilt frame lighted by a small pink glass lamp. Along the wall two beds were placed, on one of which a naval officer was sleeping in his clothes; on the other, near a table on which two open bottles of wine were standing, sat the new regimental chief and an aide-de-camp. Koseltzoff was not bashful, and felt himself in nowise guilty, either towards the State or towards the chief of the regiment, and yet, at the sight of the latter—his comrade until very recently—he experienced a certain apprehension.

"It is strange," he thought, seeing him rise to listen to him. "He has commanded the regiment scarcely six weeks, and power is already visible in his bearing, in his looks, in his clothes. Not a long while ago this same Batretcheff amused himself in our quarters, wore the same dark calico shirt for whole weeks, and ate his hash and his sour cream without inviting any one to share it, and now an expression full of hard pride can be read in his eyes, which say to me, ' Although I am your comrade, for I am a regimental chief of the new school, you may be sure I know perfectly well that you would give half your life to be in my place.' "

" You have been treating yourself to a rather long absence," said the colonel, coldly, looking at him.

" I have been ill, colonel, and my wound is not yet altogether healed."

" If that's so, what did you come back for ? " Koseltzoff's bulk inspired his superior with mistrust. " Can you do your duty ? "

" Certainly I can."

" All right. Ensign Zaïtzeff will conduct you to the ninth company, the one you have already commanded. You will receive the order of the day. Be so good as to send me the regimental aide-de-camp as you go out," and his chief, bowing slightly, gave him to understand by this that the interview was ended.

On his way out Koseltzoff muttered indistinct words and shrugged his shoulders several times. It might readily be believed that he felt ill at ease, or that he was irritated, not exactly with his regimental chief, but rather with himself and with all his surroundings.

CHAPTER XV

BEFORE going to find his officers he went to look for his company. The parapets formed of gabions, the trenches, the cannon in front of which he passed, even the fragments and the shells themselves over which he stumbled, and which the flashes of the discharges lighted up without pause or relaxation, everything was familiar to him, and had been deeply engraven on his memory three months before, during the fortnight he had lived at the bastion. Notwithstanding the dismal side of these memories, a certain inherent charm of the past came out of them, and he recognised the places and things with unaffected pleasure, as if those two weeks had been full of only agreeable impressions. His company was stationed along the covered way which led to the sixth bastion.

Entering the shelter open on one side, he found so many soldiers there that he could scarcely find room to pass. At one end burned a wretched candle, which a reclining soldier was holding over a book that his comrade was spelling out. Around him, in the dim light of a thick and heavy atmosphere, several heads could be seen turned towards the reader, listening eagerly. Koseltzoff recognised the A B C of this sentence : " P-r-a-y-e-r a-f-t-e-r s-t-u-d-y. I give Thee thanks, my Cre-a-tor."

" Snuff the candle ! " some one shouted. " What a good book ! " said the reader, preparing to go on. But at the sound of Koseltzoff's voice calling the sergeant-major he was silent. The soldiers moved, coughed, and blew their noses, as always happens after an enforced silence. The sergeant-major arose from the middle of the group, buttoned his uniform, stepped over his comrades, and trampling on their feet, which for lack of room they did not know where to stow, approached the officer.

" How do you do, my boy ? Is this our company ? '

" Health to your Excellency ! We congratulate you on your return," replied the sergeant-major, gaily and good-naturedly. " You are cured, your Excellency ? God be praised for that ! for we missed you a good deal."

Koseltzoff, it was evident, was popular with his

company. Voices could immediately be heard spreading the news that the old captain had come back again, he who had been wounded—Mikhaïl Semenovitch Koseltzoff. Several soldiers, a drummer among others, came to greet him.

"How do you do, Obanetchouk?" said Koseltzoff. "Are you safe and sound? How do you do, children?" he then added, raising his voice.

The soldiers replied in chorus:

"Health to your Excellency!"

"How goes it, children?"

"Badly, your Excellency. The Frenchman has the upper hand. He fires from behind the intrenchments, but he doesn't show himself outside."

"Come, come, who knows? perhaps I shall have the chance of seeing him come out of the intrenchments, children. It won't be the first time we have fought him together."

"We are ready to do our best, your Excellency," said several voices at the same time.

"He is very bold, then?"

"Terribly bold," replied the drummer in a low tone, but so as to be heard, and speaking to another soldier, as if to justify his chief for having made use of the expression, and to persuade his comrade that there was nothing exaggerated or untrue in it.

Koseltzoff then left the soldiers in order to join the officers in the barracks.

CHAPTER XVI

THE great room of the barracks was filled with people—a crowd of naval, artillery, and infantry officers. Some were sleeping, others were talking, seated on a caisson or on the carriage of a siege-gun. The largest group of the party, seated on their cloaks spread on the ground, were drinking porter and playing cards.

"Ah! Koseltzoff's come back! Bravo! And your wound?" said divers voices from different sides.

Here also he was liked, and they were pleased by his return.

After shaking hands with his various acquaintances, Koseltzoff joined the gay group of card-players. One of them, thin, with a long nose, and a large moustache which encroached on his cheeks, cut the cards with his white, slender fingers, on one of which there was a large seal ring. He seemed disturbed, and dealt with affected carelessness. On his right, lying half-raised on his elbow, a grey-haired major staked and paid a half-rouble every time with exaggerated calmness. On his left, crouching on his heels, an officer with a red and shining face joked and smiled with an effort, and when his card was laid down, one of his hands moved in the empty pocket of his trousers. He played a heavy game, but without any money—a fact which visibly irritated the dark officer with the handsome face. Another officer, pale, thin, and bald, with an enormous nose and a large mouth, walking about the room with a bundle of bank-notes in his hand, staked money against the bank and won every time.

Koseltzoff drank a small glass of brandy and sat down beside the players.

"Come, Mikhaïl Semenovitch, come; put up your stake," said the officer who was cutting the cards; "I'll bet you have brought back a lot of money."

"Where could I have got it? On the contrary, I spent my last penny in town!"

"Really! You must have fleeced some one at Sympheropol, I'm sure!"

"What an idea!" replied Koseltzoff, not wanting his words to be believed; and unbuttoning his uniform, so as to be more comfortable, he took a few old cards.

" I have nothing to risk; but, devil take me! who can foresee luck? A gnat can sometimes accomplish wonders. Let's go on drinking to keep our courage up."

Shortly after he swallowed a second small glass of brandy, a little porter into the bargain, and lost his last three roubles, while a hundred and fifty were charged to the account of the little officer with the sweat-moistened face.

" Have the kindness to give me the money," said the banker, interrupting the deal to look at him.

" Allow me to put off paying it until to-morrow," replied the officer addressed, rising up. His hand was nervously moving in his empty pocket.

" Hum!" said the banker, spitefully throwing the last cards of the pack right and left. " We can't play in this way," he rejoined; " I shall stop the game. It can't be done, Zakhar Ivanovitch. We are playing cash down, and not on parole."

" Do you distrust me? That would be strange indeed!"

" From whom have I to get eight roubles?" the major who had just won asked at this moment. " I have paid out more than twenty, and when I win I get nothing."

" How do you think I can pay you when there is no money on the table?"

" That's nothing to me!" cried the major, rising. " I am playing with you, and not with this gentleman!"

" As long as I tell you," said the perspiring officer— " as long as I tell you that I will pay you to-morrow, how do you dare insult me?"

" I'll say what I like. This is not the way to play!" cried the major, excited.

" Come, be quiet, Feodor Feodorovitch!" shouted several players at once, turning round.

Let us drop the curtain on this scene. To-morrow, perhaps to-day, each of these men will go to meet death gaily and proudly, and die calmly and firmly.

The only consolation of a life, the conditions of which freeze the coldest imagination with horror, of a life which has nothing human in it, from which all hope is banished, is forgetfulness, annihilation of the consciousness of reality. In the soul of every man there lies dormant the noble spark which at the proper time will make a hero of him ; but this spark grows tired of shining always. Nevertheless, when the fatal moment comes, it will burst into a flame which will illumine grand deeds.

CHAPTER XVII

THE next day the bombardment continued with the same violence. At about eleven o'clock in the morning Volodia Koseltzoff joined the officers of his battery. He became accustomed to these new faces, asked questions, and, in his turn, shared his impressions with the officers. The modest but slightly pedantic conversation of the artillery-men pleased him and inspired his respect. On the other hand, his own sympathetic appearance, his timid manner, and his simplicity predisposed these gentlemen in his favour. The oldest officer of the battery, a short, red-haired captain with a foretop, and well-smoothed locks on his temples, brought up in the old traditions of the artillery service, amiable with ladies, and posing for a *savant*, questioned him about his acquaintance with this science or that, about the new inventions, joked in an affectionate way about his youth and his handsome face, and treated him like a son, all of which charmed Volodia. Sub-lieutenant Dedenko, a young officer with the accent of Little Russia, with shaggy hair and a torn overcoat, pleased him also, in spite of his loud voice, his frequent quarrels, and his brusque movements, for under this rude exterior Volodia divined a brave and worthy man. Dedenko eagerly offered his services to Volodia, and tried to prove to him that the cannon at Sevastopol had not been placed according to rule. On the other hand, Lieutenant Tchernovitzky, who had high-arched eyebrows, and wore a well-cared-for but worn and mended overcoat, and a gold chain over a satin waistcoat, did not inspire him with any sympathy, although superior to the others in politeness. He continually asked Volodia details about the Czar and the minister of war, related with fictitious enthusiasm the heroic exploits accomplished at Sevastopol, expressed his regret at the small number of true patriots, and made a show of a great deal of knowledge, wit, and exceedingly noble sentiments ; but in spite of all that, and without being able to tell why, all these discourses sounded false to Volodia, and he even noticed that the officers in general avoided speaking to Tchernovitzky. The yunker, Vlang, whom he had awakened the evening before, sat modestly in a corner, silent, but laughing sometimes at a joke, always ready to recall what had been forgotten, presenting a small glass of brandy to the officers in turn, and rolling cigarettes for all. Charmed by the simple and polite manners of Volodia, who did not treat him like a boy, and by his agreeable appearance, his large, fine eyes never left the face of the new-comer. Urged by a feeling of great admiration, Vlang divined and forestalled all his wishes, a fact which the officers immediately noticed, and which furnished a subject for unsparing jokes.

A little before dinner second-captain Kraut, relieved from duty on the bastion, joined the little company. A fair, fine-looking fellow, of a lively turn of mind, the proud possessor of a pair of red moustaches, and side-whiskers of the same colour, he spoke the language to perfection, but too correctly and too elegantly for a pure-blooded Russian. Quite as irreproachable in duty as in his private life, perfection was his failing. A perfect comrade, to be counted on implicitly in all affairs of interest, he lacked something as a man, just because everything in him was an accomplishment. In striking contrast with the idealistic Germans of Germany, he was, after the example of the Russian Germans, in the highest degree practical.

" Here he is ! here's our hero ! " shouted the captain at the moment Kraut came in, gesticulating and clanking his spurs. " What'll you have, Frederic Christianovitch—tea or brandy ? "

" I am having some tea made, but I won't refuse brandy while I am waiting, for my soul's consolation ! Happy to make your acquaintance ! Please get fond of us, and be well-disposed towards us," he said to Volodia, who had arisen to salute him. " I am second-captain Kraut ! The artificer told me you came last evening."

" Allow me to thank you for your bed, which I profited by last night."

" Did you at least sleep comfortable there ? Because one of the legs is gone, and no one can repair it during the siege. You have to keep on wedging it up."

" So you have got out of it safely ? " Dedenko asked him.

" Yes, thank God ! but Skvortzoff was hit. We had to repair one of the carriages ; the side of it was smashed to pieces."

He suddenly arose and walked up and down. It could be seen that he felt the agreeable sensation of a man who has just come safe and sound out of great danger.

" Now, Dimitri Gavrilovitch," he said, tapping the captain's knee in a friendly manner, " how are you, brother ? What has become of your presentation for advancement ? Has it been finally settled ? "

" No ; nothing has come of it."

" And nothing will come of it," said Dedenko ; I've proved it to you already."

" Why will nothing come of it ? "

" Because your statement was badly prepared."

" Ah, what a determined wrangler ! " said Kraut,

gaily. "A truly obstinate Little Russian. All right; you will see that they will make you a lieutenant to pay you for your mortification."

"No, they won't do anything."

"Vlang," added Kraut, speaking to the yunker, "fill my pipe and bring it to me, please."

Kraut's presence had roused them all up. Chatting with each of them, he gave details of the bombardment, and asked questions about what had taken place during his absence.

CHAPTER XVIII

"NOW, then, are you settled?" Kraut asked of Volodia. "But, excuse me, what is your name—both your names? It's our custom in the artillery. Have you a saddle-horse?"

"No," answered Volodia, "and I am greatly troubled about it. I have spoken to the captain. I shall have neither horse nor money until I get my forage-money and my travelling expenses. I should like to ask the commander of the battery to lend me a horse, but I am afraid he will refuse."

"You would like to ask one of Apollo Sergeivitch?" said Kraut, looking at the captain, while he made a sound with his lips which expressed doubt.

"Well," said the latter, "if he refuses, there is no great harm done. To tell the truth, there is seldom need of a horse here. I will undertake to ask him to-day."

"You don't know him," said Dedenko. "He would refuse anything else, but he wouldn't refuse his horse to this gentleman. Would you like to bet on it?"

"Oh, I know you are ripe for contradiction, you——"

"I contradict when I know a thing! He isn't

generous usually, but he will lend his horse, because he has no interest in refusing it.''

'' When oats cost eight roubles it is evidently in his interest to consent. He will have one horse the less to keep.''

'' Vladimir Semenovitch ! '' cried Vlang, coming back with Kraut's pipe. '' Ask for the spotted one ; it is a charming horse.''

'' That's the one you fell into the ditch with, eh, Vlang ? '' observed the second-captain.

'' But you are mistaken in saying that oats are eight roubles,'' maintained Dedenko, in the meantime, continuing the discussion. '' According to the latest news they are ten-fifty. It is evident that there is no profit in——''

'' You would like to leave him nothing, eh ? If you were in his place you would not lend your horse to go into town either. When I am commander of the battery, my horses, brother, will have four full measures to eat every day ! I shan't think of making an income, rest assured ! ''

'' He who lives will see,'' replied the second-captain. '' You will do the same when you have a battery, and he also,'' pointing to Volodia.

'' Why do you suppose, Frederic Christianovitch, that this gentleman would also like to reserve some small profit for himself ? If he has a certain amount of money, what would he do it for ? '' Tchernovitzky asked in his turn.

'' No—I—excuse me, captain,'' said Volodia, blushing up to his ears. '' That would be dishonest in my eyes.''

'' Oh ! oh ! what milk porridge ! '' Kraut said to him.

'' This is another question, captain, but it seems to me that I couldn't take money which doesn't belong to me.''

'' And I will tell you something else,'' said the second-captain in a more serious tone. '' You must learn that, being battery commander, there is every advantage in managing one's affairs well. You must know that the soldier's food doesn't concern the commander. It has always been like that in the artillery. If you don't succeed in making both ends meet, you will have nothing left. Let us count up your expenses. You have first the shoeing "—and the captain bent one finger; "next the medicine "—he bent a second one; "then the administration—that makes three; then the draft-horses, which certainly cost five hundred roubles—that makes four; then the refitting of the soldiers' collars; then the charcoal, which is used in great quantities, and at last the table of your officers; lastly as chief of the battery you must live comfortably, and you need a carriage, a cloak, etc."

"And the principal thing is this, Vladimir Semenovitch," said the captain, who had been silent up to this moment. "Look at a man like me, for example, who has served twenty years, receiving at first two, then three hundred roubles pay. Why shouldn't a man be rewarded for his years of service with a morsel of bread for his old days?"

"It can't be discussed," rejoined the second-captain; so don't be in a hurry to judge. Serve a bit and you'll see."

Volodia, quite ashamed of the remark which he had thrown out without stopping to reflect, murmured a few words, and listened in silence to Dedenko, who set about defending the opposite thesis. The discussion was interrupted by the entrance of the colonel's orderly announcing dinner.

"You ought to tell Apollo Sergeivitch to give us wine to-day," said Captain Tchernovitzky, buttoning his coat. "Devil take his avarice! He will be shot, and no one will get any."

"Tell him yourself."

"Oh, no, you are my elder; the hierarchy before everything!"

CHAPTER XIX

A TABLE, covered with a stained table-cloth, was placed in the middle of the room in which Volodia had been received by the colonel the evening before. The latter gave him his hand, and questioned him about Petersburg and his journey.

" Now, gentlemen, please come up to the brandy. The ensigns don't drink," he added with a smile.

The commander of the battery did not seem as stern now as on the day before ; he had rather the air of a kind and hospitable host than that of a comrade among his officers. In spite of that, all, from the old captain to Ensign Dedenko, evinced respect for him which betrayed itself in the timid politeness with which they spoke to him and came up in line to drink their little glass of brandy.

The dinner consisted of cabbage-soup, served in a large tureen, in which swam lumps of meat with fat attached, laurel leaves, and a good deal of pepper ; Polish *zrasi* with mustard, and *koldouni* with slightly rancid butter ; no napkins ; the spoons were of pewter and wood, the glasses were two in number. On the table was a single water decanter with a broken neck. The conversation did not flag. They first spoke of the battle of Inkerman, in which the battery had taken part. Each related his impressions, his opinion of the causes of the failure, keeping silent as soon as the battery commander spoke. Then they complained of the lack of cannon of a certain calibre ; they talked of certain other improvements, which gave Volodia an opportunity of showing his knowledge. The curious part was that the talk did not even touch upon the frightful situation of Sevastopol, which seemed to mean that each one thought too much about it to speak of it.

Volodia, very much astonished, and even vexed, that there was no question of the duties of his service, said to himself that he seemed to have come to Sevastopol merely to give details about some new cannon and dine with the commander.

During the repast a shell burst very near the house. The floor and the wall were shaken by it as by an earthquake, and powder-smoke spread over the window outside.

"You certainly didn't see that at Petersburg, but here we often have these surprises. Go, Vlang," added the commander, "and see where the shell burst."

Vlang went to look, and announced that it had burst in the yard. After that they did not speak of it again.

A little before the end of the dinner one of the military clerks came in and gave to his chief three sealed envelopes. "This one is very urgent. A Cossack has just brought it from the commander of the artillery," he said. The officers watched the practised fingers of their superior with anxious impatience while he broke the seal of the envelope, marked "immediately," and drew a paper from it.

"What can that be?" each one thought. "Can it be an order to leave Sevastopol for a rest, or an order to bring out the whole battery upon the bastion?"

"What, again!" cried the commander, angrily, throwing the sheet of paper on the table.

"What is it, Apollo Sergeivitch?" asked the oldest officer.

They want an officer and men for a mortar battery. I have only four officers, and my men are not up to the full number," he growled, "and yet they ask for some of them. However, some one must go, gentlemen," he continued, after a moment; "they must be there at seven o'clock. Send me the sergeant-major. Now, gentlemen, who will go? Decide it among yourselves."

"But here is this gentleman who hasn't yet served," said Tchernovitzky, pointing to Volodia.

"Yes, I wouldn't ask for anything better," said

Volodia, feeling a cold sweat moisten his neck and his backbone.

"No—why, indeed?" interrupted the captain. "No one ought to refuse; but it is useless to offer to go; and since Apollo Sergeivitch leaves us free, we will draw lots, as we did the other time."

All consented to this. Kraut carefully cut several little paper squares, rolled them up and threw them into a cap. The captain cracked a few jokes and profited by this occasion to ask the colonel for wine, "to give us courage," he added. Dedenko had a depressed air, Volodia smiled, Tchernovitzky declared that he would be chosen by the lot. As to Kraut, he was perfectly calm.

They offered Volodia the first chance. He took one of the papers, the longest, but immediately changed it for another, shorter and smaller, and unrolling it, read the word, "Go."

"It is I," he said with a sigh.

"All right. May God protect you! It will be your baptism of fire," said the commander, looking with a pleasant smile at the disturbed face of the ensign. "But get ready quickly, and in order that it may be pleasanter, Vlang will go with you in the place of the artificer."

CHAPTER XX

VLANG, delighted with his mission, ran away to dress, and came back at once to assist Volodia to make up his bundles, advising him to take his bed, his fur cloak, an old number of the "Annals of the Country," a coffee pot with a spirit lamp, and other useless articles. The captain, in his turn, advising Volodia to peruse in the "Manual for the use of Artillery Officers" the passage relating to firing mortars, and to copy it at once! Volodia set himself to work at it immediately, happy and surprised to feel that the dread of danger, especially the fear of passing for a coward, was less intense than on the evening before. His impressions of the day and his occupation had partly contributed to diminish the violence of this feeling; besides, as is well known, an acute sensation cannot last long without weakening. In a word, his fear was subsiding. At seven in the evening, at the moment the sun was setting behind the Nicholas barracks, the sergeant-major came to tell him that the men were ready, and were waiting for him.

" I have given the list to Vlang, your Excellency; you can ask him for it," he said.

" Must I make a little speech to them ? " thought Volodia, on his way, accompanied by the yunker, to join the twenty artillery-men who, with swords at their sides, were awaiting him outside—" or must I simply say to them, ' How do you do, children ? ' or, indeed, say nothing at all ? Why not say ' How do you do, children ? ' I think I ought to ; " and with his full and sonorous voice he cried boldly, " How do you do, children ? " The soldiers replied cheerfully to his salutation; his young and fresh voice sounded agreeably in their ears. He put himself at their head, and although his heart was beating as if he had just run several furlongs, his walk was light and his face was smiling. When they reached the Malakoff mamelon, he noticed, while climbing up it, that Vlang, who did not leave his heels, and who had seemed so courageous down below in their quarters, stopped and ducked his head as if the bullets and shells which were whistling without cessation were coming straight towards him. Several soldiers did the same, and the majority of the faces expressed, if not fear, at least disquiet. This circumstance reassured him and revived his courage.

" Here I am, then, I also, on the Malakoff mamelon. I imagined it a thousand times more terrible, and I am walking, I am advancing, without saluting the bullets ! I am less afraid than the others, so I am not a coward," he said to himself joyfully, with the enthusiasm of satisfied self-love.

This feeling was, however, shaken by the spectacle that speedily presented itself to his eyes. When in the dim twilight he reached the Korniloff battery, four sailors, holding by the legs and arms the bloody corpse of a man with bare feet and no coat, were in the act of throwing him over the parapet. (The second day of the bombardment they threw the dead into the ditch, because they had no time to carry them off.) Volodia, stupefied, saw the corpse strike the upper part of the rampart, and thence slide down into the ditch. Fortunately for him, he met at this moment the commander of the bastion, who gave him a guide to lead him to the battery and the bomb-proof quarters of the men. We will not relate how often our hero was exposed to danger during that night. We will say nothing of how he was undeceived when he noticed that instead of finding them firing here according to precise rules such as they practise at St. Petersburg on the plain of Volkovo, he saw himself in front of two broken mortars, one with its muzzle bruised by a shell, the other still upright on the splinters of a destroyed platform. We will not tell how it was impossible for him to get soldiers together to repair it before daylight, how he found no charge of that calibre indicated in the " Manual," nor describe his feelings at seeing two of his soldiers fall, hit before his eyes, nor how he himself, even, escaped death by a hair's-breadth twenty times. Happily for him, the captain of the mortar, who had been given him for an assistant, a tall sailor attached to these mortars since the beginning of the siege, assured him that they could make use of the gun still and promised him while he was walking on the bastion, lantern in hand, as calmly as if he were in his kitchen garden, to put them in good condition before morning.

The bomb-proof shelter into which his guide conducted him was only a great, long cavern dug in the rocky earth, two fathoms deep, protected by oaken timbers eighteen inches thick. There he established himself with his soldiers.

As soon as Vlang noticed the little low door which led into it, he darted in the first with such haste that he nearly fell on the stone-pavement; then he cowered down in a corner, and refused to come out of it. The soldiers installed themselves on the ground along the wall. Some of them lighted their pipes, and Volodia arranged his bed in a corner, stretched himself on it, lighted a candle in his turn, and smoked a cigarette. Over their heads could be heard, deadened by the bomb-proof, the uninterrupted roar of the discharges. A single cannon close beside them shook their shelter every time it thundered. Inside the shelter everything was quiet. The soldiers, still intimidated by the presence of the new officer, only exchanged a word with each other now and then to ask for a light or a little room. A rat was scratching somewhere among the stones, and Vlang, who had not yet recovered from his emotion, occasionally sighed deeply as he looked about him. Volodia, on his bed in this peaceful corner crammed with people, lighted by a single candle, gave himself up to the feeling of comfort which he had experienced as a child when, playing hide-and-seek, he slipped into a wardrobe or under his mother's skirt, holding his breath, stretching his ears, being very much afraid of the dark, and feeling at the same time an unconscious impression of well-being.

In the same way here, without being altogether at his ease, he felt rather disposed to be cheerful.

At the end of ten minutes the soldiers grew bold and began to talk. Near the officer's bed, in the circle of light, were placed the highest in rank—the two artificers, one an old grey-haired man, his breast adorned with a mass of medals and crosses, among which the cross of Saint George was wanting, however, the other a young man, smoking cigarettes which he was rolling, and the drummer, who placed himself, as is the custom, at the orders of the officer, in the background. In the shadow of the entrance, behind the bombardier and the medalled soldiers in front, the "humbles" kept themselves. They were the first to break silence. One of them, running in frightened from outside, served as a theme for their conversation.

"Eh! I say there, you didn't stay long in the street. No young girls are playing there, eh?" said a voice.

"On the contrary, they are singing wonderful songs. You don't hear such ones in the village," replied the new-comer, with a laugh, and all out of breath.

"Vassina doesn't like the shells; no, he doesn't like them!" some one cried from the aristocratic side.

"When it is necessary, it is another story," slowly replied Vassina, whom everybody listened to when he spoke. "On the twenty-fourth, for example, they fired so that it was a blessing, and there is no harm in that. Why let us be killed for nothing? Do the chiefs thank us for it?"

These words provoked a general laugh.

"Nevertheless, there is Melnikoff, who is outside all the time," said some one.

"It is true. Make him come in," added the old artificer, "otherwise he will get killed for nothing."

"Who is this Melnikoff?" asked Volodia.

"He, your Excellency, is an animal who is afraid of nothing. He is walking about outside. Please examine him; he looks like a bear."

"He practises witchcraft," added Vassina, calmly.

Melnikoff, a very corpulent soldier (a rare thing), with red hair, a tremendously bulging forehead, and light blue projecting eyes, came in just at this moment.

"Are you afraid of bombshells?" Volodia asked him.

"Why should I be afraid of them?" repeated Melnikoff, scratching his neck. "No shell will kill me, I know."

"Do you like living here?"

"To be sure I do; it is very entertaining," and he burst out laughing.

" Then you must be sent out in a sortie.   Would you like to ?   I will speak to the general," said Volodia, although he knew no general.

" Why not like it ?   I should like to go very much ! " and Melnikoff disappeared behind his comrades.

" Come, children, let's play ' beggar my neighbour ! ' Who has any cards ? " asked an impatient voice, and the game immediately began in the farthest corner. The calling of the tricks could be heard, the sound of taps on the nose and bursts of laughter.   Volodia, in the meantime, drank some tea prepared by the drummer, offering some to the artificers, joking and chatting with them, desirous of making himself popular, and very well satisfied with the respect they showed him.   The soldiers having noticed that their leader was a good fellow, became animated, and one of them announced that the siege was soon going to come to an end, for a sailor had told him for a certainty that Constantine, the Czar's brother, was coming to deliver them with the American fleet ; that there would soon be an armistice of two weeks as a rest, and that seventy-five kopeks would have to be paid for every shot that was fired during the truce.

Vassina, whom Volodia had already noticed—the short soldier with fine large eyes and side whiskers—related in his turn, in the midst of general silence, which was finally broken by bursts of laughter, the joy that had been felt at first on seeing him come back to his village on his furlough, but how his father had soon sent him to work in the fields every day, while the lieutenant-forester sent to fetch his wife in a carriage.   Volodia was amused by all these tales.   He no longer felt the least fear, and the strong odours which filled the shelter did not cause him any disgust. He felt, on the contrary, very gay, and in a very agreeable mood.

Several soldiers were snoring already.   Vlang was also lying on the ground, and the old artificer, having spread his overcoat on the earth, had crossed himself with devotion and mumbled the evening prayer, when

Volodia took a fancy to go and see what was going on out of doors.

"Pull in your legs!" the soldiers immediately said to one another as they saw him get up, and each one drew his legs back to let him pass.

Vlang, who was supposed to be asleep, got up and seized Volodia by the lapel of his coat. "Come, don't go! what is the use?" he said, in a tearful and persuasive voice. "You don't know what it is. Bullets are raining out there. We are better off here."

But Volodia went out without heeding him, and sat down on the threshold of their quarters beside Melnikoff.

The air was fresh and pure, especially after that he had just been breathing, and the night was clear and calm. Through the roar of the cannonade could be heard the creak of the wheels of the carts bringing gabions, and the voices of those working in the magazine. Over their heads sparkled the starry sky, striped by the luminous furrows of the projectiles. On the left there was a small opening, two feet and a half high, leading to another bomb-proof shelter, where one perceived the feet and the backs of the sailors who lived there, and who were plainly heard talking. Opposite rose the mound which covered the magazine, in front of which men, bending double, passed and re-passed. On the very top of the mound, exposed to bullets and shells which did not stop whistling, there was a tall black figure, with his hands in his pockets, trampling on some fresh earth which was brought in bags. From time to time a shell fell and burst two paces from him. The soldiers who were carrying sacks bent down and separated, while the black silhouette quietly continued levelling the earth with his feet without changing his position.

"Who is it?" Volodia asked Melnikoff.

"I don't know; I am going to see."

"Don't go; it is no use."

But Melnikoff rose without listening to him, went

up to the black man, and remained immovable a long time beside him, with the same indifference to danger. " It is the guardian of the magazine, your Excellency," he said, on his return. " A shell made a hole in it, and they are covering it up with earth."

When the shells seemed to fly straight upon the bomb-proof quarters, Volodia squeezed himself into the corner, and then came out, raising his eyes to the sky to see if others were coming. Although Vlang, still lying down, had more than once begged him to come in, Volodia passed three hours seated on the threshold, finding a certain pleasure in thus exposing himself, as well as in watching the flight of the projectiles. Towards the end of the evening he knew perfectly well the number of the cannon, the direction they fired from, and where their shots struck.

CHAPTER XXI

THE next day—the 27th of August—after ten hours of sleep, Volodia came out of the shelter-place fresh and well. Vlang followed him, but at the first hissing of a cannon-ball he bounded back and threw himself through the narrow-opening, knocking his head as he went, to the general amusement of the soldiers, all of whom, with the exception of Vlang, the old artificer, and two or three others who rarely showed themselves in the trenches, had slipped outside to breathe the fresh morning air. In spite of the violence of the bombardment, they could not be prevented from remaining there, some near the entrance, others sheltered by the parapet. As to Melnikoff, he had been going and coming between the batteries since daybreak, looking in the air with indifference.

On the very threshold of the quarters were seated three soldiers, two of them old and one young. The latter, a curly-headed Jewish infantryman attached to the battery, picked up a bullet which rolled at his feet, and flattening it against a stone with a piece of a shell, he cut out of it a cross on the model of that of Saint George, while the others chatted, watching his work with interest, for he did it well.

"I say, if we stay here some time longer, when peace comes we shall be pensioned off."

"Sure enough. I have only four years more to serve, and I have been here six months!"

"That doesn't count for retirement," said another, at the moment when a cannon-ball whizzing over the group struck the earth a yard away from Melnikoff, who was coming towards them in the trench.

"It almost killed Melnikoff!" cried a soldier.

"It won't kill me," replied the former.

"Here, take this cross for your bravery," said the young Jewish soldier, finishing the cross and giving it to him.

"No, brother, here the months count for years without exception. There was an order about it," continued the talker.

"Whatever happens, there will surely be, on the conclusion of peace, a review by the Czar at Warsaw, and if we are not pensioned off we shall have unlimited furlough."

Just at this instant a small cannon-ball, passing over their heads with a ricochet, seemed to moan and whistle, and fell on a stone.

"Attention!" said one of the soldiers. "Perhaps between now and night you will get your last furlough!"

Everybody began to laugh. Two hours had not passed, evening had not yet come, before two of them had, in effect, received their "last furlough," and five had been wounded, but the rest continued to joke as before.

In the morning the two mortars had been put in order, and at ten o'clock Volodia received orders from the commander of the bastion to assemble his men and go with them to the battery. Once at work, there remained no trace of that terror which the evening before showed itself so plainly. Vlang alone did no succeed in overcoming it ; he hid himself, and bent down every instant. Vassina had also lost his coolness, he was excited, and *saluted*. As to Volodia, stirred by an enthusiastic satisfaction, he thought no more of the danger. The joy he felt in doing his duty well, at being no longer a coward, at finding himself, on the contrary, full of courage, the responsibility of commanding and the presence of twenty men, whom he knew were watching him with curiosity, had made a real hero of him. Being even a little vain of his bravery, he got up on the parapet, unbuttoning his coat so as to be well observed. The commander of the bastion, in going his rounds, although he had been accustomed during eight months to courage in all its forms, could not help admiring this fine-looking lad with animated face and eyes, whose unbuttoned coat exposed a red shirt, which confined a white and delicate neck, and who clapped his hands, cried in a voice of command, " First ! second ! " and jumped gaily on the rampart to see where his shell had fallen. At half-past eleven the firing stopped on both sides, and at noon precisely began the assault on the Malakoff mamelon, as well as upon the second, third, and fifth bastions.

CHAPTER XXII

ON Telegraph Height, on this side of the bay, between Inkerman and the fortifications of the north, two sailors were standing, in the middle of the day. Near them an officer was looking at Sevastopol through a field-glass, and another on horseback, accompanied by a Cossack, had just rejoined him near the great signal-pole.

E

The sun soared over the gulf, where the water, covered with ships at anchor, and with sailing and rowing boats in motion, played merrily in its warm and luminous rays. A light breeze, which scarcely shook the leaves of the stunted oak bushes that grew beside the signal-station, filled the sails of the boats, and made the waves ripple softly. On the other side of the gulf Sevastopol was visible, unchanged, with its unfinished church, its column, its quay, the boulevard which streaked the hill with a green band, the elegant library building, the little lakes of azure blue, with their forests of masts, and the picturesque aqueducts. Overhead, clouds of a bluish tint, formed by powder-smoke, were lighted up from time to time by the red flame of the firing. It was the same proud and beautiful Sevastopol, with its festive air, surrounded on one side by the yellow smoke-crowned hills, on the other by the sea, deep blue in colour, and sparkling brilliantly in the sun. On the horizon, where the smoke of a steamer traced a black line, white, narrow clouds were rising, precursors of a wind. Along the whole line of the fortifications, along the heights, especially on the left side, plumes of thick, white smoke spurted out suddenly, torn by a visible flash, although it was broad daylight, and, assuming various forms, they extended, rose, and coloured the sky with sombre tints. These jets of smoke came out on all sides—from the hills, from the hostile batteries, from the city—and flew towards the sky. The noise of the explosions shook the air with a continuous roar. Towards noon, however, these smoke-puffs became rarer and rarer, and the vibrations of the atmosphere became less frequent.

" Do you know that the second bastion is no longer replying ? " said the hussar officer on horseback ; " it is entirely demolished. It is terrible ! "

" Yes, and the Malakoff replies twice out of three times," answered the one who was looking through the field-glass. " This silence is driving me mad !

They are firing straight on the Korniloff battery, and it is not replying."

" You'll see it will be as I said ; towards noon they will cease firing. It is always that way. Come and breakfast, they are waiting for us. There is nothing more to see here."

" Wait, don't bother me," replied, with marked agitation, the officer looking through the field-glass.

" What is it ?—what's the matter ? "

" There is a movement in the trenches ; they are marching in close columns."

" Yes, I see it well," said one of the sailors ; " they are advancing by columns. We must set the signal ! "

" But look there ! They are coming out of the trenches ! "

They could, in fact, see with the naked eye, black specks going down from the hill into the ravine, and proceeding from the French batteries towards our bastions. In the foreground, in front of the former, black spots could be seen very near our lines. Suddenly, from different points of the bastions, simultaneously spurted out the white plumes of the discharges, and, owing to the wind, the noise of a lively fusillade could be heard, like the patter of heavy rain against window panes. The black lines advanced, wrapped in a curtain of smoke, and came nearer. The fusillade increased in violence. The smoke burst out at shorter and shorter intervals, extended rapidly along the line in one light, lilac-coloured cloud. Then all sounds mingled together in one continued roar.

" It is an assault," said the officer, pale with emotion, as he handed his glass to the sailor.

Cossacks and officers on horseback went along the road, preceding the commander-in-chief in his carriage, accompanied by his suite. Their faces expressed painful expectation.

" It is impossible that it is taken ! " said the officer on horseback.

E

"God in heaven!—the flag! Look now!" cried the other, choked by emotion, and turning away from the glass. "The French flag is on the Malakoff mamelon!"

CHAPTER XXIII

KOSELTZOFF the elder, who had had time enough during the night to win and lose again all his winnings, including even the gold pieces sewn in the seams of his uniform, was, towards morning, sleeping a heavy but deep sleep in the barracks of the fifth bastion, when the sinister cry rang out, repeated by different voices, "The alarm!"

"Wake up, Mikhaïl Semenovitch! It is an assault!" a voice cried in his ear.

"A school-boy trick," he replied, opening his eyes without believing the news; but when he perceived an officer, pale, agitated, running wildly from one corner to another, he understood it all, and the thought that he might perhaps be taken for a coward refusing to join his company in a critical moment, gave him such a violent start that he rushed out and ran straight to find his soldiers. The cannon were dumb, but the musket-firing was at its height, and the bullets were whistling, not singly but in swarms, just as the flights of little birds pass over our heads in autumn. The whole of the place occupied by the battalion the evening before was filled with smoke, with cries, and curses. On his way he met a crowd of soldiers and wounded, and thirty paces further on he saw his company brought to a stand against a wall.

"The Schwartz redoubt is occupied," said a young officer. "All is lost!"

"What stuff and nonsense!" he angrily replied, and drawing his small rusty sword from its scabbard, he shouted: "Forward, children! Hurrah!"

His strong and resounding voice stimulated his own courage, and he ran forward along the traverse. Fifty soldiers dashed after him with a shout. They came out on an open place, and a hail of bullets met them. Two struck him simultaneously, but he did not have time to understand where they had hit him, or whether they had bruised or wounded him, for in the smoke before him blue uniforms and red trousers started up, and cries were heard which were not Russian. A Frenchman sitting on the rampart was waving his hat and shouting. The conviction that he would be killed whetted Koseltzoff's courage. He continued to run forward ; some soldiers passed him, then others suddenly appeared from another side and began to run with him. The distance between them and the blue uniforms, who were running back to their entrenchments, remained the same, but his feet knocked against the dead and the wounded. On reaching the outer ditch, everything became confused before his eyes, and he felt a violent pain in his chest. Half-an-hour later he was lying on a stretcher near the Nicholas barracks. He knew he was wounded, but he felt no pain. He would, nevertheless, have liked to drink something cold, and to feel himself lying more comfortably.

A stout little doctor with black whiskers came up to him and unbuttoned his overcoat. Koseltzoff looked over his chin at the face of the doctor, who was examining his wound without causing him the least pain. Having covered the wounded man again with his shirt, the doctor wiped his fingers on the lapels of his coat, and averting his head, passed to another in silence. Koseltzoff mechanically followed with his eyes all that was going on about him, and remembering the fifth bastion, congratulated himself with great satisfaction. He had valiantly done his duty. It was the first time since he was in the service that he had performed it in a way that he had nothing to reproach himself for. The surgeon, who had just dressed another officer's wound, pointed him out to a priest, who had a fine large red beard, and who stood there with a cross.

"Am I going to die?" Koseltzoff asked him, seeing him come near.

The priest made no reply, but recited a prayer, and held the cross down to him. Death had no terror for Koseltzoff. Carrying the cross to his lips with weakening hands, he wept.

"Are the French driven back?" he asked the priest in a firm voice.

"Victory is ours along the whole line," answered the latter, hiding the truth to spare the feelings of the dying man, for the French flag was already flying on the Malakoff.

"Thank God!" murmured the wounded officer, whose tears ran down his cheeks unnoticed. The memory of his brother passed through his mind for a second. "God grant him the same happiness!" he said.

CHAPTER XXIV

BUT such was not Volodia's lot. While he saw listening to a tale that Vassina was relating, the alarm cry, "The French are coming!" made his blood rush immediately back to his heart; he felt his cheeks turn pale and cold, and he remained for a second stupefied. Then looking around, he saw the soldiers button their coats and glide out one after the other, and he heard one of them, Melnikoff, probably, say, in a joking way, "Come, children, let's offer him bread and salt."

Volodia and Vlang, who did not leave his heels, went out together, and ran to the battery. On the French side as well as on ours the artillery had ceased firing. The despicable and cynical cowardice of the yunker, still more than the coolness of the soldiers, had the effect of restoring Volodia's courage.

"Am I like him?" he thought, rushing quickly

towards the parapet, near which the mortars were placed. From here he distinctly saw the French dash across an open space and run straight towards him.

Their sparkling bayonets were moving in the nearest trenches. A small, square-shouldered Zouave ran ahead of the others, sabre in hand, leaping over the ditches. " Grape ! " shouted Volodia, throwing himself down from the parapet. But the soldiers had already thought of it, and the metallic noise of the grape, thrown first by one mortar and then by the other, thundered over his head. " First ! second ! " he ordered, running across between the two mortars, completely forgetting the danger. Shouts and the musket reports from the battalion charged with the defence of the battery were heard on one side, and suddenly on the left arose a desperate clamour, repeated by many voices : " They are coming in our rear ! " Then Volodia, turning round, saw a score of Frenchmen. One of them, a fine man with a black beard, ran towards him, and halting ten paces from the battery, fired at him point-blank and went on. Volodia, petrified, could not belive his eyes. In front of him, on the rampart, were blue uniforms, and two Frenchmen were already spiking a cannon. With the exception of Melnikoff, killed by a bullet at his side, and Vlang, who with downcast eyes, and cheeks inflamed by fury, was brandishing a hand-spike, no one was left.

" Follow me, Vladimir Semenovitch ! follow me ! " shouted Vlang, in a despairing tone, defending himself with the lever from some Frenchmen. The yunker's menacing look, and the blow which he struck two of them, made them halt.

" Follow me, Vladimir Semenovitch ! What are you waiting for ? Fly ! " and he threw himself into the trench, from which our infantry were firing on the enemy. He immediately came out of it, however, to see what had become of his beloved Volodia. A shapeless thing, clothed in a grey overcoat, lay face to earth, on the spot where Volodia stood, and the whole place was filled by the French, who were firing at our men.

Vlang found his battery again in the second line of defence, but of the twenty soldiers only eight were alive.

Towards nine o'clock in the evening Vlang and his men were crossing the bay in a steamboat in the direction of Severnaïa. The boat was laden with wounded, with cannon, and with horses. The firing had ceased everywhere. The stars sparkled in the sky as on the night before, but a strong wind was blowing, and the sea was rough. On the first and second bastions flames flashed up from the ground, preceding explosions which shook the atmosphere and showed stones and black objects of strange form thrown into the air. Something near the docks was on fire, and a red flame was reflected in the water. The bridge, covered with people, was lighted up by fires from the Nicholas battery. A great sheaf of flames seemed to rise over the water on the distant height of the Alexander battery, and lighted up the under side of a cloud of smoke which hovered over it. As on the preceding evening, the lights of the hostile fleet sparkled afar on the sea, calm and insolent. The masts of our scuttled vessels, slowly settling into the depths of the water, stood out sharply against the red glow of the fires. On the deck of the steamboat no one spoke. Now and then, however, amid the regular chopping of the waves struck by the wheels, and the hissing of the escaping steam, you could hear the snorting of horses, the striking of their iron-shod hoofs on the planks, the captain speaking a few words of command and also the dolorous groaning of the wounded. Vlang, who had not eaten since the day before, drew a crust from his pocket and gnawed it; but at the thought of Volodia he broke out sobbing so violently that the men were surprised.

" Look ! our Vlang is eating bread and weeping," said Vassina.

" Strange ! " added one of them.

" See ! they have burned our barracks ! " he continued, sighing. " How many of our fellows are dead, and dead to no purpose, for the French have got possession."

" We scarcely came out alive. We must thank God for it," said Vassina.

" All the same, it is maddening ! "

" Why ? Do you think they will lead a happy life there ? Wait a bit ; we will take the place back. We shall lose some of our men, possibly, but as true as God is holy, if the emperor orders it, we will take it back ! Do you think the quarters have been left as they were ? No, the enemy only took naked walls. The intrenchments were blown up. He has planted his flag on the mamelon, it is true, but he won't risk himself in the town. Wait a bit ; we won't be behindhand with you. Only give us time," he added, looking in the direction of the French.

" It will be so, that's sure," said another, with conviction.

Along the whole line of the bastions of Sevastopol, where during long months an ardent, energetic life had been stirring, where during months death alone relieved the agony of the heroes who, one after the other, inspired the enemy's terror, hatred, and finally admiration—on these bastions, I say, there was not a single soul ; everything there was dead, fierce, frightful, but not silent, for everything all around was falling in with a din. On the ground, torn up by a recent explosion, there lay, here and there, broken beams, crushed bodies of Russians and Frenchmen, heavy cast-iron cannon overturned into the ditch by a terrible force, half buried in the ground and for ever dumb ; bombshells, balls, splinters of beams and bomb-proof shelters, and more corpses, in blue or in grey overcoats, which seemed to have been shaken by supreme convulsions, and which were lighted up at every instant by the gleam of the explosions resounding in the air.

The enemy well saw that something unusual was going on in formidable Sevastopol, and the explosions, the silence of death on the bastions, made them tremble. Under the impression of the calm and firm resistance of the last day they did not yet dare believe in the disappearance of their invincible adversary, and they waited, silent and motionless, for the end of the dismal night.

The army of Sevastopol, like a sea whose liquid mass, agitated and uneasy, spreads and overflows, moved slowly forward in the dark night, undulating into the impenetrable gloom, over the bridge across the bay, and proceeding towards Severnaïa, leaving behind it those spots where so many heroes had fallen, sprinkling them with their blood, those places defended during eleven months against an enemy twice as strong as itself, and which it had received the order that very day to abandon without a fight.

The first impression caused by this order of the day weighed heavily on the heart of every Russian; next the fear of pursuit was the dominant feeling with all. The soldiers, accustomed to fight in the places they were abandoning, felt themselves without defence the moment they left them behind. Uneasy, they crowded together in masses at the entrance of the bridge, which was lifted by violent gusts of wind. Amid the block of regiments, of militiamen, and wagons, pushing against one other, the infantry, whose muskets clashed together, and the officers carrying orders, made a passage for themselves with difficulty. The inhabitants and the military servants accompanying the baggage begged and wept to be permitted to cross, while the artillery, in a hurry to go away, rolled along noisily, coming down towards the bay. Although one's attention was distracted by a thousand details, the feeling of self-preservation, and the desire to fly as soon as possible from that fatal spot, filled each one's soul. It was thus with the mortally wounded soldier lying among five hundred other unfortunates on the flag-stones of the

Paul quay, begging God for death ; with the exhausted militiamen, who, by a last effort, forces his way into the compact crowd to make a free passage for a superior officer ; with the general who is commanding the passage with a firm voice, and restraining the impatient soldiers ; with the straggling sailor or the battalion on the march, almost stifled by the moving crowd ; with the wounded officer borne by four soldiers, who, stopped by the crowd, lay down the stretcher near the Nicholas barracks ; with the old artilleryman, who, during sixteen years, has not left the cannon which, with the assistance of his comrades and at the command of his chief, incomprehensible for him, he is about to overturn into the bay ; and, finally with the sailors who have just scuttled their ships, and are vigorously rowing away in their boats.

On reaching the end of the bridge, each soldier, with very few exceptions, takes off his cap and crosses himself. But besides this feeling he has another, more poignant, deeper—a feeling akin to repentance, to shame, to hatred ; for it is with an inexpressible bitterness of heart that each of them sighs, utters threats against the enemy, and, as he reaches the north side, casts a last look upon abandoned Sevastopol.

END OF " RECOLLECTIONS OF SEVASTOPOL "

THE COSSACKS

CHAPTER I

ALL has become quiet out-of-doors in Moscow. It is only at rare intervals that even the creak of wheels is heard along the snowy streets. There are now no lights in the windows, and the street-lamps have been extinguished. However, the sound of bells comes from the churches, and, tinkling out over the sleeping city, announces the approach of morning. The streets are almost completely deserted. Occasionally the sledge of a night *isvostchik*, with its narrow runners, sweeps over the mingled snow and sand to a corner, where the driver goes to sleep while waiting for a fare. Then an old woman goes into a church, where, reflected in the gilt frames of the holy pictures, the unsymmetrically placed tapers show an occasional red glare. The work-people are getting up after the repose of the long winter night, and are preparing to resume their arduous daily toil.

For idle gilded youths, however, it is still evening. From between the closed shutters of one of the windows of the *Restaurant Chevalier*, there comes, contrary to police regulations, a gleam of light. Carriages and sledges stand at the door, the drivers crowding together for warmth; and a posting-troïka is also waiting. The porter, who has wrapped his sheepskin coat tightly around him, is to be seen at the corner of the house.

"Why do they remain chatting about trifles?"

thinks a lackey, who sits with a sleepy face in the ante-room. " I always have the same luck when I am on service." Meanwhile one can hear the voices of three young men who are at supper in the neigh-bouring lighted room. They are seated at a table on which are the remains of their repast, and some half-empty bottles of wine. One of them, small, slight, and ugly, sits, and looks with good-natured, sleepy eyes at a companion who is about to leave. Another, a tall youth, reclines on a settee near the table covered with bottles, and twirls his watch-key. The third, in a new sheep-skin coat, walks about the room, and, stopping from time to time, cracks an almond between his thick, strong fingers, which have long, clean, carefully-pared nails. He constantly smiles at something, and both his eyes and face are flushed. He speaks with warmth and with a superabundance of gestures ; but it is evident that he hesitates for words. Those which come to him seem insufficient to express all that he has at heart. Yet he continually smiles. His name is Olenin.

" Now I can tell all ! " he says. " I am not trying to defend myself ; but I would, at least, like to have you understand me as I understand myself, and not look on this affair as a cowardly trick. You say that I am to blame in regard to her ? " he adds, turning to Smirnoff, who sits looking at him with such good-natured eyes.

" Yes, you are to blame," answers Smirnoff, the little fellow with the ugly face. And still greater affection and weariness seem to be expressed in his look.

" I know why you say that," continues Olenin. " To be loved, according to you, ought to suffice, and it is preferable to loving, one's self."

" Yes, quite sufficient, my dear fellow ; more than necessary," affirms Smirnoff, opening and shutting his eyes.

" But why cannot I love, I myself ? " replies Olenin, and then he stops to think, and looks

sympathetically at his friend. " Why cannot I love ?
I cannot ! No, to be loved is a misfortune—a misfortune when you feel that you are to blame because
you don't and can't give love in return. Oh, my
God ! " he adds, with an expressive gesture of his
hand. " If all this only happened in a rational way,
and not the reverse ! If it were only as we wish it
to be, and did not go on of itself ! I, apparently,
stole that affection ; at least you think so. Do not
deny it ; you must think so. But believe me, of all
the faults and follies I have ever committed in my
life, this is the only one that I don't repent of, and
can't repent of. Neither in the beginning nor afterwards did I lie either to myself or to her. It seemed
to me that I had at last, somehow or other, fallen in
love ; but, after all, I realised that I was deceived,
that this was an involuntary lie, and that it was not
possible to love in that way. I could not go further
though she did. Am I to blame that I could not
really love her ? What could I do ? "

" Well, it is all over now," said his friend, lighting
a cigar to drive away his sleepiness. " One thing
only ; you have never loved, and you do not even
know what it is to love."

Olenin again wished to say something, and racked
his brains how to say it ; but he could not express
what he wanted.

" I have never loved ! Yes, that's true—I have
never loved. Still I have a wish to know love,
stronger than any wish I ever had. But, again, is
there any such thing as love, such as I understand it ?
Everything is somehow unfinished. Well, what is to
be said ? I have made a mess of my life ; but all is
over now, you are quite right. I feel that a new life
is about to begin for me."

" Which you will again make a mess of," said his
tall friend Goloff, who was lying on the divan, and
twirling his watch-key ; however, his remark was not
heeded.

" I am both sad and happy to think that I am going

away," continued Olenin. "Why sad? I do not know." Then he began to speak of himself alone, not noticing that this subject was not at all interesting to the others. A man is never so egotistical as in a moment of great excitement. He then seems to think that there is nothing in the world finer and more interesting than himself.

"Dimitri Andreivitch, the driver, won't wait," said a young man-servant, wrapped up in a sheep-skin coat, and girt about with a scarf, as he entered the room. "The horses have been waiting since midnight, and it is now four o'clock."

Olenin looked at his servant Vanusha;* and in his knotted scarf, in his felt boots, and in his sleepy countenance, he seemed to hear the voice of another life calling him—a life of toil, privation, and activity.

"I really must go. Good-bye," he said, feeling his sheep-skin coat to see if it were properly hooked.

Disregarding the advice to offer a little more *vodka* (brandy) to the driver, and thus prevail on him to wait, he put on his hat, and then stopped short in the middle of the room. They all kissed each other, once, twice, stopped a minute, and then embraced a third time. Olenin went up to the table, drank a glass of champagne which was standing there, clasped the hand of Smirnoff, the ugly fellow, and blushed.

"No! Nevertheless I will say it. I must be frank with you, because I like you. You love her, eh? I always thought so. Yes?"

"Yes," answered his friend, smiling still more kindly.

"Then perhaps——"

"I beg your pardon, sirs; but I am ordered to put out the candles," said the sleepy lackey, entering and wondering why the gentlemen were always talking about one and the same thing. "To whom shall I give the bill? To you?" he added, turning to the tall young man, as though he knew in advance whom to address.

---

* One of the various diminutives of Ivan.

"To me," said Goloff. "How much is it?"

"Twenty-six roubles."

Goloff thought for a moment, but said nothing, and finally put the bill in his pocket. Meanwhile the two others talked on.

"Good-bye, you excellent, good fellow," said the little, ugly, tender-eyed Smirnoff, with a gentle smile.

Tears welled up into the eyes of both. They went out on to the steps.

"Ah!" said Olenin, finally, turning to Goloff. "You will settle Chevalier's account, eh? and then write me how much it is."

"Yes, it's all right," said Goloff, putting on his gloves. "How I envy you!" he added quite unexpectedly, when he had got outside.

Olenin now got into the posting-sledge, wrapped himself up in a fur coat, and said, "Well, then, come with me," and he moved on one side in the sledge, so as to make room for Goloff. His voice trembled.

His friend, however, rejoined, "Good-bye, Mitya! May God give you——" But he stopped short. All he wished was that his friend should go away as quickly as possible, and so he did not finish what he was saying.

They became silent. Then once again somebody said, "Good-bye!" Somebody else exclaimed, "Go on!" and at last the post-driver touched up his horses.

"Elizar! here!" now cried one of Olenin's friends. The coachman began to move, clicked to their horses, and slapped them with the reins, while the frozen carriage-wheels creaked over the snow.

"He's a nice little fellow, that Olenin," said Goloff. "But what a whim to go to the Caucasus as a *yunker*! (ensign). I wouldn't do it for any price. Are you going to dine at the club to-morrow?"

"Yes," replied Smirnoff. And then they separated.

Olenin felt warm and comfortable in his fur coat. He sat back in the sledge, and opened his coat for a little air. The three shaggy post-horses, covered with drops of frozen breath, galloped from one dark street into another, past the scarcely visible houses. It seemed to Olenin that only people who were going away ever went through such streets as these. Around him everything was dark, still, and lonely; and meanwhile his soul was full of recollections, of love, sympathy, and regrets!

CHAPTER II

"WHAT excellent fellows! How I like them!" he constantly exclaimed, feeling as if he were about to cry. Why should he feel like that? Who were excellent fellows? Whom did he like so much? He did not quite know himself. Sometimes he would look at a house, and wonder why it was so strangely built; sometimes he wondered why the driver and his servant Vanusha were so near him, and together with him. Then he was roughly shaken by the galloping of the side horses, which tugged at the frozen traces; and again he said, "Excellent fellows! How fond I am of them!" Once he remarked, "How splendid it is!" And then he wonderingly asked himself, "Am I drunk?" It is true he had drunk two bottles of wine for his share, but it was not the wine alone that had affected him. He recalled all the seemingly earnest words of friendship which had been so openly, and, as it were, unexpectedly spoken before his departure. He recalled the clasping of hands, the looks, the salutations, and the sound of Goloff's voice, as he said, "Good-bye, Mitya!" when he, Olenin, had already taken his seat in the sledge. He recalled his own resolute frankness, and everything had for him a touching meaning.

Before his departure, not only friends and relatives, not only people who were indifferent to him, but even those who were at variance with him, those who wished him ill, had suddenly begun to love him, and to pardon him everything, as if during confession or before death. " Perhaps I shall never come back from the Caucasus," he thought ; and then it seemed to him that he not only loved his friends, but loved some one else beside. It was not affection for his friends that had so softened and excited his spirit that he could not restrain the senseless words that seemed to come from his lips in spite of him ; nor was it love for women (he had never yet loved) that had brought him to this condition. No, it was love for himself, warm, full of hope, young love, faithful love for everything that was good in his soul, and it seemed to him now as if there were nothing but good in it ; it was this which caused him to weep, and to stammer disjointed words.

Olenin was a young man who had never finished a course of study anywhere ; who had never served anywhere, though he had been registered for a while in some government office ; who had squandered a large part of his fortune ; and who, although twenty-four years old, had never chosen any career for himself and, in fact, had never done anything at all. He was what is called in Moscow and elsewhere " a young man of society."

At eighteen years of age Olenin became as free as only rich young Russians, left without parents from their boyhood, could be thirty years ago. For him there were neither physical nor moral shackles. He could do everything. Nothing was necessary to him : nothing restrained him. He had neither family nor country, nor faith nor wants. He believed in nothing, and admitted nothing. But, despite all this, he was not a sad, bored, and argumentative youth ; on the contrary, he constantly amused himself. He had decided that there was no such thing as love ; and yet the presence of a young and pretty woman always gave him a sort of shiver. He had for a long time been aware that honours and titles were all folly ; but he felt involuntary satisfaction, if, at a ball, the Grand Duke Sergei walked up to him, and made some complimentary or friendly remark. However, he only gave himself up to his impulse inasmuch as it never bound him to anything. When, after yielding to a desire, he began to feel that it would entail work, or a struggle—even a very slight struggle with life— he instinctively tried to tear himself away from his desire, and to regain his freedom.

Thus he started on " society " life, mingling to- gether the official service, agriculture, music, to which at one time he had thought of dedicating himself, and even love, in which he did not believe. He frequently reflected as to how he might utilise all that strength of youth which is given to a man but once in life. Should he devote it to art, to science, to love, or to practical activity ? This power of his was not strength of intellect, of heart, or imagination, but that ever-recurring impulsiveness, that force which is given once to every man, of making of himself all that he desires, whatever he wishes, and of obtaining from the world whatever he may want. There are people who try to ignore this impulse, who, when they once enter into real life, don the first yoke they find, and honourably work in it till the day of their death. But Olenin realised within himself the pres- ence of this god of youth, this capability of trans- forming himself according to a desire, an idea ; of wishing and doing ; of throwing himself into a bottomless abyss, not knowing why nor where. Experiencing this feeling, he was proud of it, and, without knowing it, felt happy in its existence.

Thus he had loved himself alone, and he could not help doing so, since he expected nothing but good from himself, and had never yet succeeded in losing his illusions as to his own capabilities. Now, how- ever, on leaving Moscow, he found himself in that happy, youthful frame of mind, when, while acknow- ledging his previous errors, a young man suddenly says to himself, that all this was not the proper thing ;

that all his past was accidental, and signified nothing ; that he had previously had no desire to live *well*, but that in future, now that he is leaving Moscow, he will begin a new life, in which there will be no more mistakes, no more remorse, and, of course, nothing but happiness.

As always happens on a long journey, during the first two or three stages, your imagination remains in the place which you have left, and then suddenly, on the next morning, your thoughts are carried afar to the end of your journey, and there you begin to build castles in the air. So was it with Olenin. When he got beyond the city, and began to look at the snowy fields, he felt glad that he was alone in the midst of them, wrapped himself up in his furs, sank down to the bottom of his sledge, grew quiet, and gradually fell into a doze. The farewell interview with his friends had touched him, and he began to think of the winter he had just spent in Moscow. Pictures of the past, interspersed with confused thoughts and reproaches, began, unasked, to rise before his imagination.

He recalled his friends who had seen him off, and his relations with the girl of whom they had spoken. That girl was rich. " How could Smirnoff love her when he knew that she loved me ! " he thought ; and then mean suspicions came into his head. " There is great lack of honour in some people, one might think. And then, why didn't I fall in love with her ? " he asked himself. " Everybody tells me that I have never been in love. Am I really a moral monster ? "

Then he began to remember the occasions on which he had thought himself in love. He recalled the first period of his life in society, and the sister of one of his friends, with whom he had passed many evenings, sitting at the table while the lamp lighted up both her tapering fingers as she plied her needle, and the lower part of her pretty, graceful face ; and he recalled his conversations with her which had so dragged on, his general awkwardness and bashfulness, and his constant feeling of anger at being so timid. A kind of voice had always said to him, " That is not right ; that is not right " : and somehow it had not come out right. After that he recalled a ball and a mazurka he had danced with one pretty girl. " How much I was in love that night ! How happy I was ! How sad and wretched, too, I felt when I woke up the next morning and realised that I was free ! Why doesn't love come to me and bind me hand and foot ? " he thought. " Ah ! there can be no such thing as love ! The lady who was our country neighbour, and who used to say the same thing to me, and to Dubrovin, and to the marshal of the nobility—that she was in love with the stars, she wasn't *the one* either."

Then he began to remember his active life in the country as a landowner ; and again his reflections gave him no pleasure. " Will people talk for long about my departure ? " he suddenly asked himself. And immediately afterwards an idea came to him, which caused him to frown, and to mutter indistinct words ; this was a recollection of the six hundred and seventy-eight roubles which he owed to his tailor ; and he remembered how he had asked the tradesman to wait a year longer, and the expression of discontent which had become visible on the tailor's face. " Oh, my God, my God ! " he repeated, frowning, and trying to drive away the unendurable thought. " Nevertheless, she loved me," he muttered again, thinking about the girl to whom the conversation at Chevalier's had referred. " Yes, if I were married to her, things would be different, and I should not now be owing money to Vasilieff," he said. And there came to him a recollection of the last evening he had spent in playing cards with Mr. Vasilieff at the club, where he had gone on leaving *her* ; and he remembered having lost, his request to go on playing, and Vasilieff's cold refusal.

" A year of economy," he reflected, " and everything will be paid ; and then the devil take them all ! " But, in spite of this feeling of assurance, he again began to count up the debts he had, and to think of how he should pay them. " Yes, I still owe money to Morel, besides Chevalier," he reflected; and there came to him the recollection of a night on which he had got greatly in debt. It was on the occasion of a drinking party with some Zigani, which some young fellows from St. Petersburg had got up. " Sashka Borch, an aide-de-camp of the emperor, and Prince Dolbenki, that important old fellow, were there. Why were they so contented with themselves?" thought Olenin; "and why did they form a special circle, which, in their opinion, everybody else ought to feel greatly flattered to enter? Because they were aides-de-camp of the emperor? It was absurd their considering everybody else to be so stupid and snobbish. I showed them the contrary, simply because I never wished to get intimate with them. Nevertheless, I think that Andrei, the steward, was very much astonished to find me at thee-and-thou with such a man as Sashka Borch, a colonel, and an aide-de-camp of the emperor. Yes; and nobody drank more than I did that evening. I even taught the Zigani a new song, and they all listened to me. Well, I have done very many foolish things, but still I am a very, very fine young fellow," he reflected.

The morning found Olenin at the third station. He drank his tea, helped Vanusha to transfer the packages and trunks, and ascertained where everything was, and how to find it,—where his money was, and how much he had; where his passport, his road-pass, and the posting receipt were: and everything seemed so well arranged, tha he began to get merry, and the long journey appeared to him in the light of a lengthy promenade.

During the morning and afternoon he sat deep in arithmetical calculations as to how many miles he had gone, how far it was to the next station, how far after to the next town, to dinner, to tea, and to Stavropol, and what proportion of the whole road he had already gone over. Then he began to calculate how much money he had, how much was necessary to discharge his debts, and what part of his income he could spend. At evening, when he drank his tea, he calculated that to Stravropol there remained but seven-elevenths of the whole road, that his debts could be paid by seven months of economy, and that they amounted to only one-eighth of his entire property; and then, growing quiet, he wrapped himself up, sank down in his sledge, and again began to doze. His imagination now was all in the future, in the Caucasus. All his dreams were blended with images of Amalat Beks, Circassian girls, mountains, precipices, fearful torrents, and dangers. Everything came up to his fancy confused; but fame which attracted, and death which threatened, constituted the interest of the future. Sometimes, with unaccustomed bravery, and with strength which astonished everybody, he killed and defeated an innumerable throng of mountaineers; sometimes he himself was a mountaineer, and with others rose for independence against the Russians. As soon as details presented themselves to his mind, his old Moscow acquaintances were always actors in the scene. Sashka Borch always made war against him, either with the Russians or mountaineers. Even (he did not quite know how) the tailor, Mr. Capel, took an active part in the triumph of the victor.

If, at this moment, he remembered any of his old weaknesses, the remembrance was rather pleasant than otherwise. It was clear that among the mountains, the torrents, the Circassian girls, and the dangers, these mistakes of his could not be repeated. He had already once confessed them to himself, and that was the end of them. Yet there was one dream, a very dear dream, which mingled with every thought of his anent his future—the dream of a woman. Among the mountains there came to his imagination a vision of a Circassian slave-girl, with a slender waist, long braided hair, and submissive blue eyes. He pictured to himself amid the mountains some lonely cabin, and on its threshold he saw *her* watching for him, as he returned tired and cove d with dust, blood, and fame ; and he gloated over her kisses, her shoulders, her sweet voice, and especially her submissiveness. She was charming, although she was uneducated, wild, and rude. In the long winter evenings he would begin to educate her. She proved sensible, full of understanding, and gifted, and quickly gained all necessary knowledge. Why not ? She could very easily learn languages, read and understand the productions of French literature. " Notre Dame de Paris," for example, would certainly please her. She would even talk French. In a drawing-room she would have more native dignity than many a lady of the highest society. She would sing simply, but with feeling and passion.

" But no, this is all folly," he finally said to himself. And then they came to another station ; and it was necessary to change sledges, and give a gratuity to the driver. However, he again sought in his fancy for the *folly* he had just been thinking of ; and again there rose to his vision the Circassian girl, with fame and return to Russia, an appointment as aide-de-camp of the emperor, and such a charming wife. " But then there is no such a thing as love," he at last said to himself. " Titles are all nonsense ! But six hundred and seventy-eight roubles owing to my tailor ? However, the subjected territory would give me far more wealth than I could spend in my life. On the other hand, one ought not to enjoy so much wealth alone. I ought to divide it. But with whom ? Six hundred and seventy-eight roubles, Mr. Capel, and then it is quite evident——" Some very confused things began to enter his thoughts ; and only the voice of his man, Vanusha, and the feeling that the troïka had stopped, disturbed him in his healthy, youthful dream. Without knowing how he changed to another sledge at the new station, and then went on farther.

Next morning it was just the same—the same stations, the same tea, the same cruppers of horses moving up and down before him, the same short conversations with Vanusha, the same confused visions and dreams in the evening, and then a healthy, youthful sleep during the night.

CHAPTER III

THE farther Olenin proceeded from the centre of Russia, the farther all his recollections seemed from him ; and, the nearer he came to the Caucasus, the more comforted he grew at heart. The idea of going away altogether, never to return, nor to show himself any more in society, sometimes came into his head. " None of the people I shall see here know me ; none of them will ever go to Moscow or mingle in the society in which I lived, and learn about my past. Moreover, no one in Moscow society will ever find out what I may do when I live among these people." Thus quite a new feeling of freedom from his whole past took hold of him as he glanced at the rude beings whom he met on the road, and whom he did not admit to be people on a level with his Moscow acquaintances. The ruder the people, the fewer the signs of civilisation, the freer he felt himself. Stavropol, through which he was obliged to pass, made him angry. The signs, especially the French ones, the ladies in open carriages, the cabs standing in the open streets, the boulevards, and a gentleman in an overcoat and a silk hat, walking along this boulevard, and staring at those who passed him, all affected him disagreeably. " Perhaps some of those people know some of my acquaintances," he thought, and he again remembered the club, the tailor, the cards, and society.

Beyond Stavropol, however, all went on satisfactorily : everything was wild, and, more than that, beautiful and warlike. Olenin kept feeling gayer and gayer. All the Cossacks, drivers, and station-inspectors, seemed to him simple beings, with whom he

could jest and talk without any effect, without
thinking as to what class of society they belonged to.
All belonged to the human race, which had become
unconsciously dear to Olenin; and all were very
amiable with him. While in the land of the Don
Cossacks, he had changed his sledge for a cart; and at
Stavropol it had become so warm that he rode without his furs. It was already spring—an unexpected,
joyous spring for Olenin. At night the postmasters
no longer let him go out of the stations, and said that
even in the evening it was dangerous. Vanusha had
begun to grow cowardly; and a loaded rifle lay at his
side. Olenin became still gayer, however. At one
station the inspector told him a story of how, not long
before, there had been a fearful murder on the road;
and as he proceeded he began to meet men who were
well armed, for safety's sake.

"It is already beginning," thought Olenin to
himself; and he constantly expected a sight of the
snowy mountains about which he had been told so
much. Once, towards evening, his Tartar driver
pointed with his whip to some heights barely visible
behind the clouds. Olenin eagerly began to look;
but it was twilight, and the clouds half concealed the
mountains. He could only see something greyish,
whitish, and wavy; and, much as he tried, he could
find nothing beautiful in the sight of these mountains,
about which he had heard and read so much. He
then began to think that mountains and clouds looked
very much alike, and that the especial beauty of
snowy mountains, of which people had told him so
much, was a mere fancy, like the music of Bach, or
love, in which he did not believe. So he ceased
expecting anything of the mountains. On the next
day, early in the morning, he woke up in his cart and
glanced indifferently to his right. The morning was
beautifully clear. Suddenly, at twenty paces from
him, as it seemed at the first moment, he saw some
pure white masses, with tender outlines, and fantastic,
distinct summits standing out against the sky. When

he began to comprehend the distance which lay between himself and the mountains, between the mountains and the sky, and the vastness of these mountains, and when he began to realise all their infinite beauty, he feared lest it was all a mirage or a dream. He shook himself to wake himself. However, the mountains were still there.

"What is that ? what is that ? " he asked the driver.

"The mountains," answered the Tartar, with indifference.

"I have looked at them a long time," said Vanusha. "How fine they look ! People would not believe it at home."

With the quick movement of the cart, the mountains appeared to run along the horizon, their rosy tops gleaming in the rays of the rising sun. At first they only astonished Olenin, afterwards they delighted him ; later, on looking more and more at the growing and receding chain of snowy heights rising straight from the middle of the steppe, he became truly penetrated with consciousness of their beauty. From that moment whatever he saw, whatever he thought of, whatever he felt, acquired with him the new and strikingly majestic character of the mountains. All his Moscow recollections, his shame and his regrets, all his trivial dreams of the Caucasus, departed, and never returned again. "Now it has begun ! " a sort of triumphant voice said to him. The road, the winding line of the Terek, now visible in the distance, the fishing stations, and the people, no longer seemed to him a mockery. He looked at the sky, and dreamt of the mountains. He looked at himself, at Vanusha, and again thought of the mountains. "There go two Cossacks on horseback," he mused, "with their guns slung over their shoulders, and swinging on their backs, and their horses regularly moving their grey-and-white legs. Ah ! but the mountains. Beyond the Terek there rises some smoke from a village. Ah ! but the mountains. The sun rises, and is reflected in the Terek, and lights up the reeds. Ah ! but the mountains. A cart is leaving the fishing station ; some pretty women, young women, are in it. Ah ! but the mountains. The Abreks* are trotting over the steppe, but I am not afraid of them. I have a gun, and force, and youth— yes, and there are the mountains ! "

CHAPTER IV

ALL along the line of the Terek, a distance of some sixty miles, over which are scattered the stations of the Grebna Cossacks, the country has the same character. The Terek, which separates the Cossacks from the Circassian mountaineers, flows turbidly and rapidly along. It is here already wide, and constantly washes some greyish sand to the low right bank, all overgrown with reeds, and undermines the abrupt though not elevated left bank, with its century-old oaks, its rotting plane-trees, and young undergrowth. On the right bank are scattered the villages of friendly but not altogether pacific Circassian tribes.† Along the left bank, at about half a mile from the water, and at a distance of four or five miles from each other, are placed the Cossack stations. In old times most of these stations were on the very margin of the stream ; but the Terek, which moves northward from the mountains, has washed them away, and now there are dimly visible various thickly overgrown gardens and orchards, with pear-trees, lindens, and poplars, woven together with brambles and wild vines. Nobody lives there now ; and on the

---

* Circassians hostile to Russia.
† The reader will bear in mind that this work was written in 1852, before the Russian domination in the Caucasus was thoroughly organised.

sand one only sees the tracks of the stags, the wolves, the hares, and the pheasants that abide there.

From station to station there goes a road cut straight through the forest. Along this road are placed the outposts, in which the Cossacks are stationed; between the outposts, on slight elevations, there are look-outs. Merely a narrow belt of woody fertile land, about half a mile wide, constitutes the property of the Cossacks. North of them come the sandy hillocks of the Nogai and Mozdok Steppes, which go straight on northward, and merge, God knows where, into the Turkoman, Astrakhan, and Kirghiz Steppes. Southward of the Terek are the Great Tchetchna, the Kotchkalosofsky range, the Black Mountains, and still another range, and, farther on, the snowy mountains, visible indeed on the horizon, but where no Cossack has ever been. On the belt of fertile country, so richly overgrown with vegetation, there has lived from time immemorial a warlike, handsome, and rich population of Russian old-believers, called the Grebna* Cossacks.

Long, long ago, their ancestors, old-believers, fled from Russia, and settled beyond the Terek, among the Circassians, at the foot of the first range of the woody mountains called the Great Tchetchna. Living among the Circassians, these Cossacks intermarried with them, and adopted the customs, manners, and morals of the mountaineers, whilst retaining in all their pristine purity their mother language and their old faith. A tradition, which is still fresh among the Cossacks, says that the Czar Ivan the Terrible came on one occasion to the Terek, summoned the old men from the Grebna, and gave them land on the Russian side of the river, covenanting to live with them in friendship, and promising never to compel them to subjection, or to change of faith. Even now the Cossack tribes consider themselves related to the Circassians; and love for

---

* Literally, mountain summit.

freedom, idleness, robbery, and war constitute the chief traits of their character. The influence of Russia is only manifested in controlling their elections, and taking away the bells of their schismatical churches, and it is exercised by the troops which pass by or are stationed there.

The Cossack, by inclination, hates the roving mountaineer who has killed his brother less than the soldier who is stationed to protect his village, but who has smoked up his cottage with tobacco. He respects his foe the mountaineer, but despises the soldier as a foreigner, and an oppressor. The Russian peasant is for the Cossack a wild and despicable being, a specimen of whom he sees in the various travelling traders and Little-Russian colonists, whom in contempt he calls " hat-wearers." For him elegance in dress consists in imitation of a Circassian. His best arms are those obtained from the mountaineers ; his best horses are bought or stolen from them. The young Cossack is proud of knowing the Tartar language ; and, when he is amusing himself, he will even talk with his comrades in Tartar. Nevertheless, this little Christian population, dwelling on a paltry stretch of territory, and surrounded by half-wild Mohammedan tribes and Russian soldiers, considers it has attained the highest degree of development, and regards no one but a Cossack as a man : on everybody else it looks with a sort of contempt.

The Cossack passes the greater part of his time at the outposts, in expeditions, in hunting, or in fishing. He very seldom works at home. His presence at the station is an exception to the rule, and then he carouses. All the Cossacks make their own wine ; and drunkenness is not so much an inclination common to all as a custom or even rite, the non-fulfilment of which would be considered a heresy.

The Cossack looks on women as the instruments of his prosperity. An unmarried girl may have the right to amuse herself, but the husband makes his wife work for him from youth to old age, and displays quite an Oriental character in exacting obedience and labour. With this system the women become strongly developed both physically and morally, and although externally resigned, acquire incomparably more influence and weight in home-life than in Western countries. Although separated from social life, and charged with heavy manual labour, they obtain more authority in home-affairs. The Cossack, who, before outsiders, considers it unbecoming to speak affectionately or unnecessarily with his wife, always feels her superiority when he is left face to face with her. His house, his property, his whole fortune, have been acquired by her toil, and are kept up only by her labour and efforts. Although he is firmly convinced that labour is shameful for a male Cossack, and is suited only for a Tartar workman or a woman, he feels, in a confused way, that all that he enjoys, and calls his own, is the product of that labour, and that it is in the power of the woman—his mother or his wife, whom he considers his slave—to deprive him of everything that he enjoys. Moreover, the constant toil of a masculine character allotted to the Cossack woman have given her an independent and manly character, and have developed in her to an astonishing degree both physical force and sound sense, decision, and firmness of character. The women, for the most part, are stronger, more sensible, more developed, and finer looking, than the men. The beauty of the Grebna Cossack woman is especially striking by the blending of the purest type of the Circassian face with the broad and powerful frame of the Northern races. The Cossack women wear the Circassian dress— Tartar shirt, *bechmet*,* and drawers ; but they tie up their heads in kerchiefs, in the Russian style. Elegance, neatness, and even beauty in their attire, and extreme cleanliness in their cottages, form a habit and a necessity of their lives. In their relations with

* Embroidered jacket.

men, the women, and especially the unmarried girls, enjoy complete freedom.

The station of Novomlinsk is considered to be the capital of the Grebna Cossacks. Here especially are preserved the manners of the old Cossacks ; and the women of this station have ever been famous for their beauty throughout the whole Caucasus. The tribe's sources of livelihood consist of its vineyards, orchards, melon and pumpkin plantations, of its fishing and hunting grounds, its maize and millet fields, and, in addition, there is the booty gained in war. Novomlinsk is two miles from the Terek, and separated from it by a thick forest. On one side of the road, which passes through the station, flows the river ; on the other lie vineyards and orchards, and the sandy hills of the Nogai Steppe. The station is surrounded by an embankment and a hedge of brambles. Everybody coming to the station, or leaving it, passes through a high stone gateway, covered with a little roof thatched with reeds. Near by, on one side, you see, on a wooden carriage, an old gun which has not been fired for a hundred years, and which was, at some time or other, captured by the Cossacks. A Cossack, in a uniform fur coat, with sabre and gun, sometimes stands, and sometimes does not stand, on guard at the gate : sometimes he salutes, and somtimes he does not salute, a passing officer. Under the reed-thatched gate, on a small board, the following inscription is painted in black characters : " Houses 266, souls of the male sex 897 ; ditto of the female sex 1,012."

Th houses of Novomlinsk are all raised upon posts two or three feet above the ground, and are nicely thatched with reeds, with steep gables. Although they are not all new, they are invariably in good condition and clean, with high porches of different styles. They are not set close to each other, but picturesquely placed along the broad streets, with plenty of room between. In front of the large windows of many houses one may see dark-green balsam-poplars, tender

F

light-green acacias, with white fragrant blossoms, as well as insolently brilliant yellow sunflowers, and luxuriant beds of vegetables, and vines. On the broad square in the centre of the village there are three shops, stocked with cotton goods, seeds, green beans, and gingerbread ; and beyond a tall fence, behind a row of old poplars, one sees, longer and higher than the others, the house of the regimental commander, with its double windows. On week days, especially in summer, there are very few people to be met walking in the streets of the station. The Cossacks are on service—at the outposts, or on expeditions. The old men are hunting or fishing, or, together with their wives, are working in the vine-yards and gardens. Only the very young, or the sick, remain at home.

CHAPTER V

IT was one of those evenings peculiar to the Caucasus. The sun had gone down behind the mountains ; but it was still light. The last rays illumined a third of the sky; and in their light the whitish mass of the mountains stood out very distinctly. The air was sharp, calm, and resonant. A long shadow stretched out from the mountains for miles over the steppe. On the steppe, beyond the river, along the roads, everywhere, all was deserted. If occasionally some horsemen were seen anywhere, the Cossacks at their outposts and the Circassians in their villages looked at the riders with astonishment and curiosity, and tried to guess who these people could be. Were they enemies ? Everybody seemed to fear one another, and did not stray from the houses : only the animals and birds who did not fear man freely traversed this waste.

The woman tying up the vines eagerly complete their task, so as to return home. Girls, braiding their whips together, hasten from the gardens, which are soon deserted, while the station becomes peculiarly animated. From all sides people come to it on foot, on horseback, and in creaking carts. Girls in tucked-up skirts, with switches in their hands, run to meet the cattle, which are hastening along in a cloud of dust, amid the gnats brought by them from the steppe. The cows and buffaloes wander along the streets, and the women, in gaily-coloured bechmets, hasten after them. We can hear loud conversation, merry laughter, cries and shouts, with the lowing of the cattle. There an armed Cossack on horseback, who has obtained leave to quit the outpost, rides up to a cottage, and leaning down to the window, knocks at it, immediately after which one can see a pretty young Cossack girl, and hear her affectionate talk. There comes a high-cheeked Tartar workman, returning with reeds from the steppe. He turns his creaking cart into the clean, broad court-yard of the captain's house, throws off the yoke from the sweating heads of the oxen, and talks in Tartar with his master. Beside the pool, which fills nearly the whole street, and past which so many people have gone, skirting the fences, there steps a barefooted Cossack girl, with a bundle of wood on her back, and lifting her petticoat high above her white ankles, while a horseman who has just returned laughingly cries, " Lift it higher, wench," and stares at her. The girl then drops her petticoat, throws down her wood, and runs away. An old Cossack, with rolled-up trousers and bare breast, who is returning from fishing, carries over his shoulder in a net some still panting silvery fish, and to make a short cut, crawls through the broken fence of a neighbour, and tears his shirt, which catches on some twigs. There an old woman drags a dry branch after her, and the blows of a hatchet are heard from round the corner. Cossack children shout as they whip their tops everywhere where there is a bit of level ground in the streets. Women clamber over prickly hedges, so as not to go round about. Smoke rises from all the chimneys. In every yard one hears the increased bustle which precedes the stillness of night.

Old Mother Ulitka, the wife of the cornet and schoolmaster, has, like the other women, come to the gate of her yard, and watches for the cattle who are being driven along the street by her daughter Marianka. She has not yet succeeded in opening the wicket-gate, when a huge buffalo-cow, surrounded by gnats, rushes forward lowing, and breaks its way through the fence, after which slowly come the cows, who familiarly turn their large eyes on their mistress, and measuredly beat their sides with their tails. That shapely beauty, Marianka, comes up to them, and, throwing away her switch, opens the wicket-gate, and with her petulant feet tries to separate and drive in the rest of the cattle. " Take off your shoes, you devil's child ! " cried her mother. " Your shoes are getting all spoiled."

Marianka does not feel in the least insulted by the appellation of " devil's child," but takes these words as an endearing epithet, and merely keeps on with her business. Her face is half concealed by the kerchief tied around her head : she wears a pink shirt and a green bechmet. She disappears under the thatched gate of the yard, behind the fat back of one of the herd ; and, through the fence, you can hear her tenderly talking to the buffalo-cow, whom she is going to milk. " Now stand !—Oh, you—Come now, little mother ! "

Soon after, the girl and the old woman enter the milk-house, each carrying two large pails of milk, the produce of the day. From the large chimney of the milk-house, the smoke of the burning dogwood soon rises ; for the milk is being made into curds. The girl attends to the fire ; and meanwhile the old woman goes to the gateway.

Twilight has now enveloped the village. The air is full of the smell of vegetables, and cattle, and pungent smoke. Along the streets, Cossack girls are running, bearing lighted rags in their hands. In the yards one hears the heavy breathing and quiet rumination of the cattle, who are now at rest; and women's and children's voices call to one another. On a week-day it is seldom you hear the voice of a man.

An old, tall, and masculine-looking Cossack woman comes out of the yard opposite to Mother Ulitka's place, and asks for a light, carrying a rag in her hands.

"Well, mother, have you done that?" she asks.

"The girl is attending to the fire. Oh! you want a light do you?" says Mother Ulitka. "Proud to be of service to you."

Both the women go into the cottage. Ulitka's coarse hands, unaccustomed to small objects, tremblingly remove the cover from the precious match-box, which is a rarity with the Cossacks. The masculine-looking Cossack woman who has just come sits down on the threshold, with the evident intention of gossiping.

"So your husband is at the school, then?" she asks.

"Yes, teaching the children, mother; but he has written that he will be here for the holidays," replies the cornet's wife.

"It is plain he is a sensible man. Well, it is all for somebody's good."

"Of course it is."

"My Lukashka is at the outposts, and they don't allow him to come home," answers the visitor, without regard to the fact that the cornet's wife knew this long ago. She feels the necessity of speaking about her son, however, who has only just entered the service, and whom she wishes to marry to Marianka, the cornet's daughter.

"So he is at the outposts?"

"Yes, mother. He has not been home since the last festival. Only a day or two ago, I sent him some shirts by Thomas. Well, there is nothing to be said, since the authorities order it. In fact, they say they are looking for the Abreks* again. Lukasha, so Thomas says, is all right. He is very merry over it."

" God be praised ! " said the cornet's wife. " Your son, in a word, is a true *Urvan*."

Lukasha was called *Urvan* for the bravery with which he had pulled a little Cossack out of the water. The cornet's wife remembered this in order to say something pleasant and complimentary to his mother.

" Yes, thank God, mother, he is a good son, a brave young fellow ! Everybody speaks well of him," says Lukasha's mother. " Only I should like to marry him, and then I could die contented."

" Well, are there so few girls in the station ? " asks the wary cornet's wife, trying with her warty hands to put on the cover of the match-box.

" There are many, many," remarks Lukasha's mother, as she nods her head. " But your girl, Marianusha ; she's the girl ! You would have to look through the whole regiment † for one like her."

The cornet's wife is acquainted with the secret wishes of Lukasha's mother ; and, although Lukasha seems to her a very good young Cossack, yet she does not care to continue the conversation. First, because she is the cornet's wife and rich, and Lukasha is the son of a simple Cossack, and fatherless orphan ; and secondly, because she does not want to part too quickly with her daughter ; chiefly, however, because propriety demands that she should act like this.

" Well, what of that ? Marianka will grow up, and then she will be a wife like the rest of them," she says with reserve.

" Oh ! I will send the match-makers ; I will send them after the vintage ; and we will come to pay our

---

* See note *ante*, p. 157.
† This refers to the military organisation of the Cossacks. It will have already been noticed that Ulitka's husband was a cornet as well as a schoolmaster.

compliments to your worship. We will come to pay our compliments to Ilia Vasilievitch."

" What has Ilia got to do with it ? " proudly says the cornet's wife. " They'll have to talk with me. But everything in its time."

Lukasha's mother sees by the stern face of the cornet's wife that it is of no use her saying anything more ; so she lights her rag with a match, and, getting up, exclaims : " Don't forget, mother : remember those words. Well, I must go home," she adds. " It is time to light the fire."

On her way to the street, while waving the lighted rag in her outstretched hand, she meets Marianka, who bows to her.

" A queen girl and a working girl," she thinks, looking at the beauty. " Grow up, indeed ! Quite time to get married already. Yes, and in a good house too : she had better marry Lukasha."

Mother Ulitka meanwhile had her own thoughts, and as she sat on her threshold she pondered deeply, until her daughter called her.

CHAPTER VI

THE male population of the stations pass their time in expeditions and at the outposts. That very Lukashka,* about whom the old women of Novomlinsk were talking that evening, was on the look-out at the post of Nijni Prototsk, on the very bank of the Terek. Leaning on the balustrade of the look-out, and blinking his eyes, he kept gazing, now into the distance beyond the Terek, and then near by at his comrades, and sometimes he talked with them a little.

---

* Lukasha and Lukashka are varying diminutives for Luka (Luke), just as Mariana, Marianka, and Marian-ushka are for Marya (Mary).

The sun was already drawing near to the snowy range, which stood out white above the fleecy clouds. The latter took darker and darker shades. The atmosphere gradually gained evening freshness. From the thick, overgrown forest there arose a pleasant coolness, although about the post it was still warm. The voices of the Cossacks became more resonant in the evening atmosphere. The swift, cinnamon-tinted Terek stood out sharply between its tranquil banks. The water had already begun to fall; and, in places, the damp sand showed grey on the banks and in the shallows. Right opposite the post, on the other bank, all was deserted; there was nothing but low, unending reeds, stretching up to the very mountains. On one hand, however, near the low bank, were to be seen the mud huts, with flat roofs and funnel-shaped chimneys, of a Circassian village. The young Cossack, who stood on the look-out, gazed with his sharp eyes through the evening smoke of the peaceful village at the moving figures of the Circassian women in blue and red dresses, dimly visible in the distance.

Although the Cossacks were constantly expecting the crossing and attack of the Abreks, especially in the month of May, when the woods skirting the Terek are so thick that a man on foot has difficulty in breaking through them, and when the river is so shallow that it can in many places be forded; and although only two days previously a Cossack had come from the regimental commander with a circular, in which it was stated that, according to information received from the spies, eight men intended to cross the Terek, and that special watchfulness was therefore requisite—no such watch was kept at the outposts. The Cossacks were as if at home, without their guns, and without their horses saddled; some had engaged in fishing, others in drinking, others in hunting. The horse of the officer of the day, the only one saddled, was walking on three legs amid the brambles by the side of the woods; and merely the Cossack on guard was provided with his musket and sabre. The corporal of the post, a tall, lean fellow, with an extraordinarily long backbone, and short legs and arms, sat, with his coat unhooked, on the terrace of the hut, and, with an expression of official idleness and laziness, shut his eyes and wagged his head from one hand to the other. An elderly Cossack, with a broad, greyish-black beard, and wearing nothing but a shirt, girt round with a black strap, lay on the water's edge, lazily looking into the monotonous, curling, and eddying Terek. Others, also, oppressed by the heat and half undressed, were either washing their clothes in the water, or weaving snares, or lying on the warm sand of the bank, humming songs. One fellow, with an ugly sunburnt face, and evidently dead-drunk, lay on his back beside one of the walls of the hut, which, two hours before, had been in the shade, but which now was exposed to the full force of the oblique sun rays.

Lukashka, who stood on the look-out, was a tall, handsome young fellow, about twenty years old, very like his mother. His face and his entire build, in spite of the angularity of youth, expressed great physical and moral strength. Although he had not long before been put on active duty, it was evident, from the look on his features, and the quiet assurance of his mien, that he had already succeeded in acquiring that military and somewhat proud bearing which is peculiar to Cossacks, and, in general, to everybody who is in the habit of carrying arms. He realised that he was a Cossack, and estimated himself at his proper value. His ample caftan was badly torn in one or two places ; his cap was knocked in behind, in the Circassian style ; his leggings were let down below his knees. His clothing was certainly not rich, but it sat on him with that special Cossack elegance, which consists in imitating the Circassian *djiguit*.* About

---

* Warrior, or more exactly "brave," as applied to the Red Indians.

the latter everything is broad, torn, and careless : his arms only are good. But this torn attire is donned and girt up, and his arms hang upon him in a special fashion, which everyone cannot manage to follow, though it immediately strikes the eye of a Cossack or of a Circassian. Lukashka had this warrior-like appearance. Resting his hands on his sabre, and screwing up his eyes, he constantly glanced towards the distant village. Taken separately, his features were not good ; but looking at his build, and at his black-browed, sensible face, every one would involuntarily have thought, " That is a fine young fellow."

" The women, the women in the village, have all scattered," he said at last in a sharp voice, showing his brilliant white teeth, and not addressing his remark to any one in particular.

A comrade, who lay on the ground under the look-out, quickly raised his head, and remarked : " They are probably merely going for water."

" If I only fired off my gun," said Lukashka, laughing, " how frightened they would be ! "

" It will not carry so far."

" Pooh ! My gun will carry farther than that. Wait a while till it is their festival, and then I will go over there and pay a visit to Ghirei Khan and drink *buza*," * said Lukashka, angrily beating off the gnats, which kept settling on him.

A slight noise in the wood now attracted the attention of the Cossacks. A spotted mongrel setter, scenting about and wagging its tail, ran up to the post. Lukashka recognised the dog as that of a neighbour, an old sportsman, Uncle Eroshka, and immediately afterwards he perceived the old man himself in the wood.

Uncle Eroshka was a Cossack of gigantic stature, with a heavy beard as white as swan's-down, and with such broad shoulders and chest that in the woods

---

* A kind of beer.

there was no one to compare with him. He did not look so tall as he was, however, for all his strong members were well proportioned. He had a torn blouse thrown over him, and on his feet he wore deer-skin sandals secured with a rag, which was wrapped about his legs, while on his head a ragged white fur cap was set. Over one shoulder he carried a net containing smoked meat for attracting falcons, while over the other hung a dead wild-cat, which was attached to a strap. Fastened to his belt there was a bag with bullets, powder, and bread, with a horse-tail for keeping off the gnats, a large dagger in a torn sheath spotted with blood, and two dead pheasants. Looking up to the post he stopped.

"Hey, Lam!" he cried to his dog, in such a stentorian voice that the echo sounded far off into the forest; and swinging over his shoulder his large, fowling-piece, called by the Cossacks a "flint," he took off his cap.

"Have you passed the day well, good people, eh?" he said, turning to the Cossacks with the same merry voice, speaking, indeed, without any effort, but as loudly as if he were calling to somebody on the other side of the river.

"All right, uncle, all right!" merrily answered the young Cossacks on various sides.

"What have you seen? Tell us!" cried out Uncle Eroshka, as with the sleeve of his coat he wiped the sweat from his broad red face.

"Listen, uncle! What sort of a falcon is it that lives in yonder plane-tree? It comes out every evening," said Nazarka, turning, and pointing to the place with his shoulder and his foot.

"You must be fibbing," suspiciously answered the old man.

"It is true, uncle. Just sit here a while," answered Nazarka, laughing.

Then the Cossacks all began to grin.

Nazarka had not seen any falcon at all; but the young Cossacks at the outpost had, for some while past, acquired the habit of teasing and chaffing Uncle Eroshka every time he came to see them.

"Oh, you fool! you never do anything but lie," said Lukashka to Nazarka, who immediately became quiet.

"If it is necessary to sit I will sit," said the old man, to the great satisfaction of all the Cossacks. "But have you seen any wild boars about?"

"Is it easy to see wild boars?" asked the corporal, very glad to have the opportunity of a little conversation, and leaning from side to side, and scratching his long back-bone with both of his hands. "We want to catch some Abreks, and not any wild boars. You have not heard anything, uncle, have you?" he added, winking without reason, and showing his white teeth.

"Abreks?" said the old man; "no, I have not heard anything about them. Have you got any fresh wine? I am awfully thirsty; it's a fact. Well, just give me a drop, and I will bring you some young wild boars very soon; indeed I will! Bring on your wine," he added.

"So you want to rest, do you?" asked the corporal, as if he had not heard Eroshka's request.

"Yes, I should like to rest at night," answered Uncle Eroshka. "I shall rest during the holidays, and, God grant, I shall kill something; and then I will give it to you; indeed I will!"

"Uncle, eh, uncle!" sharply cried Luka from above, thus drawing to himself the attention of all the Cossacks, who immediately looked at him. "You just go up stream, and you will find a fine herd of boars. Oh! I am not lying. I went the other day, and one of our Cossacks killed one of these boars. I'm telling the truth," he added, arranging his musket behind his back, and speaking in a serious tone of voice.

"Ah! so Lukashka *Urvan* is here?" said the old man, looking up. "Where was the boar shot?"

"So you hadn't seen me, then? Why, am I too

little to be seen ?" rejoined Lukashka. "The boar was near the river," he added. "As we were going along the bank, it moved in the bushes, and, as my gun was unloaded, Iliaska shot it! Yes, and I will show you where the place is, uncle; it is not so far off. Just give me time. I know the way there. Uncle Mosef," he continued, decisively, and almost commandingly, to the corporal, "it is time to change guard;" and then arranging his gun, and not waiting for any order, he began to descend from the look-out.

"Come down!" said the corporal, looking about him. "It is your turn, Gurka," he resumed. "Go up. Your Lukashka has grown very sharp," he added, turning to old Eroshka; "as soon as you come, he can never remain still. Only a little while ago, he himself killed a boar."

CHAPTER VII

THE sun had already set, and the shadows of night kept quickly advancing over the forest. The Cossacks had finished their duties about the outpost, and had collected in the hut for supper. Only the old sportsman, who was still expecting the falcon, remained under the plane-tree, dragging about a piece of smoked meat secured to his leg. But if a falcon sat on the tree, it did not come down after the bait. Lukashka, with all deliberation, was placing traps and snares for the pheasants, beyond the brambles, and was singing one song after another. In spite of his height and large hands, it was evident that he was expert even in work of the most delicate and minute description.

"Eh, Lukashka!" called Nazarka in a resounding voice, "our men have gone to supper."

Nazarka, with a live pheasant under his arm, then

made his way through the brambles, and came out into the path.

"Oh!" said Lukashka, stopping his whistling, "where did you get that pheasant? It must have been my snare."

Nazarka was of the same age as Lukashka, and had also recently come into active service. He was a short, ugly, thin and sickly-looking fellow, with a sharp voice which always resounded in your ears. He was a neighbour and comrade of Lukashka. The latter was seated in Tartar fashion on the grass, and kept on arranging his snares.

"I don't know whose bird it is. It may be yours," said Nazarka.

"Did you find it beyond the ditch, under the old plane-tree? If so, it is mine: I set the snare yesterday."

Then Lukashka rose up, and looked at the pheasant. Smoothing with his hand the dark-blue head, which the frightened bird held out to him, he took it in his hands.

"We will make some pilaf. Go and cut its throat, and pluck it," said he.

"Shall we eat it ourselves, or give it to the corporal?"

"Oh! he will eat some of it with us."

"I don't like cutting its throat," resumed Nazarka.

"Give it here, then."

Lukashka took a small knife from under his dagger, and quickly cut the throat of the pheasant, which quivered. Before it could expand it wings, its bleeding head had fallen off.

"There!" said Lukashka, throwing the pheasant on the grass. "We will have some fine pilaf to-day."

Nazarka shuddered as he looked at the pheasant. "Listen, Lukashka: that devil is again going to send us into an ambuscade," he said, taking up the bird, and by the devil meaning the corporal. "He has sent Thomushka for some brandy, and it was his turn for duty. How many more nights is this to go on? He always comes down on us."

Lukashka, whistling, went towards the outpost. " Catch hold of this line ! " he said.

Nazarka obeyed, and continued : " I will tell him this evening. I will tell him straight. Let us say that we won't go, that we are tired out, and that is the end of it. Tell it straight : he will mind you. It is a bad mess."

" You have found something now to talk about," said Lukashka, evidently thinking of some other matter. " Nonsense ! What difference does it make if he sends us out for the night ? It won't do any harm. In ambuscade you can amuse yourself ; and here what can you do ? Whether you are at the outpost, or in an ambuscade, it's all the same. You——"

" But when are you going to the station ? "

" Oh, well ! I shall go there for the holidays."

" Gurka said that your Dunaïka was flirting with Thomushka," suddenly remarked Nazarka.

" The devil take her ! " answered Lukashka, showing a whole row of white teeth, but not laughing. " Don't you think I can find another ? "

" Well, that is what Gurka said. He went, he says, to see her, and her husband was not there. But Thomushka was sitting there, and eating a pie "—— Nazarka here stopped a moment ; and then he went on——" and when he was under the window, he heard how she said, ' That devil's gone ! Why, my dear, don't you eat your pie ? There is no use your going home to sleep : stay here.' And Gurka cried under the window, ' All right ! ' "

" You lie ! "

" By God, it is true ! "

Lukashka became silent. " Well, she has found another, devil take her ! There are plenty of girls like that. Besides, I had got tired of her."

" What a devil of a fellow you are ! " rejoined Nazarka. " You ought to make up to Marianka, the cornet's daughter ; she doesn't flirt with anybody."

Lukashka snorted. "What's that about Marianka? Pooh! all the girls are the same," he said.

"You make up to her."

"What have you to say about it? There are plenty of others." Then Lukashka again began to whistle, and went back to the outpost, tearing off the leaves and twigs on either side. While passing through the bushes, he suddenly stopped, and having noticed a smooth, dark sapling, he took his dagger out, and cut it. "That will make a fine ramrod for my gun," said he, making it whistle as he brandished it.

The Cossacks were at supper within the white-washed hut, seated on the clay floor, about a low Tartar table, and the conversation ran on whose turn it was for the ambuscade. "Whose turn is it to go now?" said one of the men to the corporal, who stood at the open door of the hut.

"Yes, whose turn is it?" replied the corporal. "Burlak has gone, Thomushka has gone," he added, not quite sure. "I think you had better go, you and Nazarka," he resumed, turning to Luka. "Yes, and Ergushoff can go, if he has woke up yet."

"You would never wake up; how do you expect him to do so?" said Nazarka in a half whisper.

The Cossacks laughed.

Ergushoff was the Cossack who was drunk, and who had been sleeping outside the hut. He had only just come in, and was rubbing his eyes.

Lukashka just then stood up, and examined his gun.

"Yes, go as soon as you can. Eat your supper and go," said the corporal. And, without waiting for an expression of assent, he shut the door, evidently not much expecting to be obeyed. "If it hadn't been ordered, I wouldn't send anyone," he added. "You see, the captain has sent word. He says that eight Abreks have crossed the river."

"Well, of course it is necessary to go," said Ergushoff; "it is the regulation. One can't sit at home in a time like this. I tell you we must go, as the service requires it."

Lukashka, meanwhile, holding a large piece of pheasant to his mouth with both hands, and looking first at the corporal and then at Nazarka, seemed quite indifferent to all that passed.

The Cossacks were not yet ready to repair to the ambuscade when Uncle Eroshka, who had sat in vain under the plane-tree until it had grown dark, came up to the dark porch.

"Now, children," he said, in his resounding deep bass voice, "come, I will go with you. You can sit and watch for the Circassians, and I will watch for the boars."

CHAPTER VIII

IT was already night time when Uncle Eroshka and the three Cossacks from the outpost, in their cloaks, and with their muskets over their shoulders, went down along the Terek to the place appointed for the ambuscade. Nazarka did not want to go at all; but Luka called him, and he dared not stay behind. After taking a few steps slowly, they turned off from the road and went down to the Terek, along a scarcely perceptible path through the reeds. On the bank there was a thick black log cast up by the water; and the reeds about the log had been freshly crushed down.

"Shall we watch here?" said Nazarka.

"Of course," said Lukashka; "you watch here, and I will go on for a moment with uncle."

"This is the very best place; they won't see us, whereas we can see everything," responded Ergushoff. "Let us sit here. This will be the very best place."

Nazarka and Ergushoff spread out their cloaks, and lay down behind the log, whilst Lukashka went on a little farther with Uncle Eroshka.

"There! Near here, uncle," said the young

fellow, walking noiselessly behind the old man. " I will show you where they went by. I know."

" Show me the place. You are really my brave *Urvan*," answered the old man in a whisper.

After taking a few more steps, Lukashka stood still, leant over a pool, and whistled. " There's where they come to drink. Do you see anything ? " he said, scarcely audible, as he pointed out some fresh traces.

" Christ save you ! " answered the old man. " The boar must be lying in the mud behind the ditch," he added. " I will watch here, and you go back."

Lukashka secured his cloak and retraced his steps, looking sometimes to the left, to the wall of rushes, and sometimes towards the Terek, which was swirling past the bank. " There is somebody watching there, or creeping along the side," he said to himself, thinking of the Circassians, and suddenly a crashing noise, and a splash in the water, made him start, and seize his gun. Then a boar jumped into the water from the bank ; and its black form, after showing for an instant against the gleaming surface of the water, again became hidden by the rushes. Lukashka quickly aimed, but did not fire. The boar had already got away into the forest. Spitting from vexation, Lukashka went on, and on approaching the place of the ambuscade he again stopped and whistled softly. His whistle was replied to, and he joined his companions.

Nazarka, who had rolled himself up in his cloak, was already asleep. Ergushoff was sitting on his heels, and moved a little on one side to make room for Lukashka.

" Here, this is a very good place to watch. An excellent place ! " he said. " Did you take him to the place for the boar ? "

" Yes, I showed it to him," said Lukashka, spreading his cloak on the ground. " And what a big boar I turned into the water just now ! It must be the same one. Didn't you hear how it crackled in the bushes ? "

"Yes, I heard some animal make a noise. I immediately knew it was an animal. I thought to myself, 'Lukashka has frightened some kind of wild beast,'" said Ergushoff, wrapping himself up in his cloak. "Well, I am going to sleep now," he added. "You must wake me up directly the cocks crow. After that we must take our turn. I am going to sleep; and then you can sleep, and then I will sit up; that is the right way."

"Much obliged, but I don't want to sleep," answered Lukashka.

The night was dark and warm; there was no breeze. On one side only of the horizon did the stars shine: the other side, and indeed the greater part of the sky, towards the mountains, was covered by a large cloud. This black cloud, rising up from the mountains, without any wind, slowly moved farther and farther, being sharply separated by its jagged edges from the deep, starry heaven. Just in front of him the young Cossack could see the Terek and the bank beyond; behind him, and on either side, the view was cut off by a wall of reeds. Once in a while the reeds, without any motive, would all begin to waver, and whisper to each other. Seen from below, the waving feathers of the sedge-flowers seemed like branches of trees against the bright sky. At Lukashka's very feet there was the bank, past which the stream swirled. Farther on, the shining, moving mass of dark-coloured water broke monotonously against the shallows and the shore. Still farther on, water and bank and cloud became merged in impenetrable darkness. On the surface of the water dark shadows spread out, which the eyes of the Cossack, by this time accustomed to the obscurity, recognised as shadows produced by snags and floating logs. From time to time some heat lightning, reflected by the water, showed, as in a dark mirror, the line of the opposite bank.

The measured sounds of night, the rustling of the reeds, the heavy breathing of the other Cossacks, the buzzing of the gnats, and the rippling of the water, were broken occasionally by a distant shot, by the fall of a part of the bank which had been washed away, by the splashing of a large fish, or by the crashing of some animal through the thick, overgrown woods. Once an owl flew down the Terek, flapping slowly; above the very heads of the Cossacks it turned towards the forest, and, flying inland, began to flap more quickly, and finally, fluttering, settled on an old plane-tree. At every such unaccustomed sound the wakeful Cossack pricked his ears, his eyes blinked, and he slowly raised his gun.

The greater part of the night had passed away. The black cloud, spreading westward with its ragged edges, had disclosed a portion of the clear, starry sky; and the golden crescent of the moon shone right over the mountains. It was growing cool. Nazarka woke up, said something, and then went to sleep again. Lukashka began to feel tired, rose up, took a knife from under his dagger and began to peel the switch he had cut for a ramrod. His head was full of thoughts as to how the Circassians lived in the mountains, as to how the "braves" came to the Russian side of the river, how it was that they are not afraid of the Cossacks, and how they might cross in another place. He moved a little from his post, and looked down the river; but nothing was visible. Gazing from time to time at the stream and the farther bank, which was dimly distinguished from the water in the feeble moonlight, he at last stopped thinking about the Circassians, and was only waiting for the right time to rouse his companions and return to the station. Then he thought of his Dunaïka— "his little soul," as the Cossacks call a mistress—and he thought of her with vexation. At last came signs of morning: a silvery mist began to rise above the water; some young eagles whistled shrilly not far from him, and flapped their wings. Finally the cry of the first cock came from the far-off station, immediately after which another and more prolonged cock-crow was heard, to which the voices of other birds replied.

"It is time to wake them up," thought Lukashka, stopping his whistling, and feeling that his eyes were very heavy. He turned to his companions, and was trying to guess to which body the various legs belonged, when suddenly it seemed to him that there was some kind of a splash on the other side of the Terek; and he looked once more at the gleaming mountains, lighted up by the down-turned crescent of the old moon, at the opposite bank of the river, and at the logs floating along the Terek, which were now plainly visible. It seemed to him for a moment that he was moving, and that the stream and the logs were standing still; but this lasted only for an instant. He again began to look attentively. One large black tree-trunk, with a dry branch hanging from it, especially attracted his attention. This trunk, in some strange way, without rolling over, or turning about, floated in the middle of the river; it even seemed to him that it was not floating with the current, but was going straight over the Terek to a long sand-bank.

Lukashka stretched out his neck, and began to look at it more attentively than ever. The log floated up to the sand-bank, stopped, and then moved about in a strange way. Lukashka, feeling suspicious, thought he saw a hand on the other side of the log. "Ah! I shall kill an Abrek alone," he said, and he deliberately set up his rest, laid his gun across it, and holding it fast, cocked it without making any noise. Then, holding his breath, he began to aim, looking intently all the time. "I shall hit him," he thought. However, his heart beat so violently that he paused, and began to listen. Suddenly the log moved off from the sand-bank, and began to float straight across the current towards the Russian bank. "I am afraid I shall miss him," mused Lukashka, and then, in the dim moonlight, a Tartar's head just appeared in front of the log. The young Cossack aimed straight at this head, which seemed to him very near—just at the end of his gun. "He is an Abrek," he thought joyfully, and, suddenly falling on his knees, he righted his gun, looked at the sight, which was scarcely visible, drew a long breath, and in the Cossack way, according to a custom learned in childhood, muttered to himself, " In the name of the Father and Son." Then he pulled the trigger. The flash lighted up the reeds and the water for a moment. The sharp, sudden report was carried over the river, and from somewhere in the distance an echo was returned. The log was already floating down the river again, with the current rocking it, and rolling it over.

" Hold, I say ! " cried Ergushoff, seizing his gun, and rising up from behind the ambush.

" Keep still, you devil ! " Lukashka whispered, setting his teeth. " The Abreks."

" What did you shoot at ? " asked Nazarka.

Lukashka made no reply. He reloaded his gun, and kept looking after the floating log. Not far off it stopped on another sand-bank ; and from behind it there was seen something large, which moved up and down in the water.

" What did you hit ? Why don't you tell us ? " repeated the Cossacks.

" Abreks, I tell you," repeated Lukashka.

" Don't lie in that way. Did your gun go off accidentally ? "

" I have killed an Abrek. See what I shot ! " said Lukashka, rising to his feet, with his voice full of emotion. " A man was swimming over there," he added, pointing to the sand-bank. " I killed him. Look there ! "

" What is the use of lying ? " repeated Ergushoff, rubbing his eyes.

" I don't lie. Look ! See there ! " said Lukashka, seizing him by the shoulder, and pressing him with such force that he drew an exclamation of pain from him. Ergushoff looked in the direction in which his comrade pointed, and, seeing the body, suddenly changed his tone.

" There must be more of them, I'm sure of it,"

he said, quickly looking at his gun. " This was the first ; the advanced guard. He swam from over there, not far on the other side : I tell you true."

Lukashka nodded his head, and began to take off his caftan.

" What are you doing, you fool ? " cried Ergushoff. " Wait a little : you will risk your life for nothing. If you have killed him, he can't get away. Give me a little powder : have you got any ? Nazar, run back quickly to the outpost, but don't go along the bank. They would see you and kill you : I tell you true."

" I go alone ? Go yourself," replied Nazarka, angrily.

Lukashka, who had taken off his coat, now went down to the bank.

" Don't go down there, I tell you," called Ergushoff, putting some powder in the pan of his gun. " He won't move. I can see that he isn't alive. Let them have time to come here from the post. Go on, Nazarka, are you afraid ? Don't be afraid, I tell you."

" Luka, O Luka," said Nazarka, " tell us how you killed him."

Lukashka, however, was only thinking of getting into the water.

" Go to the post quickly, both of you," he replied. I will wait here. Tell the Cossacks to send some men by a roundabout way ; if they are on this side to catch them."

" I tell you they will get away," retorted Ergushoff, getting up. " We ought to catch them now."

Both he and Nazarka, however, after crossing themselves, went to the post, not along the bank, but scrambling through the bushes, and thence along the forest-path.

" Now, mind, Luka, don't you move," cried Ergushoff, looking back, " or else they will kill you. See that you don't budge, I tell you."

" Go on ; I know," said Lukashka, and, glancing at his gun, he sat down in ambuscade.

Once alone, he gazed at the sand-bank and listened for the Cossacks, but it was some distance to the out-post, and he was wild with impatience : he kept thinking that the Abreks who had been following the dead man would get away. Just as he felt vexed about the boar that had escaped him on the night before, so now was he vexed with the Abreks who also were getting away. He looked eagerly around him, and then at the other bank, expecting to see another man ; and, fixing his rest, he kept ready to fire. That the others might kill him was an idea that never entered his head.

CHAPTER IX

THE dawn was already breaking. The body of the Circassian was plainly visible ; having grounded on the sand-bank, it now scarcely moved. Suddenly, not far from Lukashka, the reeds crackled, some steps were heard, and the feathery tops of the sedge grass stirred. Lukashka cocked his gun, and muttered, " In the name of the Father and the Son." As soon as he did this the steps ceased.

" Eh, Cossacks, don't kill your uncle," resounded a deep bass voice ; and thrusting the reeds aside, Uncle Eroshka suddenly came up.

" I almost killed you, by God I did," said Lukashka.

" What did you fire at ? " asked the old man.

His sonorous voice echoed over the wood and down the river, and abruptly annihilated the quiet of the night and the mystery which surrounded the Cossacks. The dawn suddenly seemed to have become lighter and clearer.

" You saw nothing at all, uncle, eh ? Well, I killed an animal," replied Lukashka, uncocking his gun, and standing unnaturally quiet.

The old man, without turning his eyes for a moment kept looking at the body of the dead man, now plainly visible, and over which the water slightly broke.

" He was swimming, with a log on his back. I was looking at him, and then—Look there ! He has got blue drawers apparently, and a gun—Do you see ? " said Lukashka.

" How not see ? " solemnly said the old man ; and his face became serious and stern. " You have killed a djiguit," he added, almost sympathetically.

" I was sitting so, and looking," resumed Lukashka, " and all of a sudden I wondered what it was that seemed so black on the other side. I looked at it once more, and apparently a log went by in the water. There was nothing strange in that. But this log, a good sound trunk in fact, was floating on the water—not down with the current, but going across. Then I looked again, and saw a head behind it. What was there strange in that ? I moved a little, so that he might not see me through the reeds, and then I cocked my gun. But the beast must have heard me ; for he crawled up on a sand-bank, and looked about. ' You lie ! ' I thought, ' you won't get away.' He just crawled up and looked at me. Something resounded in his throat. I got my gun ready without moving, and waited for him. He lay there, and lay there ; and at last began to move again. When he swam into the moonlight his back was visible. ' In the name of the Father, Son and Holy Ghost,' I said, and I looked out through the smoke, and he was writhing. He groaned, or at least it seemed so to me. Then I thought, ' Please the Lord, I have killed him.' When he got to that sand-bank, he was quite visible, and tried to stand up ; but he had no strength left him. He was badly hit, and so he lay down. I could see it all quite plainly. He doesn't move now ; and so he must be dead. The other men have gone back to the outpost to tell the rest of them to come down."

" So you shot him ? " said the old man. " He is very far now ; " and again he sadly shook his head.

Just at that moment the Cossacks, both on foot and on horseback, were heard along the bank, amid a loud crackling of the bushes. " Are they bringing a boat ? " cried Lukashka.

" Luka, my brave fellow, bring him ashore," cried one of the Cossacks along the bank. Then Lukashka, without waiting for the boat, again began to undress, never taking his eyes off the body.

" Wait a minute ! Nazarka is bringing the boat," cried the corporal.

" You fool ! Perhaps he is alive. He is only pretending to be dead. Take a dagger with you ! " cried another Cossack.

" Go on and talk," replied Lukashka, taking off his breeches. He had quickly undressed himself, and crossed himself, and, giving a sudden spring, he jumped with a splash into the stream, and stretching out his white arms, and lifting his back high above the water, he cut across the current, and made for the sand-bank. The Cossacks talked aloud in excited voices. Three horsemen came up by a roundabout way. The boat was seen beyond the turn. Lukashka meanwhile reached the sand-bank, bent over the body, and turned it over twice. " He is quite dead," he cried, in a sharp voice.

The Circassian was hit in the head. He wore blue drawers, and had his shirt, his coat, his gun, and his dagger tied on his shoulders. Over all there was fastened a large branch, which was what had deceived Luka at first.

" That is the way to catch carp ! " cried one of the Cossacks, who were standing in a circle, while the body, having been pulled out of the water, lay on the grassy bank. " How yellow he is ! " said another.

" Where have our fellows gone to look ? The other Abreks are doubtless on the other bank. If he had not been the first, he would not have swam over in that way. Why did he swim over alone ? " said a third.

" Oh ! he must have been a sharp fellow, and

came out to explore before the rest.   He is evidently
one of their best warriors," said Lukashka, mockingly,
wringing the dead man's wet clothes on the bank,
and constantly shivering.   " His beard is dyed, and
cut a little."

" He put his shirt in that bag on his back : he
could swim better without it," said some one.

" Listen, Lukashka ! " exclaimed the corporal,
holding the gun which had been taken from the
dead man.   " You keep the dagger and the coat ;
and as for the gun—come, I will give you three
roubles for it.   See, it's loaded," said he, blowing
down through the barrel.   " I should like to have it
as a remembrance."

Lukashka made no answer, and this request evidently vexed him ; but he knew that he could not
refuse it.

" What a devil he was ! " he said, snorting, and
throwing the Circassian's coat on the ground.   " If
he had only had a good coat, instead of some
rags ! "

" It will be good enough to wear when you go wood
cutting," said another Cossack.

" Mosef, I am going home," exclaimed Lukashka,
evidently already forgetting his vexation, but wishing
to profit by his present to the corporal to the best
advantage.

" Well, go.   Why not ? "

" Carry the body to the outpost," said the corporal,
turning to the Cossacks, and still examining the gun.
" Yes ; and make a covering of boughs over him, to
shelter him from the heat.   Perhaps some of them
will come from the mountains to ransom him."

" It isn't warm yet," said some one.

" But a jackal might come and tear him.   That
wouldn't be nice," remarked another Cossack.

" We will put a guard over him, for they will
certainly come to ransom him ; and it would not do
to have him torn."

" Well, Lukashka, do as you please.   But you

ought to offer a gallon of vodka to the boys," added the corporal, merrily.

"Yes, that is what you ought to do," chimed in the Cossacks. "God has given you good luck ! You killed an Abrek the first time you fired."

"Well, some one buy the dagger and the coat. Give as much money as you can. I will sell the drawers too," rejoined Lukashka. "They won't fit me. What a sun-burned devil he was ! "

One Cossack bought the coat for a rouble : and another offered two gallons of brandy for the dagger.

"Drink, boys, I will send you a gallon," said Lukashka. "I will bring it myself from the station."

"You might cut up the trousers for kerchiefs for the girls," suggested Nazarka.

The Cossacks all burst into a laugh.

"You have had laughing enough," said the corporal. "Take away the body ! You cannot bring a mess like this into the hut."

"What are you standing still for ? Bring it along here, boys ! " said Lukashka in a tone of command to the other Cossacks, who seemed unwilling to take hold of the body ; and they all obeyed the order as if it had been given by the corporal. Having dragged it some steps, they dropped the legs, which, lifelessly trembling, sank to the earth ; and then walking off a little, they stood silent for some time. Nazarka, however, went up to the body, and turned the head so as to see the bloody round hole over the temple and the face.

"Oh, what a mark ! In the very brain ! " he said. "There cannot be a mistake. This fellow's people will always know him."

No one answered ; and again the angel of silence sped over the Cossacks.

The sun had already risen, and with its rays lighted up the dewy ground. The Terek murmured not far off ; in the waking forest, the pheasants hailed the morning, crowing to each other on all sides. The

Cossacks stood silent and motionless around the dead body, and looked at it. The dark-brown corpse, clad in nothing but wet, dark-blue cotton drawers, tied tight with a girdle about the fallen belly, was well built and comely. The muscular arms lay straight along the sides. The bluish, freshly-shaven round head, with the wound on the temple, was turned up. The smooth, sunburned brow showed conspicuously. The glassy eyes were open ; the pupils remaining visible, and looking, so it seemed, past every one. On the thin lips, stretched apart at the edges, contrasting with the red, half-shaven moustaches, there seemed to remain a good-natured, shrewd smile. There was some tawny hair on the small, bony hands ; the fingers were bent in, and their nails were tinged red. Lukashka had not yet dressed himself. He was still wet, his neck was redder, and his eyes shone more than usual ; his fat cheeks trembled ; and vapour seemed to rise from his white, healthy body into the morning air.

" He, too, was a man," he said, evidently admiring the corpse.

" Yes, he came to grief ; he had no luck," said one of the Cossacks.

Then the angel of silence flew away. The Cossacks moved about, and began to talk to one another. Two of them went to get some branches to cover the body : others went off to the outpost. Lukashka and Nazarka ran to get ready for their journey to the station.

Half an hour afterwards, through the thick forest which separated the Terek from Novomlinsk, they were going home, almost on a run, but talking without cessation.

" Don't tell her that I sent you, but go and see whether her husband is at home, or not," said Lukashka, in a sharp voice, to his comrade.

" All right ! I shall go to Yanka's myself. Shall we have a little spree ? " said the obedient Nazarka.

" Why shouldn't we have one ?   Now or never ! " answered Lukashka.

On reaching the station, the two Cossacks took a drink, and then lay down to sleep until the evening.

CHAPTER X

THREE days after the events which have just been described, two companies of a Caucasus infantry regiment arrived at the station of Novomlinsk, to take up their quarters there.

The unharnessed wagon-train was already standing on the square. The cooks had dug a pit, and having brought from different yards various bits of wood which had been lying about, they were already cooking the soup. The sergeants were counting the men. Stakes for securing the horses were being driven into the ground. The quarter-masters were going here and there through the streets, pointing out their quarters to officers and soldiers. On this side were some green boxes, piled up in a line : on that were the harness and the horses. Here the kettles in which the soup was boiling : there were the captain and the lieutenant, and Onesim Michailovitch, the sergeant-major. It had been ordered that the companies should be quartered at Novomlinsk ; and so the men made themselves quite at home there. " But why were they quartered at that particular station ? What sort of people were the Cossacks there ? Were they glad to have the soldiers quartered upon them ? Were they schismatical or not ? " To answer such questions was not the soldier's business. Crowds of dusty and tired infantry-men were scattered noisily and disorderly, like a swarm of bees, about the square and through the streets. Not in the least noticing the unfriendly disposition of the Cossacks, but going in batches of two and three, with merry conversation, and a great clattering of muskets, they entered the huts, hanging up their ammunition, scattering their bags and knapsacks about, and jesting with the women. On the square, near the soup-kettles, to which all soldiers are partial, there had collected a large group of smokers, with pipes between their teeth. They were looking, now at the smoke, which rose up towards the warm sky, and grew and thickened like a white cloud ; now at the flame of the soup-fires, which, like melted glass, quivered in the clear atmosphere ; and they joked and laughed about the Cossacks because they did not live exactly as the Russians did. In every yard soldiers were to be seen, and everywhere one heard their laughter, as well as the sharp, shrill cries of the Cossack women, who were defending their houses, and refusing to give water and dishes. Boys and girls crept close to their mothers, and with frightened astonishment watched each movement of the soldiers, people such as they had never seen in all their lives ; while others were running after the troops at a respectful distance. Old Cossacks came out of their huts, sat down on the terraces, and darkly and silently gazed at the bustle of the soldiers, as though they submitted to the vexation in spite of themselves, and did not understand what the result of it would be.

Olenin, who for three months now had been a yunker of this Caucasus regiment, had had quarters assigned to him in one of the best houses of the station—that of the cornet Ilia Vassilievitch, the husband of old Mother Ulitka.

" What sort of a business will this be, Dimitri Andrevitch ? " said Vanusha, the valet, to his master, as the latter, arrayed in a Circassian uniform and bestriding a Kabarda pony bought at Grozni, finished a five-hours' march by riding gaily into the yard of the house where quarters had been assigned to him.

" What, Ivan Vassilitch ? " he asked, patting his horse, and looking in amazement at Vanusha, who was covered with sweat, with his hair disordered and his face dejected. He had arrived with the train, and was now unpacking his things.

Physically, Olenin seemed quite another man. Instead of shaven cheeks, he wore whiskers and a beard. Instead of having a yellowish face, the result of late nights, a ruddy, healthy tan appeared on his cheeks, on his forehead, and even behind his ears. Instead of a brand-new black dress coat, he wore a dirty white Circassian uniform, with broad pleats; and he carried a gun. Instead of a freshly-starched linen collar, one could see the red neckpiece of his silk shirt, buttoned around his sunburnt neck. He was, indeed, dressed in Circassian style, but badly. Anybody would at once have set him down as a Russian, and not as a djiguit. All was right, and yet all was wrong. However, his whole exterior was radiant with health, gaiety, and self-content.

"It may be laughable enough for you," said Vanusha; "but just come yourself, and talk to these people. They won't give one entrance. Yes, and that is not the end of it—you can hardly get a word from them." And Vanusha angrily threw his iron pail down on the threshold. "They are not Russians, these fellows!"

"But have you spoken to the chief of the station?"

"Ah, I don't know were he lives," said Vanusha in a tone of vexation.

"Well, who has been insulting or annoying you?" asked Olenin, looking round.

"Oh! the devil take them! Whew! The master is not at home. They say he has gone to some *kriga** or other; and the old woman is such a devil that the Lord preserve us from her!" answered Vanusha, clutching hold of his head. "How we are going to live here, I don't know. They are worse than Tartars, by God! It is all nonsense their calling themselves Christians: why, even Tartars would

---

* A fishing place.

behave better. Gone to a *kriga*, indeed! What sort of a thing do they mean by a *kriga*? Nobody knows," concluded Vanusha, as he turned away.

" So matters are not the same as they would be in our village at home ? " said Olenin, looking about, but not alighting from his steed.

" Let me take your horse," said Vanusha, evidently puzzled by what for him was a new order of things, but nevertheless resigned to his fate.

" So a Tartar is better ? Oh, Vanusha ! " repeated Olenin, finally getting off his horse, and slapping the saddle with his hand.

" Oh ! you may laugh as much as you like. It may be mere fun for you," rejoined Vanusha, in an angry voice.

" Come, come ; don't get angry, Ivan Vassilie-vitch ! " answered Olenin, continuing to smile. " Wait a minute. I will go to the people of the house ; I will arrange everything ; we shall live here very comfortably, I'm sure ; only don't get excited."

Vanusha did not reply, but, blinking his eyes, he looked contemptuously at his master, and shook his head. Vanusha considered Olenin to be merely his master, and Olenin looked on Vanusha merely as his servant. They would both have been very much astonished if any one had told them that they were friends ; and yet they were friends, without either of them knowing it. Vanusha had been taken into the house when only eleven years old, and when Olenin was of the same age. When the latter became fifteen, he occupied himself with educating Vanusha, and taught him how to read French, of which Vanusha was very proud ; and nowadays Vanusha, when he was in a contented frame of mind, said a French word or two with a very stupid smile.

Olenin now ran up to the steps of the cottage, and knocked at the front door. Marianka, wearing nothing but a pink shirt (just as Cossack girls are usually dressed at home), jumped in a frightened way from the door, and, standing against the wall, covered

G

the lower part of her face with the broad sleeve of her garment. Upon opening the door a little farther Olenin espied in the half-light the tall and stately figure of the young girl. With the quick and envious curiosity of youth, he involuntarily noticed her strong virginal figure defined by the creases of her thin calico shirt, and her pretty black eyes, which were gazing at him with childish horror and wild inquisitiveness.

"That is she," thought Olenin. "Yes; but there must be many such," it immediately occurred to him. And then he opened an inner door. Old Mother Ulitka, who also wore nothing but a shirt, was bending over, with her back turned to him; she was sweeping the floor.

"Good-day, mother! I have come about the quarters."

The Cossack woman, without straightening herself, turned a stern but still handsome face upon him.

"What have you come about? You want to laugh at me? Eh? I will make you laugh, the plague take you!" she cried, looking askance at the intruder from under her frowning brows.

Olenin had at first thought that the brave regiment of the Caucasus would be received everywhere with delight, and especially be treated by the Cossacks in true comrade fashion; and so this reception puzzled him. Putting on a brave face, however, he tried to explain that he intended to pay for the rooms; but the old woman would not allow him to finish.

"What have you come for? We have no need of you, with your wry face. Wait a little. The master will come home; and he will show you a place. I don't need your filthy money. You come to spoil the house with your tobacco-smoke, and then you offer to pay for it with money. Have I not seen just such rascals? May they shoot you through the heart! May a thousand bombs perforate your intestines!" she shrilly cried, pushing Olenin out of the room.

"It is evident that Vanusha is right," thought the

young officer. "Even a Tartar would be more digni-
fied"; and, amid the shouts of Mother Ulitka, he
went out of the cottage. As he was going out,
Marianka, still dressed in her pink shirt, but with her
head swathed to her very eyes with a white kerchief,
unexpectedly darted past him. Quickly pattering
down the steps with her bare feet, she ran off, then
stopped, suddenly looked at the young man with
laughing eyes, and concealed herself behind a corner
of the house. Her firm, youthful walk, and wild look,
her flashing eyes seen under the white kerchief, and
her lithe form, acted still more strongly than before
on Olenin. "It must be she," he thought; and
thinking much less about his quarters than about
Marianka, he went back to Vanusha.

"What a wild sort of a girl!" said the latter, who
was still busying himself with his master's luggage,
but seemed to be in a little better humour. "She
is just like a young colt in the pasture. The woman!"
he added in French, in a loud and triumphant voice,
and then he giggled.

CHAPTER XI

TOWARDS the evening the master of the house
returned from fishing, and, learning that he
would be paid for his rooms, he appeased his wife, and
satisfied the demands of Vanusha. Everything was
soon arranged. The family went to occupy their
winter cottage, and let their summer one to the yunker
for three roubles a month. Olenin ate something,
and then took a nap. When he woke up, just before
evening, he washed and brushed himself, dined, and
smoking a cigarette, sat at the window which over-
looked the street. The heat had somewhat abated.
The oblique shadow cast by the cottage, with its

carved gable, stretched across the street to the wall of the opposite house, of which the steep reed-thatched roof shone in the rays of the setting sun. The atmosphere became fresher. In the village everything was quiet; the soldiers had retired to their quarters; the herds had not yet been driven home; and the workpeople had not yet come back.

Olenin's quarters were almost at the edge of the village. From time to time, from the Tchetchna, or the Kumik plain, somewhere far beyond the Terek, the spot from which Olenin had recently come, shots were faintly heard. The young fellow felt very well after his three months' campaign. His freshly-washed face was cool; he experienced a feeling of cleanliness unusual during the campaign; and in all his rested members he was conscious of quiet strength. In his mind, too, everything seemed fresh and clear. He remembered the campaign, and the dangers which he had escaped: he remembered that, at the time of danger, he had conducted himself very well; that he had behaved no worse than the others who had received him as a comrade in the brave army of the Caucasus. His Moscow recollections were already God knows where. His old life had been wiped out, and a new one had begun—a wholly new life, in which there had as yet been no mistakes. Here, like a new man among new people, he could deserve a new and good opinion of himself. He felt youthful delight in living; and looking first out of the window at the boys who were playing with balls in the shadow of the houses, and then at his newly-arranged quarters he thought how pleasantly he was situated and how he should enjoy this station-life, which was still new to him. He also looked at the mountains and at the sky; and amid all his recollections and dreams there were mingled a strong feeling of the grandeur of nature. His life had begun, not as he had expected it would on leaving Moscow, but unexpectedly well. Mountains, mountains, mountains, were mingled in all that he thought and felt.

" He has kissed the pot ! He has licked the pitcher !
Uncle Eroshka has kissed the pot ! " suddenly cried
out some Cossack boys, who had been playing under
the window, as they turned to a side street. " He
has kissed the pot ! He has drunk up his dagger ! "
they cried, crowding together, and retreating.

These cries were directed at Uncle Eroshka, who,
with his gun on his shoulder, and with three pheasants
dangling from his belt, was returning from shooting.

" I have sinned, my children ; I have sinned ! " he
replied, boldly looking at the windows of the huts on
both sides of the street. " Yes, I have drunk away
my dagger : it is my fault," he repeated, affecting
indifference, but, in reality, sorely vexed with the
children.

Olenin was astonished at the way the boys treated
the old sportsman, and still more surprised by the
expressive face and the strong build of Uncle Eroshka.

" Hallo ! Cossack ! " he said, turning to him,
" come here ! "

The old man looked up towards the window, and
stopped.

" Good-day, good man ! " said he, lifting his cap
from his closely-clipped head.

" Good-day, good man ! " answered Olenin.
" What are the boys calling out at you for ? "

Uncle Eroshka came up to the window. " They
are teasing me, an old man. Well, it is of no account.
I am fond of them. Let them have a little amusement with their old uncle," he said, in the firm and
resonant tone which is to be expected from old men
of high positions. " Are you the army commander ? "

" No, I am a yunker. Where did you kill those
pheasants ? " asked Olenin.

" Oh ! I shot these three hens in the woods,"
answered the old man, turning so as to show his
broad back, on which hung three pheasants, whose
heads were twisted into his belt, while they splashed
his caftan with their blood. " Haven't you ever
seen any before ? " he asked. " If you like take a

brace of them. Come !" And he held two pheasants towards the window. " Are you a sportsman, too ?" he asked.

" Yes, I am very fond of shooting," replied Olenin ; " during the campaign I killed four pheasants."

" Four ! What a number !" laughingly replied the old man. " Are you a drinker too ? Do you like new wine ? "

" Why not ? I like a little at times."

" Ah ! I see that you are a fine young fellow. We shall be very good friends," said Uncle Eroshka.

" Come in," rejoined Olenin, " and we will drink a little new wine together."

" Very well, I'll go in," said Eroshka. " But you must take the pheasants."

It was evident, from the old man's face, that the yunker pleased him ; and he had immediately understood that he could drink some wine for nothing, and thus afford to give a brace of pheasants.

A moment afterwards Uncle Eroshka appeared at the door of the hut. Then only did Olenin realise the immense stature and strength of this old man, whose bushy beard was perfectly white, and whose dark red face was covered with deep wrinkles. The muscles of his legs, arms, and shoulders were as full and firm as those of a young man. On his head, under his short hair, deep scars were visible. His thick, sinewy neck was covered with creases, like an ox's, and his warty hands were bruised and scratched. He quickly and lightly stepped over the threshold, rid himself of his gun, set it down in a corner, and then, with a quick glance, took in and estimated the furniture and effects in the cottage. With his legs swathed in rags, he walked slowly into the middle of the room. There had come with him a strong but not unpleasant odour of wine, vodka, powder, and dry blood.

Uncle Eroshka bowed to the eikons, arranged his beard, and approaching Olenin, gave him his thick black hand.

" *Koshkildy*," he said. " That means, in Tartar, I wish you health. Peace to you, as they say "

" I know," answered Olenin, giving him his hand ; " *Koshkildy* ! "

" Ah ! you don't know how to reply," said Uncle Eroshka, nodding in disapproval. " When any one says to you ' *Koshkildy* !' you must say, ' *Allah razi bo sun* ! '—' God keep you ! ' That's the right way, my father, and not ' *Koshkildy*.' I will teach you everything. You are just like Ilia Moseitch, one of your Russians who was here. We two were great friends. He was a fine fellow ; a drunkard and a thief and a sportsman—ah, what a sportsman !—and I taught him everything."

" What will you teach me ? " asked Olenin, feeling more and more interested in the old man.

" I will teach you how to shoot ; I will teach you how to fish ; I will show you the Circassians ; and I will find you a pretty girl, if you want one. That is the kind of man I am. A real joker ; " and then the old man began to laugh. " Can I sit down, my father, I am tired ? *Karga* ? " he added, interrogatively.

" What does *karga* mean ? " aked Olenin.

" Oh ! that means ' good ' in Georgian. I alway say *karga* ; it is one of my sayings—my favourite word. *Karga*, when I say it, means that I'm in a good humour. Well, father, tell them to bring me some wine. Have you got a soldier or servant here ? "

" Yes ; Ivan ! " cried Olenin.

" All you fellows are always called Ivan," said Eroshka.

" Ivan is my man's real name. Here, Vanusha, get some wine from the mistress, and bring it here."

" It is all the same, eh ?—Vanusha or Ivan. Why, among you soldiers, is everybody called Ivan ? " repeated the old fellow. " You, my good man, ask for some wine from the cask already tapped. They have the best in the village. But see you don't pay more than thirty kopeks the quart. She, that old witch, would be glad to—— Ah ! our people are great fools," continued Uncle Eroshka in a confidential tone, when Vanusha had left the room. "They don't consider you as people at all; they think that you are worse than the Tartars; you are worldly, and Russians. However, from my point of view, although you are a soldier, you are a man; you still have a soul in you. That is my way of looking at things. Ilia Moseitch was a soldier; and yet what a golden heart he had! Is not that so, my father? That is the reason that our people don't like me. To me it is all the same, however. I am a merry fellow, I, Eroshka. I love everybody. That's right, eh, father?" And then the old man affectionately patted Olenin on the shoulder.

CHAPTER XII

VANUSHA, meanwhile, was in the very best of humours. He had succeeded in arranging all his belongings, in getting shaved at the barber's, and in letting his trousers down outside of his boots—a sign that the company was now in commodious quarters. He had attentively, and in a measure malevolently, looked at Eroshka, as at some wild beast that he had never seen before. Then, having shaken his head at sight of the muddied floor, he took two empty bottles from under a bench, and went to the people of the house.

"Good evening, good people!" he said, having decided to be especially agreeable. "The master has sent me to buy some new wine of you. Pour it out for me, good people."

The old woman made no answer at first. The girl, who stood before a small Tartar mirror, was arranging a kerchief on her head; she turned towards Vanusha.

"I will pay money, respected people," said Vanusha.

shaking the copper-pieces in his pocket. " You be good, and we will be good ; that is the best way to act."

" How much do you want ? " abruptly asked the old woman.

" A gallon."

" Pour it out for him," said Mother Ulitka, turning to her daughter. " Draw it from the cask that is tapped, my dear."

The girl took the keys, and went quickly out of the cottage, together with Vanusha.

" Tell me, please, what young woman is that ? " said Olenin to Eroshka, and pointing to Marianka, who was then passing the window.

The old man winked, and nudged Olenin with his elbow.

" Wait ! " said he, and he looked out of the window " Hem, hem ! " he coughed, and then he called, " Marianka, O sister Marianka ! Love me, my little soul ! What a jester I am," he added in a whisper to Olenin.

The girl, without turning her head, but giving a strong and decided gesture of dissent, went past the window with that masculine gait peculiar to Cossack girls. She slowly glanced at the old man with her dark, shaded eyes.

" Love me, and you will be happy," cried Eroshka, and, winking, he looked at Olenin in a questioning way. " What a young fellow I am still. What a jester I am," he added. " She is a queen of a girl, is she not ? "

" A beauty ! " said Olenin. " Call her here."

" Come, now. Now, now," said the old man. " They want her for Lukashka. Lukashka is a brave young fellow, a djiguit. The other day he killed an Abrek. I will find you some one better. I will get you one who will be all in silk, and will walk in silver. Whatever I promise I do. I will find you a beauty."

" You are an old man, and yet you talk like that ? " replied Olenin. " That is sinful."

" Sin, where is the sin ? " answered the old man decisively. " Is it a sin to look at a pretty girl ? Is it a sin to go about with her ? Or is it a sin to love her ? Do you Russians think that ? No, my little father : that isn't sin, but salvation. God made you ; God made the girl too ; he made everything, father ; so it is not a sin to look at a pretty girl. It is intended that she should be loved and admired. That is my way of looking at things, my good man."

Going through the court, and into the dark outhouse full of casks, Marianka went up to a cask, and put a dipper in it. Vanusha, standing at the door, smiled, as he looked at her. It seemed to him very funny that she wore nothing but a shirt, which was drawn tight behind and loose in front when she bent over, and still funnier that she had some half-roubles strung round her neck. He thought that at home, among the serfs, everybody would laugh if they saw such a girl as that. " I shall tell my master that *la fill com cé très biê, pour changer*,"* he reflected.

" What are you standing still for, you fool ? " suddenly cried the girl. " Give me the bottles ! "

Having filled the bottles with the cool, red wine, she gave it to Vanusha. " Give the money to mother," she said, pushing back Vanusha's hand, with the money in it.

Vanusha burst out into a laugh. " Why are you so angry, my dear ? " he said good-humouredly, standing there while the girl put the bung back into the cask.

She began to laugh. " Are you good, by chance ? " she asked.

" My master and I are very good," replied Vanusha. " We are such people that, wherever we have lived, the people have always been contented with us. That's because he is a nobleman."

---

* Count Tolstoy pens this passage in bad French, to give an idea of Vanusha's faulty pronunciation. The servant means he shall tell his master that a girl like that would do very well for a change.—Ed.

The girl stopped as she listened.

" And is he married—your master ? " she asked.

" No ; my master is too young to marry. Noblemen never marry when they are young," said Vanusha in a didactic tone.

" Stupid ! He's as big as a buffalo, and yet he's too young to marry ! Is he the commander of all of you ? " she asked.

" My master is a yunker, which means that he is not yet an officer, but personally he is much greater than a general, and a high personage, for not only our colonel, but even the Czar, knows him," proudly exclaimed Vanusha. " We are not such people as the other officers. Our father is a senator : he has more than a thousand serfs of his own ; and they send us money by thousands at a time. That is the reason everybody always likes us. Sometimes you will find a captain without any money at all ; but what is the use of any man like that ? "

" Come, I am going to shut up," interrupted the girl.

Vanusha then took the wine to Olenin, explained to him that *la fill c'est tré juli* (the girl very pretty), and immediately afterwards went out with a stupid laugh.

CHAPTER XIII

MEANWHILE they were beating the retreat on the great square. People were coming back from work in the fields. The cattle were crowding through the gateways amid a great cloud of dust. The girls and the women were bustling about the streets and in the yards, collecting their cattle. The sun had set behind the distant snowy range. The twilight was settling over earth and sky. Above the dark orchards the stars came out one by one, almost invisibly; and the sounds of life in the village gradually died away. When the Cossack girls had collected the cattle, they went to the corners of the streets, and, crunching sunflower seeds, sat down on the embankments of the huts. Marianka, who had milked two cows and a buffalo, came up to one of these groups, which consisted of several women and girls, with one old man.

Talk turned on the Abrek who had been killed. The old man told the story, and the women asked him questions.

" He will have a big reward, I suppose ? " said one woman, referring to Lukashka.

" Why, of course. They say they are going to send him a cross."

" Mosef wanted to injure him. He took away the Abrek's gun; but the authorities at Kizliar have found it out."

" What a mean fellow, that Mosef ! "

" They say that Lukashka has come back," said one girl.

" He is at Yamka's," [Yamka was a loose Cossack woman who kept a drinking-house] " drinking with Nazarka. It is said they have drunk two gallons between them."

" Oh, that *Urvan's* luck ! " said one of the women. " He is really a *Urvan*. Such a nice young fellow. His father, Kiriak, was just like him—he was father to everybody. When they killed him, all the village went to his funeral. See, there they come ! " added the woman, pointing to three Cossacks coming along the street towards the group. " Ergushoff, somehow, has joined them. What a drunkard he is ! "

Lukashka, with Nazarka and Ergushoff, now came up to the girls. All three of them were redder than usual. Ergushoff staggered, and, laughing loudly, punched Nazarka in the side.

" Why don't you sing us a song ? " he cried to the girls. " I say, sing us something, as we are on the spree."

" Have you passed the day well ? Have you passed the day well ? " was inquired on all sides.

" Sing ? Why ? Is it a festival ? " asked an old woman. " You are swollen with drink. Sing something yourself."

Ergushoff laughed, and punched Nazarka. " You sing, and I will sing too," said he. " I am good at it, I tell you."

" Why have all the pretty girls gone to sleep ? " said Nazarka. " We have come back from the outpost to drink good luck. We have been drinking good luck to Lukashka."

Lukashka, coming up to the group, slowly pushed back his cap, and stood before the girls, His broad cheeks and neck were quite red. He stood and spoke quietly and moderately ; but beneath his moderation, and the quietness of his movements, there was more latent life and force than in all the talkativeness and bustle of Nazarka. He reminded one of a colt, which, after throwing up its tail and snorting, suddenly stands still, as if chained and fettered. He stood in this quiet way before the girls. His eyes laughed, but he spoke little, looking first at his drunken companions, and then at the girls. When Marianka came up to the corner, he slowly lifted his cap, made way for her, and then placed himself in front of her, lightly stretching out one leg, putting his thumb in his belt, and playing with his dagger. Marianka, in answer to his salute, slightly bowed her head, then sat down on the embankment, and took some sunflower seeds out of her bosom.

Lukashka looked at Marianka without dropping his eyes, and, crunching some seeds, spat the skins out. All had become quiet when Marianka approached.

" Well, have you come for long ? " asked one of the women, breaking the silence.

" Till morning only," answered Lukashka, gravely.

" Well, God give you a good return ! " said the old Cossack. " I am very glad, as I was saying just now.·'

"And I say so, too," exclaimed the drunken Ergushoff, laughing. "We have got some guests, have we?" he added, pointing to a soldier who went by. "Soldiers' brandy is good: I like it!"

"They have sent three of the devils to us," said one of the women. "My old man went to the commander, but he said he could not help it."

"Ah, ah! So you have got some trouble!" said Ergushoff.

"Have they smoked you up with tobacco, eh?" asked another woman.

"We let them smoke in the yard as much as they please; but we won't let them into the house. Even if the commander came, I would not let him in. They would steal everything. Why doesn't the chief of the station take some of these devils himself, I should like to know?"

"There are no soldiers at his place."

"So you don't like it?" again said Ergushoff.

"And that isn't all; they say, too, that orders have been given to the girls to make the soldiers' beds, and treat them to wine and honey," said Nazarka, sticking out one leg, like Lukashka, and pushing his cap back to the nape of his neck.

Ergushoff burst out into a loud laugh, and, seizing the girl next to him, he hugged and kissed her. "Yes, it is all true," said he.

"Enough of that!" squealed the girl. "I shall tell my mother!"

"Tell her!" he cried. "Nazarka speaks the truth. There was a circular: he knows how to read, you see. It is true, I tell you." And then he proceeded to hug the girl next in order.

"Will you stop, rascal?" laughingly exclaimed the rosy, round-faced Ustenka, pushing him away.

Ergushoff moved on one side, and almost fell down. "They say that girls haven't any strength, but this one has almost killed me," he muttered.

"Now stop; go back to the post with you!" said

THE COSSACKS

Ustenka, and, turning away from him, she again burst into a laugh.

"So you went to sleep," she added, and did not see the Abrek. If he had only killed you, it would have served you right."

"Wouldn't you have mourned?" laughed Nazarka.

"No, I shouldn't," she replied.

"She has no heart, you see. It does not matter to her. She wouldn't have mourned, Nazarka!" said Ergushoff.

Lukashka in the meantime was looking silently at Marianka; and his gaze evidently disturbed the girl. "Well, Marianka, I hear they have quartered the commander at your house," he said at last, moving towards her.

Marianka, as usual, did not answer at once, but slowly raised her eyes to the Cossack's face. Lukashka was smiling, as though something especial, independent of the conversation, was going on between him and the girl. An old woman who was behind Marianka undertook to reply for her:

"Yes, it is lucky Marianka's parents are well off, and have two cottages," she said. "Thomushka only has one, and yet one of the commanders has been lodged with him. It is said they have filled the place with goods; so that Thomushka has not any room left him. It is an unheard of thing that they should send a whole horde of them to the village! But what can one do?" she added. "And what infernal business will they be up to?"

"It is said they are going to build a bridge over the Terek," remarked one girl.

"I heard," said Nazarka, coming up to Ustenka, "that they are going to dig a pit and bury all the girls in it, because they won't love the young fellows;" and then he again made the bow he was so fond of, after which they all laughed, while Ergushoff immediately began to embrace an old Cossack woman, leaving out Marianka, who followed in order.

"Why don't you kiss Marianka? You shouldn't miss one. Go in order," said Nazarka.

"No, no-o; my old woman is sweeter," cried Ergushoff, kissing the old woman, who was endeavouring to push him off.

"You are choking me," she cried, laughing.

A measured tread of feet at the end of the street interrupted the laughter. Three soldiers in overcoats, with guns over their shoulders, were going to change guard over the regimental chest. The old corporal looked angrily at the Cossacks, and brought his men along so as to make Lukashka and Nazarka move out of the way. The latter drew on one side; but Lukashka, merely frowning, turned his head and his broad back, and did not stir.

"People are standing here; go round," he said at last to the corporal, glancing contemptuously at the soldiers.

The latter silently went by, marching with measured steps along the dusty road.

Marianka burst into a laugh, and, after her, all the other girls did the same.

"Those are elegant fellows!" said Nazarka. "They look like long-skirted choir singers." And he marched along the road in odd imitation of them.

The lookers-on again burst into loud laughter.

Lukashka slowly walked up to Marianka: "So the commander is quartered on you?" he asked.

Marianka reflected for a moment: "they let him have the new cottage," she replied.

"What is he—old, or young?" asked Lukashka, sitting down by her side.

"Do you suppose I asked?" answered the girl. "I went to fetch some wine for him, and I just saw him and Uncle Eroshka sitting at the window—a red-haired sort of fellow, it seemed to me. He brought a whole cartload of luggage with him." And then she lowered her eyes.

"How glad I am that I got permission to come back from the outpost!" said Lukashka, moving nearer to the girl, and always looking straight into her eyes.

" Well, have you come for long ? " asked Marianka smiling slightly.

" Till to-morrow morning. Give me some seeds," he added, stretching out his hand.

Marianka then gave a pleasant smile, and opened the bosom of her shirt. " Do not take them all." she said.

" Really, I was very lonesome without you ; by God I was ! " said Lukashka slowly and in a quiet tone, as he took the seeds from the girl's bosom, and moved still nearer to her. Then he began to say something to her in a whisper, and with laughing eyes.

" I shan't come : I have said so once for all," suddenly said Marianka aloud, moving a little away from him.

" I assure you I have something to say to you. Come, come, Marianka."

Marianka shook her head in token of dissent, but smiled.

" Sister Marianka ! O, sister ! mother wants you. Supper is ready ! " now cried Marianka's little brother, running up to the party.

" I am coming immediately," answered the girl. " You go on ; go on alone, child. I will come very soon."

Lukashka rose, and lifted his cap. " It is time, too, for me to go home : I have better business there," he said, pretending to feel indifferent, and trying to restrain a smile ; and he soon disappeared behind the corner of the houses.

Meanwhile, night had already settled over the village. The bright stars spangled the dark sky. The streets were dark and empty. Nazarka remained with the Cossack girls, and their laughter could be heard at a long distance ; but Lukashka, after going off with a quiet step, suddenly began to run noise-lessly like a cat—holding his dagger, which rattled with his movements—and not proceeding homewards, but toward the house of the cornet.

After he had crossed two streets, and had turned a corner, he arranged his coat, and sat down on the ground in the shade of the fence. " The cornet's daughter is a fine girl," he thought. " She is proud, devil take it ! A real Khorunjikha.* But only give me time."

The steps of a woman coming near aroused him. He began to listen, and laughed to himself. Marianka with her head bent forward, came with even steps towards him, tapping the bars of the fence with a swich. Lukashka then rose up, while Marianka started and stood still.

" Oh, you devil, you frightened me so ! You did not go home, then," she said, and laughed aloud.

Lukashka embraced the girl with one arm, and with the other hand he took her by the face. " There was something I wanted to say to you, by God it's true ! " And his voice trembled and broke.

" What kind of talk would you have at night ? " asked Marianka. " Mother is waiting for me. As for you, go to your love ! "

Then, freeing herself from his hands, she darted back a few steps ; but, on reaching the gate of her yard, she stopped still, and turned toward Lukashka, who had followed her, and kept trying to persuade her to wait a little.

" Now, what do you want to tell me, you night-prowler ? " she asked, and she again began to laugh.

" Do not laugh at me, Marianka. What if I do have a sweetheart, devil take her ! Only say the word, and I will love you—do anything you want. Do you hear ? " and he rattled the money in his pocket. " We could live a little. Other people enjoy themselves ; and I—I do not get any comfort owing to you, Marianka."

The girl answered nothing, but stood in front of

* The wife or daughter of an officer.

him, and, with a quick movement of her fingers, broke her switch into little pieces.

Lukashka suddenly clenched his fists, and set his teeth. " Yes, it's all wait, wait, wait ! As if I did not love you ! Do with me whatever you please," he said suddenly, frowning, and seizing both her hands.

The quiet expression of Marianka's face did not change.

" Do not be so bold, Lukashka ; and listen to me," she answered, not pulling away her hands, but keeping the young Cossack at some distance from her. " I am only a girl ; but listen to me. It is not for me to consent ; my will is not free. But since you love me, this is what I will tell you. You let go of my hands ; I will tell you without that. I will marry you, yes ; but do not expect any folly from me."

" So you will marry me ? That will be arranged apart from us. But love me, Marianka," said Lukashka, who from dark and angry suddenly became mild and tender, and with a smile looked closely into her eyes.

Marianka drew near to him, and gave him a kiss on the lips. " Brother,"* she whispered, pressing him convulsively ; then, suddenly tearing herself away, she ran off, and without turning back entered the courtyard of the house, despite Lukashka's prayers to wait a minute longer to hear what he had to tell her.

" Go away. They will see us," she said in a low voice. " There is that devil of a lodger of ours, walking about the yard."

" O cornet's daughter !" thought Lukashka to himself. " So you will marry me ! Yes, no doubt ; but I should like her to love me first of all."

He then went to join Nazarka at Yamka's, and, after drinking a while with him, repaired to his Duniashka, with whom he passed the night, despite her recent infidelity.

---

* " Brother " and " cousin " are used as terms of endearment among the Cossacks.

CHAPTER XIV

OLENIN was really strolling across the yard when Marianka came in by the gate, and he heard her say, " That devil of a lodger is walking about." He had spent the whole evening with Uncle Eroshka on the steps of his new quarters. He had ordered a table to be brought out, the tea-urn, some wine, and a lighted candle, to be provided, and over a glass of tea and a cigar he listened to the stories of the old man, who sat at his feet on the steps. Although the air was still, the candle flickered, and the flame blew about on different sides ; now lighting up the pillars of the house, now the table and the tea-service, and now the white, closely cropped head of the old man. The moths flew about, and, scattering the dust from their wings, now beat against the table and the glasses, now flew into the flame of the candle, and now disappeared into the dark air beyond the circle of light. Olenin and Eroshka drank five bottles of new wine between them. Each time that Eroshka filled his glass, he chinked it against Olenin's, and drank his health. He talked on without intermission. He spoke of the old life of the Cossacks—of his father, the *broad* one, who could carry on his back a boar weighing three hundred and fifty pounds, and drink two gallons of wine at one sitting. He spoke of his own former life, and of his friend Girtckik, with whom, during the time of the pestilence, he had brought furs from beyond the Terek. He spoke of hunting and shooting, and related how, in one morning, he had killed two stags ; and how his sweetheart used at night-time to run out to the outpost to join him. And all this he told so eloquently and so picturesquely, that Olenin did not notice how quickly the time passed.

" So, that was how we lived, father," said Eroshka ;
" if you had only met me in my golden time, I would
have shown you everything. But now Eroshka is
done for. Then he used to be the pride of the
regiment. Who had the best horses ? Who had the
finest sabre ? Who was always asked to the drinking
bouts ? Who was the best man to go on a spree
with ? Who was sent to the mountains to kill Ahmed
Khan ? It was always Eroshka. Whom did the girls
love ? It was always Eroshka. Because I was a
real djiguit. I drank hard ; I could steal the horses
from the herds in the mountains ; I could sing songs ;
I was good for everything. Nowadays we no longer
have such Cossacks as I was. It is a pity to look at
them. They are only so high ; " and Eroshka placed
his hand about a yard from the ground. " They
wear stupid boots and amuse themselves like fools.
When they are drunk, they all swell up : yes, and
they don't drink like men, they drink like beasts.
And what was I ? I was Eroshka the clever. People
knew me, not only in the villages, but in the mountains. Circassian princes, who were friends of mine,
used to come and see me. I was friends with all
of them. With the Tartar I was a Tartar ; with the
Armenian, an Armenian ; with a soldier, a soldier ;
with an officer, an officer. It was all the same to me,
so long as I had something to drink. People used to
say to me, ' You must purify yourself, for you are
contaminated by all this intercourse. You must not
drink with a soldier, or eat with a Tartar.' "

" But who said that ? " asked Olenin.

" Why, our commanders. But listen to the Tartar
Mullah or Cadi. He will tell you, ' You infidel giaours,
why do you eat pork ? ' It all signifies that each
person has his own customs. In my opinion, it is all
alike. God made everything for man's pleasure.
There is no sin in anything. Take, for example, an
animal. He lives in the Tartar reeds as well as in
ours. Wherever he goes, he is at home there. What
God gives him, he eats it. And yet our people say

that, for things like this, we shall have to lick pots-herds. I say, though, that it is all nonsense," he added, becoming silent.

"What is stupid nonsense ? " asked Olenin.

"Why, what our commanders tell us. At Tchervlen I had a Cossack, who was an intimate friend of mine. He was a brave fellow, just like me. The enemy killed him in the Tchetchna. He used to say that our commanders made up all these things out of their own heads. You will die, he said, and the grass will grow on your grave, and that is all there is in it." Then the old man laughed. "He was a desperate fellow ! " he added.

"But how old are you ? " asked Olenin.

"God knows ! Seventy, about. When we had an empress,* I was already a big fellow. You can count how much it would be since then. Would it be sixty years ? "

"Yes, fully. And still you are strong and hearty."

"Well, thank God ! I am well ; I am perfectly well : only a witch cast a spell over me."

"How ? "

"Why, ruined me, spoiled me."

"So, when we die, the grass will grow over us,". repeated Olenin.

Eroshka evidently did not wish to express this idea more clearly. He kept silent for a little while.

"And what do you think of it ? But, come, drink," he cried, smiling, and offering some wine.

CHAPTER XV

"AND so——What was I talking about ? " con-tinued Eroshka, trying to remember. "Yes, this is the kind of man I am. I am a hunter ; and

---

* Catherine the Great, who reigned from 1762 to 1796.

there isn't another hunter in the regiment like me. I can find and show you every kind of animal, and every kind of bird—what they are and where they are. I know all about them. And I have got dogs, and two guns, and nets, and a mare, and a falcon; got every thing I want, thank God! You, perhaps, may become a real hunter, but don't boast of it. I will show you everything. That's the kind of a man I am! I will find the scent for you. I know the beast; and I know where his lair is, and where he goes to drink or lie down. I will make a shooting hut, and I will sit there all night and keep watch for you. What is the use of sitting at home? One only gets warm, and gets drunk. And then the women come and make a row; and the boys cry at you; and one gets angry. Whereas there, at dawn you go out, and you choose a place, and you smooth down the reeds, and you sit there and watch there, like a brave young fellow, and wait for them. In any case, you know what goes on in the woods. You look up at the sky and see the stars; you look at them and guess the time. Then you look around you. The wood stirs, and you hear a little noise; and a boar comes out to roll in the mud. You hear how the young eagles cry, and how the cocks or the geese in the village answer them—geese only until midnight, of course. All that I know. And somewhere in the distance you hear the sound of a gun, and thoughts come to you. You think: ' Who fired then? ' A Cossack, just like me, has perhaps watched for an animal, and has killed it, or perhaps he has only wounded it; and the animal dashes angrily into the weeds to wipe off the blood, all to no purpose. But I don't like that! I don't like that! What is the use of hurting an animal? Kill it at once, fool! ' Perhaps one thinks: ' A Circassian has killed some poor little Cossack.' All that comes into your head. Once, I remember, I was sitting at the waterside, and saw a cradle floating along—only one side of it was a little broken —and the thought came to me: ' Whose cradle is that ? " It must be, I thought, that those devils of soldiers came to a Circassian village, and robbed the Circassian women, and that some devil killed a child, and took him by the feet and threw him into the fire. Don't they do things like that ? Some people have no souls. When such thoughts came into my head I felt sorry. I thought to myself : 'They threw away the cradle, drove away the old woman, and burned the house ; and now the djiguit will take his gun and come over to our side of the river to rob.' You see, one has to think when one sits there. Yes ; and, as you listen, a lot of grice break from the wood, and you start, and say : 'Come on, my dears!' They are smelling about, you think, and you sit with-out moving a muscle ; and your heart goes 'Thump, thump, thump !' That is the way it moves inside you. This last spring, a lot of grice, quite black, came up to me in the woods ; and I said to myself, 'To Father and Son,' and was just about to fire, when one of the old sows snorted somehow to her little ones, as much as to say : 'Take care, my children ; there is a man there ;' and then they all scampered off into the bushes."

"How did the sow explain to her grice that there was a man sitting there ? " asked Olenin.

"What ? Do you think that an animal is a fool ? No, an animal is far more cunning than a man: it is great folly to call him a swine. He knows every-thing. Just take an example. A man goes along a track without noticing it. But as soon as a sow comes on your track, she smells it out, and runs off. That means she has got sense in her : that you don't know your own tracks, and she does. Yes ; and you want to kill her, and she wants to walk alive in the woods. You have such an idea and she has another. She is a sow ; and for all that she is no worse than you : she is also a divine creation. Eh ! man's a fool ; man's a fool !" repeated the old fellow several times, and then letting his head sink down, he became absorbed in thought.

Olenin also began to think, and descending the steps with his arms behind his back, he began to walk about the yard.

When Eroshka roused himself, he raised his head, and began to look at a nightmoth which was hovering about the flickering flame of he candle, almost falling into it.

" You fool, you fool ! " he said, " where are you flying to ? You fool, you fool ! " Then he got up, and, with his thick fingers, began to drive away the moth. " You will get burnt, you fool ! come, fly away here. There is plenty of room," he added in a tender voice, trying to take it by its wings so as to place it out of harm's way. " You are killing yourself, and I am sorry for you."

He sat there for a long time, talking to himself, and drinking out of the bottle ; while Olenin continued to walk up and down the yard. Suddenly a noise at the gate roused the young fellow : involuntarily holding his breath, he listened to a girl's laugh, to a man's voice, and to the sound of a kiss. Purposely rustling the grass with his feet, he retreated to the other side of the yard. Soon afterwards, the fence creaked ; a Cossack (Lukashka), in a dark uniform and a white cap, went along the fence ; and a tall woman in white went past Olenin. " I have nothing to do with you, nor have you anything to do with me," this is what Marianka's decisive stride seemed to say to him. He watched her go to the family cottage, and still observed her, even through the window, as she took off her kerchief, and set down on the bench. Then suddenly a feeling of loneliness, confused wishes and hopes, and a kind of envious desire seized upon Olenin's soul.

The last lights were extinguished in the cottages : the last sounds in the village had died away. The fences and the cattle (which seemed mere white masses in the yards), the roofs of the houses, and the rows of poplar-trees, all seemed to be in a healthy, quiet sleep. All that an attentive ear could detect was the incessant croaking of the frogs resounding from the damp distance. In the east the stars became fewer, and it seemed as if they were merging in the growing light : overhead they clustered more thickly and shone more brilliantly. The old man leant his head on his arm, and sat listening. A cock began to crow in the opposite yard. Olenin was still walking up and down absorbed in thought. At last the sound of several voices came to his ear. He went to the fence, and began to listen. Some Cossacks were singing a merry song ; and one young voice was heard above all the others.

" Do you know who that is singing ? " asked the old man, rousing himself. " That is Lukashka the djiguit. He has killed a Circassian and he is making merry over it. What is the use of being glad of it ? "

" Have you ever killed any people ? " asked Olenin.

The old man suddenly rose up on both his elbows, and brought his face nearer to Olenin's. " The devil ! " he cried. " Why do you ask that ? It is no use talking about such things. Is it sensible now, yes, is it sensible now to ruin a man's life ? Good-bye, father, I have had enough to eat and drink," he said, rising. " Would you like me to fetch you to go shooting to-morrow ? "

" Come."

" See that you get up early then. If you oversleep, you will be fined."

" I daresay I shall get up earlier than you," answered Olenin.

The old man went off. The song was finished : but steps were heard, and merry talk. A little while later, the song again resounded, but farther off ; and Eroshka's deep voice joined the others. " What people ! what a life ! " thought Olenin, and with a sigh he went into his room.

CHAPTER XVI

UNCLE EROSHKA was past active service, and lived by himself. His wife, some twenty years previously, had become converted to the Orthodox faith, and had run away from him, and married a Russian sergeant. He had no children. He was not boasting when he said that he had held the first place among the Cossacks of the village. Everybody in the regiment knew him for his former bravery. The death of more than one Circassian, and even Russian, was on his soul. He had gone out into the mountains ; and he had stolen from the Russians, and had twice been in prison. The greater part of his life had been passed in hunting in the forests, where he lived for days on a bit of dry bread, and drank nothing but water. To make up for that, however, whenever he was in the village he got drunk from morning till night.

Upon leaving Olenin he slept for two hours, and, waking up long before light, he lay on his bed, and passed judgment on the young man with whom he had so recently become acquainted. Olenin's simplicity pleased him greatly—simplicity in the sense that he did not grudge wine—and Olenin himself pleased him. He wondered why the Russians were all so simple and rich, and why they all knew nothing, and were yet so very learned. He thought these questions over by himself, and reflected as to what he might ask Olenin to give him. Uncle Eroshka's cottage was tolerably large, and not old ; but the absence of a woman was very evident. Contrary to the usual Cossack character for cleanliness, his whole room was dirty, and in the greatest disorder. On the table lay a blood-stained caftan, half a roll, and close by a jay intended as food for the falcon. On the benches, some shoes, a knife, a dagger, a bag, some wet clothes, and rags were scattered in disorder. In one corner, in a basin of dirty, foul-smelling water, a pair of sandals were soaking; in another corner stood a rifle with its rest. On the floor a net and several dead pheasants were thrown, and round the table wandered a hen, tied by one leg, and pecking at the refuse on the dirty floor. Near the stove, which was not alight, there stood an earthenware pot, filled with some thickened milk; and on the stove itself was perched a hawk, trying to free itself from the cord which held it; while a small grey falcon sat quietly on the edge, glancing from time to time at the hen, and moving its head from right to left.

Uncle Eroshka himself lay on his back on the short bed, which was placed between the wall and the stove. He was wearing nothing but his shirt; and, resting his strong feet against the stove, he rubbed his hands, which had been badly scratched by the falcon which he was in the habit of carrying without wearing gloves. In the whole room, and especially in the immediate neighbourhood of the old man himself, the atmosphere was impregnated with that same strong, not unpleasant, mixed odour which accompanied him everywhere.

" Are you at home, uncle ? " suddenly exclaimed a sharp voice outside the window—a voice which Eroshka immediately recognised as that of his neighbour Lukashka.

" At home. Come in ! " cried the old man. " Well, neighbour Marka, Luka Marka, why have you come to see uncle ? Are you going back to the outpost ? "

The falcon roused itself on hearing its master, and fluttering its wings, tried to free itself from its leash.

The old man was fond of Lukashka, whom he alone excluded when he expressed his contempt for the young Cossacks. Moreover, Lukashka and his mother, being neighbours, not unfrequently gave the old man some wine, some sour cream, and other things from their household provisions, which Eroshka lacked. The old fellow, who had followed his impulses throughout his life, always explained his feelings in a practical way. " Well," he would say to himself, " they are well-to-do people. I give them some fresh game, and a chicken or two, and they don't forget me : they send me a pie or some rolls."

" How are you, Marka ? Glad to see you ! " he now merrily cried, as with a quick movement he slipped out of the bed, jumped up and took a couple of steps over the creaking floor. He looked at his crooked legs, and suddenly seemed to be very much amused at them. He burst into a laugh, stamped his bare heels once, twice, and then made a salute. " Did I do it well ? " he asked, twinkling his little eyes. Lukashka laughed.

" Well, are you going to the outpost ? " asked the old man.

" I have brought you the wine, uncle, that I promised you."

" Christ be merciful to you ! " said old Eroshka, picking up his trousers and blouse, which lay on the floor. Putting them on, and girding himself with a strap, he poured some water from the basin on his hands, wiped them on a pair of old trousers, parted his beard with a small piece of comb, and then came and stood before Lukashka. " I am ready," he said.

Lukashka found a glass, wiped it, filled it, and, sitting down on the bench, handed it to Eroshka.

" Here's to your health ! In the name of the Father and the Son ! " said the old man solemnly, accepting the wine. " May you obtain everything you wish ! May you be a brave fellow, and get a cross ! "

Lukashka also drank his wine with a prayer, and set the glass on the table. The old man got up, brought a dried fish, laid it on the threshold, beat it with a stick so as to make it softer, and after placing it on a blue earthenware plate (the only one he possessed), set it on the table.

" You see, I have got everything I want, even a bit of something to eat, thank God ! " he said, proudly. " Well, what about Mosef ? "

Lukashka related how the corporal had taken the Abrek's gun, evidently wishing to know the old man's opinion of the matter.

" Oh ! don't bother about the gun," said Eroshka. " If you don't let him keep the gun, you won't get the reward."

" How, uncle ? They say they don't give rewards to young fellows who are not yet mounted.* And the gun was a good one, a Crimean one, worth eighty roubles."

" Well, never mind ! Once I quarrelled with my captain : he wanted me to give him a horse. ' Give me the horse,' he said, ' and I will have you made a cornet.' I didn't give it him, however, and so I never got on."

" Well, uncle, now I have got to buy a horse ; and they say that, across the river, you can't get one for less than fifty roubles : and mother has not sold her wine yet."

" Oh, that didn't trouble us ! " said the old man. " When Uncle Eroshka was of your age, he had already carried off herds and horses from the Tartars, and driven them over the Terek. They were so plentiful, that you had to sell an excellent horse for a gallon of brandy, or for a sheep-skin cloak."

" Why did you sell them so cheap ? " asked Lukashka.

" Oh, what a fool you are ! A fool, Marka ! " said the old man, contemptuously. " A man can't be stingy with what he has stolen. I suppose you have never seen anybody drive off horses ? Why don't you answer ? "

" What should I say, uncle ? " said Lukashka. " It is plain we are not such people as you were."

* The Cossacks look on those who have not yet served on horseback in the field as " infants," or under age.

"You are a fool, you are a fool, Marka! 'Not such people!'" answered the old man, imitating the young Cossack. "Yes, I was not that kind of a Cossack at your age."

"Well, what can we do?" asked Lukashka.

The old man contemptuously shook his head. "Uncle Eroshka was simple," said he. "He was never stingy about anything. For that reason, all the Tchetchna were good friends with him. One of my friends would come to me: I would make him drunk, talk smooth with him, put him to sleep in my bed, and, when I went to see him, I made him a present. That is the way for people to act, and not as they act now. The only amusement the young people now have is to nibble seeds, and then spit out the husks," said Eroshka, derisively moving his lips in imitation of the way in which the present Cossacks nibbled the sunflower seeds, and spat out the husks.

"Yes, I know that," said Lukashka; "that is true."

"If you wish to be a true Cossack then, be a djiguit, and not a moujik. A moujik will buy a horse, pay down the money, and take the horse away with him. That doesn't require any cunning."

They were both silent for a while.

"Well, uncle, it is very dull both in the village and at the outpost," resumed Lukashka at last. "Everybody is so timid! Take Nazarka, for instance. Not long ago, we were in a Circassian village; and Ghirei Khan suggested we should go among the Nogais and carry off some horses: but no one went. I could not go alone."

"And your uncle? Do you think I have dried up? No, I haven't dried up. Give me a horse, and I will go to the Nogais at once."

"What is the use of talking nonsense?" said Lukashka. "Tell me how to act with Ghirei Khan. He says: 'Only bring the horses to the Terek, and I will find a place to hide them.' But you see he is slippery. It is hard to believe him."

"You can believe Ghirei Khan. All his family are excellent, worthy people : his father was my true friend. Only listen to your uncle. I won't teach you anything bad. Make him swear an oath to you, and then you can believe him. And when you go along with him, always have your pistol ready, especially when you begin to divide the horses. Once a Tchetchna man almost killed me because I asked ten roubles of him for a horse. Yes, you can believe Ghirei. But never go to sleep without your gun."

Lukashka listened attentively to the old man. "Well, uncle, people say you have got the bursting-weed," he added, after a moment's silence.

"No, I haven't got the bursting-weed ; but I can teach you how to find it. Be a good boy, and don't forget what an old man says. Shall I tell you ? "

"Yes, tell me, uncle."

"You know a tortoise—a kind of devil, you know —a tortoise ? "

"Of course I know."

"Well, you find its nest, and make a little wicker-work fence all about it, so that it cannot get inside ; then it goes all about in a circle, and immediately starts to find the bursting-weed. It brings it, and the wicker-work all breaks into pieces. You go there quickly on the next morning, and look carefully where the wicker is broken ; there the bursting-weed will lie. Take it with you, and carry it wherever you like : there will be neither lock nor bolt for you then."

"Did you ever try it, uncle ? "

"Perhaps I did ; perhaps not : at all events, good people told me about it. I had only one charm. I used to recite ' Hail to you,' when I got on my horse."

"What sort of a ' hail to you,' uncle ? "

"So you don't know it ? Oh, what people ! You see you have to ask your uncle. Now listen, and say it after me." Thereupon the old man began to recite : "' Hail to you who live in Zion ! '" continuing with some gibberish, and finally asking, "Well, can you remember it ? Come, repeat it."

Lukashka laughed. "Why, uncle! you don't mean to say that this kept you from being killed?" said he. "Perhaps though——"

"Oh, you have grown wise! You must learn it, and then say it: it won't do you any harm at all events." And then the old man laughed to himself. "However, don't you go among the Nogais, Lukashka," he added.

"Why not?"

"The times have changed, and you people also. You Cossacks are good for nothing. Besides, remember the Russians who have been sent here. They would find fault with you, and try you. You had better give it up. Why should you go? It was different when I was with Girtchek." And the old man seemed about to begin one of his endless stories.

Lukashka looked out of the window. "It is quite light, uncle," he interrupted. "It is time for me to go; come and see me."

"Christ preserve you! I am going to see that officer. I promised to take him out shooting; he's a good fellow, it seems to me."

CHAPTER XVII

LEAVING Eroshka, Lukashka went home. As he went out, the raw, dewy mist was rising from the ground, and covering the village. Invisible cattle began to move on various sides: cocks crew oftener and more sharply. Finally the air began to clear; and the people began stirring. It was only when quite near that Lukashka perceived the fence of his yard quite wet with the mist, the roof of the hut, and the open gate. In the yard, through the haze, he heard the noise of a hatchet, with which some one was chopping wood. Lukashka went into

H

the cottage. His mother was already up, and, standing before the stove, was putting some wood into it. His little sister was still asleep on the bed.

"Well, Lukashka, have you come on leave?" said his mother, quietly. "Have you amused yourself? Where did you spend the night?"

"I was in the village," quietly answered her son; taking his gun out of its case, and looking at it carefully.

His mother shook her head.

Putting some powder into the pan, Lukashka removed several empty cartridges from a bag and began to fill them, closing them with bullets rolled up in a rag; then, after biting the ends of the cartridges together with his teeth, and finally inspecting them, he put them in the bag.

"Well, mother, I told you to mend the baskets; have you mended them?" he asked.

"How could I? The dumb one mended something last night. Why, you are surely not going back to the outpost already? I have not seen you at all."

"Well, I have just come, and I have got to go," answered Lukashka, tying up his powder. "Where is the dumb one? Has she gone out?"

"She must be chopping wood. She is always lamenting over you. 'I don't see him,' she says— 'I don't see him at all;' and she somehow puts her hands to her face and chuckles, and then presses her hands to her heart, and wrings them to show that she is sad. Shall I go and call her? She understood everything about the Abrek."

"Call her," said Lukashka. "Yes; and there was some tallow of mine there: bring it here. I want it to grease my sabre."

The old woman went out; and a few minutes later, with a creaking tread, the dumb sister of Lukashka entered the cottage. She was six years older than her brother, and would have been extremely like him; had it not been for the dull expression of her face; such as is common to all mutes. She wore a coarse

shirt, patched in several places. Her feet were bare
and scratched; and on her head there was an old
blue kerchief; her neck, her arms, and her face were
as muscular as a man's. It was evident by her clothing, and everything about her, that she constantly
performed a man's hard work. She had brought in
an armful of wood, which she threw on the stove;
then she went up to her brother, with a glad smile
covering her whole face, patted him on the shoulder,
and began with her hands, her face, and indeed her
whole body, to make repeated signs to him.

"Well, well, good, good! You are a good girl,
Stepka," answered her brother, nodding his head.
"You have got everything ready; you have mended
everything; good girl! Here's something for you;"
and taking two ginger-bread cakes out of his pocket
he gave them to her.

The face of the dumb girl grew red, and she chir-
ruped with delight. She made still more signs,
pointing at the cakes, and then bringing her thick
fingers to her eyebrows and face. Lukashka understood her, and kept on nodding, and slightly smiling.
She meant to say that her brother gave nice things
to the girls, and that the girls all liked him; and that
one of them, called Marianka, was better than all the
rest, and loved him. She indicated Marianka by
pointing in the direction of her yard, then, at her own
eyebrows and face, and chuckling, and nodding her
head. Love she indicated by putting her hand to her
breast, kissing it, and pretending to embrace something.
The mother returned to the hut, and on seeing what the
dumb girl was talking about, she smiled, and nodded
her head approvingly. The dumb girl showed her the
cakes, and again chuckled with joy.

"I told Ulitka not long ago that I should come to
propose on your behalf for her daughter," said the
mother. "She received my words well."

Lukashka looked at his mother. "Well, mother,"
he said, "the wine must be taken to market; and
I must have a horse."

H 2

"I will take it when the time comes. I will arrange the casks," said the mother, evidently not wishing that her son should meddle in the household affairs. "When you go," added the old woman, "take the bag which is in the passage. I got it for you, and have something ready for you; or will you put it with the saddle-bags?"

"All right," answered Lukashka. "If Gherei Khan comes from over the river, you must send him to the outpost; for they won't let me leave again for a long time. I have got some business to transact with him."

Then he began to get ready.

"I will send him, Lukashka; I will send him; You were amusing yourself last night at Yamka's, weren't you?" asked the old woman. "I got up to see about the cattle, and listened, and I felt sure I heard you singing songs."

Lukashka did not answer. He went out into the passage, threw his bag over his shoulder, with his cloak over it, took his gun, and then paused on the threshold.

"Good-bye, mother!" he said. "Just send a little cask of wine by Nazarka," shutting the gate behind him. "I promised it to the boys there. He will come and get it."

"Christ preserve you, Lukashka! God be with you! I will send it: I will send some out of the new cask," answered the old woman; and then going up to the fence, and leaning over it: "Listen a bit," she added.

Lukashka stood still.

"You have been enjoying yourself here—well, thank God! Why shouldn't a young man enjoy himself a little? God gives happiness. That's all right. But over there, my son, look out: don't do such things too often. More than all, keep on good terms with your commander. It is necessary; you cannot do otherwise. I will sell the wine, and get some money for you to buy a horse, and I will get a wife for you as well."

" All right, all right ! " answered her son, frowning.

The dumb girl now cried out in order to attract attention. She first pointed to her head and her hand, which meant shaven head, or Tchetchna man ; then, contracting her brows, she pretended to load a gun, cried out, and began to chirrup, shaking her head. She meant that Lukashka ought to kill another Circassian.

Lukashka understood her, laughed, and then with quick, light steps, holding his gun under his cloak, he disappeared from view amid the mist. After standing silently at the gate for some moments the old woman turned back to the hut, and immediately began her work.

CHAPTER XVIII

LUKASHKA started off for the outpost ; and at the same time Uncle Eroshka whistled to his dogs, and, crawling through the fence, went by some back lanes to Olenin's quarters, for when he went on a hunting expedition he never liked to meet women. Olenin was still asleep ; and even Vanusha, although awake, was still looking about him, wondering whether it were time to get up or not, when Uncle Eroshka with his gun over his shoulder, and in full hunting costume, opened the door.

" Get up ! " he cried, in his bass voice. " There is an alarm. The Circassians have attacked the village. Ivan, get the tea-urn ready for your master. Get up, quick," cried the old man. " That's how it's here with us, my good fellow. Even the girls have got up. Look out of the window. Look out there : there's one girl going for water, and yet you are still asleep."

Olenin woke up, and jumped out of bed. He felt

fresh and merry at the sight of the old man and the sound of his voice.

"Sharp, sharp, Vanusha!" he cried.

"So this is the way you go shooting! People are breakfasting, and you are still asleep. Lam! where are you going?" Eroshka cried to his dog. "Is your gun ready?" And he went on shouting just as if there were a whole crowd of people in the cottage.

"Well, it's my fault: there is nothing to be done. Powder, Vanusha, quick. Load the gun!" exclaimed Olenin.

"A fine," said the old man.

"*Du té voule vou?*" said Vanusha, grinning; he meant "Will you have some tea?"

"You are not one of our people: you don't talk in our way, you devil!" cried the old man to him, showing his yellow teeth.

"One is forgiven the first time," laughed Olenin, who was now putting on his great boots.

"Yes, you can be forgiven for the first time," answered Eroshka: "but the second time you oversleep I shall fine you a gallon of wine. As soon as it begins to get warm, one doesn't find a stag."

"Even if we do find one, he will be wiser than we are," said Olenin, repeating what the old man had said the night before: "we shan't be able to deceive him, he will get away all right?"

"You laugh, eh? But kill him, and then talk. Come along with you. Look, there is the master of the house coming to see you," added Eroshka, looking out of the window. "He has been and dressed himself up, he has put on his new caftan, so that you may see that he is an officer. Oh! what people!"

Indeed Vanusha now came in to say that the master wanted to see Olenin. "*L'argean,*"* he said mysteriously, by way of telling his master the meaning of the cornet's visit. Immediately afterwards, the

_____

* The money—implying that the landlord had come for his rent.

cornet himself, in a new caftan, with officer's shoulder-straps, and freshly blackened boots (a rarity among the Cossacks), came rolling into the room with a smile on his face, and congratulated Olenin on his arrival.

The cornet, Ilia Vassilievitch, was a " civilized " Cossack, who had been in Russia ; he was a school-teacher, and, more than that, of noble blood. Knowing this, he wished to appear noble ; but despite his assumed polish, his assurance, his would-be easiness of demeanour, and his absurd style of talking, one guessed that he was much the same man as Uncle Eroshka. This was indeed evident from his sunburnt face, his hands, and his red nose. Olenin asked him to sit down.

" Good-morning, father ; good-morning, Ilia Vas-silievitch ! " said Uncle Eroshka, standing up, and, as it seemed to Olenin, bowing ironically low.

" How are you, uncle ? So you are already here ? " answered the cornet, carelessly nodding to the old man.

The cornet was a man of about forty, with a little grey, wedge-shaped beard ; he was dry, thin, but good-looking, and still very fresh, in spite of his age. On entering Olenin's quarters, he had evidently felt afraid lest he should be taken for a common Cossack, and wished to let the young man realise his importance at once.

" This is our Egyptian Nimrod," he said, with a smile of self-satisfaction, turning to Olenin, and bowing to the old man—" a hunter before the Lord; our first man in everything. Have you already found him out ? "

Uncle Eroshka, looking at his feet, which were shod with damp leather sandals, meditatively nodded his head, as though he were astonished with the adroit-ness and learning of the cornet, and he repeated to himself : " Egyptian Nimrod—what does he mean by that ? What will he invent next ? "

" Yes : we are going shooting together," said Olenin.

"Just so!" remarked the cornet. "And I have a little business affair with you."

"At your service."

"As you are a nobly-born man," resumed the cornet, "and as I can myself understand, being an officer, we can settle matters with each other, just as all nobly-born people do——" Here he paused, and looked with a smile at the old man and Olenin.

"If you wish to arrange this affair with my consent, for my wife is a stupid woman of feeble intellect, and cannot quite understand your words of yesterday—I mean that my quarters could have been let to the regimental adjutant, without the stable, for six roubles. As a nobly-born man, however, I could always get along without letting the place at all; still, as you wish it, I, also holding the rank of officer, can come to an understanding with you about everything. The inhabitants of this region don't have the same usages as we have, but I should like to fix the proper conditions in every respect——"

"He speaks well and plainly," muttered the old man.

The cornet talked on still more, in the same style. From all this prattle, Olenin, with some little trouble, finally understood that the cornet wished to receive six roubles a month for his quarters. He readily accepted the terms, and asked his landlord if he would take a glass of tea.

The cornet refused.

"According to our stupid customs," he said, "we consider it a sin to use a glass which does not belong to us. Certainly, with my education, I could understand one's doing so; yet my wife, in her human weakness——"

"Well, will you have some tea?"

"If you will allow me, I will ask for my own glass, my special one," answered the cornet, and he went out on to the steps. "Bring me my glass!" he cried, in a loud voice.

A few minutes afterwards the door opened, and a

sunburnt young hand and arm, with a pink sleeve, appeared through the opening, holding a glass. The cornet went to the door, took the glass, and whispered something to his daughter. Olenin poured some tea for the cornet into his *special* glass, and for Eroshka in a *worldly* glass.

" There, I don't wish to detain you," said the cornet, burning his mouth as he hastily attempted to swallow the scalding tea. " I myself, indeed, am exceedingly fond of fishing ; and I am here only for a little while, as it were, on leave from duty. So I also wish to try my luck, to see whether some of the gifts of the Terek will not fall to my share. I hope that you will sometimes visit me, and drink a paternal glass, according to the custom of our village," he added.

He then bowed, shook Olenin's hand, and went out. While Olenin was getting ready he listened to the commanding voice of the cornet, who was heard giving some orders to his household ; and, a few minutes afterwards, the cornet himself, with his trousers rolled up above his knees, and dressed now in a ragged coat, with a net over his shoulder, passed by the window.

" The rascal ! " said Uncle Eroshka, drinking his tea from the worldly glass. " What ! are you really going to pay him six roubles ? Was ever such a thing heard of ? Why, they give the best cottage in the village for two roubles. What a beast ! I'd give you my own cottage for three roubles."

" No, I'll stay here now," said Olenin.

" Six roubles ! It is evident that you are rolling in money, eh ? " said the old man interrogatively. " But give us some wine, Ivan."

After eating a little, and drinking a glass of vodka for the journey, Olenin and the old man went out into the street together. It was a little past seven o'clock. At the gate they met a cart, and a girl whose head was covered down to the eyes with a kerchief, and who wore a jacket over her shirt. She also had shoes, and carried a long switch in her hand. It was Marianka, and she was trying to drag the oxen along by means of a rope tied to their horns.

"Oh! little sister!" exclaimed Eroshka, making believe that he was going to hug her.

Marianka struck at him with her switch, and looked merrily at both of them with her lovely eyes.

Olenin became still merrier. "Let us go, let us go!" he said, putting his gun over his shoulder, and feeling happy that Marianka was looking at him.

"Ghi, ghi!" called the girl to the oxen, the summons being immediately followed by the creaking of the cart as it began to move.

So long as the road from the village skirted along the pasture-land, Eroshka talked a great deal. He again spoke of the cornet, and constantly scolded at him.

"But why are you so angry with him?" asked Olenin.

"He's so stingy! I don't like such people," answered the old man. "He will die some time or other, and won't take any money with him. For whom does he save it all up? He has built two houses; he has got another garden from his brother; and, as for writing papers, what a dog he is! People come here, even from the other villages to get him to write petitions for them. He doesn't stop to think about it: he does it at once, and goes away. For whom is he heaping all this money up? He has only one little boy and a girl: she will get married, and then there won't be anybody."

"Why, he must be saving it up for her dowry," said Olenin.

"What dowry? The girl will be taken fast enough. She's a nice girl. But he is such an old rascal, that he wants to marry her to some rich fellow: he himself would like to get a lot of money for her. No, there's a Cossack called Luka, a neighbour of mine, and a brave young fellow, the one who has just killed a Circassian. He's been wanting to marry her for a long time; but the old man won't give her to him.

First there's one reason, then there another, then a third. The girl is too young, he says. But I know what he's thinking about : he wants people to bow down to him. What nonsense he's making about this girl ! But in spite of it all, they are all wooing her for Lukashka. He is the first Cossack in the village. He's a djiguit, and has killed an Abrek, for which he will get the cross.

" When I went into the yard yesterday, I saw the girl being kissed by a Cossack," said Olenin.

" That is not true ! " cried the old man, stopping short.

" I swear 'tis true," said Olenin.

" Women are devils," said Eroshka, meditating. " But what sort of a Cossack was it ? "

" I did not see what sort of a looking fellow he was."

" Well, what kind of a cap did he wear ? Was it white with long fur ? "

" Yes."

" And a red caftan ? Was he about your height ? "

" Well a little taller."

" Oh ! then it was he ; " and Eroshka broke into a laugh. " Yes, it was he—my Marka. I mean Lukashka ; but I call him my Marka, as a joke. It is the very fellow. Oh, I am so fond of him ! I used to be just such another fellow as he is, father. But what's the use of looking after these women ? Once my sweetheart slept with her mother and her sister-in-law ; and still they were unable to keep me out. Another time she lived very high up ; and her mother was a witch, a very devil, who hated me fearfully. I came with my friend—Girtchik they called him. Well, I came under the window, and I climbed upon Girtchik's shoulders. I reached the window, and groped about. She was inside, and was sleeping on a bench. I woke her up all of a sudden. Oh, how she began to scream ! She didn't know me, you see. Well, what ? I couldn't say anything ; for the mother was already beginning to wake up. I just took off my cap and pressed it down upon the girl's face, when she at once knew me—by the cap, you see. So she jumped up and came out to join me. Yes, once I could get anything I wanted. They would give me sour milk, and grapes, and everything," he added, explaining matters in a practical way. " And—and she was not the only girl I have been in love with. Oh, no! I used to live well, then."

" And now ? "

" Now I go along with my dog, and wait in the wood for the pheasants, and then I shoot them."

" Do your court Marianka for Lukashka."

" Just look at the dog. See ! I shall have shown you something by this evening," said the old man, suddenly pointing to his favourite Lam.

Both became silent. After going another hundred yards, the old man again stood still, and pointing to a switch which lay across the road. " What do you think of that ? " he said. " What do you think of that ? Do you suppose that is nothing ? Do you fancy that switch has fallen there like that by chance. No, there's some witchery about it."

" How's that ? "

Eroshka burst into a laugh. " You don't know anything ! When a stick lies like that you must not step over it, but either go round it, or push it out of the way, so "—thrusting it on one side with his foot —" then say a prayer, ' in the name of the Father, Son,' &c., and go on. Then no harm will befall you. That is what the old people taught me."

" What folly ! " exclaimed Olenin. " You'd better tell me about Marianka. Does she go about with Lukashka ? "

" Hush, be quiet, now ! " interrupted the old man again, in a whisper. " Attention ! Let us go through the wood here."

The old man, stepping lightly and silently in his sandals, went in front, along the narrow path which led into the thick forest, pushing aside the wild under-growth as he made his way forward. Sometimes

he would look back with a frown at Olenin, who made
the bushes rustle as, treading heavily with his big
military boots, he carried his gun so carelessly that
it occasionally caught on the twigs, which, in different
places, stretched across the path.

" Don't make a noise ; walk quietly, soldier ! "
said Eroshka to him in an angry whisper.

One could feel by the temperature that the sun had
risen. The mist, although fast disappearing, still
covered the tops of the trees, making the forest seem
immensely high, and at every step forward the scene
changed ; what in the distance at first appeared to
be a tree turned out to be merely a bush, and a reed
looked as high as a sapling.

CHAPTER XIX

THE mist was rising, disclosing to view the damp
reed roofs of the distant village, and covering
the road and the grass along the fences with dew-
drops. Smoke was everywhere curling from the
chimneys of the houses, and people were leaving the
village in all directions, some going to work, others
to the river, and others to the outpost. The two
sportsmen went along the damp path overgrown with
weeds and grass, while their dogs trotted alongside,
joyfully wagging their tails as now and again they
looked at their masters. Myriads of gnats danced
up and down in the air, following the sportsmen, and
alighting upon their shoulders and their hands, and
flying into their eyes. There was an odour of vegetation and forestial dampness. Olenin constantly
looked back at the cart in which Marianka was sitting, switching her oxen. All around was very quiet.
The various cries and noises which had previously
been heard near the village no longer fell upon the

ear : no sound was audible except that raised by the dogs as they scrambled through the brambles, or the occasional notes of the birds calling to each other.

Olenin knew that it was dangerous in the forest, as the Abreks always concealed themselves in such places ; and he also knew that, for a man on foot in the woods, a gun was a necessary weapon. It was not that he felt frightened ; but he felt that another person in his place might feel frightened. And looking ahead into the damp and misty forest, listening with a special effort to the few faint sounds that were perceptible, he seized hold of his gun, and experienced a new and pleasant sensation. Uncle Eroshka, going ahead, halted at every spot where traces were visible of some animal, and after looking attentively at them, pointed them out to Olenin. He said but little, merely making from time to time some observation in a whisper. The road along which they went had at some time or other been crossed by carts ; but it had long ago been overgrown with grass. The elms and plane trees on either side were so thickly planted, and were covered with such luxuriant foliage, that nothing could be discerned through them ; and almost every tree was clothed from top to bottom with wild vines and other creepers. Below, the brambles grew in profusion : every little opening between the bushes was partly closed by briars and reeds, with grey nodding plumes. In some places there were large tracks, which had been made by wild animals ; and here and there small tracks of pheasants led into the thick wood. The luxuriant vegetation surprised Olenin ; he had never seen anything similar to it. This forest, the danger, the old man with his mysterious conduct, Marianka with her shapely figure, and the mountains—all seemed to Olenin like a dream.

" Ah ! a pheasant," whispered the old man, looking intently ahead, and pulling his cap down over his face. " Cover your face ! A pheasant ! " And he angrily motioned to Olenin, while he crawled onwards upon all-fours. "A pheasant doesn't like to see a man's face," he added.

Olenin was still behind, when the old man stopped, and began to look up into a tree. A cock pheasant was screaming from a branch at the dogs, which were barking at it; and Olenin suddenly caught sight of it. At the same time he heard a shot, as if from a cannon, but which came from Eroshka's heavy fowling-piece. The bird started to fly off; but as it spread its wings, it fell heavily to the ground. Walking towards the old man, Olenin started another bird, and, quickly raising his gun, took aim and fired. The pheasant flew straight up, and then, like a stone rustling through the branches, fell into the wood.

"Splendid!" cried the old man, laughing. He himself could not hit a bird upon the wing.

Picking up the pheasants, they went on farther; and Olenin, excited by the exercise and by the old man's praise, continually talked to him. "Stop! Let us go here," Eroshka interrupted. "Yesterday I saw the traces of a deer near here."

Turning into the wood, and proceeding some three hundred yards, they came to an opening overgrown with reeds, and partially covered with water. Olenin kept at some distance from the old man; and the latter went twenty paces further, bent down, and then significantly nodded and beckoned with his hand. Going up to him, Olenin saw the track of human feet, to which the old man seemed to be drawing his attention.

"Do you see that?"

"I see. Well, what of it?" trying to speak as calmly as possible. "It is the track of a man."

Then there involuntary came into his head sundry thoughts of Cooper's "Path-finder," and the Abreks; but, on account of the mysterious manner of the old man, he could not decide to question him; he was in doubt whether the danger or the sport made this mysteriousness necessary.

"Yes, that's my track," simply said Eroshka, again

pointing to the grass, on which the track of an animal was scarcely visible beside the footprint.

The old man then went on farther. Olenin kept up to him now. After taking a few steps they came upon a split pear tree, round which the ground was black, and where they saw the fresh droppings of a stag. The place was so overgrown with vines that it was like an arbour, dark and cool. " The animal must have been here this morning," said Uncle Eroshka. " You see that is quite fresh."

Suddenly a fearful rustling was heard in the wood ten paces from them. They both started and clubbed their guns, but nothing was visible, though they plainly heard how the reeds were being broken. The quick, measured beat of a gallop was heard for an instant, then the rustling turned into a dull noise, sounding still farther and farther away in the quiet of the wood. Something seemed to break loose in Olenin's heart. He peered anxiously into the green forest, and at last glanced at the old man.

Uncle Eroshka, with his gun against his breast, stood immovable. His cap was thrown back ; his eyes burned with unusual fire ; and his mouth, from which his yellow teeth stood out in a malicious way, remained fixedly open.

" A stag ! " he said ; and then despairingly throwing his gun on the ground in front of him, he began to pull his grey beard. " It stood there ; and we ought to have approached by the path. Fool ! fool ! that I was," and he angrily plucked his beard. " Fool ! pig ! " he affirmed again, once more pulling his beard. Something seemed to soar over the forest, in the mist ; and still farther and farther away resounded the gallop of the deer.

It was already twilight when Olenin returned home with the old man tired, and hungry, but happy. Dinner was ready. He ate and drank with Uncle Eroshka, and then beginning to feel warm and merry, he went out on the steps. Again the mountains rose before his eyes in the sunset, again the old man told him his unending stories of sport, Abreks, girls, and the careless, wild life he had led. Again the beautiful Marianka came out, went in, and passed through the yard. Through her shirt Olenin detected more clearly than ever the outlines of her lovely virginal form.

CHAPTER XX

THE next day Olenin went alone, without the old man, to the place where they had started the stag. To avoid going out by the gate, he, like everybody else in the village, crawled through the prickly hedge. He had not yet succeeded in getting rid of the thorns which had pricked through his coat, when his dog, running on in front, started two pheasants, and he had only just got among the blackberry-bushes, when other pheasants began to rise on every side. The old man had not shown him this spot, which he had meant to keep for himself. Olenin killed five pheasants in twelve shots, and, crawling after them through the brambles, he became so warm, that the perspiration streamed off him like rain. He called his dog away, uncocked his gun, and brushing the gnats off with the sleeve of his coat, he quietly set out towards the place where he had been the day before. It was not possible, however, to restrain the dog, which, even on the road, kept getting on scent ; and so he killed still another brace of pheasants ; and being thus delayed, it was noon before he was able to find the place for which he was seeking.

It was a clear day, quiet and warm. The morning dew had already dried up, even in the woods ; and myriads of gnats alighted upon his face, his back, and his hands. The black dog became quite grey from being so thickly beset with them. Olenin's coat, through which they could sting him, also became grey.

He did not know how to escape them. It seemed to him that in summer time it would be impossible to live in the village. He was already starting for home, but remembering that other people contrived to live, he decided to be patient, and let himself be devoured. Strange to say, by noon he even began to like the buzzing. It seemed to him that if there were not this atmosphere of gnats surrounding him on all sides, this paste of gnats, which he crushed with his hands whenever he wiped his sweaty face, and this itching over his whole body, the forest would have lost its wild character and charm. These myriads of insects were so suited to the wild, luxuriantly-rich foliage ; to the abundance of animals and birds which filled the thickets ; to the dark-green trees, the odorous, hot air, the rivulets of muddy water which everywhere ran down from the Terek, and murmured under the leaves hanging over them, that what had previously seemed to him horrible and unendurable now began to be pleasant.

After inspecting the spot where on the day before he had come upon the stag, and not finding anything, he thought of resting. The sun was right over the woods, and its rays streamed down on his head and back whenever he came into an opening, or into the road. Seven heavy pheasants weighed him down at the waist. He searched for the tracks of the stag which he had seen the day before, crawled under the bushes into the wood, to the very spot where the animal had lain, and lay down in his bed. He then looked round about him at the dark green verdure ; at the lair, at the marks left by the knees of the stag, at the clods of black soil turned up by his hoofs : it was cool and comfortable there. He was not thinking about anything in particular, and did not wish for anything. Suddenly there came over him such a strange feeling of happiness, and of love for everything, that with his old childish habits he began to cross himself, and thank some one. Then at last, he realised the sensation with special clearness. " Here

I, Dimitri Olenin, an individual distinct from all others, now lie alone, God knows where, in the very place where there lay a stag—a handsome old stag, that has never perhaps seen a man, and in a spot where no person has ever sat before, or has even thought of sitting. I sit, and around me rise young and old trees, one of them covered with wild wreathing vines. Around me, too, whirl pheasants, chasing one another, and mourning, perhaps, over their killed brothers."

Then he took up his pheasants, looked at them, and wiped his scratched, blood-stained hand on his coat. "Perhaps the complaining jackals sniff the smell of blood, and retire with disappointed faces. About me, the gnats flying among the leaves, which seem to them immense islands, dance in the air, and buzz,—one, two, three, four, a hundred, a thousand, a million gnats; and all these, for some reason or other, are hanging about me; and each of them has just as much a separate existence, separate from all the rest, as I have." Then he reflected as to what the gnats hummed and thought about. "'Here, here, children! Here's where you can eat some one,' they buzz, and then they settle down upon me." Then it seemed to him that he was not at all a Russian nobleman, a gentleman belonging to Moscow society, and the friend and relation of this and that person. He thought he was simply a being just like a gnat, and just like a pheasant, or a stag, as those now about him. "Just like them, and just like Uncle Eroshka; I live and I die," said Olenin. "The old man spoke the truth indeed, when he said that the grass would grow over one, and that that would be the end."

"Well, what of it if the grass will grow over me?" he thought. "Everything must live, everything try to be happy; for I only wish for one thing—happiness no matter what I be; whether I be an animal or an insect, or an envelope in which is enclosed a part of the divinity. I must live in the best way I can and be happy. Ah! and how can one be happy? and why was not I happy before ? " Then he began to think over his past life, and felt sorry for himself. He thought of himself as an egotist, who had demanded too much ; whereas in reality he needed nothing. Then he looked around him at the verdure lighted up by the setting sun, and on the clear blue sky, and felt as happy as he had felt before.

"Why am I so happy ? and why have I lived so far ? " he thought. "How I always used to demand things for myself ; how whimsical I was ! I never did anything for myself, except caused myself shame and sorrow ! And now I find out that nothing is necessary for happiness." Suddenly a new world seemed to open before him. "Happiness is not this," he said. "Happiness consists in living for others : that is clear. Every one aspires to happiness : therefore it must be a lawful desire. When a man satisfies himself in a selfish way, that is, seeks riches and fame, comfort and love for himself, it often happens that circumstances do not permit him to satisfy his wishes. They are unlawful. But the demand for happiness is not unlawful. What are the wishes that can always be satisfied in the eternal condition of things ? What ? Love, self-abnegation ! "

He became so glad and excited upon discovering this, as it seemed to him, new truth, that he jumped up, and, in his impatience, began to ask himself, for whom he should sacrifice himself, to whom he should do good, and whom he ought to love. "Nothing is necessary for me," he thought : "so why should not I live for others ? "

He then took up his gun, with the intention of returning home to think all this over, and seek an opportunity of doing good. He left the thicket, and when he had reached a glade he looked around him. The sun was no longer visible, it had sunk below the tree-tops. The temperature seemed cooler, and the spot appeared quite unknown to him, and not at all like any place near the village. All had suddenly changed, both the weather and the character of the forest. The sky was covered with clouds ; the wind whistled over the crests of the trees ; around him he only saw reeds and deadwood. He began to call his dog, which had run after some animal or other ; and his voice sounded hollow amid the solitude. He was strangely oppressed, and began to feel frightened. There came into his head various thoughts of the Abreks, and of the murders about which he had heard ; and he expected he would see a Circassian come out of every bush, and have to defend his life, and die—or prove a coward. Then he began to think of God, and a future life, as he had not thought for a long time. Around him there was still the same sombre, stern, wild scene. " It is worth while living for one's self," he thought, " when at any moment one may die suddenly, die without having done any good to anybody, and in a way that nobody would know about ? "

He then went on in the direction in which he supposed the village to be. He no longer thought about sport ; he felt almost tired to death, and gazed with special attention, almost horror, at every tree and object, expecting at every minute that he would have to engage in a conflict for his life. After wandering about for a long time he came to a ditch, through which flowed some cold sandy water from the Terek, and he resolved to follow it without knowing where it would lead him. Suddenly, as the reeds began to rustle behind him, he started, and clutched his gun. But he soon felt ashamed of himself. His tired dog, which was panting heavily, had jumped into the cold water and begun to lap it.

Olenin drank with the dog, and then continued walking beside the ditch, supposing that it would bring him to the village. But, despite the companionship of his dog, everything seemed to him to be more sinister. The forest began to grow darker ; the wind blew with greater strength and fury into the hollow trunks of the old trees. Some large birds whirled shrieking about their nests in the tree-tops. The forest vegetation became more scanty, the reeds were more abundant, and bare, sandy patches of plain could be seen, covered with the tracks of wild animals.

Amid the howl of the wind there rose up another sad and monotonous noise which he could not account for. His spirits drooped more and more. He felt behind him for his pheasants, and found one of them missing. It had got torn off, and had fallen down ; and nothing but its bloody head and neck remained fastened to his belt. Then in an unaccountable manner he began to feel more frightened than he had ever felt before. He began to pray to God, and especially feared one thing—that he would die without having done any good ; and he so much desired to live, to live so as to accomplish some great victory of self-sacrifice.

CHAPTER XXI

SUDDENLY sunlight began to dawn on his soul. He heard sounds of conversation in Russian, and the quick and measured flow of the Terek ; and, at a few paces before him, he saw the dark-brown swiftly-flowing waters of the river, with the greyish-white sand of the banks and shallows, the distant steppe, the mountains, the roof of an outpost rising above the water, and a saddled horse grazing among the brambles. The red sun appeared for an instant from behind the clouds, and with its last rays shone gaily over the river, the reeds, the roof, and a group of Cossacks, among whom Lukashka, by his fearless air, involuntarily attracted attention.

Olenin already felt thoroughly happy again. He had reached the Lower Prototsk post on the Terek, opposite a peaceable Circassian settlement on the other side. He saluted the Cossacks, and went into their hut. The Cossacks received him coldly. Then he

went out upon the terrace and lighted a cigarette.
The Cossacks still paid but little attention to him—
in the first place, because he was smoking ; and,
secondly, because they had something very different
to think about that evening. Some hostile Circassians—the relations of the Abrek who had been killed
—had come from the mountains with a flag of truce
in order to ransom the body. They were waiting for
the Cossack authorities from the village. The brother
of the dead man, a tall, stalwart fellow, with his beard
dyed red, looked as calm and haughty as a king, in
spite of his ragged coat and cap. He was very
similar in features to his dead brother. He did not
honour any one with a look, and did not even once
glance at the corpse. Sitting on his heels in the shade,
he spat from time to time as he smoked his pipe, and
in a gutteral voice, gave occasional commands which
his companions respectfully obeyed. It was evident
that he was a djiguit, who had seen the Russians
before, not exactly under the same circumstances ;
and therefore he was now not so surprised at anything
he saw in them, and did not even occupy himself about
them. Olenin went up to the dead body, and began
to look at it ; whereupon the brother, glancing from
under his brows with quiet contempt, abruptly and
angrily said something. The flag-bearer hastened to
cover up the dead man's face. Olenin was surprised
at the djiguit's majesty and sternness of expression
He tried to say something to him, to ask him from
what village he came ; but the Circassian, scarcely
looking at him, spat on the ground in contempt, and
then turned away. Olenin was surprised that the
mountaineer showed no interest in him, and explained
his indifference by attributing it to his stupidity or
his ignorance of the Russian language. He then
turned to the bearer of the flag of truce, who also
acted as a spy and interpreter whenever occasion
required, and who was just as ragged as the djiguit,
but dark and not red-haired, agile, with extremely
white teeth, and black, sparkling eyes. This fellow

willingly entered into conversation, and asked for a cigarette.

"They were five brothers," he said to Olenin, in broken Russian. "This is now the third one that the Russians have killed. Only two remain. That one is a djiguit, a very great djiguit," he continued, pointing to the Circassian warrior. "When they killed Ahmed Khan (for that was the name of the dead Abrek), his brother was on the other side among the reeds. He saw it all—saw how they put him in a boat, and how they brought him to shore. He sat till night-time in his hiding place, and wanted to kill the old man, but the others would not let him."

Lukashka now went up to Olenin and the interpreter, and sat down beside them.

"From what village?" he asked.

"Over there in those mountains," answered the interpreter, pointing beyond the Terek to a blue, misty defile. "Do you know Suyuk-Su? It must be about eight miles from there."

"Ah! at Suyuk-Su do you know Ghirei Khan?" asked Lukashka, evidently proud of his acquaintance; "he is a friend of mine."

"He is my neighbour," answered the interpreter.

"A splendid fellow!" and Lukashka, evidently much interested, began to talk in Tartar to the interpreter.

Soon afterwards the captain and the chief of the station rode up with two Cossacks. The captain, a newly appointed officer, saluted the Cossacks; but, contrary to custom, no one received him with the words, "We wish you health, your excellency"; however, a few of them greeted him with a simple bow. Some, and among them Lukashka, stood up and stretched themselves. The corporal reported that all was in order at the post. All this seemed laughable to Olenin; indeed, as if the Cossacks were playing at soldiers. However, formalities soon made way for simpler intercourse; and the captain, who was just as good a Cossack as the rest, began to talk freely in Tartar with the interpreter. Some kind of document was drawn up, and given to the interpreter, some money was received from him, and they went up to the body.

" Which of you is Luka, the son of Gavriloff ? " asked the captain.

Lukashka took off his cap, and stepped forward.

" I have sent a report about you to the colonel. What will come of it I don't know. I have also written for a cross, but it is too soon for you to be made a corporal. Do you know how to read ? "

" No."

" What a fine fellow he is ! " said the captain, still continuing to play the commander. " Put on your cap ! To what Gavriloff family does he belong ? That of Gavriloff Cheraki ? "

" His nephew," answered the corporal.

" Ah ! I know, I know," answered the captain. " Now carry the body off. Help each other," he added, turning to the Cossacks.

Lukashka was radiant with joy, and seemed handsomer than usual. Leaving the corporal, and again putting on his cap, he sat down by the side of Olenin.

When the body had been placed in the boat, the dead man's brother went to the bank. The Cossacks involuntarily separated, so as to make room for him. With a spring he jumped into the boat. Then, as Olenin noticed, he for the first time surveyed the Cossacks with a quick glance, and, abruptly asked something of the interpreter. The latter replied, and pointed to Lukashka. The Circassian looked at the young fellow for a moment, and, then slowly turning away, began to gaze at the other bank. It was not hatred, but cold contempt, that was expressed in his look. He said a few words more. " What does he say ? " asked Olenin of the interpreter.

" That your people have killed ours ; but ours will be equal with you. Altogether it is a sad mess," answered the interpreter, as he laughed, showing his white teeth, and jumped into the boat.

The dead man's brother sat there motionless, constantly looking at the other bank. He so despised the Cossacks that he had no curiosity about them. The interpreter, standing at the stern of the boat, moving the oar first on one side, and then on the other, guided it, and talked without cessation. Cutting obliquely across the current, the frail skiff looked smaller and smaller. The voices of those on board became barely audible; and, finally, the Circassians reached the other bank, where their horses were. They took out the body, threw it across a horse, which reared and plunged, vaulted into their saddles, and then went at a walk along the road, past the village, from which a crowd of people emerged to look at them. The Cossacks meanwhile were unusually contented and merry: there was laughter and jesting on every side. The captain and the chief of the station went into the hut, to have a little snack. Lukashka, with a merry face, and vainly trying to assume a staid expression, sat opposite Olenin, with his elbows on his knees, peeling a little stick.

"Why do you smoke?" he said, feigning curiosity. "Is it good?" He addressed Olenin, because he had noticed that the young fellow felt ill at ease among the Cossacks.

"I am accustomed to it," answered Olenin.

"H'm! If we fellows dared to smoke, there would be a terrible noise about it. But do you see these mountains over there?" added Lukashka, pointing to the defile; "they seem near, but you wouldn't be able to get to them. How will you manage to get home, too, alone? It is dark. I will show you the way, if you like," he added. "Just ask the corporal to let me go with you."

"What a splendid fellow!" thought Olenin, looking at the Cossack's merry face. He remembered about Marianka, and the kiss he had heard behind the gate, and began to feel sorry for Lukashka—sorry for his want of knowledge and education. "What folly and stupidity!" he thought. "One man has

killed another, and he is as happy and contented as
if he had achieved the greatest feat in the world. Is
there nothing that tells him that there is no reason
for delight—that happiness is to be found in self-
sacrifice, not in killing ? "

"Come, now, don't fall in his way, brother," said
one of the Cossacks who had gone over to the boat,
turning to Lukashka. "Did you hear what he asked
about you ? "

Lukashka raised his head. "My godson ? " he
said, meaning the dead Circassian.

"Oh ! your godson will not rise again, but his red-
haired brother."

"Let him pray to God to get off safe himself," said
Lukashka, laughing.

"Why do you laugh ? " asked Olenin of Lukashka.
"If they had killed your brother, would you have
been glad ? "

There was still a smile on the Cossack's face as he
looked at Olenin. He seemed to understand what
the latter had implied, but he was far above such
ideas.

"Well, what ? " said he. "It may happen.
Don't they kill some of us fellows occasionally ? "

CHAPTER XXII

THE captain and the chief of the station had gone
    off ; and Olenin, so as to do a favour to Luk-
ashka, as well as to avoid going home alone through
the dark forest, obtained permission from the corporal
for Lukashka to accompany him. Olenin thought
that Lukashka wished to see Marianka, and besides
he was very glad of the companionship of such a
pleasant-looking and talkative Cossack. Lukashka

and Marianka were somehow or other mixed up in his imagination, and he found a certain satisfaction in thinking about them. "He loves Marianka," he thought to himself; "and I myself could love her." Then a strong and novel feeling of happiness took possession of him as they went home through the dark wood. Lukashka was also happy in soul. Something like friendship seemed springing up between these two young men, who were so different in disposition and manners. Every time they looked at each other, they smiled.

"By what gate do you enter the station?" asked Olenin.

"The middle one. But I will take you as far as the swamp: you won't have anything to fear when you are there."

Olenin laughed. "Do you fancy I am afraid? Go back. Much obliged to you. I will go alone."

"Oh! no. What have I got to do? Why shouldn't you be afraid? Why *we* are afraid sometimes," said Lukashka, also smiling.

"Come to my house: we will talk, and drink some wine, and you can go home in the morning."

"Don't you suppose I can find a place to stay all night?" laughed Luashka. "Besides, the corporal told me to come back."

"I heard you yesterday singing songs; besides I saw you——"

"Oh! I do like the others," said Lukashka, nodding.

"Are you going to get married?" asked Olenin.

"My mother wants me to marry; but I haven't any horse as yet."

"Are you not in the regular service, then?"

"No, I am preparing for it. I have only just joined, and I haven't got any horse, and I don't know how to get one. That's the reason why I can't get married."

"How much does a horse cost?"

"I bargained for one the other day, on the other

side of the river ; but they wanted sixty roubles,—
a Tartar horse too."

" Will you come to me as an orderly ? I will give
you a horse," suddenly said Olenin. " I will, really.
I have a couple, and I don't need them both."

" You don't need them ? " said Lukashka, laughing. " But why should you give me one ? I will
get one somehow. God will help me."

" Won't you come with me as an orderly ? " said
Olenin, delighted that it had occurred to him to offer
a horse to Lukashka. However, he felt rather awkward and ill at ease. He wanted to say something
else, and did not know how to do so.

Lukashka first broke the silence. " Have you got
a house of your own in Russia ? " he asked.

Olenin could not resist the temptation of saying
that he had several houses of his own.

" A big one, bigger than ours ? " good-humouredly
asked Lukashka.

" Much bigger, ten times bigger," replied Olenin.

" And have you any horses like ours ? "

" I have a hundred horses, worth three and four
hundred roubles each. Only not like yours—
trotters, you know. Still, I like these horses here
better."

" But why have you come here ? Were you sent
or did you come of your own free will ? " asked
Lukashka, with a touch of irony. " Ah ! here's
where you lost your way," he added, pointing to a
path beside which they passed. " You should have
gone to the right."

" I came to this district of my own accord," answered Olenin. " I wanted to look at your country,
and take part in a campaign."

" Ah ! I should like to join in a campaign," said
Lukashka. " Do you hear the jackals ? " he added,
listening.

" Haven't you any regret at having killed a man ? "
asked Olenin.

" Why should I regret it ? Ah, if I could only go

on a campaign!" repeated Lukashka. "That is what I should like."

"Perhaps we will go together. Our company will start off before the festival, and your sotnia too, perhaps."

"But what an idea it was of yours to come here—you with houses and horses and serfs? I should have amused myself if I had been in your place. What rank have you?"

"I am a yunker, and shall soon be promoted."

"Well, if you are not bragging when you say that you are so well off, why, in your place, I should never have left home. I am sure I should never have come to such a country as this. Do people live well in your part?"

"Yes, very well," said Olenin.

It was already dark, when, while chatting in this manner, they eventually came to the village. The mist of the forest still surrounded them; the wind still howled aloft in the trees; the jackals seemed to walk along beside them, so distinctly could they be heard, laughing and yelling. In the village, too, voices resounded, together with the barking of dogs, and the outlines of the huts were visible against the sky. Lights were burning in the windows; and the atmosphere was charged with the smell of burning kizyah.* It seemed to Olenin, that evening, that here in this village all his happiness was contained, his house, his family, and that he would never live so happily elsewhere. He was fond of everybody, and especially of Lukashka, that evening. On reaching his quarters, to the astonishment of the young Cossack, he brought out of the shed a horse which he had bought at Groznoï—not the one he usually rode, but another. It was a very fair animal, although no longer young, and he gave it to Lukashka.

---

* Combustible matter prepared with the dung of sheep and goats.

"But why do you give it to me?" asked the latter. "I have not done you any service."

"Really it isn't worth anything to me," answered Olenin. "Take it, you can give me something or other in exchange. We shall be able to go on the campaign together."

Lukashka was confused. "But what can I give you?" said he. "That mare is certainly worth a good deal," he added, after looking at the animal.

"Come, take it, take it! If you don't take it, you will insult me. Vanusha, lead the grey mare home for him."

Lukashka, however, took it by the halter. "Well, thank you!" said he. "This is something that I never dreamed of."

Olenin felt as happy as a child. "Tie her up here for a moment. She is a good horse," he said. "I bought her at Groznoï, and she gallops splendidly. Vanusha, give us some wine. Let us go into the house."

The wine was served. Lukashka sat down and took up a glass. "God grant that I may serve you in some way!" he said, as he finished his wine. "How am I to call you?"

"Dimitri Andreitch."

"Well, Mitri Andreitch, God keep you! We will be good friends. Come to see us sometimes. Although we are not rich people, still, as good friends, we will entertain you. Yes; and I will tell my mother that if you want anything, any curds, or grapes, she is to send them to you. And, if you come down to the outpost, I shall be at your service. We can go shooting across the river if you like. It is a pity I did not know you a day or two ago! I killed such a boar, and I had to divide it among the Cossacks! I might have brought it to you."

"Thank you! Much obliged! Only don't harness the mare to a cart: she has never gone that way."

"Harness a horse! Never! But this is what I

propose," said Lukashka, lowering his voice. " If you like, I will take you to see my friend, Ghirei Khan. He invited me to meet him on the road over there, where one goes down from the mountains. We will go together. I won't let him molest you ; I will be your protector."

" All right ; we will go there some day together."

Lukashka now seemed quite calm and self-possessed as if perfectly understanding his relations with Olenin. His quiet simplicity astonished the latter, and even seemed unpleasant to him. They talked together for a long time, and it was already very late when Lukashka rose up. He was not drunk (for he was never drunk), but he had imbibed a good deal of liquor when he grasped Olenin's hand and went away.

Olenin looked out of the window to see what he would do as he went off. The young Cossack went along quickly, with his head bowed. Then, after letting the mare out of the yard, he sprang upon her like a cat, raised a kind of war cry and dashed off down the street. Olenin had thought that he would impart his good luck to Marianka ; but, although he refrained from doing so, the yunker felt gladder at heart than he had ever felt before. He rejoiced like a boy, and could not help telling Vanusha, not only that he had given Lukashka a horse, but why he had done so, and all about his new theory of happiness. Vanusha did not approve of this theory, however, declaring that as there was no mention of money in it, it must be all nonsense.

Lukashka having ridden home, jumped down from his horse, and gave it to his mother, telling her to send it out to the Cossack pasture. He himself had to return to the outpost that night. The dumb girl came up to lead the mare away, and informed her brother, by signs, that if she knew the man who had given him the animal, she would bow down to his feet. The old woman, however, only shook her head on hearing her son's story, and made up her mind that Lukashka had stolen the horse ; accordingly she ordered the dumb girl to take it to the pasture before daylight.

Lukashka went back alone to the outpost, and on his way he constantly thought over Olenin's conduct. Although the horse was not a very good one, in his opinion it must have cost at least forty roubles; and he was content with it. But he could not understand why this present should have been made to him, and so he did not feel the least gratitude. On the contrary, some confused suspicions of a bad design on the yunker's part ran through his mind. What this design might be he could not explain to himself; however, he would not admit for a moment that a stranger had given him a horse worth forty roubles merely out of good feeling. This seemed to him impossible. If Olenin had been drunk, why, then he could have understood it: he would have done it out of brag. But the yunker had been sober, and he probably wanted to secure his, Lukashka's, services for some bad business. "However, that will soon be seen," reflected the young Cossack. "The horse is mine now, and I shall soon see what he is after. I cannot be easily fooled. Yes, we shall see, who is the sharper of the two," he added, feeling the need of setting himself on his guard against Olenin, and trying to awaken some unfriendly feeling in his heart.

He did not tell any of his comrades how he had procured the horse. He said to some that he had bought it; and to others he replied in an evasive way. In the village, however, the truth was soon known. Lukashka's mother, Marianka, Ilia Vassilievitch, and other Cossacks, did not know what to make of Olenin's present, and began to feel afraid of the yunker. Despite this suspicion, however, Olenin's action caused them to feel great respect for his simplicity of heart and his wealth.

"Have you heard that the yunker who lives with Ilia Vassilievitch has given Lukashka a mare worth fifty roubles?" said one Cossack. "He must be a rich fellow."

I

"Yes, I have heard it," answered another. "But what of that? Lukashka must have rendered him a service. We shall see. We shall see what will come of it. Ah! that *Urvan* is a lucky fellow·"

"And what a reckless feather-brain that yunker is," rejoined a third Cossack; "I only hope that he won't set the village on fire."

CHAPTER XXIII

OLENIN led a calm, monotonous life. He seldom saw his superior officers and comrades. The position of a rich yunker in the Caucasus is very advantageous in this way. He is never ordered about for work or drill. After the late expedition Olenin had been presented for promotion as an officer, and had since been left quiet. The other officers considered him an aristocrat, and therefore kept a little at a distance. Their card-playing and drinking and singing parties, of which he had had some experience, had no attraction for him; and, he in his turn, kept clear of the officers' society, and lived in the village. Military life in a village station has long had its special character. Just as every yunker or officer in a fortress regularly drinks porter, and gambles, and talks of promotions and decorations, so at a station he regularly drinks wine with his landlord. flirts with the girls, offers them honey and mead, goes about with them, and gradually falls in love with them, and sometimes even marries them. Olenin, however, had always lived in his own way, and had an unconscious aversion for beaten tracks. So he did not follow the beaten track of the life of an officer in the Causasus.

He woke up at daylight. After he had drunk his tea, and satiated himself with the sight of the mountains, the freshness of the morning, and occasional glimpses of Marianka, he used to put on an old coat, and some limp wolf-skin sandals, gird on his hunting-knife, take his gun, a little bag containing some lunch and tobacco, call his dog, and set out at six o'clock in the morning for the forest behind the village. At seven o'clock in the evening he would return, tired and hungry, with five or six pheasants hanging from his belt, sometimes with some bigger game, and with his bag, containing his lunch and cigarettes, untouched.

He used to come home morally fresh and strong, and perfectly happy. He could not even tell what he had thought about all the time. He had not indulged in recollections, dreams, or profound reflections; but fragments of all these had floated in his head. He would stop to ask himself what he had been thinking about. At one moment he had imagined himself to be a Cossack, working in the gardens with his wife, or an Abrek in the mountains, or a boar, running away from himself. He had listened to everything, looked at everything, and watched for a pheasant, a boar, and a deer.

In the evenings Uncle Eroshka constantly used to sit with him. Vanusha brought them a quart of wine; and they quietly talked and drank, and then went off to sleep, contented. Next day there was more shooting, more healthy weariness, and again they drank and chatted and felt happy. Sometimes, on a festival or a day of rest, Olenin would remain at home all the time. Then his chief occupation was Marianka, whose every movement he anxiously and almost unconsciously followed from his windows or porch. He used to look at her and love her (so it seemed to him), just as he loved the beauty of the mountains and the sky, and he never thought of any other intercourse with her. It seemed to his mind that between him and her there could not exist such relations as were possible between her and young Lukashka, and still less those which would be possible between a rich officer and a Cossack girl. It seemed to him that if he had tried to act like his comrades he would have exchanged his contemplative delights for a life of torture, disenchantment and despair. Besides, in regard to this woman he had already gained a victory of self-sacrifice, which afforded him great satisfaction. He somehow feared and respected Marianka, and nothing would have tempted him to say to her a word of love in jest.

Once, in the summer, when Olenin, instead of going shooting, had remained at home, a Moscow acquaintance unexpectedly came in—a young man whom he had met in society.

" Ah, my dear fellow ! How glad I was to learn that you were here ! " the visitor began in Moscow French, and he continued in the same strain, interspersing his talk with French expressions. " They told me ' Olenin was here.' ' What Olenin ? ' I asked. and I felt so glad ! So fate has brought us together. Well, how are you ? What are you doing ? Why are you here ? "

And then Prince Beletsky began to tell his own story—how he had joined his regiment for a while ; how the commander-in-chief had asked him to be his aide-de-camp ; and how he was going to accept the post after the campaign, although he did not at all care for it.

" Having decided to serve here, in this hole," he added, " I must at least make my way—get a cross, or a promotion, or be transferred to the Guards. All that is indispensable, not for myself, but for my family and my friends. The prince received me very well. He is a very gentlemanly kind of a man," continued Beletsky, after an instant's silence. " For the expedition I am to be presented with the cross of St. Anne. And I shall stay here until the campaign begins. It is splendid here, and, by-the-way, what women there are ! Well, and how do you live ? Our captain told me—you know Startseff, a good-hearted stupid fellow—he told me that you lived a horribly lonely life ; and that you saw nobody. I can imagine that you don't care about being intimate with the other officers here, and I am glad of it, because we shall see more of each other. I am living over there at the corporal's house. What a girl there is there—Ustenka! She's charming!"

And faster and faster the French and Russian words flowed on, like an echo from that world which Olenin had thought he had left for ever. The common opinion about Beletsky was that he was a pleasant, good-natured little fellow. Perhaps he really was so; but to Olenin, despite his handsome, frank face, he seemed in the highest degree repulsive. He seemed so full of all that worldly nonsense of which Olenin had tried to rid himself. What vexed the latter more than all was that he was not able, that he really lacked strength enough to repel this man decisively. It was as though the old world in which he had formerly moved still had irresistible claims upon him. He felt angry with Beletsky and with himself, and yet he speedily introduced French phrases into his own talk, and got interested in the commander-in-chief and his Moscow acquaintances. At last, simply because he had an opportunity of talking in a Frenchified dialect, he again began to look with contempt on his comrades and on the Cossacks, and became very friendly with Beletsky, promising to go and see him, and asking him to call frequently. Olenin, however, did not go to visit Beletsky, of whom Vanusha greatly approved, saying that he was a real gentleman.

Beletsky accustomed himself at once to the usual life of a rich officer. In a single month he had become like an old inhabitant of the village. He made the old men drunk, gave evening entertainments, went to the parties of the Cossack girls, boasted of his conquests, and even went so far that the women somehow called him "grandfather." The Cossacks considered it only natural that a young man should be fond of wine and women, so they grew accustomed to him, and even liked him better than Olenin, who was a puzzle for them.

CHAPTER XXIV

IT was five o'clock in the morning. Vanusha, on the steps, was fanning the coals in the *samovar*. Olenin had already gone to bathe his horse in the Terek. The old woman was in her cottage, from the chimney of which rose the thick black smoke of the freshly-lighted stove. Marianka was milking a buffalo-cow in the cattle-pen. She could be heard saying impatiently, " Stand still, you beast ! " and immediately afterwards the measured sound of the milking began. At last the tread of hoofs was heard in the street ; and Olenin, on a handsome dark-grey horse, still wet and shining from his bath, rode up to the gate. Marianka's pretty head, covered with a simple red kerchief, peered over the fence, and then disappeared again. Olenin wore a red silk blouse, a tall cap, and a white Circassian coat girt with a strap, from which a dagger was hanging. He sat somewhat affectedly on his full-fed horse, and, holding his carbine, bent over to open the gate. His hair was wet ; his face shone with youth and health. He thought that he was handsome, with quite the bearing of a djiguit ; but in the latter respect he was mistaken. At a glance, every experienced Cossack could see that he was merely a soldier. Noticing Marianka as she peered over the fence, he bent down boldly, threw open the gate, and, tightening the bridle, gave a crack with his whip, and rode into the yard. " Is tea ready, Vanusha ? " he cried gaily, without looking towards the door of the cattle-pen. He realized with satisfaction that his handsome horse, who was straining and stretching every muscle, was ready to leap over the fence ; however, he made him advance at a walk over the dry clay of the court-yard.

" It is ready ! " answered Vanusha. Then it seemed

to Olenin that Marianka's pretty face was still peering out of the cattle-pen; but he did not look at her. Jumping off his horse, he hung up his firearm in the porch, and then with an awkward movement, glanced in a frightened way towards the pen; but no one was visible, only the same regular pounds of milking were to be heard.

Going into the house, Olenin came out a little later with a book and a pipe, and sat down to drink his glass of tea on the top of the steps, selecting the side which the oblique rays of the morning sun had not lit up. He intended to spend the whole morning at home, to write some long deferred letters; but somehow he disliked leaving his seat, the house seemed to him a dungeon. The old woman had now heated her stove. Marianka drove the cattle to pasture, and, on coming back, began to collect the *kizyak*, or dung fuel, along the fence. Olenin read, but he understood nothing of the book that lay open before him. He constantly raised his eyes, and looked at the young and stalwart woman moving about in front of him. Whether she remained in the damp morning shadow which fell from the house, or advanced into the middle of the courtyard, illumined by the joyous light, and where her shapely figure in its bright costume shone out, casting a dark shadow on the ground, he feared losing a single one of her movements. He delighted in seeing how freely and gracefully she bent over; how her pink shirt, which was her only garment, draped itself over her breast and along her muscular legs; how, when she straightened herself up, the outlines of her heaving bosom were strongly defined under the tightly drawn shirt; how firmly her narrow feet, shod in old red slippers, trod the ground without losing their form; how skilfully her strong bare arms, the muscles of which seemed to be straining angrily, wielded the hoe; and how she turned her deep black eyes at times on him. Although her brows knitted, yet those eyes of hers expressed her satisfaction at being admired and a consciousness of her beauty.

"Well, Olenin, have you been up long?" asked Beletsky, as in the uniform of a Caucasus officer he entered the yard, and turned to his friend.

"Ah, Beletsky!" exclaimed Olenin, stretching out his hand. "How early you are!"

"What can one do! I have been driven away. A ball is to be given in my rooms. Marianka, you'll come to Ustenka's?" he added, turning to the girl.

Olenin was astonished that Beletsky could address this girl so simply. But Marianka bent her head as though she had not heard, and, throwing her hoe over her shoulder, went with her bold, muscular step into the house.

"Ashamed, sister, ashamed!" called Beletsky after her. "You are ashamed to be caught like that," and then, smiling merrily, he ran up the steps.

"You are going to have a ball, you say? Who drove you away?" asked Olenin.

"Ustenka, my landlady. You are invited to the ball. That is, there will be cakes, and an assembly of the girls."

"But what can one do there?"

Beletsky smiled knowingly, and then winking, jerked his head towards the cottage which Marianka had entered.

Olenin shrugged his shoulders, and flushed.

"By God! you are a strange fellow," Beletsky said. "Come, don't pretend there's nothing between you."

Olenin frowned. Beletsky noticed it, and smiled insinuatingly. "Well, really," he said, "you live in the same house, so to say, and she is such a splendid girl, such a fine girl!—a perfect beauty."

"A wonderful beauty! I never saw such a woman before," said Olenin.

"Well, then, why not?" asked Beletsky, having no idea of the state of the case.

"It is perhaps strange," answered Olenin; "but why shouldn't I tell you how I feel? Since I have been living here, it is just as if women did not exist for me. And I feel so free and well, I really do! Besides, what is there in common between us and these women? Eroshka is another matter: we have a common passion—sport."

"Oh! what is there in common between us, you say? Well, what is there in common between me and Amalia Ivanovna? You may say that the women here are not very clean; I will agree with you in that, but *à la guerre, comme à la guerre!*"

"I never had to deal with Amalia Ivanovna—I never had anything to do with such people," replied Olenin. "Those it would be impossible to respect: but this girl I do respect."

"Well, respect her if you like. Who prevents you?"

Olenin did not reply. He evidently wanted to finish saying what he had begun. He had too much on his heart. "I know I am an exception," he resumed, extremely agitated; "but my life has become so ordered that I see no need of altering my habits. And I could not live here—I could not live as happily as I live now—if I lived as you do; and, besides, I seek something altogether different: I see something different in them from what you see."

Beletsky raised his eyebrows, as though he did not quite believe Olenin. "Well, all the same, come to see me to-night. Marianka will be there. I'll make you acquainted. Please come. If you feel bored you can go away. Will you come?"

"I would come; but to tell you the truth, I am seriously afraid of being led away."

"Oh, oh, oh!" cried Beletsky. "Only come, and I'll quiet you. Will you come? Word of honour?"

"I would come; but really I don't understand what part we should play there."

"Come, I beg of you. Will you?"

"Well, I'll come, perhaps," said Olenin.

"Well, now, here are some charming women, such as one finds nowhere else, and you live like a monk. What is the pleasure in that? Why should you spoil your life, and not enjoy what there is? Have you heard that our company is going to Vozdvizhensky."

"Really? They told me the Eighth company was going," said Olenin.

"No, I received a letter from the adjutant. He writes that the prince himself will take part in the campaign. I shall be glad to see him. I'm already beginning to feel bored here."

"They say that there will be an expedition soon."

"I haven't heard of that; but I heard that Krinovitsin has got a St. Anne cross for the last campaign. He expected to be made a captain," said Beletsky, laughing. "And he's disappointed. He has gone on the staff."

It was getting dark when Olenin thought about the entertainment. The invitation tormented him. He wanted to go; but it frightened him somewhat to think of what might happen there. He knew that no male Cossacks, no old women, no one but girls would be there. What would take place? How should he act? What should he say? What would they talk about? What intercourse could he have with these wild Cossack girls? Beletsky had alluded to strange, cynical, and at the same time strictly proper relation. He trembled at the thought that he would be in the same room as Marianka, and able to talk with her. That seemed to him quite impossible, when he remembered her haughty bearing. Beletsky, indeed, said that all this was very simple, and, by the way, how would *he* act with Marianka? "It would be interesting to ascertain that," thought Olenin.

"But, no, I had better not go. It would be wrong and cowardly, and, moreover, there could be no object in it." However, again he was tormented by the question as to what it would be like; and his promise, too, seemed to bind him. At last he started out without deciding positively on anything; but, when he arrived at Beletsky's, he went in.

The house in which Beletsky resided was just such a cabin as Olenin's. It stood on piers, raised some four or five feet from the ground, and contained two rooms. In the first one which Olenin entered, after ascending some steep steps, there were several feather-beds, Cossack pillows and rugs, elegantly arranged along the wall facing the entrance. On the side-walls hung some brass basins and arms ; under the bench there were some water-melons and gourds. In the second room there was a large stove, a table, some benches, and " old-believer " images. Here Beletsky had placed his camp-bed and his trunks. His weapons hung against a rug draping the wall ; and toilet articles and portraits were scattered over the table. A silk dressing-gown was thrown on a bench, and Beletsky himself, looking clean and handsome, lay on the bed in his shirt and drawers, reading Dumas' " Three Musketeers."

He jumped up on seeing Olenin, and exclaimed : " You see how I am settled. Good ! I am so glad that you have come. They are already hard at work. Do you know what the pie is being made of ? Of dough, with pork and raisins. But no matter. See what a state of excitement they are in ! "

In truth, on looking out of the window, they saw an unusual bustle in the landlady's cottage. The girls, one carrying one thing, and one another, kept running in and out. " Will you be ready soon ? " cried Beletsky.

" Immediately. Are you hungry already, grand-father ? " And a loud laugh was heard in the cottage.

Ustenka, pretty, fresh-tinted, plump, and with her sleeves rolled up, now came to Beletsky's cabin for some plates. " Oh, come ! Take care, I shall break the plates," she suddenly squealed. " You should come and help us," she added, laughing to Olenin. " And you ought to procure some goodies for the girls."

" Has Marianka come ? " asked Beletsky.

" Of course. She brought the dough."

" Do you know," said Beletsky to his friend, " if this girl Ustenka were dressed up, cleaned, and set

off a little, she would be better than all our beauties ?
Do you ever see that Cossack woman Borstcheff,
who married a colonel ? She is charming, with such
an amount of dignity, too. I wonder where she got
it."

" I never saw her ; but I don't believe anything
could be prettier than this costume."

" Well ! I can adapt myself to every kind of life ! "
said Beletsky, sighing merrily. " I'll go to see what
they're doing."

He then threw on his dressing-gown and ran off.
" You must send to buy the dessert," he said.

Olenin sent his friend's orderly for some gingerbread
and honey ; but at the moment when he handed him
the money it seemed to him wrong to give it—indeed,
as though he were buying some one ; and he made no
decided answer to the question of the old soldier, as to
how many gingerbread cakes and how much honey he
should purchase.

" As you please," he answered.

" For all of them ? " asked the old soldier. " Gingerbread cakes are dear."

" For all, for all," said Olenin, and he sat down near
the window, astonished that his heart beat so fast, as
though something important and bad were going to
happen. He heard shouting and a bustle in the other
cottage when Beletsky went in, and, some minutes
later, he saw him jump out, amid cries and laughter
and run down the steps.

" They turned me out," said he.

Then, soon afterwards, Ustenka again came into
Beletsky's room, and triumphantly invited the young
men, explaining that everything was ready.

When they entered the cottage all was indeed ready,
and Ustenka was arranging the beds along the wall.
On the table, which was but partially covered by a small
napkin, there stood a decanter of wine and some dried
fish. There was a smell of pastry and raisins. Half
a dozen girls, in holiday gowns, and with their heads
bare, instead of being tied up in kerchiefs as usual,

crowded in a corner behind the stove, whispering, laughing, and giggling.

"We humbly beg of you to do honour to my guardian angel," said Ustenka, inviting the guests to the table.

Amid the crowd of girls, all of whom were, without exception, pretty, Olenin looked for Marianka; and he was sad and vexed at meeting her under such circumstances. He felt stupid and awkward, and resolved to do whatever Beletsky did. The latter, rather solemnly, but with perfect, self-assurance and ease, went to the table, drank a glass of wine to the health of Ustenka, and invited the others to do the same. Ustenka, however, declared that girls did not drink.

"We might taste a little with honey, though," said some one in the throng. And then they called out to the orderly, who had only just returned from the shop with the honey and cakes. The old soldier, glancing out of the corners of his eyes—was it with envy or contempt?—at his superiors, who, in his opinion, were having a spree, carefully and conscientiously handed over the piece of honeycomb and the cakes, which were wrapped up in some coarse grey paper, and then began to enter into lengthy explanations about the price and the change; however, Beletsky sent him out.

Mixing the honey with some wine poured into the glasses, and sumptuously scattering three pounds of gingerbread cakes over the table, Beletsky forcibly pulled the girls from their corner, made them sit down, and began to help them to the cakes. Olenin involuntarily noticed how Marianka, with her small, sunburnt hand, seized hold of two of the cakes, and then seemed uncertain what she was to do with them. The talk was constrained and far from pleasant, in spite of the freedom displayed by Ustenka and Beletsky, and their efforts to enliven the company. Olenin became confused, thought as to what he could possibly say, hesitated, realised that he inspired curiosity, and that perhaps he seemed ridiculous, and was communicating his shyness to the others. He became red in the face, and it seemed to him that all this was especially awkward for Marianka. "They are probably expecting us to give them some money," he thought. "How shall we give it? and how can we manage it most quickly and so get away?"

CHAPTER XXV

"WHY, don't you know your lodger?" suddenly said Beletsky, turning to Marianka.

"How should I know him, when he never comes to see us?" replied Marianka, looking at Olenin.

Olenin, who was slightly frightened, started, and, without quite knowing what he was saying, replied: "I am afraid of your mother. She scolded me when I first arrived."

Marianka burst out laughing. So you got frightened?" she said, and then, after glancing at him, she turned away.

This was the first time that Olenin saw the beauty's whole face; hitherto he had only seen her covered with a kerchief down to her eyes. Not without good reason was she considered to be the first beauty in the village. Ustenka certainly was a pretty girl, short, full-faced, with rosy cheeks, merry hazel eyes, a constant smile on her red lips, and always laughing and chattering. But Marianka was not merely *pretty*, she was a *beauty*. Her features might have seemed too masculine, and almost coarse, had it not been for her tall, shapely form, and her powerful chest, and shoulders, and especially for the alternately stern and tender gleam of her long black eyes, shaded by dark brows, and for the caressing expression of her mouth and smile. She seldom smiled, but whenever she did, she invariably charmed one. She was aglow with virginal force and with health. All the girls were pretty, but even they, just like Beletsky and the old soldier who had brought the cakes, involuntarily looked at Marianka, and then, after turning to the others, gazed back at her. She seemed a proud and happy queen among her subjects.

Beletsky, trying to infuse a little life into the entertainment, talked incessantly, made the girls pour out the wine, and constantly addressed Olenin with unbecoming remarks in French about Marianka's beauty, calling her " Yours," and urging him to follow his example. Olenin felt more and more uncomfortable, and he was trying to think of a pretext for going away when Beletsky proposed that, as it was Ustenka's birthday, she ought to hand some wine round and kiss them. She consented, but on condition that some money should be put on her plate, as is done at weddings. " What devil brought me to this repulsive feast ? " said Olenin to himself. And he rose up to go away.

" Where are you going ? "

" Oh ! I am going to get some tobacco," he replied, intending to decamp ; however Beletsky caught him by the arm.

" I have some money," he said in French.

" Well, I can't go away ; for I must pay something," thought Olenin, and he got vexed with his own awkwardness. " Can't I act like Beletsky ? It wasn't necessary to come ; but, being here, there is no need of my spoiling their enjoyment. I must drink in the Cossack way ; " and then taking up a big wooden bowl, of the capacity of eight glasses, he filled it with wine, and nearly drained it. The girls did not understand his conduct, but looked at him almost with horror. It seemed to them strange and improper. Then Ustenka brought each of the young fellows a glass of wine, and kissed them. " Come, girls, now we shall amuse ourselves ! " she said, rattling on the plate the four roubles which the friends had laid on it.

Olenin no longer felt awkward. He began to talk.

"Now, it's your turn, Marianka; bring some wine and kiss us," said Beletsky, seizing her by the hand.

"Well, I'll kiss you, so!" she said, jestingly, raising her hand against him.

"Oh! we can kiss 'grandfather' even without being paid," interposed another girl.

"You're sensible!" said Beletsky, and he kissed the girl, who tried to get away from him. "But, come, pass the wine," he insisted, turning to Marianka. "Pass it to your lodger;" and, taking her by the hand, he led her up to the bench, and made her sit beside Olenin.

"What a beauty!" he said, turning her head so as to show her profile.

Marianka did not try to escape, but, smiling haughtily, turned her long eyes full on Olenin. "A lovely girl!" repeated Beletsky.

"Am I beautiful?" Marianka's glance seemed to repeat, and Olenin, without really accounting for what he was doing, put his arms around her, and tried to kiss her. But she suddenly tore herself away, pulled Beletsky off his legs, and the cloth from the table, and ran to the stove. Then a cry, and a burst of laughter broke forth. Beletsky whispered something to the other girls; and suddenly they all ran out of the cabin, and shut the door.

"Why did you kiss Beletsky, and won't kiss me?" asked Olenin.

"I won't, that is all," she answered, protruding her lower lip, and raising her brows. "He is 'grandfather,'" she added, smiling, and then going to the door, she began to knock on it. "What did you shut it for, you devils?"

"Oh! let them be there, and we'll stay here," said Olenin, drawing near her.

She frowned, however, and sternly motioned him away with her hand. And again she seemed to Olenin so majestically beautiful that he remembered himself, and began to feel ashamed. He went to the door, and began to push it. " Beletsky, open the door ! What foolish trick is this ? "

Marianka again laughed her radiant, happy laugh. " Ah ! you are afraid of me ? " she said.

" Yes : you're as bad as your mother."

" Well, sit a little more with Eroshka, and the girls will begin to like you." And then she smiled, looking him straight and close in the eyes.

He did not know what to say. " And if I came to see you ? " he said suddenly.

" That would be another thing," she replied, shaking her head.

At that moment Beletsky suddenly opened the door, and Marianka jumped away, her hip pressing against Olenin's.

" What I thought before was all nonsense—love, and self-sacrifice, and Lukashka. There is only one happiness : he who is happy is right." These thoughts confusedly whirled through Olenin's head, and with a force of which he himself was unconcious he seized Marianka, and kissed her on the forehead and cheek. She did not get angry, but only burst into a loud laugh, and then ran away to the other girls.

With that the evening ended. The old woman— Ustenka's mother—came back from her work, began to scold, and drove all the girls away.

CHAPTER XXVI

" YES," thought Olenin, on returning home, " if I only gave myself the rein a little, I should become madly in love with that girl." He went to to sleep with this idea, but he thought that it would all pass off, and that he would speedily return to his old life.

However, the old life did not come back to him.

His relations with Marianka became different. The wall which had divided them had been broken down. Olenin already exchanged a word with her every time he met her. The landlord, having received his rent, and learned about Olenin's wealth and generosity, invited him to come and see them. The old woman received him kindly ; and from that time the young fellow frequently went of an evening to the family cabin, and sat there till night.

He apparently lived as before in the village ; but in his soul everything was turned upside down. His days he spent in the woods. But at about eight o'clock, as it began to get dark, he used to go to the landlord's, either alone, or with Uncle Eroshka. The family had already got so used to him that they were astonished when he did not come. He paid properly for his wine, and was a quiet fellow. Vanusha would bring him some tea, and he would sit in a corner by the stove. The old woman, without minding him, went on with her work, and over the tea and the wine they talked about Cossack affairs, about the neighbours and about Russia, concerning which the old people asked questions, whilst Olenin told stories. Sometimes he brought a book, and read to himself. Marianka, like a wild goat—drawing her feet up under her—used to sit on the stove, or in a dark corner. She took no part in the conversation ; but Olenin saw her eyes and face, watched all her movements, heard her crunching seeds, and felt that she was listening with her whole being while he talked. He also felt her presence while he read. At times it seemed to him that her eyes were turned upon him, and when he met their bright glance, he involuntarily became silent, and looked at her. Then she immediately averted her face : and he, pretending that he was very much taken up with the talk of the old woman, listened to her breathing, watched her movements, and again waited for her look. In the presence of others she was generally gay and pleasant with him ; but when they were alone she was wild and rough. Sometimes he arrived before Marianka had come in : and suddenly her firm tread was heard, and her blue calico shirt appeared in the open doorway. She came into the middle of the room, espied him, and her eyes smiled tenderly, but scarcely noticeably, while he began to feel happy, though strangely nervous.

He sought for nothing, wished for nothing from her ; but every day her presence became more and more necessary to him.

Olenin had so entered into the life of the station that the past seemed to him wholly foreign, and the future, especially outside of the world in which he lived, never occupied him at all. On receiving letters from home, from his relations and friends, he felt offended that they should pity him as a lost man ; he himself felt that every one was lost who did not lead a life like his own. He felt certain that he should never repent of having torn himself away from his former existence, and of having settled down in such a lonely and peculiar way at the station. During the campaign, and in the forts, it had been well enough ; but here, under the wing of Uncle Eroshka, in the forest, in the cottage at the edge of the village, and especially in the presence of Marianka and Lukashka, all the world in which he had formerly lived seemed false to him. It had troubled him even formerly, and now it seemed inexpressibly wretched and ridiculous. Every day he felt himself more free, more and more of a man. The Caucasus appeared to him very different from what he had imagined. He found nothing like what his dreams had been, or like the descriptions he had heard or read. " Here there are no dark-brown steeds, or precipices, or Amalat-Beks, or heroes and great villains," he thought. " People live as nature lives : they are born, get married, and procreate ; they fight, drink, eat, enjoy themselves, and die ; and there are no special laws, excepting those unchangeable ones which Nature has set to the sun, the grass, the animals, and trees. Other laws they do not have." And, for that reason, these people in comparison with himself seemed good, and strong, and free ; and, when he looked at them, he felt ashamed and sad for himself.

Sometimes it seriously came into his head to throw up everything, to inscribe himself among the Cossacks, to buy a cottage and cattle, to marry a Cossack girl (but not Marianka, whom he had given up to Lukashka), and live with Uncle Eroshka, to go about hunting and fishing with him, and accompany the Cossacks on their expeditions. " Why shouldn't I do that ? What am I waiting for ? " he would ask himself. And he would worry himself, and feel ashamed of himself. " Am I afraid to do what I consider reasonable and right ? Is the wish to be a simple Cossack, to live in accordance with nature, to do no harm to any one, but, on the contrary, to do good to people—is it more foolish to dream of all this, than to dream as I did previously of becoming a minister or the commander of a regiment ? " However, a mysterious voice seemed to tell him to wait, and not to decide : he was restrained by a confused consciousness that he could not wholly live the life of Eroshka and Lukashka, because he had another idea of happiness, which consisted in self-sacrifice. His gift to Lukashka had never ceased to make him feel happy, and he was constantly on the look-out for an opportunity of sacrificing himself for others ; but this opportunity never came. Sometimes he would forget his newly-discovered recipe for happiness, and feel able to live the life of Uncle Eroshka ; but then he would suddenly remember himself, and again seize hold of his idea of self-sacrifice, basing himself upon which he could look calmly and proudly on everybody else, and on their happiness.

CHAPTER XXVII

A SHORT time before the vintage, Lukashka came to Olenin's on horseback. He looked more like a djiguit than ever.

"Well, when are you going to get married?" asked Olenin, gaily greeting him.

Lukashka did not answer directly. "See, I have exchanged your horse on the other side of the river. This is a splendid animal, a Kabarda of the Tavro breed," he said.

They examined the new horse together, and trotted it about the yard. It was really an unusually fine gelding—broad and long, with a shiny iron-grey coat, a feathery tail, and a fine mane. It was so well fed, that, as Lukashka expressed it, "you could lie down on its back to sleep." The hoofs, eyes, and teeth, everything about the animal plainly indicated that it was a horse of the purest blood. Olenin could not leave off admiring it: he had never yet met such a beauty in the Caucasus.

"And his gait," said Lukashka, patting the beast on the neck. "Such a gait he has! and he is such a knowing horse! He follows one about."

"Did you give much to boot?"

"Well, I did not count it," answered Lukashka, smiling. "I got the horse through my good friend over there."

"It is really a beauty of a horse. What will you take for it?" asked Olenin.

"I have been offered one hundred and fifty roubles; but I will give it to you for nothing," said Lukashka merrily. "Only say the word, and you shall have it. I will unsaddle it, and you can take it. Let me serve you in some way or other."

"No, not for anything."

"Well, at least take this present I have brought for you," and Lukashka unfastened his belt, and took one of two daggers which hung from the strap. "I got it over the river."

"Thank you very much."

"And my mother has promised to bring you some wine."

"All that isn't necessary. We will make up our accounts some other time. I am not going to give you any money for your dagger."

"How can you? We are friends. Ghirei Khan invited me to his house, and said, 'Choose something'; and I selected this dagger. It is our custom."

They then went into the cottage and drank a glass of wine together.

"Well, are you going to stay here now?" asked Olenin.

"No, I came to bid you good-bye. I am sent to the outpost across the Terek. I start to-day with Nazarka, my comrade."

"And when is the wedding to be?"

"Well, I shall come home again soon, and then there will be the betrothal, and then I shall have to go on service again," answered Lukashka unwillingly.

"What! won't you even see your sweetheart?"

"Well, what is the use of looking at her? When you start on the expedition, ask at our sotnia for Lukashka the broad-shouldered. There are plenty of wild boars over there, by-the-way. I have killed two; and I will take you to the place."

"Well, good-bye! God preserve you!"

Lukashka mounted his horse, and, without going to see Marianka, rode away, caracoling down the street, where Nazarka was already waiting for him.

"Shall we go there?" asked Nazarka, pointing in the direction in which Yamka lived.

"You go," said Lukashka, "and take the horse there; and, if I delay coming, give him some hay. I will come to the sotnia before daybreak."

"Did the yunker make you another present?"

" No. I paid my thanks to him with a dagger ; he wanted the horse," said Lukashka, as he alighted and gave the reins to Nazarka.

He slipped under Olenin's very window without being seen, glided quietly through the yard and came to the family cottage. It was already quite dark. Marianka, wearing nothing but her shirt, was combing her hair at the window and getting ready to go to bed.

" It is I," whispered the Cossack.

Marianka's face had expressed complete indifference; but it grew peculiarly animated as soon as she heard herself called. She opened the window, and, with a frightened but happy look, peered out of it.

" What do you want ? " she asked.

" Let me in for a minute," said Lukashka. " I am tired of living without you."

He embraced her through the window, and taking her face in his hands, he kissed her. " Come, do let me in."

" What stupid things you are saying ! I have told you already that I won't let you in. What is it to wait a little ? "

He did not answer, but continued kissing her ; and she made no further resistance.

" You see it isn't easy to kiss through the window," said Lukashka.

" Marianushka ! " the old woman was heard calling ; " whom are you talking with ? "

Lukashka quickly took off his cap, so that he might not be known by it, and crouched down under the window.

" Go off as quickly as you can," whispered Marianka ; and then she answered her mother : " Lukashka has just called. He asked for father."

" Well, send him in here."

" Oh ! he has gone away. He said he hadn't time to wait."

And, indeed, Lukashka, bending down under the window, had already darted through the yard. He was off to Yamka's. No one had seen him except Olenin. After drinking a couple of pints of wine, the young djiguit and Nazarka left the village. The night was warm and dark and still. For a time they rode along silently; nothing was heard save the horses' steps. Finally Lukashka began to sing the song of the Cossack Mingal; but, after finishing the first verse, he stopped and turned to Nazarka. "She would not let me in," said he.

"Oh!" answered his comrade; "I knew she wouldn't. Yamka told me that the yunker is always going there, and that Uncle Eroshka has been bragging that he had got a musket from the yunker for arranging matters with Marianka."

"He lies, the old devil!" angrily answered Lukashka. "She is not a girl of that kind. I will break that old fellow's ribs;" and then he began to sing his favourite song, popular throughout Russia:

"Forth from Ismailovo village,
Where the queen has gardens peerless,
Flew a swift and keen-eyed falcon,
Followed by a youthful huntsman.
And the huntsman called the truant,
Bade him on his right hand settle;
But the falcon keen responded:
'In a golden cage thou had'st me,
Yet thou knew'st not how to keep me;
And on thy right hand 'tis certain
That thou could'st not now retain me.
I shall fly to the far ocean,
Where the waves are azure-tinted;
There a white, white swan I'll kill me,
And upon his flesh I'll feast me,
Gorge myself with luscious meat.'"

CHAPTER XXVIII

THERE was company at the cornet's. The betrothal took place. Lukashka had come to the village, but he did not go to see Olenin; and Olenin would not go to the entertainment at the cornet's invitation. He was sadder than he had felt at any time since his arrival in the village. He saw Lukashka, wearing his best clothes, and accompanied by his mother, repair, a little before evening, to the cornet's, and he was troubled as to why Lukashka treated him so coldly. Having shut himself up in his rooms, he began to write his diary.

" I have greatly reflected, and I have greatly changed in recent times," he wrote, " and have come back to what is written in one's primers. In order to be happy, one thing is necessary—to love, and to love with self-sacrifice, to love all, everybody, everything, to spread around the spider-web of love : who ever falls into it is one's brother. Thus I have caught in my web Vanusha and Uncle Eroshka, Lukashka and Marianka."

Just as Olenin had finished penning these words, Uncle Eroshka came in.

The old sportsman was in his merriest mood. A few days before, on going to see him, Olenin had found him in the yard, before the carcase of a wild boar, which, with a proud and happy face, he was skinning with a small knife. The dogs—among them his favourite Lam—lay about him, and gently wagged their tails, as they looked at what he was doing. The little boys peeped at him through the fence with great respect, and did not mock at him, as they usually did. His neighbours, who as a rule were not well disposed towards him, exchanged greetings with him, and brought him—one a pitcher of fresh wine ; another some curdled milk ; and another, some wheat-cakes. On the next morning, Eroshka sat at his gate all covered with blood, and gave out his boar's meat by the pound—to some for money, to some for wine. On his face was written the words, " God has given me good luck. I have killed a wild boar ; and now Uncle Eroshka had become necessary to everybody." The result of all this was that he became drunk ; and, indeed, for four days he drank without going out of the village. Having, moreover, indulged in numerous

libations with the company at the cornet's, he came
into Olenin's quarters, with a red face and dishevelled
beard, but wearing a new red caftan decorated with
galloon, and carrying a three-stringed guitar, which
he had brought from across the river. He had long
previously promised Olenin this amusement, and he
was in the mood for it. Seeing that Olenin was busy,
however, he became gloomy.

"Write, write, my father!" he said in a whisper,
as if he suspected that there was some sort of spirit
between him and the paper; and fearing to drive it
away, he cautiously and quietly sat down on the floor.
When Uncle Eroshka was drunk the floor was his
favourite seat. Olenin looked at him, ordered some
wine to be given to him, and then went on writing.
However, it bored Eroshka to drink alone: he
wanted to talk. "I was at the cornet's party," he
said. "What swine they all are! I did not care for
it, so I came to see you."

"Where did you get your guitar?" asked Olenin,
continuing to write.

"Oh! I went across the river, father, and I got the
guitar there," Eroshka replied very quietly. "I am
a great fellow for playing. I will play you a Tartar's,
a Cossack's, a gentleman's, or a soldier's song, just
as you like."

Olenin looked at him again, laughed, and continued
writing.

This smile encouraged the old man.

"Oh, now, stop, father, stop!" he said suddenly,
in a decided way. "Has any one worried you?
Well! let them go; spit at them. Come, why go on
writing? what is the use of it?" And then he gave
Olenin a little nudge, beat time with his thick fingers
on the floor, and twisted his thick lips in to a derisory
grimace. "What is the use of writing charms?
Better go and amuse yourself, and be a gay young
fellow." He had very funny ideas about writing,
which he always associated with charms and witchcraft.

Olenin burst into a laugh, and Eroshka did the same, jumping up from the floor, and beginning to show his skill by playing on the guitar and singing Tartar songs.

"What is the use of writing, my good fellow?" he repeated. "You had better listen: I will sing to you. If you died of writing, then you would not hear any songs. Come, amuse yourself."

Then he sang a ditty of his own composition, with accompaniment:—

> " Ah, di-di-di-di-di-di,
>   Where did you see him?
>   In a shop and at the fair,
>   Pins he was a-selling there!"

After this he sang a song which he had learned from a former friend, the sergeant-major:

> " 'Twas Monday when in love I fell;
>   All Tuesday suffered pains of Hell;
>   On Wednesday I my passion stated;
>   On Thursday for the answer waited;
>   On Friday the decision came,
>   The maid would not requite my flame.
>   On Saturday so sad I felt
>   My thoughts on self-destruction dwelt;
>   But, luckily, though thus inclined,
>   On Sunday morn I changed my mind."

Then he resumed:

> " Ah, di-di-di-di-di-di,
>   Where did you see him?

Finally winking, shrugging his shoulders, and again dancing, he sang:

> " I will kiss thee, I will clasp thee,
>   Red ribbons I will give to thee;
>   I will call thee Nadezhenka;
>   Dearest little Nadezhenka,
>   Tell me dost thou really love me,
>   Wilt thou be ever true to me?"

He then walked about, playing vigorously; then suddenly he made a leap in the air, and again began to dance about the room. What he considered to be gentlemen's songs, such as "di-di-di," he sang for Olenin only; but afterwards, having drank two or three more glasses of wine, he remembered the good old times, and sung the real Tartar and Cossack songs. In the middle of one of his favourite airs his voice began to tremble, and he stopped short, continuing, however, to strum upon the guitar.

"Oh, my friend!" he said, and his voice sounded so strangely that Olenin looked up. The old man was crying. Tears had started from his eyes, and one was rolling down his cheek.

"You have passed, my good old times, and will never return!" he continued, sobbing; and then, without wiping away his tears, he suddenly cried out in his deafening voice: "Drink! Why don't you drink?"

One Tartar song especially moved him. There were but few words in it, and all its charm consisted in its sad refrain—"Aï, daï, dalalaï!" Eroshka translated the words for Olenin's benefit, as follows: "A young brave rode gaily away, away far into the mountains. The Russians came in his absence and fiercely burned down the hamlet. They slaughtered the men, and they led the women off into bondage. When again the young brave returned, riding back home from the mountains, lo! where the village had flourished there was but ruin and cinders. No home, no cabin was left him; dead were his mother and brother. Only one tree was still standing. The brave sat under it weeping. He, too, was alone like the tree, that lonely tree still remaining; and sadly he wept as he sang, 'Aï! daï! dalalaï!'"

This refrain, which was affecting, and involuntarily remained in the memory, the old man repeated several times. After singing the last verse, he suddenly took down a gun from the wall, ran into the yard and discharged both barrels into the air. Again, in a still sadder voice, he once more sang the same refrain, and then became silent.

Olenin had come out after him on to the steps, and looked upon the dark, starry sky in the direction where the shots had been fired. Lights were still visible in the windows of the cornet's house, and voices were heard. Girls were crowding about the entrance and the windows, and running from the kitchen into the vestibule. Several Cossacks jumped down from the steps, and raised the usual shouts in response to the refrain and the shots of Uncle Eroshka.

" Why are you not at the party ? " said Olenin.

" God be with them ! God be with them ! " answered the old man, whom they had evidently offended in some way or other. " But I do not love them. I do not love them. Oh, what people they are ! Let us go into the house. They are having a good time on their side, and we will amuse ourselves together."

Olenin returned into the house. " Well, does Lukashka look happy ? Won't he come to me ? " he asked.

" What, Lukashka ! No ! They have lied to him, and told him I tried to influence the girl for your sake," said the old man in a whisper. " Well, what sort of a girl is she after all ? She can be ours if we like. With plenty of money, she will be ours. I will manage it for you ; really I will ! "

" No, uncle, money won't do anything ; she does not love me. I will not talk about it."

" Oh, what poor orphans we are ! " suddenly exclaimed Uncle Eroshka. " Nobody loves us." And again he began to cry.

Olenin drank more than usual as he listened to the tales told by the old man. " How happy Lukashka must be ! " he thought ; but he himself felt sad. The old man drank so much that evening, that at last he fell upon the floor ; and Vanusha was obliged to call some soldiers to carry him away. He was so angry with Eroshka for his misconduct that he even forgot to speak in French.

CHAPTER XXIX

IT was in the month of August. For several days in succession there had not been a cloud in the sky. The burning rays of the sun were unendurable, and from morning till evening there blew a warm breeze, which raised up clouds of dust and drove the heated sand across the plains, along the roads and gardens, and scattered it through the air over the reeds, the trees, and the village. The grass and the leaves were covered with dust. The fields and the salt-marshes were dry and bare, and hard under the feet. The water had long since fallen in the Terek, and was quickly disappearing, and drying up in the ditches. The muddy banks of the village pond were trodden hard by the cattle; and all day long one could hear the cries of the little boys and girls as they splashed in the remaining water. On the steppes the reeds and the rushes were already withered; and the cattle, overpowered by the heat ran into the fields. The wild beasts had decamped to the mountains, away from the Terek. Gnats and mosquitoes hovered in clouds over the villages and fields. The snowy peaks were covered with grey mist; the air was heavy and pestiferous. The Abreks, it was said, had forded the shallows of the river, and were galloping about on our side. The sun set every evening in a warm, red glow.

It was also the season for the harvest work. The entire population of the village was busy in the watermelon fields and the vineyards. The gardens, thick with rank vegetation, alone offered a cool, pleasant shade. Everywhere ripe bunches of black grapes hung down among broad, semi-transparent leaves. Along the road which led to the gardens creaking carts, heaped to the very top with black grapes, were slowly dragged, and bunches of grapes, mashed by the wheels, lay about in the dust of the highway. Little boys and girls, in shirts spotted with grape-juice, and holding bunches in their hands, ran about after their mothers. Along the road one constantly met ragged workmen, carrying baskets of grapes on their strong shoulders, and stained to their eyes with grape-juice. With their heads bound down to their eyes in kerchiefs the young girls led the oxen, harnessed to the high carts, laden with the fruit of the vines. The soldiers, on meeting the carts, would ask the girls for some grapes; and a Cossack damsel, jumping on the cart while it was in motion, would seize a handful of grapes and throw them to the soldiers, who held up the skirts of their coats to receive them. In some court-yards the peasants had even begun to press the grapes, and the smell of new wine filled the air. Casks, red, as if covered with blood, could be seen under the awnings; and Tartar workmen, with rolled-up sleeves and trousers, and stained legs, were espied in the yards. Snorting hogs fell upon the pressed grape-skins, and wallowed in them. The flat roofs of the cottages were quite covered with the large clusters, which were drying in the sun. Jackdaws and crows collected on these roofs, pecking among the grapes, and flew cawing from place to place.

The fruit of the year's labour was being collected; and this year the vintage was unusually abundant and good. In the shady green gardens, amid the sea of vines, on every side one heard laughter and merry voices, and amid the leaves one obtained glimpses of the light-coloured garments of the women.

It was midday, and Marianka was seated in her garden in the shade of a peach-tree, preparing the family dinner, which she had taken out of the laden cart. Opposite to her, on a blanket spread upon the ground, the cornet, who had just returned from school, sat, pouring some water out of a pitcher on to his hands. Marianka's little brother, who had just run in from the pond, was wiping himself with his sleeves; and breathing heavily, he looked anxiously at his sister and mother, in expectation of his dinner. The old woman, with her sleeves turned up over her brown, sunburnt arms, was setting out some grapes, dried fish, curdled milk and bread on a low, round Tartar table. The cornet, after washing his hands, took off his cap, crossed himself, and came up to the table. The boy seized hold of the pitcher, and eagerly began to drink. The mother and daughter, crossing their legs under them, sat down on the grass. Even in the shade, the heat was unendurable. The atmosphere was hazy and heavy. The strong, warm breeze which blew between the branches brought no coolness with it, but merely the monotonous sound made by the waving pear trees, peach trees, and mulberry bushes. The cornet again crossed himself, took a pitcher of fresh wine covered with vine-leaves from behind him, and, after imbibing a long draught, handed it to the old woman. The cornet was stripped to his shirt, which was open about the neck, disclosing his muscular and hairy chest. His thin, cunning face wore a very merry expression. Neither in his pose nor his conduct was there any sign of his usual politic bearing; he was simply merry and natural.

"By this evening we shall finish the whole vineyard," he said, wiping his wet beard.

"Yes, we shall gather them all," answered the old woman, "provided the weather does not prevent us. The Demkins have not yet picked half of their grapes," she added. "No one but Ustenka is working; and she is half dead."

"How could they?" said the old man.

"Come, take a drink, Marianka," said the old woman, handing the pitcher to the girl. "God grant that we shall have something for the wedding!" she added.

"That is for future consideration," said the cornet, frowning slightly.

The girl hung her head.

"Why do you say that?" asked the old woman. "The matter is quite concluded, and the time is not far off."

"Don't you make any guesses about that," said the old man. "Come, it is now time to clear off."

"Did you see Lukashka's new horse?" asked the old woman. "He no longer has the one that Mitri Andreivitch gave him: he has changed it for another."

"No, I have not seen it. But I was talking to-day with our lodger's servant," said the cornet; "and he says that his master has just received another thousand roubles."

"In one word, he is a rich fellow," said the old woman.

The whole family was merry and contented. The work was progressing successfully. There were more grapes and finer ones than they had anticipated.

Marianka, after eating her dinner, gave some grass to the oxen, rolled up her jacket as a pillow for her head, and lay down under the cart on the down-trodden and juicy grass. She wore a red silk kerchief over her hair, and merely a long blue calico shirt about her body; however, she was fearfully warm. Her face glowed, and her eyes were overcome with heat and weariness; her lips involuntarily opened, and her breast heaved.

The working season had already begun two weeks previously, and the young girl's time had been occupied with heavy, constant toil. At daybreak she jumped out of bed, washed her face with cold water, bound her kerchief over her head, and ran barefooted after the cattle. Then she hastily put on her shoes and her jacket, and, taking a little bread in her satchel, harnessed the oxen, and went off to the vineyard for the whole day. There, resting only for a short hour, she cut off the bunches of grapes; and in the evening, merry, if tired, she returned to the village, leading the oxen by a rope, or driving them on with a switch. After unharnessing the cattle in the twilight,

K

she would take a few seeds in the sleeves of her shirt, and go to the corner of the street to laugh and chat with the other girls. But as soon as twilight had died out she was back in the hut, supping in the dark room with her parents and young brother. Careless and healthy, she sat down on the stove, and half-dreamingly listened to Olenin's talk. As soon as he went off she threw herself upon her bed, and slept until the morning—a quiet, unbroken sleep. Lukashka she had not seen since the day of her betrothal, and she was quietly waiting for the time of the wedding. She had got accustomed to Olenin, and felt with satisfaction his constant gaze upon her.

CHAPTER XXX

ALTHOUGH the heat was overpowering, and the gnats were whirling about in swarms even in the shade of the cart, and although the little boy in turning about disturbed her, Marianka, with her kerchief over her face, was already beginning to doze off, when suddenly Ustenka, her neighbour, came up, and crawling under the cart lay down by her side.

" Now let's sleep," said Ustenka, as she settled herself. " But wait a minute," she added, starting up again ; " it is not comfortable like that." And then she jumped up, tore down some green branches, fastened them to the wheels of the cart on either side, and threw some cloaks over them.

" Be off ! " she cried to the little boy, as she again crawled under the cart. " Are Cossacks allowed to be in the same place as girls ? Be off ! "

When they were under the cart together, Ustenka suddenly embraced Marianka with both arms, and drawing her towards herself began to kiss her on her

cheeks and neck. " The dear little brother,"* she
said, bursting into a laugh.

" You have learned that from ' grandfather,' "
said Marianka, trying to get away. " Come, stop ! "
and then they both laughed, so that Marianka's
mother cried out to them.

" She is envious," said Ustenka.

" You stupid, let me sleep ! Why did you come ? "

However, Ustenka did not cease caressing her
friend. " I will tell you why," she said. " Listen."

Marianka raised herself up on her elbow, and ad-
justing her kerchief, which had been hanging over
her face, she asked : " Well, why ? "

" I know something about your lodger."

" There is nothing to know," answered Marianka.

" Oh ! what a hypocrite you are ! " said Ustenka,
nudging her with her elbow, and laughing. " You
won't tell anything. He goes to see you."

" Yes, he comes sometimes. What of it ? " said
Marianka, and she suddenly blushed.

" Well, I am a simple-minded girl ; I believe in
everybody. Why should I conceal anything ? "
asked Ustenka. And her merry, rosy face assumed
a thoughtful expression. " Do I do any harm to
anybody ? I love him ; and that is all."

" Who ? ' Grandfather ? ' "

" Yes."

" That is a sin," exclaimed Marianka.

" Ah, Mashinka ! When can one have a good time
except when one is a girl ? By and by, why I shall
get married to a Cossack, and begin to have children
and a bad time of it. When you have got married to
Lukashka, you will no longer be able to amuse yourself : you will have children too, and hard work."

" Well, others get married, and live happily. It
is all the same," quietly answered Marianka.

" Come, do tell me what has happened between
you and Lukashka."

---

* See note *ante*, page 211.

K 2

"What has happened? Why, he has proposed for me. Father put him off for a year, but now they have betrothed me to him, and we are going to be married in the autumn."

"And what did he say to you?"

Marianka smiled. "What everybody says, that he was in love with me. He was always asking me to go out and walk with him in the orchard."

"You didn't go, I hope? What a fine young fellow he has become; the first brave there is. He amuses himself in the sotnia. Not long ago our Kirka came and said that he had got such a fine horse, but that he was very lonesome on your account. Well, what else did Lukashka say to you?"

"So you want to know everything," replied Marianka. "Well, once he came up to the window at night time drunk, and wanted to come in."

"Did you let him in?"

"Why should I let him in? I told him that I would never let him in, and I will keep my word," seriously answered Marianka.

"Oh, but he is a splendid fellow! No other girl would despise him like that."

"Then let him go after the others," proudly answered Marianka.

"Don't you like him?"

"Yes, I like him; but I'm not going to make a fool of myself for his sake. That would be wrong."

Ustenka suddenly let her head fall on her friend's breast, hugged her with both arms, and trembled all over with restrained laughter. "What a stupid you are!" she suddenly exclaimed, bursting out. "You refuse happiness," and then she began to tickle Marianka.

"Let me go!" cried Marianka, amid her laughter.

"Why can't you girls keep still, instead of making such a noise?" asked the old woman behind the cart, in a sleepy voice.

"You refuse bliss," again said Ustenka in a whisper. "Ah, God! you are happy all the same. How they all do love you! You are a bad girl; and yet they all love you. If I had been in your place I should have got hold of your lodger. I looked at him that evening when you and he were at our house, and it seemed to me that he devoured you with his eyes. My 'grandfather' has given me lots of presents, but it's said that your lodger is the richest of all the Russians here, and his servant say she has serfs."

Marianka rose up and smiled in a meditative way. "Do you know what he said to me once?" she remarked, biting a piece of grass. "He said, 'I wish I were the Cossack Lukashka, or your brother Lazutka.' Why should he say that?"

"He only said it because it happened to come into his head," answered Ustenka. "What doesn't mine say? He is such a funny fellow!"

Marianka lay down again, placed both her hands on Ustenka's shoulders, and shut her eyes. "To-day he wanted to come to the vineyard to work: father invited him," she said, after a short spell of silence, and then she went to sleep.

CHAPTER XXXI

THE sun came out from behind the pear-tree which shaded the cart, and its oblique rays, penetrating through the branches placed by Ustenka, burned the faces of the sleeping girls. Marianka awoke, and began to bind up her head with her kerchief. On looking round she saw, just beyond the pear-trees, Olenin, who, with his gun over his shoulder, was standing there, and talking with her father. She nudged Ustenka, and, smiling, pointed to the young man.

"I did not find one yesterday," so Olenin was

saying, as he anxiously looked about him, not seeing Marianka behind the branches.

" Go over there to that corner strip, pass round it, and you will find an overgrown garden, where there are always a number of hares," said the cornet, who had assumed his official manner.

" Is it easy to find hares at vintage time ? You had much better come and help us. You can work with the girls," merrily called the old woman. " Come, girls, get up ! " she cried.

Marianka and Ustenka were whispering together, and could scarcely keep from laughing under the cart.

As soon as it had become known that Olenin had given Lukashka a horse worth fifty roubles, the people of his house had been much more amiable with him. The cornet especially had noted with satisfaction Olenin's growing acquaintance with his daughter.

" But I do not know how to work," said Olenin, averting his eyes from the green branches beside the cart, through which he had at last espied the blue shirt and red kerchief of Marianka.

" Come, I will give you some peaches," answered the old woman.

" That's according to the rules of Cossack hospitality in the old times. My wife stupidly clings to the old customs," said the cornet, explaining the words of the old woman. " However, in Russia you not only have plenty of peaches but pine-apple preserves."

" So there are some hares in the abandoned gardens, are there ? " asked Olenin. " Well, I'll go there," he added, and then casting a quick glance through the branches, he adjusted his cap, and went off between the rows of green vines.

The sun had sunk behind the hedges, and its broken rays were shining through the transparent leaves, when Olenin again returned to his landlord's orchard. The wind had quieted down, and a fresh coolness was spreading over the place. Whilst still afar, by some instinct or other, Olenin had recognised Marianka's blue shirt amid the rows of vines, and, picking some grapes as he walked along, he went up to her. His tired dog also snapped at times with his foaming mouth at the bunches which hung low down. Marianka blushing, turned down her sleeves, and adjusted her kerchief lower over her forehead; then she went on cutting off the bunches, and arranged them in a basket. Still keeping hold of the branch she was stripping, she stopped cutting as Olenin approached nearer, smiled pleasantly and then again set to work. Olenin came on, and threw his gun over his shoulder so as to set his hands at liberty. "Where are your people? God help them! Are you alone?" he wished to say, but in reality he said nothing at all, and only pushed back his cap. It was very awkward for him to find himself alone with Marianka; however, live a voluntary martyr he went straight up to her.

"If you carry your gun like that, you will kill some one." said Marianka.

"No, there's no danger," replied Olenin, and then they both grew silent.

"Why don't you help me?" said the girl.

He then took a knife, and began cutting off the clusters. Drawing from beneath the leaves a heavy bunch, weighing fully three pounds, and all the grapes of which were pressed against one another, he showed it to Marianka.

"Shall I cut it off? Is it ripe?" he asked.

"Give it here!"

Their hands met. Olenin took hold of Marianka's, and she looked at him smiling. "So you are soon to be married?" he said.

Without answering, she looked at him with quiet eyes, and then turned aside.

"Well, do you love Lukashka?"

"What affair is that of yours?"

"I am envious——"

"Absurd!"

"Really, you are such a beauty!"

And suddenly he felt conscience-stricken at having

said this. His words seemed to him so cowardly. However, he drew a long breath, summoned his courage, and took her by both hands.

"Well, whatever I may be, I am not for you. Why do you deride me?" answered Marianka. But her glance revealed how well she knew that he was not jesting.

"How deriding you? If you only knew how——"

His words seemed common-place to him, and sounded discordant, as if they did not correspond sufficiently well with his feelings. However, he continued: "There's nothing that I would not do for you."

"Go away, you tormenter!"

But her face, her burning eyes and heaving bosom, said something very different. It seemed to him that she understood the puerility of all he said to her, and stood far above such ideas. It seemed to him that she had long ago known all that he wished, and had not dared to say to her, and yet wanted to hear how he would say it. And why should she not know? he thought. But she would pretend not to understand, and would not answer, he reflected. "Ho!" suddenly cried Ustenka, who was not far off behind the vines, and then her light laugh resounded. "Come here, Mitri Andreivitch, and help me. I am alone!" she called to Olenin, as her round, childish face peered through the leaves.

Olenin, however, did not answer, and did not move from his place. Marianka meanwhile continued cutting off the grapes, but constantly looked at him.

He began to say something or other; stopped short, however, and then having shrugged his shoulders and adjusted his gun, went off with a quick step.

CHAPTER XXXII

TWICE he stopped, listening to the light laughter of Marianka and Ustenka, who were calling out something to each other. Olenin passed the whole of the afternoon in the woods, and, without having killed anything, he returned home in the twilight. On passing through the yard, he noticed the door of his landlord's cottage open, and caught a glimpse of a blue shirt.

He immediately called to Vanusha, so as to let him know that he had arrived, and sat down in his usual place on the steps.

The people of the house had already come back from the vineyard: they came into the yard, and then went back into the house, and did not invite him in. Marianka twice went out to the gate. Once in the dim light it seemed to him that she was looking at him. He eagerly watched her every movement, but could not decide to approach her. When she had returned into the cottage, he came down the steps and began to walk about the yard; but Marianka did not come out again. Olenin passed the whole night sleeplessly, in the yard, listening to every sound in the cornet's cottage. He heard them chattering in the evening; taking supper together; pulling out the mattresses and pillows, and lying down to sleep. He heard how Marianka laughed at something or another, and how all grew still again. The cornet talked something over in whispers with the old woman and somebody drew a long breath. At last Olenin went into his own rooms. Vanusha had fallen asleep, without undressing. Olenin envied him, and again took to walking up and down the yard, always expecting something or other; but nobody came, and nobody stirred.

He heard nothing but the heavy breathing of three people. He recognised that of Marianka, and constantly listened to it, and heard the beating of his own heart. All was quiet in the village. The moon had risen; and the cattle became visible as they went breathing loudly about the pens, now lying down, and now standing up again. Olenin angrily asked himself: "What do I want?" and could not tear himself away from his thoughts. Suddenly he clearly heard steps, and the floor in the cornet's house creaking. He darted towards the door; but again nothing was heard save the even breathing. In the yard the heavy buffalo cow turned round, rose first on her fore-legs, then on all fours, whisked her tail about, walked measuredly over the dry clay soil, and finally with a sigh laid down in a place shaded from the moon.

Again Olenin asked himself: "What am I about?" and at last he resolved to go to sleep. But at that moment he heard some fresh sounds, and in his imagination there rose up before him the form of Marianka, coming out into the moonlit but misty night, and again he drew near the window and listened to her steps. At last, just before dawn, he went to her window and tapped on the pane. Then he ran to the door and really heard the deep-drawn breath of Marianka and her footsteps. He took hold of the latch, and moved it gently. Bare feet, scarcely making a creak, were cautiously drawing near the door. The latch moved; the door was set ajar; there came forth an odour of gourds and warm air; and then Marianka appeared on the threshold. He saw her only for a moment in the moonlight, for she hastily shut the door, and, whispering something, ran off with light steps. Olenin began to knock gently; but no one answered. Then he went to the window, and listened. Suddenly he was astonished to hear a man addressing him in a sharp, shrill voice.

"All right," said a short Cossack with a white cap, approaching Olenin. "I have seen it all. All right!"

Olenin recognised Nazarka and became silent, not knowing what to do or say.

" This is nice ! I shall go to the chief of the station ; I'll tell him, and I'll let her father know about this. Oh ! what a girl that cornet's daughter is ! So she hasn't enough with one lover ? "

" What do you mean ? What do you want from me ? How much ? " asked Olenin.

" Nothing. I shall only tell the head of the village," said Nazarka, and he laughed. " Oh, what an adroit yunker this is ! "

Olenin trembled, and grew pale. " Come away, come here," he said and he caught Nazarka firmly by the arm, and drew him towards his quarters. " Come, nothing happened at all. She would not let me in, and I did not do anything. She is perfectly virtuous."

" Well, we shall see," said Narazka.

" I will give you something to keep quiet. Wait a bit ! "

Nazarka became silent, and Olenin went into his room, and brought out ten roubles which he gave to the Cossack.

" Come, now, nothing happened whatever ; but, all the same, I am to blame, and so I will give you something : only, for God's sake ! don't let anybody know of it. Really there was nothing at all."

" Well, God keep you. Good-bye," said Nazarka, laughing, and he went away.

The young Cossack had ridden that night to the village, commissioned by Lukashka to prepare a place for a stolen horse, and, on his way home along the street, he had heard the sound of Olenin's footsteps. On the next day he returned to his company, and bragged about the affair, telling his comrades how cleverly he had made ten roubles.

Olenin on the following morning saw the people of the house, and it was evident that nobody knew anything about the matter. To Marianka he did not speak ; and she merely laughed as she looked at him. That night also he passed sleeplessly, walking uneasily up and down the yard. The following day he purposely spent in hunting, and in the evening, in order to escape from himself, he went to Beletsky's. He felt afraid of himself, and even made solemn vows to himself not to go any more to Marianka's. The next night, however, he was roused by a sergeant. The company was ordered to start on an expedition at once. Olenin was very glad of this occurrence; for he thought that it would furnish him with a pretext to leave the village, and never return. The expedition only lasted four days, however. The commander was anxious to see Olenin, who was a distant relation of his; and he offered to keep him on his staff. But Olenin refused. He found that he could not live without his village, and he asked to return there. For the expedition he was decorated with the soldier's cross of St. George, which he had previously so much longed for; but now he was quite indifferent to this cross, and still more indifferent as to the promotion which he had not yet obtained. On the way back, without any reason, he rode in advance with Vanusha, preceding his company by some hours. He spent the whole of that evening on his steps, looking at Marianka; and far into the night he again walked aimlessly up and down the yard.

CHAPTER XXXIII

THE next morning Olenin woke up late. None of the people of the house were to be seen. He did not go shooting, but went out on to the steps for a time with a book, and at last returned into the house and lay down upon his bed. Vanusha thought he was ill. Towards the evening, however, he at last got up, again sat himself at his table, and continued writing until late at night. He wrote a letter, but he did not send it, because no one would have understood what he said in it; and, indeed, how could any one have understood it all, excepting Olenin himself? This, however, is what he wrote:

"I keep on receiving sympathetic letters from Russia. People fear I am going to ruin, burying myself in this wilderness. They say of me, 'He is growing coarse and wild; he is letting everything go; he is taking to drink; and, what is worse, he is going to marry a Cossack girl.' They add that General Yermoloff remarked advisedly, that ' a man who lives for ten years in the Caucasus will either drink himself to death, or marry a woman of bad character.' How terrible, and in fact am I not ruining myself, when I might have had the great good fortune of becoming the husband of the Countess B., of being appointed as chamberlain, or as marshal of the nobility? Ah, how paltry and pitiable you all seem to me. You do not know what happiness is, or what life is. Understand that it is necessary to make one's self acquainted with the unartificial beauty of existence; It is necessary to see and understand what I see before me every day—the eternal, inaccessible snows of the mountains and a magnificent woman of that original and simple beauty which the first woman must have possessed when she came from the hands of the Creator. Then you would clearly understand who is ruining himself, and who is living rightly or wrongly—you or I.

" If you only knew what contempt I have for your illusions! When I look at my cottage, my woods, and my love there, and then think of the drawing-rooms of society full of women with their hair elaborately dressed, with plenty of false curls mixed with it, whose lips lie, and whose figures are pressed and squeezed out of shape, and whose gossip is called conversation, though it has no right to the name, I become utterly disgusted. I can picture those stupid faces, those wealthy beauties—whose expression of countenance seems to say: 'Don't be alarmed; it is all right; you can approach me even although I am a rich girl.' I recall the effrontery with which couples

in society plot together and make love to each other ;
the eternal gossip and pretence ; those rules as to
whom one can give the hand to, and to whom one can
nod, and with whom one can exchange a few words of
talk ; and finally, all that eternal *ennui* in the blood
which descends from generation to generation, whilst
people believe that it cannot be avoided, and is really
indispensable.

"Remember one thing, it is necessary to see and
to understand what truth and beauty are ; everything
else must crumble to dust. True happiness is to live
in communion with nature, to see her, to hear her,
and talk with her. I can imagine people saying
about me, with sincere compassion : ' He is going to
marry a simple Cossack girl, and will become lost to
the world.' Well, yes ; I only wish one thing—to be
really lost in your sense ; I do wish to marry a simple
Cossack girl ; and I shall not be able to do so, because
it would be the height of happiness, of which I am not
worthy.

"Three months have elapsed since I first saw the
Cossack girl, Marianka. The ideas and prejudices
of the world from which I came were still fresh within
me. I did not then believe that I ever could love this
girl. I admired her as I admired the beauty of the
mountains and the sky ; and I could not help admiring her, because she was as beautiful as they are.
Then I felt that the contemplation of this beauty
became necessary to my life ; and I began to ask
myself, ' Do I love her ? ' However, I found in myself nothing like love as I had imagined it to be. I
had no longing for a lonely life, or a desire of marriage,
or a Platonic, still less a sensual love, such as I had
already experienced. I simply needed to see her, to
listen to her, to know that she was near me, and then
I did not become happy but quieted.

"After the evening when I was for the first time
near her and sat by her side, I felt that between me
and her there existed an indissoluble although un-
acknowledged bond, against which it was impossible

to struggle. And yet I struggled—struggled saying to myself, 'Can I really love a woman who will never understand the spiritual interests of my life? Can I really love a woman for her beauty alone—love a statue?' I asked myself this. But I already loved her, although I did not suspect it.

"After the evening when I spoke with her for the first time our relations changed. Previously she had merely been for me a strange but magnificent object of nature. After that evening, however, she became in my eyes a human being—a woman. I began to meet her; I talked with her; I went sometimes to her father's, and sat there the whole evening with them; and in this closer intercourse she remained in my eyes just as pure, as unapproachable, and as magnificent as before. To every question, and at all times, she answered in the same way—quietly, proudly, and with joyous equanimity. On rare occasions she softened; but generally her every look her every word, her every gesture showed an equanimity that was not contemptuous, but at once crushing and enchanting. Every day, with a feigned smile on my lips, I tried to conceal my feelings; and, with the torture of passion and desire in my heart, I laughed and jested with her. She saw that I was pretending; but merely looked at me and smiled. My position became unendurable. I did not wish to lie to her; I wished to say all that I thought, all that I felt. I was particularly excited. This happened in the vineyard. I began to speak to her of my love in such words as I am now ashamed to recollect. I am ashamed to recollect them, for I ought never to have dared to say them to her, because she stood immeasurably higher than those words, and the feeling which I wished to express by them. I became silent through shame, and from that day my situation has become still more unendurable.

"I do not wish to lower myself by remaining on my former footing of mere good fellowship, and being in despair I ask myself, 'What am I to do?' In my disturbed dreams I sometimes imagine her to be my mistress, sometimes my wife ; and, in disgust, I repulse both one and the other idea. To make her my mistress would be horrible : it would be equivalent to murder. To make her a lady, the wife of Dimitri Andreivitch Olenin, just like one of the Cossack women here whom one of our officers married, would be still worse. Ah ! if I could make myself a Cossack, a Lukashka ; could steal horses, drink new wine, sing songs, kill people, creep up to her window at night-time when drunk, without any thought of what I am about, or why I exist, that would be another matter. Then we could understand each other ; then I might be happy. I have tried that kind of life, and still more strongly have I realized my weakness and incapacity. I could not forget myself, and my complicated, inharmonious, monstrous past. My future appears to me hopeless. Every day I see before me the distant snowy mountains, and this magnificent, happy woman ; and I say to myself that the only happiness possible in the world is not for me—that this woman will never be mine. What is at the same time the most horrible and the most pleasing thing in my position is that I feel that I understand her, and that she will never understand me. She fails to understand me—not, however, because she is beneath me ; and, after all, she ought not to understand me. She is happy. She, like nature, is even calm, and herself. I am a broken, weak being ; and yet I could wish her to understand my monstrous nature and my sufferings. I have spent sleepless nights, and, without any aim, have walked up and down under her windows, reflecting as to what was the matter with me, but all to no purpose.

" On the 8th our company started on a little expedition. I passed four days away from the village. I was sad, but indifferent to all that went on around me. On the march the songs, the cards, the drinking-parties, the talk about decorations—all seemed more hateful than ever. Now I have returned here, and I have seen her again, with my cottage, and Uncle Eroshka, and the snowy mountains, visible from my porch, and such a strong, new feeling of delight has seized hold of me, that I understand everything. I love this woman with real love—for the first and only time of my life. I now know what is the matter with me. I do not wish to relieve myself of this feeling. I am not ashamed of my love ; no, I am proud of it. I am not to blame if I love. It has come about independently of my will. I tried to save myself from it by self-sacrifice. I imagined that I could take a delight in the love of Lukashka for Marianka ; whereas I have only exasperated my heart and roused my jealousy. This is not the ideal, so-called exalted love which I previously felt ; not that feeling conjured up by the imagination and fanned by thought at leisure. I have experienced that also. This is still less a wish for sensual satisfaction. It is something else. Perhaps in her I love nature, the incarnation of all that is beautiful ; but I do not love her of my own free-will—it is as if the force of the elements constrained me to love her. The whole world of God, all nature, imposes this love upon my soul and says : 'Love.' And I love her, not with my intellect, not with my imagination, but with my whole being. And loving her, I feel that I am an inseparable part of all the happy world of God !

" I once wrote of the new beliefs I had acquired while leading a lonely life. No one can ever know with what trouble they were worked out in me, with what delight I recognized them, and saw a new path in life opened. Nothing was ever dearer to me than those beliefs. But now, love has come, and I have them no longer ; and I have no regret for them. It is even difficult for me to understand that I ever could prize such a one-sided, cold, and intellectual condition of mind. Beauty has appeared in all her splendour, and has annihilated all the work of my brain ; and I have no regret for what has disappeared. Self-sacrifice !—that is all nonsense, a wild idea. It is all pride, a refuge from deserved misfortune—refuge from envy of another's happiness. Live for others! Do good! Why?—when in my soul there is nothing but love for myself, and but one wish—to love her and live with her, and share her life? Not for others, not for Lukashka, do I now wish for happiness. Now I do not love those others. I should previously have said to myself that this was a bad feeling. I should have tortured myself with questions—what would happen to her? to me? what would become of Lukashka? But now, that is all the same to me. I live now for myself; and something stronger than myself draws me onward. I suffer; but formerly I was dead, and now only do I live. I shall go to her to-day, and I will tell her all."

CHAPTER XXXIV

AFTER writing this letter, Olenin went to visit the cornet's family. It was late in the evening. The old woman was sitting on a bench behind the stove, and reeling cocoons. Marianka, with uncovered hair, was sewing by the candle-light. As soon as she saw Olenin, she jumped up, took her kerchief, and went towards the stove.

"What's the matter? Sit down with us, Marianushka, said her mother.

Olenin could see her knee and her shapely calf. He treated the old woman to some tea, and she offered him some clotted cream, for which she sent Marianka. The latter, however, jumped up again on the stove as soon as she had placed the plate on the table; and Olenin merely felt her eyes upon him. They talked about housekeeping and farming, while Mother Ulitka came and went, and became enthusiastically hospitable. She brought Olenin some grapes, and some of her best wine; all with that especial, simple, rough, and proud hospitality which is only met with among people who earn their bread by physical toil. The old woman, who had at first so surprised Olenin by her roughness, now often touched him by the simple tenderness with which she spoke of her daughter.

" Praise God, father, we've got everything we require—wine and salt meat. We have made our new wine, and can sell three casks of grapes, and still have enough to drink. Just wait a while. You will amuse yourself at the wedding."

" When will the wedding be ? " asked Olenin, while the blood suddenly rushed to his face, and his heart beat painfully. He could hear a movement and the crunching of seeds behind the stove.

" We might have it next week. We're ready," answered the old woman, simply and quietly, as though Olenin did not exist. " I have provided everything, and got everything ready for Marianushka. We shall give her away in proper style. Only, there's a little hitch. Our Lukashka is too wild, quite too wild. He does foolish things. Not long ago a Cossack came from the sotnia and told us he had gone into the Nogai country."

" He must look out not to get caught," said Olenin.

" So I say. Take care, Lukashka ; don't be foolish ! To be sure, he's a young man, and must be up to something. But there's a time for everything. He has proved his mettle, he has carried off horses, and he has killed an Abrek, a djiguit. Now, he ought to live quietly ; otherwise matters will turn out badly."

" Yes, I saw him twice on the expedition. He was always up to some freaks. He has sold another horse," said Olenin, and he glanced at the stove.

Marianka's large black eyes glittered at him in a stern, unfriendly way, and he began to feel sorry for what he had said. " What of it ? He doesn't do harm to any one," suddenly said the girl. " He amuses himself with his own money," and she hastily jumped off the stove and went out, slamming the door after her.

Olenin followed her with his eyes as she darted across the cottage, and when she had gone he looked at the door and waited, scarcely understanding a word of what Mother Ulitka said to him. A few minutes afterwards some visitors came in—an old man, the housewife's brother, and Uncle Eroshka, and, after them, Marianka and Ustenka.

"Have you passed the day well?" whispered Ustenka. "What do you do out of doors?" she added, turning to Olenin.

"I amuse myself," he answered, and, for some reason or other, he felt ashamed of himself, and awkward.

He wanted to go away, and could not. It also seemed to him impossible to keep silent. Mother Ulitka's brother fortunately helped him out of the difficulty; for he asked him to drink, and they drank together. Then Olenin drank with Eroshka, then with the other Cossack again, and then again with Eroshka. The more he drank, the heavier his heart became. The old men, however, were enjoying it. The girls sat on the stove, and whispered as they looked at them. Olenin said nothing, but drank more than the others. Finally the Cossacks became noisy, and the old woman drove them away, and refused to give them any more wine. The girls laughed at Uncle Eroshka; and it was already ten o'clock when they all went out on to the steps. The old men then invited themselves to go and drink the night out at Olenin's, and Ustenka ran away home. Eroshka having taken the other Cossack to Vanusha, Mother Ulitka went to the outhouse, and Marianka remained alone in the cottage.

Olenin felt as fresh and comfortable as though he had just woke up. He noticed everything; and, letting the old men go on alone, he turned back into the cottage. Marianka was retiring for the night. He went up to her, wishing to say something; but his

voice broke down.   She crouched upon the bed, drawing her feet up under her, creeping into the farthest
corner, and looking at him with a wild frightened
look.   She was evidently afraid of him.   Olenin felt
this, and he began to feel sorry and ashamed, at the
same time experiencing a proud satisfaction that he
had aroused even this feeling in her.

"Marianka," he said, "will you never take pity
on me ?   I can't tell you how much I love you ! "

She moved still farther off.   "It is the wine that
makes you talk so," she answered.   "You will get
nothing ! "

"No, it is not the wine.   Don't marry Lukashka.
I will marry you."

"What is it I am saying ? " he thought, as he
pronounced the words.   "Shall I say the same to-
morrow ?   Yes, I shall say it, in truth I shall," his
conscience answered.

"Will you marry me ? " rejoined Marianka, and
she looked at him seriously ; her fright seemed to
pass away.

"Marianka, I shall go out of my mind," he answered.   "I am not my own master.   Whatever
you order, I will do ; " and senselessly tender words
came to his lips of their own accord, without any
control or volition on his part.

"Now, don't talk nonsense," she interrupted, suddenly grasping his hand, which he held out to her.
She pressed it vigorously between her strong, rough
fingers.   "Do noblemen every marry Cossack girls ? "
she added.   "Come now ! "

' Will you marry me ?   I will do all——"

"But what shall we do with Lukashka ? " she
replied laughing.

Then he tore away his hand, which she was still
holding, and gave her a close embrace.   But she
started up like a young fawn, jumped down bare-
footed, and ran out on to the steps.   Olenin recovered
his senses, and felt horrified with himself.   It again
seemed to him that he was inexpressibly vile in

comparison with her. However, without repenting for a moment of what he had said, he went home, and, without glancing at the old men who were drinking there, he lay down, and slept more soundly than he had done for a long, long time.

CHAPTER XXXV

THE next day was a festival. Towards evening everybody was out in the streets, their holiday attire brilliant in the rays of the setting sun. More wine had been pressed than usual, and everybody had finished work. The Cossacks were to start on an expedition in a month's time, and in many families preparations were being made for weddings. On the square, about a couple of shops, at one of which seeds and cakes were sold, while the other was full of prints and kerchiefs, quite a large crowd was collected. On the turf terrace which surrounded the government house sat and stood various old men in long grey and black caftans, such as are worn on the steppe, without braid or embroidery. These old men, quietly, and in measured voices, talked with one another about the harvest, the young fellows, their family affairs, and the good old times, looking haughtily and sneeringly at the young generation. In passing them, the women and the girls sometimes stopped and bowed their heads. The young Cossacks, too, respectfully slackened their pace, and, taking off their caps, kept them for some moments in front of their faces. The old men became silent. Then some sternly, and some affectionately, looked at the passers-by, and slowly took off their caps and put them on again.

The Cossack girls had not yet begun to dance, but collecting in groups, in their bright-coloured growns,

with white kerchiefs bound round their heads, they
sat on the ground, and on the terraces of those houses
which were shaded from the oblique rays of the sun,
and chattered and laughed noisily. Little boys and
girls played at *lapta*, tossing the ball high up into the
clear sky, and running in all directions over the square
with gay cries. Some girls who were just growing
up were already beginning to dance in one corner of
the square, and were starting their songs in shrill and
timorous voices. The young officials, and the boys
who were being educated at the government expense,
and who had come back for the festival in fine linen
and in new red coats, edged with galloon, had merry
holiday faces, and, hand in hand, in couples or trios,
they went from one group of women and girls to
another, resting and playing. The Armenian shop-
keeper, in a caftan of fine blue cloth, edged with galloon, stood at his open door, through which one espied
rows of coloured kerchiefs, and with a consciousness
of his own importance calmly waited for customers.
Two black-bearded, bare-footed Circassians, who had
come from beyond the Terek to amuse themselves at
the festival, sat on the mound of the house of one of
their acquaintances, and were carelessly smoking
their small pipes, and spitting from time to time as
in gutteral voices they exchanged occasional words
and looked at the people. Once in a while a soldier,
wearing an old overcoat, passed between the diversi-
fied groups on the square. At times, also, one heard
the drunken songs of carousing Cossacks. All the cottages were shut up, and their steps had been washed
clean the evening before. Even the old women were
out of doors. Along the streets, everywhere amid
the dust under foot, the husks of melon, sunflower,
and pumpkin seeds were scattered. The air was
warm ; the sky was blue and transparent. The range
of mountains seen beyond the roofs appeared very
close, and grew rosy in the rays of the setting sun.
Once in a while one heard the report of a musket-
shot across the river ; but in the village nothing was

audible save the confused, varied, merry bustle of the festival.

Olenin had walked about the courtyard all that morning waiting to see Marianka. But, when she had finished attending to her household duties, she had gone to service at the church, and had afterwards seated herself on a terrace with other girls, crunching seeds. She had run back home once or twice, looking merrily and carelessly at the lodger; but as she was accompanied, Olenin had felt afraid of talking to her. He wanted to repeat to her what he had said the night before, and to get a decisive answer from her. He watched and waited for such another minute as he had had the previous evening; but the minute did not come, and he felt unable to remain in such a state of suspense any longer. He went out into the street, and after waiting a little while, without knowing where he was going, he followed the young girl. He passed the corner where she seated herself, radiant in her blue satin gown, and, with a pain in his heart, he listened to the laughter of the girls as he passed.

Beletsky's quarters were on the square, and as Olenin went by he heard himself called and went in. He and Beletsky sat down at the window and talked. Uncle Eroshka, who wore a new caftan, joined them, and sat down on the floor beside them.

"There is an aristocratic crowd for you!" said Beletsky, pointing with his cigarette to the variegated group in the corner, and smiling. "My girl is there too, in a red dress—a new one which she has just had made. Why don't you begin the dancing?" he cried out of the window. "When it begins to get dark we will go too, afterwards we will invite them all to Ustenka's. We must give them a ball."

"I will go to Ustenka's too," said Olenin in a decisive way. "Will Marianka be there?"

"Of course. Will you come?" said Beletsky, not feeling in the slightest degree astonished. "Look! it is really very pretty," he said, pointing to the motley crowd.

"Yes," assented Olenin, trying to appear indifferent. "On such festivals," he added, "I always feel astonished. For instance, it is now the 15th.* Everybody has become contented and merry; the festival is visible in everything—in the eyes, faces, voices, and movements of all the girls. The air, the sun, all is holiday like. But *we* ourselves don't have any holidays."

"Yes," Beletsky said, not liking such reasonings. "But you are not drinking, old man," he added, turning to Eroshka.

Eroshka winked to Olenin, and, referring to Beletsky, said: "Your comrade isn't proud."

Beletsky took a glass. "*Allah birdi*," he exclaimed, and drank. *Allah birdi* means "God gave," and is the usual salutation among the Cossacks when they drink together.

"*Sau bul!*" (be in good health!) replied Eroshka, smiling and draining his glass.

"You talk about holidays," he said to Olenin, rising and looking out of the window. "But what sort of a holiday is this? You ought to have seen how one caroused in the old times. The women used to come out dressed in sarafans, all embroidered with gold braid. Their breasts were covered with rows of gold. They had gold tiaras on their heads, and went past with a rustling noise. Every one of them was like a princess. They used to come out like a whole herd of fillies and sing songs; and there was such a noise, they made merry all night. The Cossacks brought barrels of wine down into the courts, sat down opposite to them, and drank until dawn, or else they joined hand in hand and went around the village, and took everybody they met with them. Sometimes they would carouse in this way for three whole days together. I still remember how my father used to come home quite red and puffy, without his cap, and all in rags and done up. Then he would lie

---

* August 15th is the Festival of the Assumption.

down. My mother knew very well what had happened, and she would bring out a little fresh caviare and some brandy to set him right, and then go down through the village to find his cap. He would sleep in that way for two whole days. That is the kind of people we used to be; but now, what do you see?"

"And the girls in their sarafans—what did they do? Did they amuse themselves alone?" asked Beletsky.

"Alone? No. The Cossacks would sometimes come, riding on horseback, and cry, 'Let us go and break up the dances,' and they would go, and the girls would take up sticks and beat both the men and their horses. The ranks were broken, and the young fellows would seize their sweethearts and hoist them up, and start off at a gallop, saying: 'My beauty, my darling!' Ah! one could love as one listed in those times. And what beautiful girls they were—those wenches—perfect queens!"

CHAPTER XXXVI

MEANWHILE, out of a side street there came two men on horseback. One of them was Nazarka; the other Lukashka. The latter sat a little sideways on his well-fed Kabarda steed, which trotted lightly along the road, and tossed its head, with its glossy mane, up and down. The gun which was slung over Lukashka's shoulder, the pistol at his back, and the sheep-skin coat twisted round his saddle, showed that he had not come from any peaceful locality. The nonchalant manner in which he sat sideways on his saddle, and the careless movement of his hands, as he struck the horse's flanks with his whip, and especially his gleaming, proud black eyes—all expressed the consciousness of youthful strength and self-reliance.

" Have you ever seen such a brave young fellow ? " his eyes seemed to say, as they looked first on one side, and then on another. His fine horse, with its silver-decked bridle, his gun, and he himself, the handsome fellow, attracted the attention of everybody in the square. Nazarka, ugly and stunted, was not dressed as well as his comrade. As they went past the old men seated on the terrace, Lukashka stopped, and raised his white sheep-skin cap from his black, shaven head.

" Well, did you drive off many Tartar horses ? " asked a little old man, with a dark, frowning look.

" Would you have counted them, uncle ? " answered Lukashka, turning away.

" You do wrong to take that fellow along with you," said the old man, still more crossly.

" Oh ! the old devil knows everything," muttered Lukashka to himself ; and his face assumed a thought-ful expression. Then, looking towards the corner, where a number of Cossack girls were standing, he turned his horse in that direction.

" Have you had a good day of it, girls ? " he cried, in a strong, sonorous voice, reining in his steed. " Why, you have grown old without me, you witches." And then he began to laugh.

" How do you do, Lukashka ? How are you, old fellow ? " repeated merry voices. " Have you brought a lot of money ? You ought to buy some sweets for the girls. Have you come for long ? We have not seen you for an age."

" Oh ! Nazarka and I have come on a flying visit—for the night—to amuse ourselves a little," answered Lukashka, striking his horse with his whip, and riding straight to the girls.

" Marianka has had time to forget you," hissed out Ustenka, nudging Marianka with her elbow, and burst-ing into a shrill laugh. Marianka moved away from the horse, and throwing her head back, looked quietly at the Cossack with her large, lustrous eyes.

" You have not been here for a long time. Why do

you beat your horse like that ? " she asked dryly, turning away.

Lukashka had arrived in a particularly merry mood, with his countenance radiant with delight and knowledge of his worth. Marianka's coldness now worried him, and he frowned. " Step on the stirrup and I will take you up," he cried suddenly, as if to drive away his bad thoughts ; and, curvetting amongst the girls, he bent down towards Marianka. " I'll kiss you, I'll kiss you ! Come, now," said he.

Marianka looked him in the face, and then blushing, turned away. " It is just like you. You will crush my feet," she said ; and, bending down her head, she looked at her shapely legs, on which she wore blue stockings with white stripes, while new red-leather shoes, embroidered with silver braid, encased her feet.

Lukashka then turned to Ustenka, and Marianka sat down by the side of the Cossack girl who held a child in her arms. The child reached out its arms, and with its fat little hands seized hold of the necklace which hung over her blue dress. Marianka bent down over the baby, but continued looking at Lukashka out of the corners of her eyes. Meanwhile, the young fellow produced from his pocket of his jacket a packet of sweetmeats and some seeds.

" I will give all to you," he said, handing the packet to Ustenka, but looking at Marianka with a smile.

The girl's face again betrayed great embarrassment. Her beautiul eyes were as dark as a thunder-cloud ! She pulled her kerchief down, and suddenly lowered her face to that of the child who was holding her necklace, and began to kiss it wildly. The little one then caught hold of her neck and screamed out, opening its toothless little mouth.

" What are you smothering the boy for ? " asked the mother of the child, taking it away from Marianka, and unhooking her gown so as to give it the breast. " You would do better to kiss that young fellow."

" I must go and put up my horse ; and then I'll come back with Nazarka, and we will amuse ourselves all night," said Lukashka. Then, touching his horse up with the whip, he rode off from the girls.

He turned into a by-street with Nazarka, and they went up to two houses which stood side by side.

"Here we are. Come back as soon as you can," cried Lukashka to his companion who alighted at the next yard, and carefully led his horse through the wickerwork gates. "How are you, Stepka?" added the young Cossack to the dumb girl, who, also dressed up in holiday style, came out to take his horse. He then showed her by signs that she must give the horse some hay, and not unsaddle him. The dumb girl gave a chuckle, pointed to the horse, and kissed him on the nose. This meant that she loved the horse, and that it was a good one.

"How are you, mother? What, haven't you gone out into the street yet?" cried Lukashka, taking off his gun, and going into the house, the door of which the old woman opened for him. "Well, I did not think you would come," she said; "Kirka said you wouldn't."

"Well, bring us some wine, mother. Nazarka is coming with me. We are going to keep holiday a little."

"Immediately, Lukashka, immediately," his mother answered. "The women are all out holiday-making. The dumb one and I were just going out too." And then taking the keys, she hastily went to the outhouse. Nazarka, having put up his horse, and divested himself of his gun, came over to Lukashka's.

CHAPTER XXXVII

"HERE'S your health," said Lukashka, taking from his mother's hands a full bowl of wine, and carefully raising it to his mouth, as he craned his neck forward.

"Did you notice?" said Nazarka. "That old fellow suspects something. He asked, 'Did you steal many horses?' So plainly he knows about it."

"He is in league with the witches," curtly replied Lukashka. "Well, what of it?" he added, shaking his head. "They are already beyond the river. Let him look for them."

"It is annoying, all the same."

"Why? Take him some wine to-morrow. That is the best way to manage; and then nothing will happen. Now is the time for amusing ourselves. Drink!" cried Lukashka, in a voice like that of old Eroshka. "Let us go into the streets for a while, to the girls. But you must first go and get some mead, or else I'll send the dumb girl for it. We'll carouse till morning."

Nazarka smiled. "Shall me stay here long?" he said.

"Never mind! let us have a good time of it. Run and fetch some vodka. Here's some money."

Thereupon Nazarka obediently ran off to Yamka's.

Uncle Eroshka and Ergushoff, like true birds of prey, scenting out where there would be some amusement, now entered the cottage, one after the other, and both of them drunk.

"Give us another half-gallon of wine," cried Lukashka to his mother, in answer to their salutation.

"Now, tell me, devil, where did you steal them?" asked Uncle Eroshka. "Ah, you are a brave fellow. I like you!"

"Like me?" answered Luskahka, laughing. "Why, you take the girls treats from the officers. Ah, you old villain!"

"It is not true; it is not true, Marka!" And the old man burst out into a laugh. "I don't know how many times that yunker begged of me to arrange matters for him. 'Come,' he said, 'and arrange things a little for me. I will give you a gun.' But no, God be with him! I wouldn't do it; I thought

of you. But come, tell me, where have you been ? "
and the old man began to speak in Tartar.

Lukashka answered him without any concealment.
Ergushoff, who did not know the Tartar language
well, put in a word of Russian from time to time.

" I know you have been driving off some horses. I
know it for sure," he insisted.

" Yes, we went off, Ghireïka and I," continued
Lukashka, and in calling Ghireï Khan Ghireïka, he
displayed his intimacy with him, and at the time same
a desire to show off. " And he was all the time boasting that he knew the whole steppe, and could go
straight to the place. Well, we went out one dark
night, but suddenly Ghireïka lost the way, and began
to wander about. It was of no use talking and complaining, we could not find the village, and all was
confusion. We had evidently gone too far to the
right. We looked about until midnight, when unluckily the dogs began to howl."

" Fools that you were ! " exclaimed Uncle Eroshka.
" So you get lost at night on the steppe, do you ?
Devil take them ! Well, once upon a time I got lost
upon the steppe in that way ; and I remember how
the wolves barked all about ! " Then he began to
imitate the howls of a pack of wolves. " The dogs
immediately began to answer them," he continued.
" But go on, what did you capture ? "

" We escaped with our skins. Some old Tartar
women came near catching Nazarka."

" Yes, they did nearly catch me," said Nazarka,
who had just come back, in an offended tone.

" Well, we went out once more, and got lost again,"
resumed Lukashka. " We got quite confused among
the reeds. Everything looked as though we were
going towards the Terek ; but, on the contrary, we
were going just the other way."

" But you ought to have looked at the stars,"
exclaimed Uncle Eroshka.

" So I say," added Ergushoff.

" But come, it was quite dark. I wandered about,

and wandered about, and finally I got hold of some mares and then turned round, letting my horse go as he listed. I thought he would take us back; and, indeed, what do you think? Why, he began to smell about, with his nose to the ground, and then he ran off, and brought us straight to the station; but by ill luck, daylight was just breaking, and we hardly had time to hide our horses in the woods. Nazim came, however, and took them across the river."

Ergushoff nodded. "Well, it was very well done," said he. "Were there many of them? Much money?"

"Oh! it is all here," replied Lukashka, slapping his pocket. Just then, however, the old woman came back into the cottage, and the Cossacks stopped talking. "Drink!" cried Lukashka.

"Well," began Eroshka, "Girtchik and I went out late one night, just in the same way——"

"Come, come, nobody has time to listen to you. I am going," interrupted Lukashka; and then draining the wine bowl, and drawing the strap of his belt tighter, he rose up and went outside.

CHAPTER XXXVIII

IT was already dark when Lukashka reached the street. The autumn night was fresh and still. The full golden moon sailed out from behind the dark poplar-trees which stood on one side of the square. Smoke rose from the chimneys, and, mingling with the mist, hung over the village. In some of the windows, lights were burning. Talking and laughing, songs, and the crunching of seeds, were heard confusedly, but more plainly than during the day. The white kerchiefs and caps of the Cossacks were visible in the darkness, about the fences and the houses.

On the square, opposite the open doors of the lighted shop, there was a crowd of Cossacks and girls, from whom came sounds of laughter and talking. Holding each other's hands, the girls circled about over the square with a wave-like motion. A thin wench, one of the ugliest of them all, led the song :—" From the forest, the dark, green forest, *aï, da, liuli !* From the garden, the gay, green garden, *aï, da, liuli !* There came, there came two brave young gallants ; two brave young gallants both unmarried. Around they sauntered, then they halted ; they halted and began to quarrel. But soon there came a maiden lovely, a maiden lovely, who addressed them : ' Come, one of you two, I will marry ; but shall it be the fair or dark one ? ' Ah ! 'tis the fair one she has chosen, the fair one with the curly ringlets. And look, her right hand he has taken, around the circle now he leads her, and, boasting, calls unto his comrades : ' See, brothers, see my bride so comely ! ' *Aï, da, liuli !* "*

The old women stood round listening to the singing, while little boys and girls ran about in the darkness, chasing one another. The Cossacks also were gathered around, and pinched the girls as they passed by, and sometimes broke the ring apart, and entered it. In a dark corner stood Beletsky and Olenin, in Circassian coats and caps, talking with each other in a subdued tone, for they felt that they were attracting attention. Plump Ustenka, dressed in a red gown, and stately Marianka in blue satin, were seen side by side in the dance. Olenin and Beletsky were consulting as to how they should yet them away. Beletsky thought that Olenin merely wished to amuse himself a little ; but the latter was thirsting for the decision of his fate. He desired to see Marianka alone that night at any cost, so as to tell her all, and ask her whether she could and would become his wife. Although this question would probably be decided against him, he

---

* This is a specimen of the Russian *khorovod* or popular choral dance.

L

hoped that he would be able to tell her all he felt, and that she would understand him.

" Why did you not speak to me sooner ? " said Beletsky. " I would have arranged matters for you through Ustenka. But you are such an odd fellow ! "

" Well, what is to be done ? Some time or other, I will tell you all about it ; only now, for God's sake, arrange matters somehow to get her to come to Ustenka's."

" Very well, that is easily done. Here ! Marianka, why don't you choose the fair-haired fellow, and not Lukashka ? " said Belestky, alluding to the words of the song, and addressing her, just to save appearances ; for immediately afterwards he went up to Ustenka, and began to ask her to bring Marianka home with her. He had not finished talking, when another song was struck up, and the girls dragged each other off.

" Behind the garden, behind the orchard," they sang, " a gallant young fellow walked on and on. Right down to the end of the street he strolled, and with his right hand to me he beckoned. Yet a second time did he thus go by, and the sheepskin cap on his head he jerked ; and when the third time he once more came near, he halted, and, turning around, he said : ' I was coming to see you, darling mine, coming to chide you. Oh ! why won't you go for a stroll in the garden gay and green ? Can it really be true, O darling mine, that you have become too proud to have me ? Well, dear, put your heart at rest ; ne'er worry, for I shall send to ask you in marriage. I'll come to woo you and I'll marry you, and to punish your pride I'll make you weep.' I knew quite well what I ought to answer, though never a word did I dare to say ; but to the garden so green I sauntered, and there to the ring I bowed me down. And he was there, and low his bow made ; and threw a kerchief, and said to me : ' Come take it, my darling, come take it now. Ay, take it quick in your white, white hand—your lily-white hand—and love *me*, love *me*. Ah ! why is it that I feel so strange ; and what shall I give to the girl of my love ? Ah !

I will give her a kerchief brave—a kerchief brave to the girl I love ; it shall be as fine and as large as a shawl, and she shall let me kiss her and kiss her, at least five times for that kerchief brave ! ' "*

As the song came to an end Lukashka and Nazarka broke through the ring and began to walk about among the girls. The former kept up the song in a high-pitched voice, and, waving his hand, sauntered along in the centre of the ring.

"Come, one of you," he said ; whereupon the girls gave Marianka a push, but she did not wish to go to him. Amid the singing one would hear shrill laughter and a confused sound of blows, kisses, and scuffling.

Passing Olenin, Lukashka nodded to him in a familiar, pleasant way : " Well, Mitri Andreitch, so you have come to look on ? "

" Yes," answered Olenin, dryly.

Beletsky leaned over to Ustenka, and whispered to her. She wished to answer, but lacked the time ; however, when she came round again, she said, " Very well, we will come."

" And Marianka too ? "

Olenin himself now leant towards Marianka, and said, " Will you come ? Please do, if only for a minute : I have something I must say to you."

" If the other girls come, I will come too."

" Will you tell me what I asked you ? " he resumed, again bending towards her. " What a good humour you are in now ! "

She was already moving away from him, and he went after her. " Will you answer ? " he said.

" Answer what ? "

" What I asked you on the day before yesterday," and, bending close to her ear he added : " Will you marry me ? "

Marianka reflected for a moment, " Yes, I will tell you," she said, " I will tell you to-night ; " and in the darkness her eyes gazed joyously and affectionately

---

* Another specimen of the *khorovod.*

L 2

at the young man. He kept walking all the time behind her. It seemed delightful to him to get near to her.

However, Lukashka, continuing to sing, caught her firmly by the hand, and pulled her out of the chain into the middle of the ring. Olenin was only able to repeat : " Come to Ustenka's," and then he went to join his comrade.

The songs at last ended. Lukashka wiped his lips ; Marianka did the same, and then they kissed each other. " No, fully five times," said Lukashka, as he turned aside. Talking, laughing, and running about now took the place of the regular sounds and motion of the choral dance. Lukashka, who seemed to be already pretty well drunk, began to divide some sweets among the girls. " I will give some to everybody," he remarked, with a proud, half-comical, half-solemn expression of face. " However, any one who goes after the soldiers must clear out of the ring," he suddenly added, looking maliciously at Olenin.

The girls seized hold of the sweets, and, laughing, snatched them away from ane another. Beletsky and Olenin retreated on one side.

Lukashka took off his cap, wiped his brow with his sleeve, and then went up to Marianka and Ustenka. " Are you grown too proud to have me ? " he repeated, in the words of the song which had just been sung, and, turning to Marianka, he resumed angrily : " When we are married, to punish your pride, I'll make you weep." Then he began hugging Ustenka and Marianka at the same time. The latter finally tore herself away, and dealt him such a blow on the back that she almost put her wrist out of joint.

" Aren't you going to have another dance ? " he asked.

" If the other girls like they can dance," answered Ustenka. " But I am going home ; and Marianka is coming with me."

The Cossack, still hugging Marianka, drew her out of the crowd into a dark corner.

Don't go, Mashinka," he said. " This is the last time we shall amuse ourselves, perhaps. Go home, and I will come to you."

" What have I got to do at home ? What is the use of a holiday, except to enjoy one's self ? I am going to Ustenka's," replied Marianka.

" Well, it's all the same ; I shall marry you, remember ! "

" All right," said Marianka ; " we shall see ! "

" Won't you really go home ? " asked Lukashka seriously, and, clasping her to him, he kissed her on the cheek.

" Oh, stop ! let me be ! " cried Marianka, and, breaking loose, she darted away from him.

" Ah, girl, it will end badly," said Lukashka reproachfully, and he shook his head. " I will make you weep, remember." Then turning away from her, he called out to the girls to play at something or another.

His last words had half frightened Marianka, and she stopped short.

" What will end badly ? " she asked.

" Why, what you are about."

" What do you mean ? "

" Why, that you amuse yourself with that soldier, your lodger, and don't love me any more."

" I do what I please. It doesn't concern you. You are not my father, or my mother, are you ? What do you want ? I will love whom I choose."

" So it's true ! " said Lukashka. " Well, remember my words." And then he went up to the shop. " Girls," he cried, " why are you standing still ? Have another dance. Nazarka, run and bring some wine."

" Well, will they come ? " said Olenin to Beletsky at this moment.

" Yes, they are coming immediately," answered Beletsky. Let us go. We have to get everything ready."

CHAPTER XXXIX

IT was already late at night when Olenin left Beletsky's cottage following Marianka and Ustenka. The girl's white kerchief was visible in the dimness; the moon, of a glowing yellow, was nearing the horizon on the steppe, and a silvery mist hung over the village. All was quiet. The lights had been extinguished. Nothing was heard but the steps of the girls as they walked away. Olenin's heart beat violently: his face began to cool in the damp night air. He looked at the sky, he looked at the cottage from which he had just come: the candle which had lighted it had already been put out. Then he began to look at the distant shadowy figures of the girls. Their white kerchiefs became lost to view in the mist. It seemed terrible to him to remain alone, although he was so happy! He darted down from the steps and ran after the girls.

" Go away; some one will see us," said Ustenka.

" Never mind."

And Olenin turned to Marianka and embraced her. She made no resistance.

" That's enough," said Ustenka. " When you are married you can kiss her as much as you like; but now you ought to wait."

" Well, good-bye, Marianka," said Olenin. Tomorrow I will go to your father, and tell him all about it. Don't you say anything."

" What is there for me to say to him? " answered Marianka, and then both girls ran away.

Olenin remained alone, and recapitulated all that had happened. He had spent the whole evening alone with her in the corner, near the stove. Ustenka had been joking and chatting all the time, with the other girls and Beletsky. Olenin had talked to Marianka in a whisper.

"Will you marry me?" he asked.

"You are deceiving me: you won't take me," she answered quietly, with a smile.

"But do you love me? Tell me, for God's sake!"

"Why shouldn't I love you? You are not one-eyed," answered Marianka, laughing, and pressing his hand with her firm muscular fingers. "How white, how very white and soft your hands are! just like clotted cream!" she said.

"Come, don't joke. Tell me, will you marry me?"

"Why shouldn't I marry you, if my father consents?"

"Remember that I shall go out of my mind if you deceive me. To-morrow I will tell your mother and father that I have come to woo you."

Marianka suddenly burst out laughing.

"What is the matter with you?" asked Olenin.

"Why, it is so funny!"

"But I am telling the truth; I will buy a house and garden, and inscribe myself among the Cossacks."

"You will have to take care, then, and not make free with any other woman. I am very jealous."

Olenin in a transport now repeated all these words. As he remembered one thing and another, he sometimes became sad, and sometimes his spirit seemed almost bursting with happiness. He was sad because she had remained so calm all the time, talking with him in just the same way as formerly. It was as though this change in the situation had not affected her. It seemed almost as if she did not believe him, as if she had no thoughts about the future. He was happy, however, because all her words appeared to him so true, and because she had consented to belong to him. "Yes," he said to himself, "we shall only understand each other when she is wholly mine. For such a love as mine, words are not enough; one needs life, a whole life. To-morrow everything will be explained. I cannot live on like this any longer.

To-morrow I will tell everything to her father, to Beletsky, and the whole village."

Meanwhile, Lukashka, after passing two sleepless nights, had drunk so much that, for the first time in his life, his legs failed him, and he slept at Yamka's tavern.

CHAPTER XL

ON the following day Olenin woke up earlier than usual; and at once the thought came to him of what there was before him; he remembered with delight her kisses, the pressure of her fingers, and her words, " How white your hands are ! " He jumped out of bed, and would have gone at once to the other cottage, and have asked for her hand, but the sun had not yet risen, and it seemed to him that there was unusual excitement in the street: people were walking and riding about, and talking together. He hastily threw on his Circassian coat, and darted out on to the steps. The people of the house were not yet up. Five Cossacks were riding past, and noisily talking about something or other. In front of them all rode Lukashka on his broad-backed Kabarda horse. The Cossacks were all talking and shouting together; and it was impossible to understand what they referred to.

" Ride on to the upper post ! " cried one.

" Saddle your horses, and join us quick ! " said another. " It is nearer to go out by this gate."

" What nonsense ! " cried Lukashka. " We must go by the middle gate."

" Yes, that is the nearest road," said another Cossack, covered with dust, who sat on a reeking horse.

Lukashka's face was swollen with drinking; and his cap was pushed back on to the nape of his neck; he spoke with an air of command, as though he were the leader of the party.

" What is the row ? Where are you going ? " asked Olenin, with difficulty attracting the attention of the Cossacks.

" We are going after the Abreks. They are in ambush in the reeds. We are going immediately ; and, unluckily, we are not very numerous." Then, continuing to shout and gather, the Cossacks rode farther down the street.

It occurred to Olenin that it would not look well unless he went himself ; besides, he thought he would be able to come back early. He dressed himself, loaded his gun with ball, vaulted on to his horse (which Vanusha had somehow saddled), and caught up the Cossacks at the outskirts of the village. Although they were in a hurry, they had collected in a circle, and pouring some wine from a little keg, which had been brought, into a wooden bowl, they handed it to each other, and *prayed* for the success of their expedition. Among them was a young dandy of a cornet, who had accidentally come to the station, and who by right of his rank had assumed command of the nine or ten men who had collected. However, although this cornet tried to assume the airs of a general officer, the Cosascks in reality only obeyed Lukashka. To Olenin they did not pay the least attention. When they had all mounted their horses and started off, Olenin rode up to the cornet and asked him what was the matter. The officer, who was usually very polite and affable, now treated him, however, with all the dignity that he supposed his importance commanded, and it was only with great difficulty that Olenin ascertained what it was all about. A patrol which had been sent to look for the Abreks had found several of them in the reeds at about six miles or so from the village. These Abreks, who were hidden in a ditch, had fired at them, whereupon the corporal commanding the patrol had sent to the station for reinforcements.

The sun was only just rising. Two miles out from the station they stretched on this side an open and level steppe ; and nothing was to be seen save the monotonous arid plain, the sand of which was cut up in many places by cattle tracks, while here and there were scanty patches of grass, a few small pools surrounded by low reeds, and by some scarcely distinguishable paths. Some Tartar encampments were barely visible on the distant horizon. One was unpleasantly impressed by the complete absence of shade, and the sterile look of the region. On the steppes the sun is invariably red when it rises and when it sets, and whenever there is a wind this wind drives along whole mountains of sand. When the atmosphere is calm, as it was that morning, then the stillness, unbroken by a sound or movement, is especially striking. That morning, although the sun had risen, all was still and sombre indeed on the steppe : it somehow seemed to be more deserted than usual. There was no movement in the air, and nothing could be heard except the steps and the snorting of the horses ; and even these sounds seemed very feeble, and immediately died away.

The Cossacks rode along in silence. Their arms are always arranged so as not to rattle or resound. In fact, it is a great disgrace for a Cossack to have his weapons heard. Two villagers met them on the way, and exchanged a few words with them. Then suddenly Lukashka's horse stumbled against a tuft of dry grass. This is a bad sign among the Cossacks ; and the young fellows looked at one another, and hastily averted their faces, trying to avoid giving any attention to this circumstance, although in their minds it had special importance. Lukashka drew up his reins, frowned, set his teeth, and cut his horse over the head with his whip. The noble steed suddenly bounded up on all four legs, seemingly wishing to rise on wings. But Lukashka gave him a second sharp cut on his sleek flanks, and a third, and then the horse, showing his teeth, and extending his tail, snorted, reared up, and stepped forward a few paces in advance of the other Cossacks.

" That is a fine horse ! " said the cornet.

" A lion of a horse ! " rejoined one of the men.

They rode along, sometimes at a walk, and sometimes at a trot, and the change of pace was all that broke for an instant the solemn quietude of their movements. Along the whole road across the steppe, for six miles, the only living thing they met was a Tartar kibitka, a covered cart, which jolted slowly along. It belonged to a Nogai Tartar who was moving with his family, from one camping-ground to another. Farther on, near a pool, they met two ragged, high-cheek-boned Tartar women, who, with baskets on their backs, were collecting the droppings of the cattle which pastured on the steppe. The cornet, who spoke the Kumyk dialect very badly, began to ask the women some questions, but they could not understand him, and exchanged timid glances with each other.

Lukashka, however, came up, stopped his horse, and, in an off-hand way, gave the usual salutation to the Tartar women, who were evidently pleased, and began to talk with him as a brother.

" *Ai, ai, kop Abrek !* " they said plaintively, pointing in the direction where the Cossacks were going. Olenin understood that they meant there were a number of Abreks in ambush.

Never having witnessed any such affairs, and only having an idea of them derived from the stories of Uncle Eroshka, the yunker wished to keep up with the Cossacks and see everything. He admired the men, who looked about at everything, and listened to everything, paying attention to the slightest details. Although Olenin had taken a sabre and a loaded gun with him, yet, noticing how shy the Cossacks seemed of him, and how they avoided taking him into their confidence, he decided to keep aloof in the affair, the more readily as, in his opinion, his bravery had already been shown on the expedition, and especially as he was then so happy.

Suddenly in the far distance a shot was heard The cornet became excited, and immediately began to arrange how he should divide the Cossacks, and on which side they should approach. The men, however, did not pay the slightest attention to his directions, but listened only to Lukashka, and looked only at him. His face and figure expressed mingled composure and solemnity. He went on ahead with his good horse (the others not being able to keep up), and, contracting his brows, looked constantly in front of him.

"There goes a man on horseback!" he said, suddenly checking his horse, and falling back to join the others.

Olenin at once strained his eyes, but he could not see anything. But at last one distinguished two horsemen, and at a quiet pace the Cossacks went towards them.

"Are those fellows Abreks?" asked Olenin.

The Cossacks made no answer to this question, which seemed in their eyes to be devoid of sense. As if the Abreks would be such fools as to cross the river mounted!

"Uncle Rodka cannot wait," said Lukashka, pointing to two horsemen, who now became more plainly visible. "See! he is coming to meet us."

Indeed, a few minutes afterwards it was clearly seen that the horsemen were the Cossacks of the patrol. The corporal rode straight up to Lukashka.

CHAPTER XLI

"ARE they much farther off?" the young Cossack inquired; and at the same moment a sharp, quick report was heard about thirty steps off. The corporal slightly smiled.

"Our Gurka is firing at them," he said, jerking his head in the direction where the shot had been fired.

After going on a few steps farther, they indeed saw
Gurka sitting on a hillock of sand, and loading his
gun. To avoid feeling bored, he was exchanging shots
with the Abreks, who were crouching behind another
sand-hill. A bullet now whistled by them, and the
cornet became pale and confused. Lukashka got off
his horse, threw the reins to another Cossack, and
went up to Gurka. Olenin bent down and went after
him. They had hardly reached Gurka, when two
bullets whistled over their heads. Lukashka laughed,
looked at Olenin, and bent towards him.

"You will be shot, Andreitch," said he. "You
had better go away. This isn't the kind of affair for
you."

However, Olenin wished by all means to have a
look at the Abreks. Above the hillock, some two
hundred paces off, he saw their caps and musket
barels. Suddenly a cloud of smoke rose up there,
and another bullet whistled by. The Abreks were
crouching in the swamp behind the hillock. Olenin
was astonished that they had selected such a place ;
and yet on looking round the steppe he realised that
they could hardly have chosen any other.

Lukashka now returned to his horse, and Olenin
went after him. "We ought to have a cart, with
some hay," said the young Cossack, "or else they'll
kill us. Behind that hillock, there is a Tartar cart
with a load of hay."

The cornet listened to him, and the corporal consented. The cart was brought ; and the Cossacks,
concealing themselves behind it, began moving it on
in front of them. Olenin climbed the hillock, so that
he might see everything. The cart laden with hay
began to move on, the Cossacks crowding close
together behind it. The Abreks, nine in all, sat in a
row, knee against knee, and did not fire.

All was quiet. Suddenly, from the side of the
Abreks, there arose a strange and melancholy strain,
similar to Uncle Eroshka's "Aïdaï dalalaï." The
Abreks knew that they could not get away ; and, to

avoid the temptation of flight, they had tied themselves together with straps, knee to knee, and now,
having prepared their guns, they had begun to sing
their death-song.

The Cossacks, with their load of hay, drew still
nearer and nearer ; and Olenin expected shots every
minute. However, the stillness was only broken by
the melancholy song of the Abreks, and suddenly
even that came to an end. Then a shot was fired,
and a bullet struck the pole of the cart. The swearing
and the shouts of the Circassians could be plainly
heard. Soon shot followed shot, and bullet after
bullet whistled through the hay. The Cossacks
meanwhile did not fire ; they were now only five
paces off.

Another moment elapsed ; and then the Cossacks,
with a shout, started out on either side of the cart.
Lukashka was in front. Olenin heard several shouts,
a cry, and a groan. He saw smoke and blood, as it
seemed to him ; and then, springing from his horse,
he hurried after the Cossacks. Horror came upon
his eyes. He did not clearly perceive anything, but
he understood that it was all over. Lukashka, as
white as a handkerchief, was holding a wounded
Abrek in his arms, and shouting : " Do not kill him.
I will take him alive."

This Abrek was the red-bearded one, the brother of
the man whom the young Cossack had killed, the one
who had come across the Terek to fetch the dead body.
Lukashka twisted his arms, but suddenly the Abrek
tore himself away, and fired a pistol at his foe. Lukashka fell at once, and blood spurted from his breast.
He jumped up, but fell again, swearing in Russian and
Tartar. His blood was flowing fast. The Cossacks
went up to him, and began to unfasten his belt. One
of them, Nazarka, wanted to assist, but for a long time
he could not succeed in sheathing his sword, the blade
of which was covered with blood.

The Abreks, red-haired, and mostly with shaven
upper lips, lay upon the ground, massacred, cut to

pieces. Only one of them—he who had fired at Lukashka—was still alive, though badly wounded. Covered with the blood which was flowing down from his left eye, with set teeth, a pale and lowering face, threatening every one with his terrible gaze, and looking round on all sides, he seemed like an expiring bird of prey, as he crouched down, holding his dagger, evidently determined to defend himself to the very last. The cornet, however, stepped aside, avoiding a front attack, and hastily fired his pistol into his ear. The Abrek started up, but fell at once ; he was dead.

The Cossacks, who were out of breath, were separating the corpses, and appropriating the weapons of the foe. These red-headed Abreks were curious to look at : each man had his own peculiar expression of face. At last the Cossacks carried Lukashka to the cart : he scolded constantly and swore in Russian and Tartar : " You liar," he shrieked, " I will smother you with my hands ! You shall not escape me. *Ana seni !* " he added with an effort, and at last he became silent from sheer weakness.

Olenin went home. In the evening he was told that Lukashka was at the point of death, and that a Tartar from beyond the river was trying to cure him with herbs. The bodies of the Abreks had been dragged towards the village, and the women and children were going in crowds to look at them.

Olenin had come back towards twilight, and for a long time he could not forget the scene that he had witnessed. By night, however, the recollection of the previous day came back to him. He looked out of the window. Marianka was going to and fro—from the cottage to the storehouse, and working. Her mother had gone to the vineyard ; her father was at the government house. Olenin could not wait, but went to join the girl. She was then in her room, and stood with her back to him. Olenin thought that she was bashful.

" Marianka ! " he said ; " O Marianka ! can I come in ? "

She suddenly turned round : and he saw that there were tears in her eyes. Her face seemed more lovely than ever, with its expression of deep grief. She looked haughtily at Olenin.

"Marianka," he repeated. "I have come."

"Leave me," she interrupted. Her look did not alter ; but the tears flowed fast from her eyes.

"What is the matter with you ? Why do you cry ? " asked Olenin.

"What ! " she repeated with a hoarse, rough voice, "they have been killing Cossacks, and you ask me why I weep ? "

"Lukashka ? " said Olenin.

"Leave me, what more do you want ? "

"Marianka," pleaded Olenin, drawing nearer to her. "You will never have anything from me."

"Oh ! Marianka, don't say that," begged Olenin.

"Go away, you unfeeling man ! " cried the girl, angrily stamping on the ground, and stepping towards him with a threatening look. Such disgust, hatred, and anger were expressed on her face, that Olenin suddenly realised that he had nothing more to hope for. There was blood, Lukashka's blood between them ; and in despair, but without a word, he turned and left the cottage.

CHAPTER XLII

AFTER returning to his quarters, Olenin lay on his bed for a couple of hours without moving, and then he went to see the commander of the company, and asked to be allowed to join the staff. He did not bid good-bye to anybody, but he settled his account with the landlord through Vanusha. He was going to the fortress where the regimental headquarters were situated. No one but Uncle Eroshka came to see him

ff. They took a drink, a second, and even a third.
Just as when Olenin had left Moscow, three post-
horses stood at the door. But Olenin did not now
commune with himself as he had then done, and say
that all his thoughts and actions had not been fitting.
He did not again promise himself a new life. He
loved Marianka more than ever, and knew that he
could never be loved by her.

"Good-bye, father," said Uncle Eroshka. "When
you go on a campaign, be as sensible as you can, and
mind what an old man like me tells you. When you
go into action—you see I am an old wolf, and I've seen
everything—when they fire at you, don't stay in the
ranks. You see, when your fellows are a little afraid,
they all get together in a crowd; and, although it is
pleasant to be together, it is dangerous, for the enemy
fire into the mass. I always got away as far as possible from the others. I used to go alone, and that is
the reason I was never wounded. What haven't I
seen in my time?"

"But you have got a bullet in your back," said
Vanusha, who was tidying the room.

"Oh, that was a joke of the Cossacks!" answered
Eroshka.

"How a joke of the Cossacks?" asked Olenin.

"Why, they were drunk; and one of them, Vanka
Sitkin, who was very drunk, fired at me right there
with his pistol, just as if he had stuck a bayonet into
me."

"Did it hurt you?" asked Olenin. "Come,
Vanusha, are you almost ready?" he added.

"Eh! Don't be in such a hurry. Wait, and I'll
tell you. Well, he trembled as he fired, and the ball
did not damage the bones, but stayed in the flesh.
'You have killed me, brother!' I said to him. 'What
is it you have done to me? I won't let you off so
easily. You will have to give me a gallon of wine.'"

"Well, did it hurt much?" Olenin again asked,
scarcely listening to the story.

"Wait, and I'll tell you. He gave us a gallon of

wine. We drank it up and the blood still flowed. The floor of the hut was quite covered with blood. So Uncle Burlak said, ' See ! the little fellow is going to die.' ' Give us another gallon of sweet wine,' said I, ' or else I will have you judged.' They brought some more, and we got drunk, so drunk——"

" Well, did it hurt ? " asked Olenin again.

" Hurt me, indeed ? Don't interrupt. Wait till I finish. We drank and drank, and carried it on till daybreak. I went to sleep on the stove, quite dead-drunk. When I woke up in the morning, I couldn't move."

" It must have hurt you a great deal," said Olenin, still expecting an answer to his question.

" You say that it hurt. No, it didn't hurt. But I could not stretch myself, and I was unable to walk."

" Well, you lived through it," said Olenin, quietly, not even laughing ; he was so heavy at heart.

" Yes, I lived through it. But the bullet is still there. Just feel it ; " and, turning down his shirt, he displayed his broad back in which a bullet could be seen near the bone.

" See how it moves about," he said, evidently as proud of the bullet as of a plaything. " See ! it is moving back now."

" Will Lukashka live, do you think ? " asked Olenin.

" God knows ! There is no doctor. They have gone for one."

" Where will they get one—at Grozny ? " asked Olenin.

" No, father. I would have hanged all your Russian doctors long ago, if I had been the Czar. They don't know how to do anything, they can only cut one's legs off. They maimed our Cossack Baklasheff like that, they cut off his leg. It is evident that they are fools. What is Baklasheff good for now ? No, father, up in the mountains there are real doctors. Once my friend Girtchik got wounded up in the mountains, wounded right here in the breast ; and your doctors declared that they couldn't do anything for him; but a fellow named Saib came from the mountains, and cured him. Yes, the men of the mountains know the right sort of herbs."

" Come now, that is all nonsense," said Olenin. " I will send a surgeon from the staff."

" Nonsense ! " said the old man angrily. " Fool; fool ! Nonsense ! Send a surgeon. Why, if your surgeons could cure anybody, the Cossacks and the Abreks would all go to you to get cured ; but your officers, and even your colonels, all send to the mountains for doctors. Yours are all cheats, nothing but cheats."

Olenin did not answer. He was only too well convinced that everything *was* a cheat in that world in which he had formerly lived, and to which he was now returning.

" How about Lukashka ? Have you seen him ? " he asked.

" Yes : he is like a dead man. He does not eat ; he merely takes a little vodka, and breathes heavily. It is a great pity. He is a good fellow—just such a djiguit as I was. I myself nearly died once. The old women were already beginning to groan over me. My head was all hot inside, and they had put me under the eikons. I was lying quite still ; and over me, on the stove, I heard like a lot of little drums, beating as hard as they could. I tried to cry out to stop them, but they beat harder than ever. And then the old women brought in the priest, and wanted to bury me. He was a jolly fellow who amused himself with the women, and hugged and kissed them, and danced, and played the guitar. ' Confess,' he said to me ; and so I began to confess. ' I have sinned,' I said. And then he talked to me about my guitar, and said it was a perverting instrument. ' Where is the cursed guitar ? ' he asked. ' Tell me, I must break it to bits.' ' I have not got one ; said I ; but I had hidden it in the porch, under a sieve, where I knew they would not find it. The priest wanted it for himself. Well, then they let me lie and rest. And then I got well again, and played on the guitar as I had done before. But what was I saying just now?" he continued. "Ah! you listen to me. Keep as far as possible from the others when you are fighting : otherwise the enemy will kill you for sure. Really I should be very sorry for you ; you know how to drink, and that is the reason I like you so. All your fellows like to go about on the sand-hills. There was one who came here among us : yes, he came from Russia, and he was always going about on the sand-hills. As soon as he saw one, he would run up to the top of it. It somehow pleased him to get on the top of the sand-hills ; but one day an Abrek saw him, and shot at him, and killed him. Oh! those Abreks shoot very well when they have a rest for their guns—even better than I do. I don't like it when they kill a fellow. But I say, sometimes, when I look at your soldiers, I wonder at them. How stupid they are ! They go straight on, all in a crowd ; and, what's more, they wear red collars to their tunics. It is just like running into danger. One of them is killed and falls, and they drag him off, and another takes his place. What folly !" repeated the old man, shaking his head. "Why don't they separate, each one by himself ? That is the best way to manage ; it is much more reasonable. You do like that, and you won't get wounded."

"I am much obliged to you. Good-bye, uncle ! God grant we shall see each other again !" said Olenin, as he rose up and went out on to the steps.

The old Cossack remained seated on the floor. "Is that the way to bid good-bye ?" he said. "Oh! what kind of people do you belong to ? We have kept company together for a whole year—and now, good-bye—and you go off so. Come, now, I love you : you don't know how I pity you. You are so sad : you are all alone, alone. Somehow or other nobody loves you. Sometimes I can't sleep, thinking of you, and I feel so sorry for you ! As the song says, ' It is sad, dear brother, to live in a foreign land.' It is just so with you."

"Well, good-bye!" said Olenin again.

The old man rose up, and held out his hand. The yunker clasped it, and wished to go.

"No, give me your head. Here, your head!" said Uncle Eroshka; and then taking Olenin's head between his hands, he kissed him three times, with moist moustaches and lips, and burst into tears. "I love you! Good-bye!"

Olenin took his seat in the cart, which was waiting.

"Well, are you going off like that? You might make me a present, just out of remembrance, father. Give me a gun, you have got two," said the old man, still shedding tears.

Olenin took one of his guns and handed it to him.

"What! Are you giving that gun to the old fellow?" exclaimed Vanusha. "He never has enough. He is a regular old beggar. These people are never satisfied," he added, as he buttoned up his coat, and sat down on the front-seat.

"Shut your mouth, hog!" cried the old man, laughing. "It is evident you are a stingy fellow."

At this moment Marianka came out of the cottage, glanced indifferently at the post-cart, and, making a slight bow, went into an out-house.

"The girl," said Vanusha, in French, with a wink, and a stupid laugh.

"Let us be off!" retorted Olenin, angrily.

"Good-bye, father! Good-bye. I shall remember you," cried the old Cossack.

As Olenin drove away, he looked round once. Uncle Eroshka was talking with Marianka, evidently about his own affairs; and neither he nor the girl gave the yunker a last glance.

END OF "THE COSSACKS"

THE PRISONER OF
THE CAUCASUS

CHAPTER I

AN officer, named Jiline, who was serving in the
army of the Caucasus, received one day a letter
from his mother, in which she wrote :—" I am now old,
and I should like to see my beloved son again before
I die. Come and say ' Good-bye ' to me, and put me
away under the ground, and then, God willing, you
will be able to return to your duties. I have found
a wife for you. She is good and sensible, and does
not lack means. If you like her, you will be able to
retire from the army, and remain with us for the
rest of your days."

Jiline pondered over his mother's letter. " Yes,"
he thought, " my mother is certainly getting far
advanced in years. If I don't go now, perhaps I may
never see her again. I will go, and I will marry
this girl she has chosen for me, if I like her. Why
shouldn't I, indeed ? "

He obtained leave of absence from his colonel, bade
his brother officers' good-bye, gave his men four kegs
of vodka, and made ready to set off.

Hostilities were then being carried on in the
Caucasus. The roads were dangerous, not only at
night, but also during the day. If any Russian
strayed away from the fortress, the Tartars either killed

him or carried him off to the mountains. Twice a week parties of travellers were escorted by troops through the country which separated the Russian fortresses, and travellers were always placed in the midst of the escort.

It was the summer-time. A body of travellers having assembled outside the fortifications, the troops who were to accompany them took up their positions in the van and in the rear of the carriages, and the party then started. Jiline was on horseback, and the carriage containing his baggage formed part of the caravan. A distance of twenty-five versts was to be covered that day, but the *oboze** only made slow progress, for delay was frequently caused by the soldiers coming to a halt, by a wheel breaking down, or by the restiveness of a horse which had to be restrained—all things which necessitated the temporary stoppage of the whole party.

The sun had already accomplished half of his day's course when the oboze had scarcely traversed half of the appointed distance. The dust and heat were excessive, and the travellers had no means of either sheltering or refreshing themselves. Their way lay over a perfectly barren steppe ; there was not a single tree, nor even bush, along the whole line of route. Jiline, who was riding in front of the oboze, kept halting from time to time to enable his travelling companions to come up with him. At length, however, he grew impatient, and he began to wonder whether it would not be preferable to risk going the rest of the stage alone to enduring these wearisomely frequent stoppages.

" I have a good horse," he said to himself, " and if I happen to meet any Tartars I shall be able to escape them."

Then he checked his horse again, and began to consider the question seriously. Should he push on alone, or should he continue to submit to these

---

* The caravan, or travelling party.

continual delays ? Another officer, who, like Jiline, was also on horseback, now spurred his animal forward and joined the young man. This officer, who was named Kostiline, carried a gun slung behind his back. He was a stout, heavy man, with a red face, down which the perspiration was streaming.

" Let us push on by ourselves, Jiline," he said, as he came up. " I'm almost dying with heat and hunger."

Jiline reflected for a moment. " Is your gun loaded ? " he asked.

" Yes."

" Very well, then, let us push on ; but on one condition, and that is that we keep together."

They now rode forward, chatting together as they made their way over the steppe, and glancing round about them. They could see for a great distance. When they had crossed the steppe, however, the road was shut in between two hills.

" We must climb that hill," said Jiline to his companion, " and reconnoitre the neighbourhood, or else we may be surprised at some turn in the road."

" What is there to reconnoitre ? " replied Kostiline. " Come along ! "

Jiline, however, would not agree to this. He proceeded to ascend one of the hills. His horse, which he had selected out of a troop of colts and bought for a hundred roubles, was a thorough-bred hunter. It was full of spirit, and had been well trained by its master. In a few moments it brought Jiline to the crest of the hill, and almost as soon as he began to look round him, he caught sight of some thirty Tartars on horseback, scarcely a deciatine away. He at once turned his horse's head, but the Tartars had already observed him, and started in pursuit of him, brandishing their guns. Jiline fled down the hill as quickly as his horse could carry him.

" Look to your gun at once ! " he cried to Kostiline. He himself was reckoning for safety on his horse's speed.

" Now, my pet," he said mentally, " carry me well, and don't stumble, or I'm lost. If I can only reach Kostiline and his gun, they shan't have me."

Kostiline, however, instead of waiting for his comrade, rode as quickly as his horse could carry him in direction of the fortress. He lashed his steed so vigorously, now on one side and now on the other, that amidst the cloud of dust which rose up nothing but a flying saddle and a waving tail could be distinguished.

Jiline then realised that he was in a situation of great peril. There was no chance of any assistance from Kostiline's gun, and he felt that he could not do much with only his sabre to help him. He now turned his horse's head in the direction of the caravan, and tried to save himself by flight. Six of the Tartars however, had already reached the hill by a cross-cut, and intercepted his retreat. Jiline's horse was a good one, but the Tartar's were better, and they had gained further upon him by riding across the slope of the hill. Jiline then tried to turn his horse round, but the animal was galloping on so furiously that he could not check it, and was thus carried straight on to the Tartars. One of the latter, a red-bearded man, mounted on a grey horse, was posted in front of his companions. He gave a loud shout, showing his teeth, as he cocked his gun.

" I know you, you demons ! " cried Jiline. " If you take me, you will put me in a hole and flog me with your knouts. But you shall never take me alive ! "

Jiline was a lightly built man but a brave one. He drew his sabre and spurred his horse forward against the red-bearded Tartar. " I will either crush you beneath my horse, or I will hew you down with my sabre," he thought.

Just at this moment, however, several guns were discharged, and Jiline's horse fell. The young officer's leg was caught beneath it and held fast. He made an effort to release himself, but before he could do so, a couple of stinking Tartars seized hold of him and proceeded to tie his hands behind his back. He then made a sudden spring and overturned the two Tartars; however, three others had by this time dismounted, and they beat the young officer over the head with sticks. Then his sight began to fail him, and he tottered forward, whereupon the Tartars seized him again, took some ropes from their saddles, fastened them to his wrists, and dragged him towards their horses. They next snatched off his cap, pulled off his boots, rifled his pockets, took away his money and his watch, and tore his clothes. Jiline glanced in the direction of his horse and saw the poor animal lying on its side, struggling and kicking in its vain efforts to get on to its legs again. A stream of dark-coloured blood was pouring out of a great hole in its head, and the dusty road was steeped in the gore for more than an archin's distance.

A Tartar now went up to the horse and took off its saddle. The poor animal still continued to struggle, and the man drew his dagger and cut its throat. A gurgling sound was heard; the horse gave a convulsive spring, and finally fell down stiff and motionless. Then the Tartars removed the rest of the trappings, after which they hoisted Jiline up on to the red-bearded man's saddle, fastening him to it with a leather strap so as to keep him from falling, and at last carried him off with them to the mountains.

Jiline lurched backwards and forwards, and at every moment his face kept striking against the Tartar's stinking back. He could see nothing in front of him except this broad back, surmounted by brawny shoulders and clean shaven bluish head, covered with a sheepskin cap.

Jiline's head was dreadfully bruised and the blood trickled down over his eyes. However, he was not able either to settle himself into a moderately comfortable position on the saddle, or to wipe away the blood which was blinding him. His hands were bound so tightly that the cords cut into his flesh.

In this fashion the troop travelled on from one mountain to another; and finally, after fording a river, they came out upon the high-road, at a spot where it passed between two hills.

Jiline tried to see where he was being taken, but his eyelids were now glued down by the flowing blood, and he could not move in the slightest degree. The night fell. The troop crossed another stream, and then ascended a stony mountain. At last some rising smoke was seen, and the barking of dogs could be heard. They had reached an *aoul*.*

The Tartars now dismounted, while several children ran up and surrounded Jiline, throwing stones at him, and breaking out into cries of glee as they did so. However, the Tartars drove the children away, took Jiline off the horse, and summoned a serving-man.

He came up when he heard himself called. He was a Nogaï, with projecting cheek-bones, and wore merely a pair of trousers and a ragged shirt, through which his naked breast could be seen. The Tartars said something to him, whereupon he went away, returning again almost immediately with two pieces of wood, to which were attached iron rings, furnished with locks. They now unbound Jiline, put his legs through the rings, secured the locks, and then thrust the young officer into a shed, and locked the door upon him.

Jiline fell down upon a heap of horse's litter, where he lay for some time without moving; but at last he began to grope about in the dark, and when he had succeeded in finding a spot where the straw was more plentiful, he stretched himself at full length upon it.

---

* A Tartar village.

CHAPTER II

THE young officer had no sleep that night, and the nights were very short at that time of the year. When he saw the day breaking through a chink in the boards he rose up, widened the chink with his fingers, and looked out. He could see a road winding down from a mountain. On the right there was a *saklia** between two trees. A black dog was lying by the door ; and an ewe, accompanied by its lambs, was roaming up and down, flicking its tail. Then Jiline observed a Tartar girl coming down the mountain. She wore a coloured shirt, a pair of trousers, a belt and boots. Her head was covered with a caftan, on which there was a cross of silvered iron. She walked along with a waddling gait, holding by the hand a little Tartar child, who had a shaved head and wore nothing but a shirt.

The young girl entered the saklia. Just at that moment the red-bearded Tartar came out of it. He was enveloped in a silk *bechmett*.† His dagger was attached to a silver belt. His stockingless feet were encased in shoes, a high sheepskin cap was set upon his head. He stretched himself, stroked his short red beard, stood still for a moment or two, then gave an order to a servant and walked away.

Two children on horseback now rode up to the horse-pond. Other children, all with shorn heads and wearing nothing but shirts, came up and approached the shed. They got a long stick and pushed it through the chink in the wall. Jiline shouted out, and the children then scampered off as fast as they could, screaming loudly. All that Jiline could see of them was their knees gleaming in the sun.

---

* A Tartar hut. † A long Oriental mantle.

The young officer now felt terribly thirsty; his throat was quite parched. "Why don't they come to me?" he wondered.

Suddenly he heard the door of the shed open. Then the red-bearded Tartar made his appearance, accompanied by a short brown man. The short brown man's eyes were black and gleaming; his complexion was bright, his beard was carefully trimmed, and his face had a pleasant, smiling expression. He was more richly clad than his companion. His blue silk bechmett was decked with lace, and at his waist he carried a large silver dagger. Over a pair of shoes of red, delicate leather, ornamented with silver embroidery, he wore another stronger pair. His big astrakhan cap was white.

As the red bearded Tartar entered the shed he began to speak in words which Jiline could not understand, but which sounded like threats and abuse. Leaning against the wall, he began to finger his dagger, and cast a wolf-like glance at the young officer. The little dark man, whose movements were as jerky and as lively as though he were full of springs, now approached Jiline, and, squatting down in front of him, smiled, patted the young man's shoulder, and muttered a few wards in his own language. Then, winking his eye and clucking his tongue, he began to speak in a spasmodic sort of way.

"A fine *Ourous*,"* he remarked.

Jiline did not understand him, however. "Give me something to drink," he said; "I want something to drink."

The little dark man continued his clucking. "A fine Ourous!" he repeated.

Jiline then raised his hands to his lips, and tried to make them understand that he was thirsty. The Tartar understood, and smiled. He went to the door and called out: "Dina!"

A young girl now ran up. She was thin, indeed

---

* Tartar for "a Russian."

scranny, and seemed about thirteen years old. From her striking resemblance to the little dark man, it was easy to see that she was his daughter. She had the same bright black eyes, and her face was a pleasant one. She wore a long blue chemise with large sleeves, ungirded by any belt, but trimmed with red at the breast and cuffs. She also wore a pair of drawers, and her thin shoes were protected by an outer pair of high-heeled ones. Round her neck there was a circlet composed entirely of Russian half-roubles. Her head was uncovered, and a long tress of black hair, knotted with a ribbon, to which a few metal ornaments and a silver rouble were attached, hung down over her back.

Her father said a few words to her, and she went away, returning shortly with a small jug of silvered iron. She handed this jug to Jiline, and then, quickly squatting down, in such a fashion that her knees were higher than her shoulders, she watched him drink, opening her big eyes widely, as though some strange wild beast were before her.

When Jiline, after his draught, held the jug towards her, she bounded back like a wild kid. Her father, however, broke out into a laugh, and then gave her some order. Then she took up the jug and ran out of the shed, returning almost immediately with some unfermented bread on a wooden platter. Then she again squatted down and gazed earnestly at the prisoner.

The Tartars at length went away, locking the door upon Jiline. Shortly afterwards the Nogaï came into the shed.

" Up ! master, up ! " he said to Jiline, in Tartar. He knew no more Russian than the others did.

Jiline guessed, however, that the Nogaï bade him get up and follow him. So he left the shed, limping along, on account of his shackled legs, and as he reached the threshold he saw before him a Tartar vilage, consisting of half a score of huts and a tower-shaped minaret. Some children were holding three saddled horses near one of the huts, from which the dark Tartar emerged, and motioned with his hand to Jiline to enter. Then, still chattering in his own language and smiling, he went inside again, and Jiline followed him.

The room in which the young officer now found himself was well and comfortably furnished. The walls were washed with yellow ochre. Several feather beds of different colours were piled up at the end of the room, and on the side-walls some richly-worked tapestry was suspended. Over this tapestry were hung sabres, guns, and pistols, all mounted in silver, while in a recess in a corner of the room there was a small stove.

The hardened earth, which formed the only flooring, was scrupulously clean. One corner was covered with a piece of felt, upon which a carpet was laid, and upon this carpet were cushions stuffed with feathers. Five Tartars, amongst whom were the little dark man and the one with the red beard, sat leaning their backs against the feather cushions. In front of them were some round wooden platters containing a sort of pancake made from millet, with cups of melted butter, and a jug of *bouza*, the Tartar beer. They all ate with their fingers.

The little dark man rose up and ordered Jiline to take a place apart from the others, not on a carpet, but on the bare ground. Then he resumed his seat, and invited his guests to help themselves to the pancakes and bouza. The Nogaï assisted Jiline to the place which had been assigned to him, took off his shoes, placed them near the door by the side of those belonging to the guests, and then seated himself on the felt by his master, whom he watched eating, with lips which watered with hungry desire.

When the Tartars had finished their pancakes, a woman, dressed just like Dina, came in and took away the butter. She returned, carrying a big pail, and a jug with a narrow neck. The men first washed the butter-grease off their hands, and then fell on their knees, puffing and wheezing, and began to say their prayers. After this, they mumbled amongst themselves for a moment or two, and then one of them addressed Jiline in Russian.

" It was Kazi-Mohammed," he said, pointing to the red-bearded man, " who took you. He has given you to Abdul-Mourad."

Then, pointing to the little dark man, he added : " This is he who is now your master."

Jiline remained silent.

Abdul-Mourad now said something in his own language, ending with the remark : " Good Ourous ! Soldier Ourous ! "

The interpreter then began to translate what had been said. " He orders you," said he, " to write home and request your ransom to be sent. As soon as the money comes, you will be set at liberty."

Jiline reflected for a moment. " Will the ransom be a heavy one ? " he asked. " How much will be required ? "

The Tartars again consulted amongst themselves, and then the interpreter translated their reply. " Three thousand pieces," he said.

" It is quite impossible for me to pay that sum," replied Jiline.

Abdul then rose up, and with a deal of lively gesticulation began to speak to Jiline, as though the latter were able to understand him.

" How much can you give ? " now resumed the interpreter.

" Five hundred roubles," replied Jiline, after having considered the matter.

Upon hearing this answer, the Tartars all began to speak together. Abdul raved at the red-bearded man, and screamed so loudly that his lips grew covered with foam. The red-bearded man, however, remained perfectly unmoved. He closed his eyes and clucked his tongue. At length they all grew silent once more, and the interpreter again addressed Jiline.

" That is not sufficient," he said. " Abdul, your

M

master, will not be satisfied with that. He has paid two hundred roubles for you to Kazi-Mohammed, who was indebted to him in that sum. He cannot give you your liberty for less than three thousand roubles. If you don't write for them, you will be put into a hole and flogged with a knout."

"Well," said Jiline to himself, "with fellows like these, the more one seems afraid, the worse it is for one;" and so he sprang up sharply on to his feet.

"Tell this dog," he exclaimed to the interpreter, "that if he thinks he's going to frighten me, he shall not have a single copeck, for I will not write. I'm not afraid of you, dogs that you are, and I never shall be!"

The interpreter translated this speech to the Tartars, who all began to talk together again.

After chattering for some considerable time, the little dark man rose up once more, and approached Jiline. "Ourous," he said; "djiguit, djiguit Ourous."

In the Tartar language "djiguit" means brave.

Still continuing to laugh, Abdul next said a few words to the interpreter: "Give a thousand roubles," now translated the latter.

But Jiline would not give way. "I will not give more than five hundred roubles; and if you kill me, you will get nothing at all."

The Tartars again began to talk together. Then they gave an order to the Nogaï, who left the room while the others resumed their conversation, glancing alternately at Jiline and the door.

The servant came back, accompanied by a stout man. This latter had bare feet, and his legs were shackled like Jiline's. The young officer immediately recognised him as his companion Kostiline. They placed Kostiline beside his comrade, and the two officers related their adventures to each other, whilst the Tartars watched them in silence. Kostiline told Jiline that his horse had stumbled, and that his gun had missed fire, and that it was Abdul who had taken him prisoner.

Abdul now got up, and, pointing to Kostiline, said a few words, which the interpreter proceeded to translate.

" You both belong to the same master," he said. " The one who pays his ransom first will be liberated first. You are very headstrong," he continued, addressing himself to Jiline. " Your comrade is more sensible, and has already written for five thousand pieces to be sent to him. He will be well treated in consequence."

" My comrade acts as he thinks best," replied Jiline ; " perhaps he is a rich man, but I am not. As far as I am concerned, it will be as I have said. Kill me, if you like, but if you do so you will get nothing at all. I shall not send for more than five hundred roubles."

There was now an interval of silence. Then Abdul suddenly rose up from his seat, produced a little casket, from which he took a pen, some paper, and some ink, and handed them to Jiline, tapping the young man on the shoulder and signing him to write. He accepted the five hundred roubles.

" Wait a moment," said Jiline to the interpreter. " First of all make him understand that we expect to be well fed and well clothed, and to be allowed the pleasure of each other's society. And, moreover," he added in conclusion, pointing to his shackles, " we must be freed from these lumps of wood."

Then he looked at Abdul and smiled. Abdul replied, with an answering smile : " I will give you a *tcherkeska*,"* he said, upon hearing Jiline's words translated, " and some boots. You shall live together as though you were a married couple. I will feed you like princes, and you shall occupy the same shed. But I cannot take off the shackles, for if I did you would escape. They can only be removed during the night."

---

* A long coat.

Then he again stepped up to Jiline and tapped him on the shoulder. " You, good fellow," he said; " I good, too." Jiline wrote his letter, but inscribed a fictitious address upon it so that it should never be delivered. " I will manage to escape somehow or other," he thought.

The prisoners were then removed to a hut, where they were supplied with some maize straw, bread and water, a couple of old tcherkeskas, and some old and sadly worn boots, which had probably been taken from the bodies of slain soldiers. At night-fall the shackles were removed from their legs, and the door of the shed was locked.

CHAPTER III

FOR a month Jiline and his comrade lived in this fashion in captivity. Their master always had a laughing expression on his face when he came to see them

" You, Ivan, are good fellow ; I, Abdul, am good fellow too," he kept repeating ; although he only allowed his prisoners very spare diet. He gave them nothing but unfermented bread made of millet-flour baked into cakes, the very crust of which was often quite soft from lack of sufficient cooking.

Kostiline had written home a second time. He was longing for his money to arrive, and was growing sick at heart. For whole days he never stirred out of the shed, but spent his time in sleeping and counting the hours. On the other hand, Jiline, who knew that his letter could not have reached its address, had not taken the trouble to write again.

" Where could my mother find the money for my ransom ? " he asked himself. " She depends upon what I send her for the greater part of her livelihood. It would absolutely ruin her to get those five hundred roubles together. No, God helping me, I'll contrive to get myself out of this, somehow."

He occupied his time wandering about the aoul, reconnoitring, asking questions, and spying about for some means of escape. When he was not out doing this, he occupied himself in making clay dolls, or in weaving rushes, for he could turn his hand to anything.

One day he carved a doll, dressed it in a Tartar shirt, and stuck it on the roof of the shed. Dina observed it, and called out to the young girls who were passing by, on their way to fetch some water.

They all put their pitchers down, and laughed admiringly at it. Jiline then took it down and offered it to them. They all continued to laugh, but they did not venture to approach and take it, so Jiline set it on the ground, and retiring into the hut, waited to see what would happen.

Dina now ran up, glanced around her, and then seized the doll and hurried away with it.

Early the next morning she was to be seen on the threshold of her father's saklia, carrying and rocking the doll, which she had dressed in some bright-coloured rags. An old woman, however, came out, and after scolding the girl, snatched the doll away from her, broke it, and sent Dina off to work.

Jiline now made a still prettier doll and offered it to Dina.

One day the young girl came to the hut with a little pitcher, and, squatting down before him, smilingly signed that it was for himself. "Why does she look so gay?" wondered Jiline.

He took a draught from the pitcher, thinking that it contained water. It was milk, however. "That is very good!" he exclaimed, as he finished drinking.

Dina seemed transported with joy. "It is good, Ivan, it is good!" she cried. Then she abruptly sprang up, clapped her hands, snatched the pitcher from Jiline's grasp, and ran off.

From that time forward she brought him some milk every day in secret. Sometimes the Tartars made cheeses from the milk of their sheep, and upon those occasions Dina always managed to bring some to her new friend. One day when the master had killed a sheep the girl brought the young man a piece of the meat concealed in her sleeve. She threw it down before him, and then ran off. On another occasion, there was a violent storm, and the rain fell in torrents for some hours. The little streams became swollen, and rushed along violently, so that in spots where, as a rule, one had not the slightest difficulty in crossing, the water was now three archins in depth, and the current so strong that it swept heavy stones along with it ; the torrents roaring downwards with a noise which was increased a hundred-fold by the many echoes of the mountains.

When the storm was over, several pools of water were left in the village. Jiline asked his master for a knife, and then he carved a little boat out of a piece of wood. He attached to it a wheel made of feathers, and placed two little dolls inside it. The young girls brought him some rags with which he dressed these dolls, one of which was made to represent a moujik, and the other a baba. Then Jiline placed his boat in a little stream, and the wheel began to turn, and the dolls to dance. All the village quickly crowded around : the children, the babas, and the men all ran up, chuckling and crying out : " Aï, Ourous ! aï Ivan ! "

On another occasion Jiline had noticed in Abdul's hut a watch of Russian manufacture which was completely out of order. " Give it to me, and I will set it right for you," he said to his master.

Then he took the watch to pieces with the aid of a pen-knife. He put it together again, and it went all right. Abdul was so delighted with this that he gave

Jiline his old bechmett, which was all in rags. The young officer, however, thought that he might just as well accept the gift. "It will come in usefully to cover myself with at night time," he thought.

Jiline soon won the reputation of being able to do anything, and people came from the most distant villages to see him. One person would bring him a gun which required repairing, another would bring a pistol, and another a watch. His master provided him with a pair of pincers, a gimlet, and a file. Once even, when a Tartar fell ill, his relations came to Jiline and asked for his help, and the young man, who knew absolutely nothing about medicine, at once promised assistance. "Perhaps the sick man will get well again of his own accord," he thought to himself.

Then he retired into his shed, took up some earth and ashes, and mixed them with water. He muttered a few words over the muddy mixture and gave it to the invalid, who swallowed it ; and it very fortunately chanced that he quickly got well again.

Jiline now began to understand the language of the district a little ; and such of the Tartars as had grown familiar with him addressed him simply as " Ivan." The others, however, still continued to look askance at him. He was no favourite, for instance, with the red-bearded Tartar ; whenever the latter saw him, his face darkened, and he either turned away or else cowardly abused him.

Amongst the Tartars there was one old man who was not an inhabitant of the aoul. His saklia stood at the foot of the mountain, and Jiline only saw him whenever he came to the village mosque to say his prayers. This old fellow was short ; he wore a cap covered with a tchalma—a piece of white linen—and his short beard and moustache were as snow-white as swan's-down. His face, which was covered with wrinkles, was of a brick-red colour ; his nose was curved like a kite's beak, and there was a wicked expression in his grey eyes. Of his teeth, only a couple of the canine ones remained. As he passed along, with his tchalma-adorned cap on his head, and supporting himself on a thick staff, he looked about him with the glance of a hungry wolf; and whenever he caught sight of Jiline he turned away and began to mutter.

One day Jiline walked in the direction of the mountain to see the house where this old man dwelt. As he went down a sloping path, he espied a little garden enclosed by a stone wall. Behind the wall there was some cherry, peach, and apricot trees, and a saklia with a flat roof. As Jiline approached still nearer he noticed some straw hives round which the bees were humming. He then raised himself on the tips of his toes to get a better view, and, as he did so, the shackles on his legs clattered somewhat noisily. The old man, who was in his garden, thereupon turned round, and when he saw Jiline he utter a shout, drew his pistol from his girdle, and fired at the young officer. Jiline had only just time to slip behind a big pear tree for refuge.

Furious with anger, the old man went to complain to Jiline's master. Abdul summoned his prisoner before him, and, still smiling as usual, he asked him why he had looked over the wall.

" I had no intention of wronging the old man in any sort of way. I merely wanted to see how he lived," replied the young officer.

The old man, who was fuming with anger, showed his two canine teeth, and said something in a hissing voice, while he pointed with his hand towards Jiline. The young man understood that he was asking Abdul either to kill him or to send him away from the aoul.

After giving vent to his rage, the old fellow finally returned home; and then Jiline asked his master who this very violent tempered person might be.

" He is a man of great importance," replied Abdul. " He was our chief djiguit. In past times he killed many Russians, and he used to be very rich, and had three wives and eight sons. They all lived together in the same aoul. One day, however, the Russians came, destroyed the village, and slew seven of his sons, The eighth, the only survivor, went over to their side. The old man then surrendered himself to the foe, and pretended to give them his allegiance. For three months he lived in their midst ; then he came across his son, killed him, and fled away. He has never fought since then, but he made a pilgrimage to Mecca to pray to Allah. That's the reason why he is entitled to wear the tchalma on his head, for every one who has been to Mecca is a hadji and wears the tchalma. He hates you Russians, and he has asked me to kill you. But I can't do that. I have paid hard cash for you ; and, besides that, I have grown very fond of you, Ivan, and not only I won't kill you, but I would not even let you go away, if I had not given my word to do so."

Then he began to laugh, repeating several times over in Russian : " You, Ivan, good fellow ; I, Abdul, good fellow, too."

CHAPTER IV

JILINE continued living in this way for another month. In the daytime he wandered about in the aoul, or devoted himself to some kind of work. When night fell, and everything became quiet, he excavated soil at the foot of the wall of his shed. The number of stones made the work very laborious, and he was often obliged to employ his file. In time, however, he succeeded in making a hole large enough to give passage to a man's body.

" Now I must reconnoitre the country, so as to be

able to know which way to steer my course," he said to himself. "But I am afraid there's no one who would give me any information."

One day in the afternoon, when his master was absent, he strolled off to the outskirts of the aoul, and then he began to ascend the mountain to obtain a view of the neighbourhood. Abdul, who had gone off on an expedition, had told one of his children to keep a watch on Jiline, and to follow him wherever he went. So, when the child saw the direction the young officer was taking, he called out to him : "You mustn't go up there! my father has forbidden it. If you don't come back I shall go and call the others."

Thereupon Jiline began to argue with him. "I'm only going a little way," he said. "I'm just going up there, that's all. I'm looking for a herb I want to find for some medicine. Come with me. I can't escape, you know, with these shackles on my legs. I will make you a bow and some arrows to-morrow."

The child agreed, and they set off together.

From the foot of the mountain it did not seem a difficult thing to reach the summit, but Jiline found that it was really no easy matter, especially with his shackled ankles.

When he reached the top, he sat down and looked round him. Southward, behind the shed, he saw a road running between two hills. A flock of sheep was passing along it. Quite low down there was another aoul, and behind this aoul came another mountain, far more precipitous than the one upon which Jiline was sitting : and then, again, behind that one, there was another. Between the two mountains lay a dark-looking wood. Farther away there were other heights rising up, one after another, till they faded away on the horizon.

Several of the mountains were covered with snow and had peaks as white as sugar-loaves. One of them, shaped like a conical cap, rose high above all the others and stood out clearly from the rest of the chain. To the east and west, on each side that Jiline gazed at, did the mountains rise up, and here and there smoke of aouls ascended from the valleys between them.

" I am in the midst of a hostile country," thought Jiline.

He now turned and looked in yet another direction. Far away in the distance he could espy a little river and a village surrounded by gardens. Some babas, who looked very small in the far distance, were washing their linen on the banks of the stream. Behind this village, also, there rose a mountain. Then, further away still, there stretched some forests. Between two mountains there lay a bluish smooth plain, which looked like a drift of smoke lying on the ground.

To assist him in taking his bearings, Jiline recalled the position of the rising sun as he had seen it from the fortress where he had been quartered. He fancied that there must be a Russian fortress on the plain that he saw before him ; and, accordingly, he considered it was in that direction that he must steer his course.

The sun was now sinking. The snow-white mountains were assuming a purple tinge, and the black ones were growing still darker and gloomier. A mist began to rise up from the valleys, and the plain where Jiline thought there must be a Russian fortress glowed brightly in the setting sun. The young officer strained his eyes, and he fancied he could see some little columns of smoke rising up as though they were proceeding from chimneys. This strengthened his conviction that the fortress lay in that direction. It was already late and the mollah had summoned the faithful to their prayers. The flocks were wending their way home, and the cattle could be heard lowing. Several times already had the child requested Jiline to return to the aoul, but the young officer could not tear himself away from the view he was contemplating. At last, however, he consented to return.

" I now know which way I must take," he thought to himself.

He determined to put his project into execution before another day dawned. It happened that the approaching night would be quite moonless. Unfortunately, however, the Tartars were to return that evening from their expedition. As a rule, they returned with a great many noisy demonstrations of delight, especially when they brought back a drove of cattle. That day, however, they brought no booty with them ; and, what was worse, they had lost one of their party, one of the brothers of the red-bearded man, who had been killed in a skirmish. They were all greatly excited, and began to prepare for the dead man's burial.

Jiline left his shed and went out to look on. The Tartars had wrapped the corpse in a linen covering. Using no bier, they carried it outside the aoul, and laid it on the grass beneath a plane-tree. Then the mollah came. The old men, wearing their turbans, clustered together, took off their shoes, and squatted down in a single line in front of the body. In front stood the mollah. Behind him were three old men, and behind these came all the other Tartars. For a long time they remained thus in silence, Then the mollah raised his head. " Allah ! " he exclaimed.

Then he abruptly relapsed into silence, and everyone remained perfectly still for another considerable space of time. At last the mollah raised his head again.

" Allah ! "

" Allah ! " repeated all the others, and then they once more relapsed into silence.

The corpse, which lay stiff and rigid beneath its linen covering, was not more motionless than the mourners. There was not a sound to be heard save the rustling of the leaves of the plane-tree. The mollah next said a prayer. Then the Tartars took the corpse in their arms and carried it towards a grave which was not excavated vertically, after the ordinary custom, but horizontally, like a sort of cave.

The Tartars took the body up by the arm-pits, bent it double, and then pushed it into the cave, crossing the arms over the breast. The Hogaï then brought some freshly cut reeds, and the mouth of the grave was covered with them. Then some earth was thrown in and smoothed over; a huge stone being set up against the spot where the dead man's head rested. Finally the whole party clustered round the grave, squatting down and keeping perfect silence for a time

"Allah! Allah! Allah!" they all cried, after a long pause, and then they all arose.

The red-bearded Tartar, who was named Kazi, next gave some money to the old men. Then he struck his brow three times with his whip and went off to his own house.

On the following morning the red-bearded Tartar took a mare, and, followed by three other Tartars, led it behind the aoul. When they had got outside the village, he took off his bechmett, turned up his sleeves, drew out his poniard with his muscular hands, and sharpened it. The other Tartars raised the mare's head. Kazi stepped up to it, cut its throat, and then, throwing it on its side, began to flay it. Some women and young girls then came up and washed the animal's intestines. Then they cut them into small pieces and carried them into the red-bearded man's saklia. The whole village assembled in his dwelling to pay honour to the deceased. During three days they ate the mare's flesh and drank bouza, and during these three days not a single Tartar left the aoul.

On the fourth evening Jiline saw them making preparations for a journey. The horses were brought out; and half a score of men, among whom was the Tartar with the red beard, rode off. Abdul remained in the village. The moon was still young, and the nights were gloomy.

"I must make a start to-night," thought Jiline to

himself, and thereupon he revealed his plan to Kostiline, who seemed more frightened than otherwise.

"How is it possible for us to escape? We don't know which way to go," he said.

"Yes, I do."

"But the nights are not long enough for us to get out of reach before morning."

"Well, we will make a halt in the forest. I have secreted some cakes. What good will you get by stopping here? If the money comes, you may be all right; but if your people cannot get it together, what then? The Tartars are very fierce just now; our people have killed one of them, and I have heard some talk of their avenging his death upon us."

Kostiline reflected for a moment or two. "Very well," he said, "let us have a try."

CHAPTER V

JILINE increased the size of the hole to enable Kostiline to pass through it. Then they sat down and waited till they thought every one in the aoul would be asleep.

As soon as every sound had died away, Jiline made his way through the hole, and left the shed, telling Kostiline to follow him. The latter crept through in his turn, but, in doing so, he caught against a stone, which he loosened from the wall, and which fell down with a noisy clatter. Ouliachine, a very fierce dog belonging to Abdul, gave the alarm; and then all the other dogs in the aoul followed his example and began to bark.

Jiline had foreseen the possibility of some such accident as this, and had taken his precautions. He had made friends with Ouliachine by showing him some little kindnesses; and, accordingly, he now had merely to whistle to him and throw him a piece of cake, to induce him to become quiet.

However, Abdul had heard the barking as he lay in his saklia. "Hait! hait, Ouliachine!" he shouted, without coming out.

Jiline scratched the dog's ears, and Ouliachine rubbed himself against his friend's legs, and wagged his tail.

The fugitives sat down and waited for a moment or two. All was quiet again. No sound was to be heard save the snuffling of the sheep in their sheds, and, further away in the distance, the murmur of the stream as it flowed over the stones. The night was dark, and the stars seemed very high up in the heavens. The new moon was sinking behind the mountain. A mist, as white as milk, filled the valleys.

Jiline now rose to his feet. "Come, my friend, let us be off!" he said to his companion.

They started, but they had only taken a few steps when they heard the mollah's call sounding from the minaret—"Allah! Resmillah! Ilrakhman!" This meant that every one ought to repair at once to the mosque. The fugitives again halted, and sat down at the foot of a wall. For a long time they remained hiding themselves in this position, waiting until all the faithful had gone by. Then again everything became quiet and still.

"Let us try again once more, and may God help us!" thought the officers.

They crossed themselves and set off again. They passed through the farm-yard, made their way down towards the stream, which they crossed, and then entered the valley. The mist was thick, and lay low. Nothing could be seen excepting the stars, which served Jiline as guides, enabling him to steer his course. The air was fresh and pleasant for walking, but the fugitives were sorely troubled by their old boots. Jiline took his off, threw them away, and continued his journey with bare feet. He sprang from one stone to another, and kept glancing at the stars.

Kostiline followed him with pain and difficulty. "Don't go quite so quickly," he said. "These confounded boots have rubbed all the skin off my feet."

"Take them off, then; you'll get on much better without them," replied Jiline.

Kostiline then threw the boots away, and, like his companion, walked on with bare feet; however, he suffered still more pain than before. He cut his feet against some stones, and kept checking his companion's progress.

"Never mind about cutting your feet," remarked Jiline to him when he complained; "they will heal again; whereas, if we get caught, there's no saying what will happen."

Kostiline made no reply, but continued walking in the greatest pain. For a long time they went on in this manner; but suddenly they heard the barking of dogs on their right hand.

Jiline stopped, then he climbed a hillock and looked around him. "Ah! we have made a mistake," he said; "we have gone too far to the right. There is another aoul here; I have just seen it. We must turn back, and strike out towards that mountain on the left, where I fancy we shall find a forest."

"At any rate, let us take a moment's rest," groaned Kostiline. "Let me get my breath, my feet are streaming with blood."

"Oh, you'll soon get better, my friend," replied his companion. "Walk more lightly; like that! Come along!"

Jiline now went back in the direction from which they had come, at a running pace. Then he abruptly struck out to the left, towards the mountains. Kostiline in the meanwhile continually lagged behind, and never ceased groaning.

At last the fugitives reached the summit of the

mountain, and, as Jiline expected, came upon a forest. They forced their way through several dense thickets, which tore their clothes, and at length discovered a road. Suddenly, however, they heard a clattering. They then stood still and listened.

The sound seemed as though it were made by a horse. As soon as the fugitives halted, the noise ceased ; but immediately they began to walk again, the noise also sounded once more. Again they stopped, and again the noise ceased. Jiline then crept softly towards the road, where he caught sight of a gloomy form which looked like a horse, though it did not quite resemble one. Upon this horse, if it indeed it were a horse, there was something which did not look like a man.

" What can it be ? " said Jiline to himself.

He whistled softly. The shadowy creature gave a start, and then fled away like a hurricane amid a noisy smashing of branches. Kostiline had dropped down with fright.

" It is a stag ! " cried Jiline, laughing at him. " It is a stag ; don't you hear him crashing along with his horns ? We have frightened him quite as much as he frightened us."

They then proceeded on their way again. The daylight was now beginning to break ; but the two fugitives were quite uncertain as to whether they were really advancing in the direction of the Russian camp.

At last they came to a clearing where Kostiline sat down. " You can please yourself," he said, " but I shan't go a step further. I can't put one leg before another."

His companion tried to encourage him.

" No, indeed," replied Kostiline, " I am quite exhausted. I can go no further."

Jiline felt vexed, and began to reproach his comrade. " Very well, then," he ended by saying, " I shall go on by myself. Good-bye."

Kostiline, however, now sprang up briskly, and walked along.

They went on for another four versts in this manner. The mist had grown thicker; the surrounding country was quite invisible, and the stars could scarcely be seen. Suddenly they heard the sound of a horse's steps behind them. Jilne lay down on the ground and listened.

"It is a horseman coming towards us," he muttered.

They hastily left the road, and concealed themselves amongst the trees. Presently Jiline crept towards the road, and there he caught sight of a Tartar on horseback driving a cow before him, and muttering to himself. The Tartar passed on, and Jiline returned to his companion.

"God has saved us from being seen," he said. "Get up, and let us push on."

Kostiline tried to rise, but he fell down again immediately. "I can't go another yard; I swear to you that I can't. I have no strength left me," he moaned.

Jiline pulled him up roughly, whereupon he broke out into such a loud cry of pain, that his companion turned quite pale as he heard it. "Don't shout like that," he said. "The Tartar is still near, and he will hear us." Then, as though speaking to himself, he continued: "The poor fellow is quite done up; but I can't desert a comrade."

"Get up, and climb on to my shoulders," he resumed, speaking aloud again. "I will carry you, since you can't walk."

Then he assisted Kostiline on to his back.

"Hold on to my shoulders," he said, "but don't grip hold of my throat."

Jiline, too, was tired, and his feet were cut and bruised like Kostiline's. However, he stooped forward so that his comrade might be in a more comfortable and less fatiguing position, and then strode onward.

But the Tartar had heard Kostiline's cry, and the two fugitives were now alarmed by a shout behind them. It was the Tartar calling out in his own language. Jiline hastily dived into a thicket. The Tartar fired his gun in the direction which the two officers had taken, but, fortunately, he did not hit them. Then he shouted again, and finally trotted off.

"We are lost, my friend," said Jiline. "That dog will go and tell the other Tartars, and they will set out and pursue us. If we can't get over another three versts, we are lost!"

"The devil take me," he thought, "for having encumbered myself with this lump of a fellow! If I had been alone, I should have been far away by this time."

"Go on by yourself," now said Kostiline. "Why should your safety be imperilled on my account?"

"No, indeed," replied Jiline, "I can't desert a comrade."

He hoisted Kostiline on to his shoulders once more and struggled on for another verst, through a forest of which he could not see the end. The mist was now beginning to evaporate, and the stars were growing very pale; they were vanishing one by one. Jiline was almost exhausted.

They happened at last to come across a little spring which welled up near the road-side. Here Jiline stopped, and laid Kostiline down on the ground.

"We'll have a short rest here, and a drink," he said, "and then we will eat our cake. We must be nearly at our journey's end by this time, I should think."

Jiline had just stooped down to drink, when a noise like the sound of some one quickly approaching was heard. The two officers immediately sprang into a thicket, and lay down. Several Tartars could be heard talking together. They halted near the spring, and then, after a short deliberation, set their dogs loose. A rustling of branches made the two fugitives look round. They saw a dog standing in front of them. It began to bark.

The Tartars then came up, and perceived Jiline and Kostiline. They at once seized them, bound them with cords, and set them upon their horses. After the party had gone some three versts or so, Abdul made his appearance, accompanied by several other Tartars. He conversed for a few moments with the men who had recaptured his prisoners; then he ordered the latter to be transferred to his own horses, and returned with them to the aoul.

Abdul did not say a single word during the journey, and his habitual smile had vanished from his face. The party reached the village during the morning, and the prisoners were left in the street. The children clustered around them, shouting loudly, and amusing themselves by throwing stones at the prisoners, and lashing them with their whips.

At last the Tartars collected themselves in a circle, which the old hadji of the mountain joined, and began to deliberate. Some of them urged that the two officers ought to be sent further away among the mountains, while the old man advised that they should be put to death. Abdul, however, protested against this latter course. He had bought the prisoners, he said, and he was expecting to get their ransom, and did not wish to lose his money.

"They will never pay you anything," replied the old hadji, "and they will only bring us misfortune, for it is a sin to nourish a Russian. Those men ought to be killed."

The group now dispersed, and Abdul went up to Jiline.

"If I don't receive your ransom within a fortnight," he said to him, "I shall have you both flogged to death. If you try to escape again, I will kill you like dogs. Write another letter each of you, and see that you write proper ones."

Some paper was brought to the captives, and the

letters were written.   Then shackles were put upon their legs again, and they were led away behind the mosque.   Here a pit had been dug, five archins in depth, and into this pit the two prisoners were ordered to descend.

CHAPTER VI

THE prisoners' lives were now made much harder for them.   Their shackles were never removed, and they were no longer permitted to walk about. Pieces of half-baked bread were tossed down to them as though they were mere dogs, and water was lowered to them in a jug.   The hole in which they were confined was damp and malodorous.   Kostiline fell ill at once. His body swelled out, and he was racked with pain. He spent his whole time in groaning and sleeping. Jiline also was very low-spirited.   He realised the evil plight into which he had fallen, and saw little hope of eventual freedom.   He had commenced to make a tunnel, but he was troubled by his inability to conceal the soil which he scooped out ; and one morning Abdul noticed it, and threatened to kill him.

At last, one day while Jiline was squatting on the soil dreaming of escaping, a cake suddenly fell upon his knees then another, and then some cherries.   He raised his head and caught sight of Dina.   She looked at him with a smile and then ran off.

" Perhaps Dina might help me to escape ! " thought Jiline.

He cleared a little corner of the pit, collected some clay, and then set to work making dolls.   He modelled some men and horses and dogs.

" I will toss them up to her when she comes again," he said to himself.

Dina did not come the next day. Jiline heard the tramping of horses, and he caught sight of the Tartars assembling together near the mosque in animated consultation. They were talking about the Russians. The old hadji's voice could be heard above all the others. Jiline could not clearly distinguish what it was that they were discussing, but he guessed that the Russians were close at hand, and that the Tartars were deliberating as how they might best defend their aoul, and felt embarrassed on account of their prisoners.

The sound of the voices in discussion suddenly ceased. Then a slight rustling was heard. Jiline raised his head, and saw Dina squatting down, and with her head between her knees, bending forward so that her necklet hung over the pit. Her little eyes gleamed like stars. She took a couple of pieces of cheese from her sleeve, and threw them down to the officer.

" Why haven't you been before ? " Jiline asked her. " I have made you some playthings. Here they are. Catch them." Then he threw up, one after another, the little figures which he had modelled for her.

The girl, however, shook her head. " I don't want them," she said.

Then she remained silent for a moment, and appeared absorbed in thought. " They mean to kill you, Ivan," she suddenly exclaimed ; and she imitated the action of cutting a man's throat.

" Who means to kill me ? "

" My father. The old men have ordered him to do so. I am so sorry about it."

" If you are sorry," said Jiline, " get me a long pole." The girl made a sign that it was impossible.

Jiline clasped his hands together with a supplicating gesture. " Dina, my little Dina, I beseech you to get me a pole," he said.

" I can't ; they would see me from the house." And then she disappeared.

Jiline was absorbed in thought for the whole of the

evening. " What shall I do ? " he kept asking himself.

He looked up at the sky. It was quite calm and serene. The stars were already beginning to appear, but the moon had not yet risen. The mollah now ascended the minaret and summoned the faithful to prayers.

Jiline at last began to feel drowsy. He had given over hoping for Dina's return. Suddenly, however, some small pieces of clay fell on to his head, and roused him with a start. He raised his eyes to the mouth of the pit, and he saw a long pole coming down.

He joyfully seized hold of it and drew it towards him. It was a strong and substantial one, which he had noticed some days previously on the roof of Abdul's house. He looked up again. The stars were shining far aloft in the heavens. Over the edge of the pit, Dina's eyes were gleaming like a cat's. She stooped still further forward.

" Ivan ! Ivan ! " she said, in a low voice, and then she signed to the young officer to speak very softly.

" Well ? " he said.

" They have all gone away. There are only two men left in the aoul ! "

" Come, then, Kostiline," said the young man, turning to his comrade, " let us make a last attempt. I will help you on."

Kostiline, however, would not hear of another attempt to escape. " No," said he, " it is my destiny never to get away from this place. How could I possibly escape, I who haven't even the strength to turn round ? "

" Very well, good-bye, then."

Jiline kissed his comrade. Then he grasped hold of the pole, told Dina to hold it firmly, and began to climb up it. Twice he fell down, however, being hampered in his movements by his shackles. Finally he stood upon Kostiline's shoulders, and at last succeeded in gaining the mouth of the pit. Dina laid hold of the collar of his shirt and pulled him out with all the strength of her little hands, laughing with pleasure as she did so. Then Jiline drew up the pole.

" Take it back to its place again," he said to Dina ; " for if it were found here you would be beaten."

Dina then went off, dragging the pole after her, and Jiline made his way across the mountain. When he reached the valley, he took up a sharp stone and struck it against the lock of his shackles. The lock, however, was very strong, and he coul not break it.

Suddenly he heard some one coming down the mountain, and speaking. It was Dina.

" Give me the stone," she said, and then she dropped on to her knees and began to batter at the lock. But her little fingers were no thicker than twigs, and she threw down the stone and burst into tears.

The young man now again began to strike the lock with the energy of desperation. Dina stooped over him and kept her hand upon his shoulder. Jiline turned round, and saw a fiery glow in the heavens. It was caused by the moon which was just about to rise.

" I must get across the valley and into the forest before the moon is fully risen," he thought, and thereupon he rose to his feet, threw away the stone, and prepared to start on again with his legs still shackled. " Good-bye, Dinouchka," he said : " I shall never forget you as long as I live."

Dina detained him searching for his pockets, into which she put some cakes.

" Thank you, you thoughtful little creature," said the young man. " Who will make dolls for you now ? " he added, caressing the girl's head.

Dina, hiding her tearful face in her hands, sprang up the hill with the agility of a young kid. Amid the gloom nothing could be heard of her save the tinkling of the coins as they jingled together in her scanty hair.

Jiline crossed himself. Then he raised the lock of his shackles with his hand to prevent it from making a noise, and set out. He hurried along as quickly as his impeded legs would allow him to do, glancing every moment at the spot where the moon was on the point of rising. He clearly discerned which way he ought to take. He must go straight ahead for some eight versts; and it was absolutely necessary that he should gain the forest before the moon appeared. As he crossed the stream, the light was growing brighter behind the mountain. One side of the valley was brighter than the other, and the shade cast by the mountain was gradually disappearing.

Jiline kept carefully in the shadow as he pushed along. He made all haste he could, but the moon moved more quickly than he did. He could see it already appearing above the crest of the mountain, and just as he gained the forest, the full orb shone out brightly. Everything became as bright and clear as though it were daytime. Every leaf on the trees could be distinguished. The mountain stood wrapt in a bright and peaceful quietude, and a death-like silence reigned all around. Not a sound of any kind was to be heard, save the gentle murmur of the little stream as it flowed along through the valley.

Jiline entered the forest without having met any one. He found a shady spot, where he sat down to rest for a moment, and ate a cake. Then he looked about for a stone, and again began to batter at the lock, but he only bruised his hands, without succeeding in breaking it. At last he rose up and resumed his journey. By the time he had gone another verst he was quite exhausted, although he had halted every ten yards.

"What shall I do?" he thought. "I must drag myself onward as long as I have any strength left me, for if I once sit down I shall never be able to get up again. However, I shall certainly never reach the fortress to-night. I will rest during to-morrow, and then, when the night falls, I will push on again."

He walked on during the whole night, meeting no

one but two Tartars on horseback. He had heard them approaching in the distance, and had been able to conceal himself in time. The moon was now beginning to pale, and the morning mist was rising. Daylight would appear very soon, and Jiline had not yet got through the forest. "Well, I will just go thirty yards further," he said to himself, "and then I will creep into a thicket and lie down and rest."

However, when he had gone the thirty yards, he found himself on the outskirts of the forest. The day had dawned. In front of him he saw the steppes and the fortress. To the left, near the mountains, there were some fires burning, round which a number of men were clustering. Jiline looked more attentively, and he could distinguish the gleam of the guns of the Cossacks and Russian soldiers. Transported with delight, he summoned all his strength, and began to descend the mountain slope. "May God protect me!" he thought to himself. "If a mounted Tartar should happen to see me in this open space, I should not be able to escape him, near as I am to my own people."

He had scarcely made this reflection when he caught sight of three Tartars on a hill on his left. They were about two deciatines away from him. As soon as they observed him they started in pursuit. Jiline's heart throbbed excitedly. He waved his hands over his head, and shouted at the top of his voice: "Help, comrades! help!"

Fortunately, the Russians heard him, and some mounted Cossacks started off at full gallop to intercept the Tartars. These Cossacks, however, were a long way off, whereas the Tartars were gradually nearing Jiline.

The young officer, summoning all his remaining strength, and holding up his shackles in his hand, ran desperately towards the Cossacks, repeatedly crossing himself as he sped along. "Quick, my brothers, quick!" he cried.

The Cossacks were about fifteen in number, and the Tartars, seemingly afraid, at last checked their horses, so that Jiline managed to reached his people. The Cossacks surrounded him, inquiring who he was, and where he came from. But Jiline seemed quite dazed. He could only sob, and cry out : " Friends ! friends ! "

One of the soldiers at last brought him some bread, another brought him some kacha,* and a third some vodka. Then, after breaking his shackles, they wrapped a cloak around him.

The officers recognised him, and led him away to the fortress, where the soldiers joyously collected to see him. He told them how he had been captured by the Tartars.

" And this is the end," he said in conclusion, " of my journey home—and maybe of my marriage. It was clearly my destiny that those things should not be."

Thus he continued to serve with the army of the Caucasus.

A month later Kostiline was ransomed for five thousand roubles ; but, when he returned to his friends, he was in a dying condition.

---

* Cooked oatmeal.

END OF " THE PRISONER OF THE CAUCASUS "

THREE DEATHS

CHAPTER I

IT was autumn. Two carriages were rolling along the high road. In the first, two women were seated ; one, the mistress, who looked pale and thin ; the other, her maid, who was plump and florid.

The latter had short, wiry locks, which escaped from under her well-worn bonnet, and which she hurriedly tucked up with a red hand covered with a torn glove ; her full bosom, well protected by a thick shawl, bespoke robust health ; her bright black eyes rested on the fields which she saw flying by through the carriage window, and then reverted to her mistress, or wandered uneasily round the corners of the vehicle. Just in front of her swung the lady's bonnet in a net ; on her knee lay a young dog ; and several parcels were piled up at the bottom of the carriage, so that she could not settle her legs comfortably. The noise made by the jolting of these packages mingled with the creaking of the wheels and the rattling of the windows.

The lady tossed about on her cushions, shaken by an internal cough, as she sat there with her hands resting on her knees, her eyes closed, and her brows knit. She wore a white nightcap on her head, and a pale blue silk handkerchief tied round her pale and delicate throat. A straight line, half concealed by the cap, parted her fair hair, which was plastered down with pomade. There was something dry and unhealthy about the whiteness of this broad parting, and, moreover, the lady's wrinkled skin had a yellow tinge and hung loosely over her fine delicate features. There were hectic spots also on her cheek-bones. Her lips were parched and mobile ; her scanty eyelashes drooped vertically. A cloth travelling cloak fell in long folds over her hollow chest. Although her eyes were closed, her countenance conveyed an impression of weariness, irritability, and habitual suffering.

The footman was dozing as he leant against the rail of his seat. The yamstchik kept urging forward with his cries his four big steaming horses, turning round occasionally towards the other yamstchik, who might be heard behind the first carriage. The wheels left wide parallel tracks on the muddy sand of the road. The sky was grey and cold, and the fields and the highway were shrouded in a damp mist. A close atmosphere prevailed inside the vehicle, in which the scent of Eau de Cologne mingled with the dust, which entered from outside. At last the invalid threw her head back, and slowly opened her eyes. They were brilliant and splendidly dark.

"Again !" she said, as with her beautiful wasted hand she pushed aside the end of her maid's fur cloak which had rubbed against her knee. Then her lips contracted with a sickly expression.

Matriocha, the maid, then raised the fur, rose upon her sturdy legs, and drew a little farther away. Her fresh face turned scarlet. The invalid, with her beautiful, dark eyes eagerly watched the movements of the maid, and then resting her two hands on the seat, she tried to raise herself and sit a little higher up. Her strength, however, was not equal to the effort. Her mouth again contracted, and an expression of mingled exhaustion, irony, and spite overspread her countenance. "If you would but help me ! But no, I do not want you. I can do it myself. Only I must

beg of you not to put those bags behind me. But no,
do not touch them if you cannot understand ! "

The lady then closed her eyes; then, suddenly
raising them again, she gazed at the maid. Matriocha
was not looking at her mistress, but biting her ruddy
lips. A deep sigh came from the lady's sick breast;
but it was cut short and transformed into a cough.
She then averted her frowning countenance and held
both hands to her chest. When the fit of coughing
had subsided, she again closed her eyes and remained
motionless.

Both carriages entered the village. Matriocha
drew her big hand from under her shawl and made the
sign of the cross.

" What is it ? " asked the lady.

" The place where we change horses, madame."

" I asked why you were crossing yourself ? "

" There is a church, madam."

The invalid turned towards the village and began
to cross herself deliberately, fixing her eyes upon the
large church which the carriage was now passing.

Both vehicles pulled up at the post-house. From
the second alighted the invalid's husband with the
doctor ; they both came up to the first carriage.

" How are you ? " asked the doctor, as he felt the
lady's pulse.

" Well, you are not over-tired, are you, love ? "
said the husband in French. " Would you like to
get out a little ? "

Matriocha pushed the packages away and drew
close into her corner, in order not to be in the way
of the conversation.

" It does not signify ; I am always the same,"
rejoined the invalid. " I will not get out."

The husband waited a little longer, and then turned
his steps towards the post-house. Matriocha, skipping
down from the carriage, made her way on tiptoe
through the mud to the court-yard entrance.

" Because I feel ill, there is no reason why you

shouldn't have your breakfast," said the invalid with a smile to the doctor, as he stood near the carriage door. "No one cares anything about me," she added to herself, as she saw the doctor walk slowly away and then run up the steps of the post-house. "They are all well, and what do they care? Oh, my God!"

"Well, Edward Ivanovitch," said the husband, advancing to meet the doctor and rubbing his hands, "I have ordered my travelling-case to be brought in here; what do you say to that?"

"That suits me," returned the other.

"And what about her?" asked the husband with a sigh, lowering his voice and raising his eyebrows.

"I have already told you that she will never reach Moscow, let alone Italy, especially in such weather as this."

"But what are we to do, then! Alas! Alas!" And the husband buried his face in his hands. "Give it to me," he added, addressing the man who had brought in the lunch-basket.

"We ought never to have set out," answered the doctor, as he shrugged his shoulders.

"But what was I to do, tell me?" rejoined the husband. "I did everything in my power to keep her at home. I talked of our income, the children whom we should have to leave behind us, and my business matters; but she would not listen. She makes plans for her life abroad as if she were not ill, and if I had objected on the score of her state of health, I should simply have killed her."

"She is dying already! You must know the truth, Vassili Dimitrich: it is impossible to live without lungs, and lungs never grow again. It is very sad, very unfortunate, but how can it be helped? All that either of us can do is to soothe her last moments so far as we are able; what she most needs is a priest, a physician of the soul."

"Ah! But enter into my position, and you will see how difficult it is for me to mention anything of the sort to her. I cannot broach the question, whatever may happen. You know how good she is——"

"Make an effort, however, to detain her till the roads are settled after the winter," observed the doctor, with a significant shake of the head, "for something might happen to her on the journey!"

"Aksinsha! Here, Aksinsha!" now cried the postmaster's daughter, as she threw a wrap over her head and trod down the mud on the back steps. "Come along! Come and have a look at the lady of Schirkinsky! They say she is being taken abroad on account of her lungs. I have never yet had a good look at a consumptive person."

Aksinsha came out, and the pair, holding each other by the hand, walked through the court-yard. Then slackening their pace, they passed close by the carriage, and looked in through the open window. The invalid turned her head that way, but when she observed their curiosity, she frowned, and averted her face.

"Little mother!" said the postmaster's daughter, staring with all her might, "how handsome she was, and see what she has become now! It is terrible! Did you see her, Aksinsha? Did you see her?"

"I should think I did! How thin she is!" responded Aksinsha. "Let us take another peep; we can pretend that we are going to the well. Did you see how she turned away? But I managed to catch sight of her, all the same. What a pity, Macha!"

"Ah! how thick this mud is!"

And then they turned back and ran towards the court-yard.

"I am enough to frighten any one now, I have no doubt of it," thought the invalid. "Let us make haste to another land. There I shall get well again."

"Well, and how are you, my love?" said the husband, as he came up to the carriage munching his last mouthful.

N

" The eternal question," thought the sick woman. And to see him eating, too ! "

" It is nothing," she murmured between her teeth.

" Do you know, my love, I am afraid that this journey, in such weather as this is, will only make you worse. Edward Ivanovitch thinks so too. What do you say to retracing our steps ? "

She felt vexed and said nothing.

" The weather will improve, and so will the roads ; and by that time you will feel better, and then we can all go together."

" Excuse me. If I had not listened to you, I should have reached Berlin before now, and have been restored to perfect health."

" But what could I do, darling ? You know how impossible it was. And now, if you would but wait another month, you would get well, I should be able to settle my affairs, and we might take the children with us——"

" The children are not ill, and I am."

" But then fancy, my love, in such weather as this, supposing you were taken worse on the road ! In the other case we should at least be at home."

" And what good would it do me to be at home ?— Die at home ? " rejoined the invalid, pettishly.

The word *die*, however, evidently frightened her, for she now cast an imploring glance of inquiry at her husband, who cast down his eyes and made no reply. Then the invalid's mouth quivered like a child's, and the tears rolled from her eyes. Her husband covered his face with his handkerchief, and walked away without speaking a word.

" No, I will go on," she said, looking upwards, and then she clasped her hands and uttered a few incoherent words. " Why, oh why, my God ? " she said ; and meanwhile her tears fell faster and faster.

She prayed fervently for some time ; but she still felt her chest greatly oppressed ; the sky, the fields, and the road, looked grey and mournful, as far as her eyes could reach; the autumnal mist still kept brooding over the muddy road, the roofs, the carriage, and the sheepskins of the yamstchiks, as the latter greased the wheels and put in fresh horses, chatting meanwhile in their joyous, sonorous voices.

CHAPTER II

THE carriage was ready, but the yamstchik who was to drive it was in no hurry. He entered the yamstchiks' isba; it was hot, heavy, and gloomy there; it smelt of its inhabitants, of sheepskins, bread baking, and sauerkraut. Several yamstchiks were assembled there; the cook was busy at the stove, on the top of which there lay a sick man wrapped in sheepskins.

"Uncle Feodor! Uncle Feodor, I say," cried a young yamstchik to the invalid, as he entered in his touloup, with his knout passed through his belt.

"What do you want, Schabala? What have you to say to Fedka?"* returned a voice. "Isn't your coach waiting for you?"

"I wanted to ask him for his boots. Mine are worn out," replied the young man, as he tossed back his hair and played with the fingerless gloves which hung from his belt. "Is he asleep? Hi! Uncle Feodor, I say!" he repeated, coming close up to the stove.

"What is the matter?" asked a feeble voice, as a thin brown face peeped out from the top of the stove; and then the speaker, with a large, white, lean, and very hairy hand, pulled a caftan over his shoulder, which had been covered merely with a dirty shirt.

---

* Diminutive of Feodor.

"Give me some drink, brother," he resumed. "What is it you want?"

The young yamstchik handed him a pitcher of water. "Look here, Feodor," said he shifting uneasily from one foot to the other; "you can't have any need of your new boots just now, so let me have them. You are not likely ever to put them on again."

The sick man lowered his weary head to the brim of the enamelled pitcher, and wetting his thin, drooping moustache in the dark-coloured water, he drank greedily, although with some difficulty. His beard was dirty and unkempt. He raised his dull, sunken eyes with an effort to the young man's face, and when he had done drinking he tried to raise his hand to his wet lips; however, he had not strength enough to do so, so he wiped his mouth with the sleeve of his caftan. Silent and exhausted, he looked into the yamstchik's eyes, while he paused to gather strength.

"Perhaps you have already promised them to some one else?" the young man now resumed. "Well, it does not matter—only it is damp outside and I have to work. So I said to myself: 'I will go and ask Fedka for his boots; he isn't likely ever to want them again.' But perhaps you may, only say so——"

A noise came from the invalid's chest; he bent down, suffocated by a cough which he could not get out.

"And what could he do with them?" now cried the cook, angrily, filling the isba with her voice. "This is the second month that he has been lying on that stove. See how he is choking. It is enough to make one feel ill to hear him. What is he to do with his boots? He won't be buried in them, surely. High time, too, that he was in his grave. May the Lord pardon me for saying so. But you see how he is choking. Perhaps we shall have to remove him to another isba or somewhere else. It seems there are hospitals in the town. Is it right to take possession of the whole stove without a thought for any one else?

We have no room left us, and yet we are expected to keep everything clean."

"Hey, Serioga! come along, the gentleman is waiting," cried the postmaster from the doorstep.

Serioga—the young yamstchik—was going off without waiting for the sick man's reply, but the latter, though coughing all the time, intimated by his eyes that he meant to make one.

"Take the boots, Serioga," he said at last, suppressing his cough and getting his breath again. "Only listen—you must buy me a gravestone," he added, with a rattle in his throat.

"I am much obliged to you, uncle. Then I may take them? And I swear I'll buy you the stone."

"There, children, You hear him," articulated the sick man with difficulty, and bending forward as his cough came on again.

"All right, we hear," said one of the yamstchiks. "Be off, Serioga, here comes the starosta* again. You knew how ill the lady of Schirkinsky is."

But Serioga now hurriedly pulled off his big tattered boots and tossed them under a bench. Uncle Feodor's new boots just fitted him, and he admired them as he went back to the carriage.

"Ah! what fine boots! Let me grease them," said a fellow-yamstchik, brush in hand, as Serioga mounted his box and took up the reins. "Did you get them for nothing?"

"Are you jealous?" rejoined Serioga, as he stood up to tuck the flaps of his caftan round his legs. "Gee up, my darlings!" he added to the horses. Then he raised his little knout, and the two carriages, with their passengers and trunks, vanished into the grey autumnal mist, rolling rapidly along the muddy road.

The ailing yamstchik, who was lying on the stove in the close atmosphere of the isba, was still unable to get his cough out. At last he turned himself over

---

* Postmaster.

with some difficulty and held his peace. People passed to and fro and dined in the isba till evening came, and yet the sufferer made no sound. Just before night the cook mounted on to the stove and took the sheepskin off his legs.

" Don't be angry with me, Nastasia," pleaded the invalid. " I shall soon be leaving your corner free."

" All right ; all right. It does not signify," murmured Nastasia. " Where do you feel bad, uncle ? Tell me."

" Something seems gnawing at my inside. God only knows what it is."

" And your throat must hurt you, too, when you cough ? "

" I feel ill all over. It is death that is coming on me ; that's what it is. Oh !—oh !—oh ! " groaned the sick man.

" Cover your legs up. There—like that," said Nastasia, as she arranged his caftan. And then she got down from the stove.

A night-light glimmered faintly in the isba until the morning. Nastasia and a dozen yamstchiks snored loudly on the ground or on the benches. The only person awake was the invalid, who kept coughing and tossing about on the top of the stove. Towards morning, however, he became perfectly still.

" It is an odd thing," said the cook to the others, as she stretched herself in the faint early dawn. " Do you know I fancied I saw Feodor come down from the stove and go to chop some wood. ' Leave it, Nastia,' he said to me, ' I am going to help you ! ' And I replied, ' But how can you manage to chop the wood ? ' However, he seized hold of the axe and began to chop at such a rate that you could see nothing but the splinters flying. ' What does this mean ? ' said I, ' you were so ill ! ' ' No,' said he, ' I am quite well now.' And then he raised the axe, and I felt so frightened that I began to scream, and it awoke me."

"Maybe he is dead. Uncle Feodor! Hey! Uncle!" cried one of the yamstchiks.

Feodor made no reply.

"Can he really be dead? Let us go and see," said another of the party.

Feodor's thin, hairy arm, which hung down from the stove, was stiff and livid.

"We must go and tell the postmaster. I really believe he is dead," said one yamstchik.

Feodor had no relations there. He came from a distance. They buried him on the morrow in the new cemetery behind the little wood. And for many days after, Nastasia told every fresh comer about her dream, and how she had been the first to give the alarm.

CHAPTER III

SPRING had come. Streams murmured over the wet pavement of the town as they floated away the icicles; the voices of the busy crowd rang clear, and their dress was bright. Behind the hedges of the little gardens gems were swelling on the trees, the boughs of which swayed softly, caressed by the breeze. Transparent drops were dripping and falling everywhere. The sparrows seemed to outvie each other in chirping, and kept fluttering their tiny wings. In the sunshine, on the hedges and houses, and in the trees, everything seemed twinkling with life and motion. Youth and joy were sparkling in the sky, on the ground, and within the human heart.

Some fresh straw had been spread in one of the principal streets in front of a lordly mansion. Within lay the dying woman who had been hastening to another land. Just outside the closed door of her chamber there stood her husband and an elderly lady.

On the sofa sat a priest with downcast eyes, concealing something under his stole. An old lady, the mother of the sick woman, had sunk into a low chair in one corner, and was weeping bitterly. By her side stood a maid, holding in her hand a clean handkerchief ; another one was rubbing her temples and blowing on her grey head beneath her cap.

" Well, may the Saviour bless you, my dear ! " said the husband to the elderly lady. " She trusts you so implicitly, you know so well how to talk to her—persuade her, my dear ; go to her."

He was about to open the door, but the elderly lady —the sufferer's cousin—detained him ; she raised her handkerchief to her eyes several times and shook her head, saying : " I think no one will see that I have been crying." Then, opening the door herself, she went in.

The husband seemed distracted, as though he could not tell what to do. He advanced first towards his wife's mother, but when within a few paces of her he turned back, and crossing the room, went up to the priest. The latter looked at him, cast his eyes upwards, and heaved a sigh. His little grey beard also rose and then fell again.

" My God ! my God ! " said the husband.

" What can be done ? " sighed the priest, as his eyebrows and beard again rose and fell.

" And the mother, too, who is here," said the husband, on the verge of despair. " She will never get over it. She is so fond of her, so very fond, that—I don't know. You might at least try to soothe her, father, and persuade her to go away."

The priest rose and went up to the old lady.

" Of course no one can fathom the anguish of a mother's heart," said he, " yet God is merciful——"

The old lady's features contracted ; she was shaken by a spasmodic hiccough.

" God is merciful," continued the priest, as he saw her recover breath. " I must tell you that in my

parish I knew of a case more desperate even than
Maria Dimitrievan's. Well, will you believe me? A
simple *mechtchanine* (a petty tradesman) cured her in
less than no time, and merely with some herbs. This
mechtchanine is in Moscow now. As I was saying to
Vasilli Dimitrich, you can just try him. It would at
least soothe the invalid, and God is all-powerful,
remember."

" No, she will not live," returned the old lady.
" Ought not I to have been taken instead ? " Then
her spasmodic hiccough returned with such violence
that she fainted away.

The sick woman's husband raised his hands to his
face and rushed out of the room.

The first person he met in the passage was a little
boy dashing after his younger sister.

" Am I to take the children to their mamma ? "
asked the nurse.

" No, she will not see them ; it would be too much
for her."

The little boy stopped for a moment and glanced
brightly at his father ; then he gave a sudden kick and
a joyous cry as he again broke into a run. " She is
the horse, papa ! " cried the little fellow, pointing to
his sister.

Meanwhile, in the adjoining room, the cousin,
seated by the sick woman's side, gently endeavoured
to lead her mind onwards and prepare her for the
thought of death. The doctor stood by the window
preparing some draught.

The invalid was sitting up in bed in a white cloak,
propped up with pillows, and gazing silently at her
cousin.

" Eh, my dear," she broke in abruptly, " do not try
to prepare me ; do not treat me like a child. I am a
Christian ; I know all. I know that I have not much
longer to live ; I know that if my husband had listened
to me sooner I should have been in Italy by now, and
probably—no, certainly—restored to health. Every

one told him so, but what was to be done? It must have been God's will. I know that we are all great sinners, but I have a firm trust in the divine mercy. We shall all be forgiven; it must be so. I try to examine my own heart; I have sinned greatly, but have I not atoned for it by my dreadful suffering? I have tried to bear my cross patiently——"

"Then I may bring in the father, may I not, dear? You will feel still more relieved when you have taken leave of the world," said the cousin.

The invalid bowed her head in token of assent. The cousin went out and beckoned to the priest. "God be merciful to me a sinner!" she murmured.

"She is an angel," she said to the husband, with tears in her eyes.

The husband began to weep. The priest entered the room; the old mother was still unconscious, and all was silent in the ante-room. In another five minutes the priest came out again, and taking off his stole, arranged his hair.

"Thank God she is calmer now," he said. "She wishes to see you."

The cousin and husband entered. The invalid was gently weeping with her eyes fixed on the eikon.

"I congratulate you, love," said the husband.

"Thank you. How happy I feel now. What an ineffable sense of bliss," said the sick woman. And a faint smile played on her thin lips. "How merciful God is, is he not? Merciful and almighty."

And again, dissolved in tears, she gazed on the eikon with an eager and imploring expression. Then, as if she had suddenly bethought herself of something, she beckoned her husband nearer. "You will never do what I ask you," said she petulantly, in a feeble voice.

The husband, bending over her, listened meekly. "What is it, love?" he asked.

"I have told you again and again that these doctors know nothing, but there are some good, honest, simple women who work cures. Well now—the father has been telling me—of a mechtchanine—send for him."

" But who is he, love ? "

" Good heavens ! He will not understand ! " And the invalid's face clouded over as she closed her eyes.

The doctor drew near and took her hand. The pulse was evidently growing weaker. He made a gesture to the husband. The invalid caught sight of it and gazed around in alarm. The cousin turned away and burst into tears. " Do not cry, do not distress yourself, do not distress me," said the sick woman. " You take away all my courage."

" You are an angel ! " exclaimed the cousin, kissing her hand.

" Don't kiss me there ; only the dead have their hands kissed. Oh, my God ! my God ! "

By evening the dying woman was a corpse. Her remains, lying in a coffin, were placed in one of the reception-rooms of the mansion. In this vast apartment, the doors of which were closed, there sat a sacristan reading the Psalms of David with a nasal intonation. The dazzling light of the tapers, standing in tall silver candlesticks, fell on the dead woman's white brow, on her waxen hands, which hung by her side, and on the motionless folds of her shroud, which rose impressively over her knees and toes.

The sacristan was paying no heed to what he read, but the words rose and fell in strange, monotonous cadence in the silent chamber, broken occasionally by the sound of children's voices and the patter of feet in a distant room.

" When Thou hidest Thy face," ran the psalm, " they are troubled ; when Thou takest away their breath they die, and are turned again to dust. When Thou lettest Thy breath go forth they shall be made, and Thou shalt renew the face of the earth. . . . Praise the Lord."

There was an air of severe majesty on the dead

woman's face. Neither her marble brow nor her closely-pressed lips now stirred; she seemed all attention. But did she now, at last, comprehend those grand words?

CHAPTER IV

IN another month a granite chapel had been raised over the spot where the dead woman had been interred. The yamstchik's grave, however, was still without a stone; merely green blades of grass were springing on the mound, which remained the sole vestige of a departed life.

"It will be a great shame, Serioga," said the cook at the post-house, one day, "if you don't buy Feodor a stone. You have kept on saying that it was still winter; but now, what are you about not to keep your word? You promised him in my presence. His ghost has been here once already to remind you, and if you don't buy it, he will come again and take you by the throat."

"What do you mean? Am I gainsaying it?" returned Serioga. "I will buy the stone, as I said I would. I will spend a rouble and a half over it. I haven't forgotten it, but it will have to be fetched. The first time anything takes me to town, I will buy it."

"But you ought, at least, to put up a cross," said an old yamstchik, "for you are not behaving as you ought to do. There you wear those boots."

"But where am I to get a cross? I can't make one out of the first bit of wood that comes to hand."

"What nonsense you talk about the first bit of wood that comes to hand. Take your axe and start a little earlier for the forest, and you can soon make one. Cut down a young ash, and you will have all you want. Otherwise you would have to give the woodman some vodka, and it isn't worth while paying for such a trifle. Why, yesterday, when I broke the springtree-bar of my carriage, I started off to cut myself another one, and nobody said a word about it."

Next morning, at daybreak, Serioga took an axe and made his way to the woods. A chilly, dense, continuous mist, as yet unillumined by the sun, brooded over everything. A light was gradually dawning in the east, and its pale glow was reflected in the vault overhead, veiled by light clouds. Not a blade of grass on the ground, not a leaf in the air above stirred. Occasionally a flapping of wings might be heard in the thickets, or some furtive noise on the ground, breaking the silence of the forest.

Suddenly a strange, unaccustomed sound re-echoed and died away on its outskirts. Again it was repeated recurring at regular intervals, at the foot of the trunk of one of the motionless trees. One of the tree-tops began to sway strangely. A murmur arose amid the leaves, which were full of sap ; a warbler, which had been perched on one of the branches, fluttered and piped twice, then spread its little tail and took refuge on another tree.

The strokes of the axe still resounded, growing more and more hollow ; white splinters glistening with sap fell on the green sward, and a faint crack could be heard between each stroke. The entire trunk of the tree was quivering now ; it swayed, and then suddenly rose erect again, vibrating terribly on its roots, as if with fright. Silence ensued. Then the tree tottered again ; the trunk split across, and fell prostrate on the damp earth, snapping its branches and bringing down the long boughs in its fall.

The sounds of the axe and of the woodman's footsteps ceased. The warbler piped and flew to a higher bough. One of the twigs brushed by its wings fluttered for a moment, and then all its leaves remained motionless like the rest. The trees spread their quiet branches over the vacant space, and looked even more radiant than before. The sun's first rays at last pierced through the clouds, broke forth in the blue sky, and darted over earth and heaven. The mist then floated away in wreaths, an iridescent vapour hovered over the verdant foliage, and thin white clouds sailed rapidly across the azure vault. Birds fluttered in the shade, singing wild pæans of delight. High overhead leaves full of sap were murmuring joyously, while boughs of living trees waved slowly and majestically above their fellow, cut down and dead.

THE END

WYMAN & SONS LTD., PRINTERS, READING AND LONDON

Nine Books

By

F. W. Bain

Fcap. 8vo, 3s. 6d. net each

The Ashes of a God
A Digit of the Moon
The Descent of the Sun
An Incarnation of the Snow
A Mine of Faults

Fcap. 8vo, 2s. 6d. net each

A Heifer of the Dawn
In the Great God's Hair
A Draught of the Blue
An Essence of the Dusk

Methuen & Co. Ltd., London

The Stories of F. W. Bain

MESSRS. METHUEN & Co. LTD. have much pleasure in announcing that they have arranged with Mr. F. W. BAIN to publish henceforward his remarkable series of Indian stories.

The history of these fascinating little books, which, to a few readers, have always meant so much, and which are every day becoming better known, is not the least curious in modern literature. On the appearance of "A Digit of the Moon" in 1899, the author's mystifying attributions to a Sanscrit original, and the skill with which he kept up the illusion of translation, completely took in even the best scholars, and this work was added to the Oriental Department of the British Museum Library. Later, however, the discovery was made that Mr. Bain, working with a mind saturated in Hindoo Mysticism and lore and Sanscrit poetry, was wholly its author, and it is now catalogued in the ordinary way.

To describe the charm and appeal of the stories themselves would be a hard task. They are almost indescribable. There is nothing in English literature at once so tender, so passionate, so melancholy, and so wise. The fatalism of the East, and the wistful dubiety of the West, meet in these beautiful allegories of life, which it is possible to compare only with themselves.

Methuen & Co. Ltd., London

[P.T.O.